**The long awaited sequel to *The Eyes of Katy McKade***
**by**
**Carole A. Sheller**

AF271121

# *The EYES*

# *of*

# *KANE McKADE*

Ⅴ⌀ Vision Publishing & Distributing Company
P.O. Box 686
Westminster, Colorado 80030-0868

303/403-8719 • 1-800-557-7717 • Fax: 303/940-3996

www.visionpd.com  •  (Carole Sheller e-mail) carsheller@aol.com
(Vision Publishing)    vispubdist@aol.com

ISBN 0-9662147-3-0

Cover art by        Albert M. Guida
Back cover art by    Jess E. DuBois
Layout & Design by   Diane Calkins, John Pughes & Connie Ptaszek

Printed in the U.S.A.
JM Printing Company, Inc. Denver, CO
September, 2000

# Book Reviews
## By the Most Important People Of All...
## You The Readers—Friends—Family

"I've been looking forward to reading this sequel since I closed the cover on the first book. It lived up to all my expectations. It was very enjoyable and exciting to read with resolution of many of the mysteries that enticed us in the first book. Looking forward now, to the next imaginative story line!"

*Trina Ray / North Hills, California*

"Carole Sheller has done it again...Another brilliant entertaining novel...Truly a winner."

*Connie Ptaszek / Arvada, Colorado*

"Carole Sheller writes yet another hit. This, a sequel to 'The Eyes of Katy McKade.' Kane is a wonderful pick-up to where Katy left off. It is full of great characters, fabulous story and lots of fun. Great for the family.

*Daniel L. Roth M.D. / Salem, Oregon*

"The Eyes of Kane McKade is outstanding! I loved it and couldn't put it down for a second! It was a great sequel to The Eyes of Katy McKade."

*Felicia Marti / Arvada, Colorado*

"Sheller's much awaited sequel pulls you in and keeps you there. Excellent character development and intrigue tied with a creative premise and a very imaginative story make *The Eyes of Kane McKade* a must read. Great work!! Looking forward to the next.

*Mark Fletcher / Littleton, Colorado*

"The Eyes of Kane McKade is a wonderful follow-up to The Eyes of Katy McKade. Carole's talent for creating believable characters in a present day fantasy captures the imagination in a exciting sequel you can't put down tell your finished.

*Robert M. Savidge / Arvada, Colorado*

~

"Really enjoyed *The Eyes of Kane McKade*. Very surprised, in someways it was better than Katy. Couldn't wait to see what happened next."

**Bobbie Webb / Littleton, Colorado**

"I didn't think it was possible...but Carole Sheller's The Eyes of Kane McKade was even better than her last book, The Eyes of Katy McKade!! The story of the McKades should be told on the big screen for all of us movie lovers, too. I want everybody to get to know these fascinating characters!"

**Dan Pergola / Westminster, Colorado**

"Another compelling story from author Carole A. Sheller. A great sequel with, again, unexpected twists and great characters."

**Bruce Capra / Arvada, Colorado**

"I've had the pleasure of watching the two novels-The Eyes of Katy McKade and The Eyes of Kane McKade-come to life. Twelve years in the making, and they are certainly worth the wait. The imagination of Carole Sheller in her story line and the way she makes her characters come to life is amazing. Well worth the read."

**Jake Martinez / Denver, Colorado**

"Carole Sheller has a wonderful ability to weave a great plot of twists and turns. I enjoyed *The Eyes of Kane McKade* so much that I immediately began reading Carole's earlier book, *The Eyes of Katy McKade*."

**Myke Howard / Littleton, Colorado**

"The Eyes of Kane McKade was a sequel worth waiting for. The continuance of one great story leading right into another. The way Carole Sheller develops her wonderful characters and brings you, the reader, into the many twists and turns makes this a must read for the whole family."

**Marge Burman / Longmont, Colorado**

~

"Thank you, Carole Sheller, for sharing this <u>great</u> book. I loved it – it took me away. I could not put it down. I am in awe of your ability to be able to put together such a wonderful story. I felt like I was there – in the garden – in the hospital – on Tali Island. I can't wait for your next book. Please remember me. Thanks again."

*Jerry Kinderknecht / Westminster, Colorado*

"I've watched Carole A. Sheller develop into a wonderful author. Her writing is adventurous, intriguing, and suspenseful, making The Eyes of Kane McKade a real entertaining page turner. From young to old, a truly great read."

*Trish Braddy / Denver, Colorado*

"Carole Sheller is a fresh new author that has taken me on a second page turning adventure, that I won't soon forget! <u>The Eyes of Kane McKade</u> will vividly transport you (in the same unique way <u>The Eyes of Katy McKade</u> did). I hope we will hear more from this very creative lady!"

*Vickie Galimov / Parker, Colorado*

"Carole Sheller continues the adventures of Katy McKade into her second novel 'The Eyes of Kane McKade'. After reading it you will wait-desire-a third."

*Francine Ridgeway / Littleton, Colorado*

"Carole Sheller's debut work "The Eyes of Katy McKade" was a wonderfully interesting and entertaining easy read. However as almost never happens with a sequel, "The Eyes of Kane McKade" is even better. I found myself totally engrossed with Katy and Kane, and Miss Sheller has even managed to make the background characters come to life just as she did with the fictional Island of Tali. Don't deny yourself this one. You will love it.

*Patricia McGuirre / Denver, Colorado*

~

"The Eyes of Kane McKade was a wonderful book! Rarely is the sequel as good or better than the original, but I would have to say in this case this does not apply. I enjoyed every gripping moment and found it hard to put down once I picked it up. Thank you for both books, hopefully there will be more to come."

**Chris Halling / Thornton, Colorado**

"An Excellent Sequel… With author Carole Sheller's unforgettable characters. A must to read."

**Bonnie Brough / Roswell, New Mexico**

"I really enjoyed reading both, The Eyes of Kane McKade and The Eyes of Katy McKade. I felt as if I was there with them. The suspense from one chapter to the next is so good I didn't want to put it down. Both are absolutely wonderful and I recommend them to anybody of all age groups. I can't wait for the next one."

**Natalie Counter / LaSalle, Colorado**

"Another delightful and enjoyable novel from author Carole Sheller. Fans won't be disappointed."

**Mary Ann Niccoli / Arvada, Colorado**

"I enjoyed The Eyes of Katy McKade so much, and the sequel, The Eyes of Kane McKade was absolutely terrific. I found it hard to put down. Carole Sheller's ability for developing great characters and fascinating plots and twists will keep you totally entertained."

**Robin Pergola / Arvada, Colorado**

I dedicate this in loving memory to the one that inspired me to begin writing—my big brother, Rodger L. Webb

and for
My sister Loretta Webb, Mitchell
My sister-in-law Doris Ann Webb

~

Special thanks *again* to everyone who played a part in helping me write my second novel, from the first word typed to the last word read. I could not have done it without each and everyone of you. Even though the boot seemed a little heavier this time (a little lead maybe?) I'm ready to go for the third.

# MAIN CHARACTERS

**_KANE McKADE_**  At the age of thirteen learns he has a twin sister, Katy. His father, Kevin, tells him that his mother, Meg, died when Kane was five years old. At the age of seventeen, Kane learns why he and his father live on the Tali Island...they are prisoners because of the special power they both possess, the ability to see things happen in the future but only to people they know. Kane realizes he must use this special gift to find Katy, and also help his father.

**_KEVIN McKADE_**  At the age of twenty-three Kevin, along with his son Kane, who is just over a year old, are kidnapped. They are held prisoners by Prince Tali on the island bearing his name, Tali Island. Kevin knows he could escape by himself, but there is no way he would leave his son Kane. His decision made, he abides by the rules Prince Tali gives him until the day he and his son can escape. Now almost sixteen years later, Kevin is told he's dying.

**_KATY McKADE_**  Raised on the western slope of Colorado at a place called The Ranch, Katy, at the age of seventeen, learns the truth about her identity and the existence of her father-Kevin, and twin brother-Kane. With the help of **Sister Elizabeth**, her aunt, and her Godfather, **Ben Bennett,** the decision is made—to find them.

**_PRINCE TALI_**  All his life Prince Tali is obsessed with one goal, to find a McKade--not just any McKade but a grandson or great grandson related to Jeffrey McKade. He believes they hold the power to protect his family. With the death of his father, and older brother, and now the birth of his son, Raul, Prince Tali and his young brother, **Zoric Tali,** are more determined than ever to find this McKade who holds this special gift...to see into the future.

**_RAUL TALI_**  Tortured and left for dead, Kane is able to save Raul. It was the third time Kane, along with his father, Kevin, saved Raul's life. He and Kane are best friends and raised like brothers. His life will never be the same once he finds out the real truth, not only about the McKade's, but why his mother, **Amanda**, left Tali Island—and him.

# *Prologue*
## 1994

Katy sat in the chair, looking at her reflection in the mirror. Her hands reached up and touched her face as she leaned forward to examine her features more closely. Her eyes blinked several times as a slight chill passed through her body. *I wonder if he looks like me, this twin brother that I've never known.*

She removed her hands from her face, placing them on the box that sat on her dresser. She opened the lid and removed the old photo, taken over fifteen years ago, of a man holding two babies with a woman standing by his side. *My father, Kevin. I don't even know if he's alive. And my mother, Meg. God took her away from me to soon. I was only five years old when she died.* She looked at the two babies. *Its a good thing I'm wearing a dress or I wouldn't be able to tell us apart.*

Leaning her head back against the chair, she pressed the photo to her heart. *I wonder what your life has been like? Where were you raised? Are you happy? Healthy? In love?* A smile crossed Katy's face as she touched the special locket around her neck. *Like me?*

*We'll find each other Kane, somehow...someday.*

*Carole A. Sheller*

# Chapter 1
## TALI ISLAND
## 1982

Kevin McKade sat on the porch step of the small run-down bunga-low that for the last four years he and his son, Kane, had called home. *Home! It is nothing but a prison without bars!* He watched the guards patrolling the grounds around the estate owned by Prince Tali.

There was only one entrance to Tali Island by land. The rest was surrounded by water. Over one-third of the island was covered by a jungle with several quicksand pits. It was rumored these pits were the graveyard of many bodies, compliments of Prince Tali's great-grand-father, grandfather, father, and even the prince himself.

As Kevin sat there, a strange, hollow feeling passed through his body, then he knew why...his wife Meg was dead. Her pain and suf-fering had finally ended. For that he was grateful. Tears stung his eyes as sadness ripped through him.

His mind went back to the first time they had met almost seven years ago. He had left his home in the Highlands of Scotland at the age of twenty after the death of his mother, Brenda. His father, Kurt, had died in his sleep one night at the age of seventy-eight. At the time Kevin was eighteen years old. His mother followed her husband in death the same way she had followed him through life, dying peace-fully in her sleep.

His parents had married late in life. Brenda was thirty-five. Kurt was fifty. The doctors had told her she would never be able to have children and this suited Kevin's father just fine. This "gift", or "curse" as the McKades called it, of psychic power that had been passed down from father to son, the power to see things happen in the future only to people they knew, would end with him.

They had been married almost ten years when Kurt had a vision and told Brenda she needed to see a doctor. Seven months later Kevin was born. There was no doubt he was a true McKade with eyes the same color as his father's that changed colors when experiencing a vision of the future.

After the death of his mother, Kevin decided to work his way to

Greece where he hoped to find employment on a freighter headed for the United States. There he would start a new life, never telling anyone of this gift—no—curse that possessed his body.

When he finally reached Greece he knew his destination in life was taking a new direction. He had heard about a church that helped those in need by offering food, clothing, even a new identity, if necessary, then sending them to America for the beginning of a better life.

As he stood outside the church and waited with two other men to be taken inside, Kevin had a strong feeling that this was where he would meet his future wife. The men entered the church and were taken down a flight of stairs into a room that would be their home for the next several weeks.

He noticed a woman who stood in the back. He was drawn to her instantly. He walked over and looked into her eyes, love completely consuming him. He realized she was feeling the same emotion, too. Her name was Sister Meg Riley. She was studying to be a nun and had not taken her final vows.

Father James married them a week later. They changed their name from McKade to Kincaid. Kevin hoped that would be enough to discourage anyone looking for him. He had told Meg about his life and the lives of his father and grandfathers before him; about how they lived with fear of being kidnapped because of this special gift they possessed.

They tried to keep a low profile by working at different churches, she as a teacher and Kevin as a gardener. When Meg became pregnant they decided to stay in one place until after the baby was born. When she was six months along they found out they would have twins. On July 7, 1977, Kane and Katy were born.

The babies were a little over a year old when Father James convinced Kevin and Meg it was time to go home to Colorado where Meg was originally from and where her sister and grandfather still lived. There they could begin a new life. He was returning himself the following spring and wanted them to accompany him.

It was not to be. Fate was not on their side. One day Kevin took Kane with him and stopped to get a haircut. On the way home Kevin knew they were being followed and he knew something else, too. He would never see Meg again.

The sound of his son's voice brought him back to the present. He

2

could see Kane in the distance, riding his pony and waving at him. Kevin waved back. He also waved to Raul, Prince Tali's son, who was the same age as Kane.

Ever since Kevin and Kane had been kidnapped and brought to this island, the two young boys had become inseparable. It was exactly what Prince Tali had planned. Kevin and Kane had been on the island two days when Prince Tali and his brother, Zoric, brought them to Prince Tali's private office.

As he tried not to look into eyes full of hate that stared back at him, Prince Tali said, "I'm sure I don't have to tell you why you were brought here."

"On the contrary," Kevin responded. "I need to know exactly why my son and I are here against our will." *And why I shouldn't try to kill you both with my bare hands.*

"You were brought here to fulfill a promise made by your grandfather to my great-grandfather. He saved your grandfather's life. In return, your grandfather promised that his son and sons thereafter would protect the Tali family for as long as the McKades possessed the 'gift.' I've brought you here to finally honor that promise."

"I know nothing of such a promise."

Prince Tali opened a small box that sat on his desk. He removed the contents and handed them to Kevin. They were a handwritten letter, protected in a picture frame, and a cloth family shield...the McKade shield. Kevin knew the shield was authentic. He had one exactly like it.

He reached for the letter and read:

*Let it be known on this day of June 20, 1897, that I, Jeffrey McKade, of the McKade clan do hereby make the following promise, and that this promise be known only by the McKade sons and the sons of the Tali family.*

*I am alive on this day because of the bravery of one man, Prince Vicco Tali, of Greece. The rope was around my neck when Prince Vicco risked his life for mine.*

*I have told him about the gift which the men of the McKade clan possess and have promised protection for his family as long as there is a male McKade alive to honor this promise.*

The letter was signed by Jeffrey McKade.

3

Kevin stared at Prince Tali as he handed the letter back to him. "I'd like to leave now and take my son home."

"Your home is the cottage you have lived in for the last two days. I want to make something perfectly clear to you, McKade. If you do not cooperate and do exactly as I say, I'll kill you and raise your son as my own. But as long as you do what you are told, your wife and daughter will be left alone and you'll live to see your son grow to a man. I am a man of my word. Don't ever doubt that, McKade."

"Me? Doubt the word of a killer, thief and now a kidnapper of young babies? You do your family proud, Tali." Kevin stood.

"Prince Tali to you."

"Never." Kevin turned to leave.

"McKade, another thing. You are under surveillance twenty-four hours a day. If you even whisper I'll hear you. There's only one way off this island and it's heavily guarded, so relax, enjoy your stay."

"Go to hell. Kane, come. It's time to leave."

Zoric opened the office door and motioned to the guard. "Take McKade and his son back to the cottage." He closed the door behind them, turned and smiled at Prince Tali. "I like him."

Tali smiled back at his brother. "I do, too."

"What's the plan now?"

"Time, but how much I'm not sure. If this McKade has the power to see the future, time is the only thing we've got to prove it."

In the months that followed, Kevin tried to talk to Prince Tali and his brother, Zoric, explaining as best he could how this 'gift' with which his family was blessed worked.

"It seems like with each generation," Kevin took a deep breath and continued, "this curse, as I call it, gets weaker and weaker. My father, Kurt, hoped it would die with him, but then I came along."

"Is your power as strong as your father's?" asked Zoric.

"No. In fact he was sure that it had ended with him. Then when I was fifteen I had my first dream. I saw my best friend's mother sitting and having coffee with a friend at a sidewalk cafe when a man driving a van lost control and hit the two women. My friend's mother was killed."

"Were you able to save her?" asked Prince Tali.

"Yes, with my mother's help. She went to the cafe and told the

4

woman she was on her way to pick up their sons from school, asked her and her friend to ride along. She used the excuse that she needed to talk about a problem she was having with the boys. The two women had just stepped into my mother's vehicle when this van came out of nowhere and crashed into the table where the ladies had sat. My father and I watched the whole thing happen from across the street. We barely made it home before I became very ill. The next day my father sat me down and told me all about the 'gift' of the McKade men."

"How old was your father when he experienced his first vision?" asked Zoric.

"He was young, around nine or ten years old. His vision was very mild, compared to his father's. Mine is almost non-existent, compared to theirs. My hope now is that my son, Kane, is completely free of this curse. So you see, keeping us here as prisoners is not necessary."

"I'll decide what is necessary or not, McKade. I've lost my grand-father, father and a brother and maybe—just maybe—if you and your father stood by the promise your grandfather made, my family would still be alive. My brother, Zoric, and my son, Raul, are the most important people in my life. I will do whatever is necessary to protect them. You will stay on this island, McKade," said Prince Tali.

Kevin stood, then left the room. He wondered why he even both-ered to talk with them. He knew it wouldn't help matters any.

The months had turned into years. Kane was now five years old. Kevin stood up. He would mourn the death of his wife, Meg, in his own way. He walked toward his flower garden. It was the one place that gave him peace. The only other person who seemed to find his garden a retreat was Amanda, Prince Tali's wife, and mother of Raul. She was as much a prisoner as Kevin and Kane.

Amanda had met Prince Tali when she was eighteen. Her aunt and uncle had brought her to Greece on a family vacation and ended up returning to America without her. The first two years of her marriage to Prince Tali had been wonderful. Then Raul was born and every-thing changed. Raul became Prince Tali's whole life.

Amanda wanted a divorce to take Raul back to America, but she learned quickly what was expected of her if she wanted to be with her son. She was to play the role of devoted wife and mother. Her per-

5

sonal belongings were moved into a small corner of the estate. The only thing that kept Amanda from leaving was Raul, but little by little she was losing him, too.

For the last two years she had found some contentment in the flower garden that surrounded the estate. There she had met Kevin. Their friendship was built on the mutual respect of one parent for another. Each knew that whatever was said between them was probably heard by someone else.

"Good morning, Amanda."

"Good morning, Kevin. I see the boys are out early this morning for their daily ride."

"Yes, they are. I understand that a private tutor arrives today for their schooling. Are there any other children besides Raul and Kane?" Kevin asked.

She smiled. "Only the two of them for a couple of months. Then there will be three more children joining them. They're all about the same age as our boys. You look sad today, Kevin. Aren't you feeling well?"

"I'm fine." Kevin tried to smile.

"You look like you've lost your best friend."

Kevin glanced toward the sky, then back at Amanda. "You're right, I have."

"Would you like to talk about it. I'm a good listener."

"Thanks, Amanda. This is something I have to go through by myself."

"The offer is always open in case you change your mind." Sensing that Kevin needed to be alone she turned and walked toward the small riding arena where she could watch Raul and Kane.

Kevin's eyes followed her as she left. *It's such a shame...a young beautiful girl having to live her life like this. She loves a man that only used her for one thing. To bear him a son. Her life will never be a happy one as long as she remains married to him-and lives on this God-forsaken island.*

Kevin turned. He wanted to be alone for a while and decided to walk to the lake. It was a beautiful, sky-blue lake, located in the middle of the island about half a mile from the Tali estate. The lake was about a mile wide and two miles long, surrounded by a sandy beach with only enough trees to offer perfect shade. The north side of the lake was known as Tali Town. There were two large refineries to handle all the cocoa grown on the surrounding farms. Prince Tali made sure that the people of Tali Town had all the conveniences they needed for living a good life. There were stores, gas stations, a small hospital and clinic for their health needs, the best schools and even several churches for people to practice their religious beliefs.

Kevin glanced back over his shoulder, knowing he would see the guard following him.

It was close to half an hour before he reached his destination, a small rocky hill about a hundred feet away from the lake. Kevin climbed to the top where there was a patch of grass and he could sit on one of the boulders. There he had a perfect view of Tali Town. From the side he was on, the south side, he could also see part of the Tali estate and three other estates, each with their own swimming pools, tennis courts and horse riding areas. Kevin had overheard the guards say that there were ten of these estates on this side of the island. Each cost its owner around ten million with upkeep charges of one hundred thousand a year.

Toward the west side of the island, surrounding the Tali Jungle and extending north around Tali Town, was a range of beautiful mountains, but there was one mountain that stood above all the rest, Mt. Vicco, named after Prince Tali's great-grandfather.

Kevin sat there thinking about his life, remembering Meg and the short time they had together. His hatred for Prince Tali grew. He would never forgive him for taking away what little time he would have had with Meg.

The tears stung his eyes and slowly started down his cheeks. Within minutes, sobbing rocked his body. Grief flowed from him, cleansing him on the inside. Then he felt the need to feel clean outside, too.

He was forbidden to swim in the lake, but today he didn't care. He stripped off his clothes, climbed down from the hill and ran across the sand. He stepped into the water. The guard, Mani, hollered at him.

"You better get your ass back here, McKade. If I have to come in there after you, I'll kill you."

Kevin swam until it felt like his heart would burst through his chest. Then he turned on his back, inhaling the clean air above him. He closed his eyes, feeling peace for the first time in four years.

The sound of thunder and flash of lighting startled him, but when he opened his eyes there was nothing but blue sky. He smiled to himself and headed for shore. As he stepped onto the beach, Mani grabbed his arm. "You're going to die for this, McKade."

Kevin turned and glared at Mani. "Don't ever touch me again," Kevin said.

Mani dropped his arm and jumped back as a wave of fear spread through him when he looked into eyes a color he had never seen before. He watched as Kevin headed up the hill. He yelled, "Are you some kind of freak or what, McKade?"

Kevin turned and looked down at him, a slight grin on his face. "Yes, I am." He turned away, not able to stop the chuckle that escaped his throat.

He spread his shirt out on the patch of grass and sat down. He picked up his belt buckle and ran his fingers across the wings of an eagle. This was a sign of freedom Meg had told him when she gave it to him on their first anniversary. He wore it every day. It was the only thing he had that reminded him of her, and of course, Kane. There was something about Kane that resembled Meg, especially when he smiled at you with those dimples in each cheek. His sister, Katy, had dimples too. Kevin sighed. Katy, his beautiful little Katy, who looked like her mother except for her eyes. Kane and Katy had his eyes—the family curse.

Kevin laid back on the grass and stared at the blue sky. Feeling sleepy, he shut his eyes and drifted off to sleep. He dreamed again of lighting and thunder. When he opened his eyes he saw only blue skies, just like before. For the first time in months he had a happy grin on his face.

He finished dressing and made his way down the hill. He could see Mani, the guard, lying in the sand under a tree, sound asleep. *Falling asleep on the job, Mani? Shame on you.* Kevin headed for the bungalow.

It was two hours later when Kevin saw Mani stomping up the path from the lake. Kevin could tell he was madder than hell.

Kane was sitting on the porch swing, coloring in a book. He looked up and smiled when he saw Mani approach. The smile left his face and fear replaced it when Mani grabbed his arms and pulled him off the swing, shaking him violently in the air.

"Where the hell's your old man?" Mani screamed at him.

Tears streamed down Kane's face. "You're hurting me."

Mani dropped Kane to the ground and then slapped him so hard, it knocked him back against the swing. "I asked you a question, brat. Now answer me." He drew back his hand to slap Kane again just as Kevin came out the door. Kevin grabbed Mani's arm and twisted it behind him, slamming him into the porch railing post. Blood spurted from Mani's nose. Kevin pulled back and slammed him into the post again, then threw him down the stairs. Mani slid across the gravel at the bottom. Kevin cleared all four stairs and grabbed Mani by his shirt, pulling him over onto his back. Grabbing Mani by the hair, he pounded his head against the ground.

"You ever touch my son again, I'll kill you." Kevin stared into Mani's eyes. "Understood, asshole?" Then Kevin stood and walked up the stairs to comfort his son.


Amanda walked around the small horse arena, waiting for Raul and Kane while they put their ponies away. When they finished, Kane ran up to her.

"Amanda! Amanda!" Kane said excitedly. "Did you know we start school today?"

She knelt down to welcome him into her arms. He wrapped his little arms around her neck as she picked him up and swung him around.

"Isn't it super?"

"Yes it is, Kane."

Raul walked more slowly up to his mother. "I don't want to go to school."

Amanda put Kane down and placed the palm of her hand softly against Raul's cheek. He pulled away.

A hurt, empty feeling passed through Amanda as it had a hundred times before. He was Prince Tali's son and she knew that no matter what she did or said nothing would give Raul back to her.

"Your father said it's an important day. It means you're on your way to becoming a young man."

Raul stared at her. The questioning look on his face soon changed to a smile. "I will make my father proud," said Raul.

"I will make my father proud of me, too," said Kane. "Will you be proud of us, Amanda?"

"Yes, I will. Shall we get something to drink?"

The boys ran in front of her. *They're so much alike, yet so different. Kane is lovable and affectionate, while Raul hides his feelings except when it comes to his father.*

They even looked somewhat alike with both having curly, dark brown hair, a stocky build and about the same height. Raul had her gray eyes. Kane had hazel ones, exactly like his father's. They were the most beautiful eyes Amanda had ever seen.

It was an hour later when Amanda walked the two boys across the yard to the smallest of the Tali Estate guesthouses. It had been remodeled to use as the school.

Prince Tali watched them from the window of his private office, Zoric at his side.

"It's time for Raul to have a baby brother, don't you think, Tali?" asked Zoric.

"I would have to get another wife if I wanted that. Amanda had such a hard time with her first pregnancy that the doctor didn't think it advisable to try again."

"Maybe now that Amanda is older the risk wouldn't be so high."

Tali smiled at his younger brother.

"Possibly, but we haven't shared the same bed for five years. She asked for a divorce three years ago. She wanted to move back to America and take Raul with her. I told her she could have the divorce, but once she left this island, she gave up all rights to our son."

"It looks like she decided to stay," said Zoric. "Maybe you two should try again. I hate to see Raul grow up an only child. I know from experience how important family is."

Tali smiled. "I'll think about it, little brother."

Later Prince Tali sat in his chair, thinking about Amanda and the possibility of having more children. He would visit her that evening.

A loud knock on his door startled him.

"Who is it?"

"Mani."

"Come in."

Prince Tali stood when Mani entered the room, concern sounding in his voice. "What the hell happened to you?"

He heard the hatred in Mani's voice as the man answered. "It's that bastard, McKade. You're going to have to talk to him. He threatened to kill me."

"Why?"

"He's crazy, that's why."

"Is he all right?"

"He's fine. I wanted to beat the hell out of him, but I held back like you told me. You better talk to him. Next time I might not be so understanding."

Prince Tali buzzed Zoric's room. "Could you come to my office? Mani is here and I think you should hear what he has to say."

"Be right there."

Prince Tali and Zoric listened while Mani told them what had happened that day.

"He's a crazy son of a bitch, that McKade. I wanted to kill him." Mani said.

"I'll have a talk with him. I think for now I'll take you off guard duty of McKade and put you somewhere else. In the meantime, take a few weeks off. You deserve a vacation." Prince Tali stood, the signal that Mani was being dismissed.

After he left, Prince Tali and Zoric made their way to a private viewing room where they could look at surveillance tapes of the day. There wasn't anything that happened on Prince Tali's estate that wasn't filmed everyday—twenty-four hours a day.

They watched and listened to the short conversation between Amanda and Kevin and Kevin's swim in the lake. Prince Tali turned it off after watching the brutal way Mani had grabbed Kane; of Kevin coming to the rescue of his son and threatening to kill Mani if he ever touched Kane again.

"I'll kill him myself," said Zoric, "if I ever see him hurt that boy again."

"Mani's my best bodyguard, brother. I'll remind him that no harm is to come to McKade or his son. Speaking of McKade, let's hear his side of the story."

Twenty minutes later, Prince Tali, sitting at his desk, watched as Kevin entered his office, walked right up and stood in front of him.

"Sit down, McKade."

"No, thanks. I prefer to look down on scum."

Prince Tali glared at him. "Stand then. Your comfort is not my concern. The reason I ordered you here is to tell you I saw and heard everything that happened today, and to let you know that no harm will ever come to Kane again. I'll see to it personally." He noticed the strange color of Kevin's eyes. It sent a chill through his body.

"You do that, Tali, because if you don't, you'll have one less bodyguard to feed. Oh, and one more thing...Tali." Kevin leaned over and put his palms on the desk. "Stay out of the rain. You might get wet. Lighting and thunder are killers." Kevin threw back his head and laughed, then turned and walked out the room. He slammed the door behind him.

Prince Tali looked at Zoric. "What the hell did that mean?" He stood and walked toward the window. Zoric came and stood by his side.

"Not a cloud in sight. What are your plans for the next couple of days?"

Prince Tali shook his head. "Not much. Tomorrow I have a meeting in Tali Town at the lodge with a couple from Sweden. They are interested in one of the estates. Tonight I plan on staying in. With any luck, Raul might have that little brother you think he needs so desperately."

A broad grin appeared on Zoric's face, "Good luck."

It was after ten. Amanda was lying on her bed reading when she heard the soft knock on her bedroom door. Thinking it was Raul, she said, "Come in." She was taken completely by surprise when Prince Tali entered the room.

"We need to talk."

Amanda watched him as he walked toward her and sat down in the chair by her bed.

"I've been thinking that we should have another child."

"It's rather hard to do that when we don't even have a marriage."

He stood, walked over to her bed and sat down beside her. He picked up her hand and raised it to his lips, placing a gentle kiss on the top of her fingers.

"We owe it to ourselves and Raul to try again."

He reached for her. Wrapping his arms around her, he started placing tender kisses along her neck, then he kissed her passionately. It reminded her of when they were first married. He was gentle and kind. She fell asleep with her head on his chest, feeling loved for the first time in five years.

When she awoke the following morning, she looked at the empty space beside her. She wondered what time he had left her bed. After she showered and dressed, she went looking for Raul. She found him in the dining room. He was eating breakfast with Zoric.

"Good morning, Raul, Zoric."

"Good morning, Amanda. You look radiant this morning," Zoric said.

His eyes met hers and she could feel herself blush, not just from embarrassment, but also from a feeling of humiliation. *He knows exactly what happened last night and why.*

"Will your brother be joining us this morning?"

"He said he would see you later. He has an appointment in Tali Town with potential residents. You looked so peaceful sleeping he didn't want to waken you."

"How thoughtful." *Did he tell you everything that happened? He's using me just like before.* Then, as if a weight was lifted from her shoulders, she realized something that would change her life forever. *I don't love him anymore.* A smile appeared on her face. *My dashing, handsome prince can go to hell for all I care.*

"I think I'll go pick a bouquet of flowers for the house before breakfast. Would you like to help me, Raul?"

Raul looked up at her. "That's for sissies."

Amanda smiled at him. "If you change your mind, you know where I'll be."

She walked out the door, stepping onto the verandah, and took several deep breaths of the morning's fresh air. She looked toward the flower garden and saw Kevin, already at work in tennis shorts and a sleeveless T-shirt. She felt sorry for this man and his son, Kane. They were prisoners here and she didn't know why. But she knew one thing. He was her best friend. Hell...who was she kidding. He was her only friend.

She walked up to where he was kneeling and burying new bulbs into the ground.

"Good morning, Kevin."

"Amanda."

"Kevin, I want to tell you how much your friendship has meant to me."

Kevin studied her for a moment. "There's no need. You're the only friend I have on this island, too. Do you think it would be all right for two friends to share a hug?" He raised his hand to her.

"Most definitely," she said as she took his hand and helped him stand. He took her in his arms and softly whispered in her ear, "You must leave this island as soon as possible. You will never find happiness here. For the sake of the child you'll be carrying, you owe it to yourself to find a life full of love. I have a feeling there's someone back home waiting for you. Go Amanda, go home to America, before it's too late."

She pulled from his embrace and looked up into his eyes. A feeling of warmth and contentment passed through her. She touched her stomach with her hand. "How do you know this?" she whispered.

He smiled at her. "I don't know how or why I know, I just know."

She stared into his beautiful, caring eyes and realized something. She loved this quiet, honorable man. She loved his son, Kane, too. This was where she belonged, next to him as his wife and the mother of his children. But she realized this would never be. Somewhere there was a woman he loved very deeply—the mother of Kane.

"I'll do as you say, Kevin, but first I have to take care of some personal business."

She turned and walked away.

# Chapter 2
## TALI TOWN

Prince Tali sat across from the wealthy couple from Sweden. They were the kind of people he liked living on his island. She was a pretty, stocky woman, completely devoted to her husband and two children, a boy of seven and a girl of three. He was the spoiled only child of a billionaire, trying to run the businesses he had inherited from his father. They were tired of the public life that followed them on a daily basis and wanted to live a normal one.

"We do not allow the media or television news personnel on my island." Prince Tali handed them several sheets of paper. "These are regulations you must follow if you want to live here. Your privacy and welfare are my greatest concerns."

"It sounds like heaven," the woman said. "Can we see our new home now?"

"Yes, you can." Prince Tali smiled at her. "When we get back I've made arrangements for you to stay here at the lodge for the next two days. Enjoy yourselves. See the town, meet the people and read the regulations. Then we'll talk again before you leave." Prince Tali stood. "Let me check to see if everything is ready. I'll be right back."

He made his way toward the entrance of the lodge. He looked out the front window and saw rain softly falling.

"Damn," he said to himself. It had been such a beautiful morning. Now as he looked at the dark gray clouds, he hesitated. Usually rain didn't bother him, but this rain seemed different.

He walked back to the table where the couple sat.

"Sorry, I think we're going to have to wait until this storm passes," Prince Tali said as he made his apologies to the couple.

"Are the storms here dangerous?" the lady asked.

"Not usually. Let's go and have breakfast. It should be over by then."

Suddenly a lightning strike lit up the whole room and the thunder that followed shook the building. Electricity went out all over town. The lightning and thunder lasted over an hour, leaving behind a trail of destruction.

Prince Tali stood at the window, looking out over his town. He was

15

thankful no one had been killed—especially himself.

He walked toward the front entrance and opened the door. The heavy downpour had now become a soft drizzle. He stood there, hesitating for a moment, thinking about what McKade had said.

Then, without warning, a bolt of lightning flashed from the sky, striking the ground about fifty feet from where he stood. It was the most beautiful and frightening thing he had ever witnessed. He knew something else, too. McKade had saved his life. His body trembled. He took several deep breaths, turned and entered the lodge, heading straight for the bar.


## TALI ESTATE


Amanda walked around her bedroom trying to decide what she would take back to the States when she went home. *Home, what a great sound.* She was humming to herself when Prince Tali entered her room.

"You seem happy today, Amanda."

"I am. I heard about the storm. It was so strange. We could hear the thunder and see the lightning, but it barely rained here."

"There was quite a bit of damage, but no one was hurt. I could go for a lifetime without seeing another storm like that one."

Amanda sat on the edge of her bed. "I've been thinking about the baby you think we should have. It looks like the best time to conceive would be a week from today."

"We'll make this work, Amanda."

He reached for her hands, pulled her into his arms and kissed her gently. "See you at dinner."

For the next four days that was the only time she saw him. It was exactly what she had expected. It gave her time to put her affairs in order and spend time with Raul, who was as distant as his father.

She knew that Raul would not forget her when she left. Kevin promised her that. He and Kane would not forget her, either. They had taken several pictures of each other the day of the storm. She took a photo of Raul and Kane, and one with Kevin and the two boys. He took another with her and the boys. Kevin would keep one picture of the boys and another one of her with the boys. All she had to do now was find a place to hide them. She was not sure what Prince Tali would do if he found the pictures. He might destroy them.

She lay down on her bed and stared at the ceiling, trying to sort out everything she needed to do before she talked to Prince Tali. Her mind drifted back to their first meeting. She was eighteen years old and vacationing with her aunt and uncle in Greece.

They were ready to order dinner in a plush restaurant in the city of Athens when six men entered the room. The owner came up to Amanda's aunt and uncle and asked if they would mind moving. It seemed they were sitting at Prince Tali's favorite table. They agreed.

Prince Tali came over and introduced himself, ordered a bottle of the best champagne, and told the owner to put their bill on his tab. Before the night was over, he invited himself to sit at their table, purchased two more bottles of champagne, then whisked the three of them away in his limo to several night spots.

For the next week he barely gave them time to catch their breath. He took them everywhere, then he took them to the most beautiful place of all—Tali Island.

That was where he proposed to her and she said yes. He had her parents and older brother, Lawrence, flown in from Vermont and, on July, 23, 1975, Amanda Dawnett Farly became Amanda Dawnett Tali. Raul was born May 19, 1977.

They had taken three trips to Vermont. The first one was six months after they were married. It was her parents' thirtieth wedding anniversary on November 21th and her brother's twenty-ninth birthday, December 3th.

On their second trip, Raul was four months old. The third and last time, Raul was almost two years old. Prince Tali didn't accompany her on that trip. *That seemed so long ago.*

Her mind went back even further in time to when she was in high school. She remembered her first love, her high school sweetheart, Glen. They had dated from the tenth grade through graduation. At their senior prom they promised their love to each other for life. *They would go to the same college and when it was the right time they would marry. It seemed like a lifetime ago to Amanda, but in reality it had been only seven years.*

*Enough of the past. It's time to take control of my life.* Her hand moved across her stomach. *Please God, let Kevin be right. Let there*

17

*be a new life inside me.*

Half an hour later, she was walking down the hall to Prince Tali's office. She knocked on the door.

"Come in."

She opened the door to find him sitting behind his desk. His brother, Zoric, was in a chair close by.

"Amanda, come in and sit down."

"I need to talk to you privately."

"I was just leaving," said Zoric. He stood and left the room.

Amanda sat in the chair at the side of Prince Tali's desk. She looked directly into his cold dark eyes.

"I've come to a decision about my life," she said.

"Really," he replied, smugly.

"Yes, I've decided I really don't want any more children."

Prince Tali leaned forward and took her hand in his. "Why is that?"

"I do not feel I'm healthy enough to carry a baby full term, and I don't want to take the chance there might be something wrong if one is born prematurely. I don't want to stand in your way of having more children, you're a terrific father to Raul. I would like to go home to Vermont."

Prince Tali dropped her hand and leaned back in his chair. "And Raul?"

Amanda could hear the anger in his voice. "He would stay here with you, of course. I hope we can work out something as far as Raul being able to visit me. I'd like to write to him, too. I think we can work out something that's agreeable to the both of us."

"How much is this going to cost me, Amanda?"

She couldn't help but smile. "You always were blunt and right to the point. I want enough money to establish myself in my own home. I don't want to live with or have to depend on my parents. I plan on going to college and maybe getting a teaching degree. I'd like to leave as soon as possible." Amanda stood. "Let me know your decision." She turned and left the room.

Prince Tali watched her walk away. He cursed to himself. Two weeks ago he would have paid anything to hear the words she just spoke, but now that he had decided he wanted another child, he was angry. He buzzed Zoric's office. "Come back in here. We have some decisions to make."

When Zoric returned, he told him what Amanda had said. "How do you feel about this?" Zoric asked.

"I was angry at first, but maybe it's for the best. As long as she's willing to give me full custody of Raul, I will try to be more than fair in a settlement." He picked up the phone and called his lawyer. They agreed to meet at Prince Tali's office on the mainland that afternoon.

Zoric smiled at his brother. "Do I sense a more compassionate understanding in my brother?"

"Maybe." Prince Tali laughed.

"And have you thanked McKade for saving your life?"

"No." The smile disappeared from Tali's face. "And I never will. Let's leave it at that."

Zoric shrugged his shoulders. "Whatever you say. Do you want me to go with you to the lawyers?"

"Yes, I think you should help keep me from making an ass of myself."

"Always here to help," Zoric said.

Prince Tali informed Amanda that he and Zoric would be spending the night on the mainland at the Tali apartment. He told her to enjoy the evening with Raul. It probably would be her last.

Amanda waited until Prince Tali and Zoric had left, then took out a long, thick, jewelry box. She removed a necklace and matching earrings. There was also a double-hooked bracelet that completed the set. They were all so beautiful. Prince Tali had given them to her on her twenty-first birthday. She would wear them on the flight home. After she had removed the gifts from the box she picked up a small package that she had wrapped and put in a plastic bag. She placed the package in the box, put the box in another plastic bag, along with a note she had written. She folded it around the box. When it was tight she took a roll of duct tape to secure it. *A present for my best friend.*

She placed the package in her pants pocket, then slipped on a long sweater. She walked out of the house, headed for the garden. Kevin was nowhere in sight. She made her way to where he had planted the new bulbs. She looked around until she found the perfect one. It had already started to grow small red buds on the top. She gently dug it up, pulled the box from her pocket and placed it deep within the hole.

Then she replaced the flower.

She was picking a bouquet for the dinner table when she saw Kevin and Kane walking toward her and not far behind, their constant shadow, the guard that followed them everywhere. Amanda noticed it was not Mani, but someone new whom she had never seen before. *Maybe my husband fired Mani. I never did like that man. I wish I knew why Kevin's a prisoner here. He must have something Tali wants very much.*

Kane came running up to her. "What are you doing, Amanda?"

"Waiting for you. Where have you been?"

"Swimming in the lake. I love swimming."

"I bet you're a very good swimmer." Her hand touched his cheek.

"Yea, I am." He smiled up at her.

She smiled back. "I was wondering if you and your dad would like to have dinner with Raul and me?"

"Can we cook outside?" Kane asked excitedly.

She looked up at Kevin and their eyes met. She saw something there she had never seen before—desire.

"I think that would have to be up to your father."

"It's okay with him. We cook out a lot."

Amanda stood there, realizing for the first time that she had never thought about how Kevin and Kane spent their time. She was so wrapped in her own self pity that she hadn't even taken the time to consider them. *I was nothing but a spoiled-rotten, little rich girl. Well, my life will be different from now on.* She smiled at Kevin. "I'll leave the decision to you."

"Can we sleep outside?" Kane asked.

Kevin picked up his son and swung him around. "Sure, but let's see what Raul wants to do."

"I'll go get him," said Kane, and off he went.

Amanda smiled at Kevin. "I see you have a new shadow. Where is Mani?"

"Lost, I hope. The new guy's name is J.J. He seems nice and he's pretty friendly. The boys like him."

It didn't take Kane long to find Raul. Amanda and Kevin laughed when they saw the two boys heading back, struggling with their sleeping bags.

The evening turned out to be fun for everyone. Even the guard, J.J., joined in. He helped with the cooking and cleaning up, too. When he finished, he said goodnight to everyone and headed for the guard's bunkhouse.

When it came time to turn in, Kevin went to get his sleeping bag. Amanda was telling the boys goodnight when he returned.

"There is no reason you can't stay, too," Kevin said. "I'm sure the boys won't mind sleeping together."

"Please stay, Mommy," Raul begged as he grabbed her hand and smiled up at her.

Amanda was surprised at the show of affection. "Okay. Sounds like fun."

Kevin rolled out the boys' sleeping bag at the far end of the porch, then put an extra one for Amanda's next to it. He took his own and walked about ten feet to the other side of the porch and rolled it out.

Everyone said their goodnights and settled in for the night. The two boys giggled and snickered for a few minutes, then not being able to keep their eyes open, fell sound asleep.

Kevin laid there for about half an hour before folding back his cover and raising his head to look at Amanda.

It only took her a minute before she crawled in next to him. He wrapped his arms around her, their bodies snuggled in close to each other.

For the next hour they lay there and talked. About the boys. About the death of Kevin's wife, Meg, and about Amanda going back to America. She told him about her life there and her plans when she returned. And she told him about the gift she had left for him buried in the ground.

"Do you think you'll ever make it to America?" she asked.

"Maybe someday when Kane is older, but for now this is our home. It really isn't that bad. He'll have a good education and he has his best friend, Raul."

"Is there any way I could help you escape from here?" she asked.

He hugged her tight. "I can't take that chance now. If I failed, Tali would kill me and raise Kane as his own. He told me that and I believe him."

"What is it that he wants from you?"

"It's not important. We have this night together and I want to spend it making love to you." His hand cupped her chin and raised her head. His lips softly touched hers. The memories they would take with them from this night would have to last a lifetime.

In the morning as the dawn softly glowed on the horizon, Amanda said good-bye. Kevin stood on the porch watching her as she walked toward the estate. *Maybe someday we will meet again.* He whispered a promise to her. *I'll take care of your son to the best of my ability.*


## TALI'S APARTMENT / MAINLAND


"Once Amanda leaves the island I will not let her return," Tali told his friend and lawyer, Sal.

Sal shook his head. "Are you planning on taking her son completely away from her? I don't believe that's the fair thing to do."

"No. If she wants to see Raul, I'll let her have this apartment and they can be together here, with supervision of course. I'd even be agreeable to taking him to America to stay with her, say two weeks in the summer."

"Would you go also?"

"Of course." Tali smiled. "I'd probably take Zoric with me. Maybe I can find a wife for him there." They all laughed.

"Let's go over the money settlement again," said Sal. "I'm to offer her one million up front, to be deposited in a bank of her choice. I can go as high as three million. You'll send her fifty thousand a year as long as she has no contact with you or Raul, but if she demands visiting rights that will drop down to twenty-five thousand a year. If she should re-marry, all money would stop. Do I have it right?"

"I think that should do it. Can you have it typed and ready to sign by tomorrow?" asked Tali.

"I'll have a rough draft for Amanda to look at in the morning, and if everything's okay, final copy by late tomorrow. What about personal things?"

"She can take what belongs to her, clothes, jewelry, nothing else."

"Is there any possibility she might be pregnant?" Sal asked.

Prince Tali sat there for a moment before answering. "I don't think so, but maybe she should take one of those pregnancy tests just to

22

make sure."

"I'll pick one up and bring it with me in the morning, say around nine," said Sal.

"Perfect. Zoric and I are staying here tonight to do some celebrating. We'll be there around ten, that will give you some time to spend alone with her. One more thing... Will you check with the airlines on flights into Kennedy Airport? She can make her own arrangements from there."

"Can do." Sal shook their hands. "See you in the morning."

Zoric looked at his brother. "Do I sense a feeling of regret in my big brother?"

Prince Tali smiled at him and shook his head. "What is it with men? The minute they think they can't have something, it becomes something they want very much."

"Do you still love her?" asked Zoric.

"Truthfully, I don't know. Maybe a small part of me always will. She gave me a terrific son. I really would like more children, but Amanda's not willing, so I guess you and I both have to find wives."

"Might as well get started," Zoric said as he stood, a big grin on his face.

Amanda looked at herself in the mirror. It was seven in the morning. She had packed everything she wanted to take home. Most of her things were in shipping cartons to be sent to her mother's address.

As she looked at herself she knew she had to leave Tali Island today. *I can't bear the thought of being so close to Kevin and Kane and not able to touch and love them.* Her hand touched the puffiness around her eyes. Anyone that looked at her could tell she'd been crying.

She had decided to leave the island and stay on the mainland until she could catch a flight out. She had showered and dressed when a knock sounded on her bedroom door. It was the butler, informing her that a man named Sal was waiting in Tali's office to talk to her.

"Thank you," she said as she closed the door behind her. *He sure didn't waste any time.*

"Good morning, Amanda."

"Good morning, Sal."

"I wish I was here under a more pleasant circumstance. Prince Tali would like to clear up this matter today."

"Yes, so would I." Amanda said.

Coffee was brought in. Sal handed her a copy of the temporary settlement.

"Changes can be made if necessary, but I think you'll find Prince Tali's been very generous."

Amanda read everything. She actually thought the settlement was more than fair. *Oh hell, might as well put up a little fight.*

"It seems Prince Tali doesn't think his son is worth nearly as much as I thought he would. I was thinking more of a five million settlement and a hundred thousand a year."

"He'll never agree to that, Amanda, and you know it."

"Well, we'll just have to meet some kind of compromise, won't we? I'll settle for half of what I originally wanted, two and a half million in a cashier check before I leave, plus seventy-five thousand a year if I don't see Raul. Twenty-five if I do and nothing if I re-marry. We agree on everything else. The only things I'm taking are my clothes and jewelry. I'll even give back the diamond ring that belonged to his mother. I've got everything that I'll be taking on the plane with me packed. The rest of my belongings need to be shipped."

Amanda stood. "I'm being more than generous, don't you think, Sal?" She smiled at him. "Let me know if this is agreeable. If it isn't, I'll start unpacking." She turned and left the room.

Sal sat back in his chair. A smile appeared on his face. *That's one hell of a woman, not only beautiful, but smart too.*

He called his office to let his secretary know the changes, confident that Prince Tali would agree to Amanda's wishes.

He refilled his coffee cup and walked out on the verandah. From there he could see the horse arena where Raul and his friend, Kane, were riding their ponies. *I wonder what the hell it is that Tali has on this McKade. He's a prisoner just as sure as I'm standing here, but why?* He had asked Tali once and all Tali said was that McKade owed him. That was all he needed to know.

The office door opened and Tali and Zoric entered. "How did it go, Sal?" Prince Tali asked.

"Better than I thought it would. She wanted five million, but I got her down to two and a half." Sal told him the rest and also what she said about unpacking.

It brought a smile to Prince Tali's face. "Thanks, Sal, you did well. Give her what she wants. I want her out of here."

"The only thing I didn't do was give her this." Sal handed him the pregnancy test.

"I'll take it to her and let her know final papers will be ready this afternoon," Prince Tali said.

He knocked on Amanda's door, then opened it without waiting for her to answer.

Their eyes met and Prince Tali smiled at her. "You're a beautiful woman, Amanda, an asset that I'll miss. I wanted you to know that I agreed to the changes. There's only one thing I need from you." He handed her the pregnancy test.

When she realized what it was, she sat down feeling weak. "Why? I'm not pregnant."

"Then I'm sure you won't mind. It's for your protection, as well as mine."

"I've never taken one of these before." *God, I have to find a way of getting out of this.*

"Read the instructions. I'm sure you can handle it. I'll wait, and take it with me to the clinic."

She pulled the container out of the box, along with a sheet of instructions. This test would work one hour to seven days after the time of conception to prove positive. They recommended to wait the full seven days.

Amanda counted the days backwards. It had been six days. She stood and walked slowly into the bathroom.

"Leave the door open, Amanda."

"There's no need for this. There's no way I'm pregnant."

"Like I said, I'm sure you won't mind then."

She took the test as instructed and handed it to him.

"What happens now," he asked.

She picked up the instruction sheet again. "The spot on top will turn blue in half an hour if I'm not pregnant."

"That seems pretty simple. I'll let you know," he said as he left the room.

It was the longest half hour in her life. *Please Kevin, please be right. My future is in your hands.* When Prince Tali returned he smiled at her. "It turned blue. You're not pregnant, and are free to leave. Sal should be here around two with the final papers. You want to come down and have some lunch?" He smiled at her again. "Maybe a bottle of champagne to celebrate. I would like to part friends. We still have a son that's part of us both. I think we should make this as easy as possible for him."

"Just tell him I went home for a visit. I think I'll lay down for a while. Wake me when Sal gets here."

"All right," he said as he closed the door behind him.

Amanda laid down on the bed, a big smile on her face. She rubbed her hand across her stomach. *Thank you, thank you, thank you.* She couldn't believe it worked, but she had faith in Kevin. Now all she had to worry about was that Prince Tali didn't take the test to the clinic, and she was pretty sure he wouldn't. She hadn't told him the truth about what the color meant. Blue definitely showed she was pregnant.

Eight o'clock the next morning found Amanda on Flight 447, high above the ocean, headed home with papers all signed and a cashier's check for two and a half million in a money belt wrapped around her waist. Part of her would always be on Tali Island, but now she had a new life inside her, and it took priority. She would always love Kevin. Maybe someday she could help him escape, as he had helped her. She closed her eyes and laid her head on the back of the seat...*yes maybe someday.* She drifted off to sleep.

# Chapter 3
## THREE YEARS LATER
## TALI ISLAND

Kane ran into his father's bedroom, crying hysterically. "I had a bad dream," he said, tears running down his cheeks. He rushed into his father's outstretched arms.

Kevin looked into his son's eyes. They had changed color. *Damn this curse.* "It's all right, Kane. I had the same dream. Everything's going to be all right." He held his son, comforting him.

Kane raised his head and looked at his father's face. His small hand softly touched Kevin's eyes. Kane stopped crying. "Your eyes look funny."

"Yes, I know. We must go tell Raul's father about our dream."

"Why?" asked Kane.

"He will know what to do and the dream will go away."

"Okay," said Kane.

Prince Tali was sitting at his desk when Kevin knocked on his door. He jumped up when he saw the look on both their faces and the strange color their eyes had become. He could tell Kane had been crying. "What happened?" He motioned for them to sit. Kevin sat down and lifted Kane onto his lap.

"We've both had a bad nightmare," said Kevin, "and we wanted to tell you about it. It seems Raul is getting on a bus and the bus is involved in a terrible accident. There's a fire and Raul is hurt— beyond help. We know that you can avoid this. You'll do something, won't you?" Kevin asked.

"Yes, of course," Prince Tali replied. "Is there anything else I should know?"

"No," Kevin said. He stood, still holding Kane in his arms, turned and left the room.

Two days later Raul was so happy that he didn't have to leave and go to a special school for a month. Instead he and Kane planned all the neat things they could do.

They were putting their ponies away for the day when Prince Tali entered the arena. Kevin stopped what he was doing and watched as he approached.

"I have sad news. There was an accident with the bus Raul was supposed to be on. Everyone on board is dead." Prince Tali reached down and picked up his son, hugging him tightly. "Thank you," he said to Kevin.

Kevin nodded his head, then picked up his own son and headed for the bungalow. It didn't take long before both of them became quite ill.

Prince Tali came to see them the next day to see how they were feeling.

"I will always be extremely grateful for what you've done. To show my appreciation I'm moving you and Kane into the west wing of my home."

"That's not necessary," said Kevin. "We like it here."

"You will be more comfortable there. I've already ordered new furnishings. I'm sure you'll find it to your liking."

"What are you going to do with the bungalow?" asked Kevin.

"I will either tear it down or use it for storage."

"And my garden?"

"Nothing will change. Actually you can use the bungalow for your tools and whatever else you need."

Kane was so excited about moving that Kevin knew he couldn't disappoint him, even though he was extremely skeptical about Prince Tali's motives for moving them into the main house. He suspected Tali wanted to be able to keep a closer watch over them now that he knew they both possessed 'the gift.'

Kevin had made a point to ask Raul once a week about his mother, Amanda. In the beginning she had sent post cards weekly and the first year there had been several letters. Now, three years later, all Raul received were cards on special holidays. Raul always showed the cards to Kevin.

"She's probably waiting for you to write." Kevin said to Raul.

"My father said I don't have to if I don't want to, besides he said he writes to her. Maybe when I'm older, I'll go visit her. Can Kane come with me?"

"We'll see."

Kevin watched as Raul walked away. He wondered what Amanda was doing. He was sure she had given birth to a baby girl. *She probably looks just like her mother...beautiful.*

Kevin and Kane had been living at the estate a little over a year when Kevin awoke one morning. *Damn,* he thought to himself. He lay in his bed going over the dream he'd had, hoping Kane did not have it too. Wishful thinking! He heard the knock on his door. As it opened, Kane peeked his head in. "Can I come in?" he asked.

"Sure son," Kevin said as he propped himself up. "Come and get under the covers."

Kane crawled into the bed and snuggled close to his father.

"I had a bad dream," Kane said. "There were guns and Prince Tali and Zoric were hurt." He started to cry.

"It's going to be all right, son. I had the same dream."

"If we go tell Prince Tali, will he know what to do?" asked Kane.

"Yes, he will."

"Will the dream go away?"

"Yes."

Kane looked up at his father. "Your eyes look funny."

"Oh yeah, well you look funny all over." Kevin started tickling Kane until laughter replaced the tears.

An hour later they knocked on Prince Tali's office door.

"Come in," he said. The smile on his face was quickly replaced with a look of fear. He stood. "Raul?" he asked.

"No, not this time," said Kevin.

"Who?" Prince Tali asked.

"You...you and Zoric."

"Please, sit down and tell me what you see."

Kevin looked at his son. "Kane, why don't you go find Raul. J.J. is probably waiting down at the stables to help you saddle your pony. I'll tell Tali about the dream, then I'll come and join you."

"Will you tell him about the guns?"

"Yes."

"You promise they won't be hurt?"

Kevin looked into his son's eyes and his hand softly touched Kane's cheek. "I promise, son."

"Okay. We're going to have a horse race today," Kane said with a big smile on his face. Off he went, the dream he had last night vanishing from his mind.

Kevin looked around the room, then walked over and sat down on the plush leather sofa. Prince Tali sat down on the matching leather chair to Kevin's left and waited for Kevin to begin.

"I understand there's going to be a parade and you and Zoric have been invited to ride with a very important man."

"Yes, he's the American Ambassador to Greece, and the parade is in three days."

Kevin laid his head on the back of the couch and closed his eyes. It was several moments before he spoke again. "There are horses in front, then several open cars, convertibles, with men and women. Some are sitting on the tops of the back seats with their feet in the seats. You and Zoric are riding like this in a long, dark blue car with some sort of seal printed on the side. You're both laughing, smiling and waving to the crowd. The buildings on both sides aren't very tall. On the roof of one of the buildings there's a man—no two men. The flash from the sun bounces off the guns they're pointing at the car you're riding in. Two deadly shots are fired. You and Zoric slump over onto the seat in front of you. No one even realizes you're both dead until the parade is over."

As Kevin opened his eyes, Prince Tali had to look away. The color of Kevin's eyes sent chills up his spine. He stood, walked over and poured them a cup of coffee. His hands were shaking so badly, he stopped and took several deep breaths until he felt himself gain control again. He picked up both cups and handed one to Kevin.

"Do you know who these men are?" Prince Tali asked as he sat down in the chair again.

"No, I don't."

"Do you know what building it is?"

"No, I don't know that either."

"If I took you to the mainland and we drove the route the parade is taking, do you think you could pick out the building?"

"I don't know. We could try."

"I'll get Mani to drive us."

"That's not a good idea."

"Why?" asked Prince Tali.

30

"Only you and Zoric know why I'm held prisoner here. I'd like to keep it that way."

"I understand. Zoric and I will handle it. Do I have your word, McKade, that you won't try anything foolish?"

"This time yes, but someday Kane and I will leave this island right in front of you and you won't even know it." Kevin stood. "Thanks for the coffee." He closed the door on his way out.

Prince Tali sat there for a long time, trying to figure out who would want to kill them, especially Zoric. *He is such an easy-going, good-natured person. Womanizer, yes. He's certainly that. No, it has to be me...but who?*

He had been sitting there about an hour when Zoric knocked on his door.

"You don't look too good, brother," Zoric said as he poured himself a cup of coffee.

"You won't feel so good, either, when I tell you what McKade told me this morning."

Prince Tali told Zoric everything McKade had relayed to him.

"And then he opened his eyes. That alone was enough to scare the hell out of me. His eyes were that strange color, but even more so. Kane's eyes had changed, too, but not as much. I think McKade's power is a little stronger than he realizes."

Zoric sat there silent for a few minutes trying to absorb what he'd just heard. He finally spoke. "You know what I don't understand. If this is true and you and I are to be killed, why would McKade even tell us? If we were dead, he'd be free."

"I thought about that, too." Prince Tali smiled. "Maybe he's starting to like us just a little. You think?"

"Me, yes, but you, I'm sure he'd just as soon see you dead."

"You're probably right. So in order to save you, he has to swallow his pride and save me too. Or he could be doing it to protect Kane." Prince Tali told Zoric the promise McKade had made to his son.

It was about noon when Prince Tali and Zoric came out of the office and went looking for Kevin. They found him at the lake swimming, with Kane and Raul. J.J. was close by.

"Are you going to swim with us?" Kane asked.

"Not today, but soon," said Zoric. "It looks like a lot of fun. Why don't you boys show us how good you are."

They watched as Kane and Raul showed off for them.

Prince Tali smiled as he watched his son. "He's very good," he said to Zoric.

They stayed and had lunch with the boys, then told Kevin they were going to the mainland and he was to go with them. J.J. offered to stay with the boys.

Kevin felt a new sense of freedom as they passed through the gate that led them off Tali Island onto a road about a mile long with water on both sides. At the end of the road was another gate, opened by a guard as he saw them approach. Kevin noticed the tight security and warning signs. Private Property. No One Admitted without Proper Identification Card.'

Kevin looked around as Zoric drove onto the mainland. It was a winding road which led them to another gate. There was no guard at this one, only a small electronic box attached to a pole. Zoric placed a card in a small slot on the side of the box and the gate opened in the middle, letting them pass through, then it closed. Kevin noticed a similar electronic box on the other side of the gate. They drove about a hundred feet and entered a residential street.

"Impressive," Kevin remarked, "but not foolproof."

They drove in silence until they came to the outskirts of the business district where the parade would begin.

"Go as slowly as you can and stop at each block for a few minutes," Kevin said as he looked around. "I need to concentrate."

When they came to the end, Prince Tali asked him, "Anything?"

"No, nothing except I do know the building is on our left somewhere between the middle and the end of the route. I need to get out of the car and walk around, maybe go into some of the buildings. I'll meet you back here." He looked at Tali, expecting an argument, but there was none.

"Okay, McKade. You gave me your word. I'll trust you just like your son, Kane, does."

"Is there anything we can do to help?" asked Zoric.

"Thanks for the offer," Kevin said. "But this is something I need to do alone."

Tali looked at him. "See that cafe on the corner? If you go around to the side there's a small, quiet bar. We'll meet you there. Take whatever time you need."

Kevin walked along the street for almost an hour before entering the first building. He looked at the information plaque on the wall. *Mostly doctors, dentists and a few attorneys. It's definitely not this one.* After the tenth building, he was about ready to give up when he entered what looked like an old hotel turned into apartments. He could see a pool room at the far end where the bar was located. A slight shiver passed through him. *This might be it.*

"Can I help you?" a woman's voice asked from behind him.

He turned and smiled at the stocky, gray-haired woman. "Maybe. Do you rent rooms here?"

"No, it's small apartments, by the month or longer. You interested?"

"Do you have anything on the top floor?"

"Sure do. Come on. I'll show it to you."

They took the elevator up to the sixth floor. As Kevin walked down the hallway, a strange feeling inside him kept getting stronger and stronger. The woman opened the door to number 606 and he went in. It was on the wrong side of the building. This apartment's windows faced the alley.

"Do you have anything on the other side. I don't particularly like the view from here."

"You and everyone else. I had two men in here yesterday that felt the same way. I only have one apartment left on that side. They said they would let me know by tonight if they wanted it. Left a nice deposit. I guess I could show it to you in case they change their mind."

When she opened the door Kevin immediately knew there was a connection with the men that wanted this apartment and the gunmen.

"This is more like what I had in mind," said Kevin. "Would it be all right if I checked back with you tomorrow? By the way, what did you say your name was?" He smiled at her.

"It's Betsy." She held out her hand to him and smiled back. "And yes, you can check with me tomorrow. I'll give those men until nine o'clock in the morning. If I don't hear from them, it's yours. How long did you say you'd be staying?"

"At least a month," Kevin said as they got on the elevator. When they were back down in the lobby, Kevin said good-bye and hurried out the door before Betsy could ask him any questions.

It had taken him over three hours. *I wonder if Tali is getting a little nervous.* He chuckled to himself.

Tali looked at his watch. It had been more than two hours since they last saw McKade.

"A little worried?" Zoric asked.

"Only that McKade won't find anything that will help us figure out who's behind this."

"Not even a little worried that he might take off and we'll never see him again?"

"Sure, it crossed my mind, but where would he go. He has no money and doesn't know anyone. Besides he'd never leave Kane behind."

"Does this mean you are going to ease up on him?"

"Never! In fact, I'm thinking about upgrading the surveillance cameras around the estate."

"Why?" asked Zoric.

"McKade told me someday he would escape and take Kane with him and he'd do it right under my nose."

Zoric laughed. "Leave it to McKade to ruffle your feathers."

Another hour passed.

"You want me to go find him?" asked Zoric.

"No, here he is now."

They watched him as he entered the bar and headed for their table. Kevin sat down. "I could use a stiff drink." His body felt drained.

Prince Tali motioned for the waitress. "What do you want?" he asked Kevin.

"Double shot of the best Irish whiskey you have and a cold beer."

They waited until she returned with his order. Kevin took a drink of the whiskey and coughed. Zoric slapped him on the back. "Not used to the liquor, are you?"

"No, it burns like hell." Kevin took another small sip. "That's much better."

"Did you find what you were looking for?" asked Prince Tali.

34

"Yes, it seems like the men you'll be looking for might be trying to rent an apartment at a place called Bryony." Kevin told them everything that had happened.

Prince Tali leaned forward. "Is there any way that you could be wrong on this, McKade?"

"Truthfully...I don't know. This is a first for me. I don't have a hell of a lot to go on. You could just not ride in the parade."

"We have no intention of riding in that parade, but no one will know that except the three of us."

"What about the police?" asked Kevin.

"I'll decide about that tomorrow. In the meantime, I want you to rent that other apartment and see if you can find access to the roof."

Kevin couldn't hold back the yawn. "That will have to be tomorrow. Right now I need sleep."

They finished their drinks and Zoric paid the tab. When they got to the car, Kevin crawled in the back seat and was sound asleep within minutes.

When they arrived back at the estate, Zoric pulled the car into the garage. They tried to wake Kevin.

"There's one man that can't hold his liquor." Prince Tali chuckled. "Let's leave him here to sleep it off."

It was two hours later when Kevin heard Kane calling to him from far away. He struggled to let go of the dream and bring himself back to reality. When he opened his eyes, a smiling little face was looking down at him.

"Father, wake up. It's dinnertime."

Kevin sat up, wondering where the hell he was. He looked around, then realized he was in the garage. He realized something else, too. He was starving.

Later that evening Kevin watched as Kane drew cartoons. Drawing was one of Kane's favorite things to do. He was always sketching Raul, then turning the sketch into some funny character.

"It's time to get ready for bed, son."

Kane looked at his father, disappointment on his face. "Already?" He folded his drawing tablet and put his pencils away. "I hope I don't have that stupid dream again."

"I hope you don't either, but if you do, come wake me, okay?"

"Okay." Kane gave his father a hug. "Good-night."
"Good-night, son."

Kevin went into the kitchen and fixed a cup of coffee. *A chance like this might not come along again. I'm going to have to take the risk. What harm is there in writing a letter? I mean what the hell could he do to me if he found it...kill me? Well, I better not think about that.*

Kevin picked up Kane's drawing book and a pencil and sat down in a chair close to the lamp. He started thumbing through Kane's drawings. A proud smile appeared on his face. *Damn, these are good.* He turned the page to look at the next one. The smile left his face. He studied it very carefully, then realized why it looked so familiar. It was a drawing of Raul's face on the body of a frog. The frog sat in an old antique chair in the middle of a room. It was the room that made Kevin catch his breath. It resembled the lobby of the apartment house he'd been in that afternoon right down to the pool table. There was even a rough sketch of a stocky woman standing behind a counter, and with a little imagination, it resembled Betsy.

*How can this be? What does it mean? Is Kane's 'gift' different than mine? No, it can't be. There has to be a logical explanation for this.* Kevin laughed. *Logical...what the hell kind of word is that for me to use. Nothing about this whole thing is logical.*

Kevin stood and went to check on Kane, who was sleeping soundly. He was walking by the door that led to the main house when he heard someone knock. "Come in."

Zoric poked his head in. "Just wanted to check and see how you're doing, if you needed anything for your hangover."

Kevin looked at him. "Actually, I do. I was headed for the kitchen to fix coffee. Would you like a cup?"

"No thanks, it keeps me awake. I need to find out how much the rent was on that apartment."

"Four hundred and deposit. The lady never mentioned how much the deposit was."

"Okay, I'll take care of it. See you in the morning. Tali wants to leave by eight-thirty." He closed the door softly, not to disturb anyone.

Kevin made another cup of coffee and returned to the chair he'd been sitting in. He picked up the tablet again and studied the sketch.

*There's only one explanation for this. Kane must have met one of these men, or both, sometime during his life.* Kevin breathed a sigh of relief.

He turned to the back of the tablet and carefully removed two pieces of blank paper. He kept the cover of the tablet open, hoping it would block the view in case anyone was watching. This would to be a short letter, but Amanda would understand.

*Hello, my darling,*

*I pray this short letter finds its way to you, and that you and your new family are doing well. I miss you terribly and think of you everyday. Kane misses you, too. I've kept the promise I made to you and will continue to keep it until we meet again...hopefully. Everything's the same as it's always been. I spend most of my time tending to the garden and the beautiful flowers. They always seem like a special gift, just like the stars.*

*With love, Kevin.*

He picked up both pieces of paper and turned them over, writing down a few things about what happened at the apartment on the blank sheet. He then turned it over, sketching the apartment itself.

He folded the pieces together in thirds and closed the tablet. He reached up and turned out the light and the room went totally dark. He opened the tablet again and pulled the two pieces of paper apart, slipping one inside his shirt. The other he left in the tablet.

He entered his room and laid down on his bed, the letter to Amanda pressed against his heart.

It was about an hour later when he heard the main door open into his living quarters. He knew whoever came in had a flashlight and was inspecting the tablet lying on the table.

It was several minutes later when he heard the intruder leave, closing the door behind him. Kevin breathed a sigh of relief and closed his eyes, hoping his dreams would be filled with memories of Amanda. It was not to be. The shooting, more vivid than the night before, flashed through his mind with an added attraction...Betsy.

*Carole A. Sheller*

# Chapter 4

The next morning Kevin awoke, realizing he still had on the same clothes he had worn yesterday. The letter to Amanda was pressed inside his shirt.

He stood, removing his belt. His fingers touched the eagle on his buckle. A smile came to his face. *I might be a prisoner here, but I have something that Tali will never have...the love of two beautiful women.*

Kevin hung the belt on a hook in the closet and picked out a nice pair of dress pants and shirt. *Might as well go in style. Who knows when I'll get to town again.* He headed for the bathroom to clean up.

When he was finished, he smiled at himself in the mirror as he ran a comb through his dark brown hair. He had a muscular frame with a small waist and he kept his body in good shape by lifting weights and other forms of exercise. He liked arm wrestling, but the only one who gave him even a little competition was Mani. They both were about the same height, around six foot one, all though Mani out-weighed Kevin by at least twenty pounds, but it was twenty pounds of fat.

"Are you in there, Dad?" Kane asked as he knocked on the door.

"Yes, come in." He watched as his son entered. Kevin studied Kane closely. "Any dreams, son?"

"No. You're all dressed up. Are you going somewhere?" asked Kane.

"I'm going into town again. Can I bring you anything?"

Kane had a worried look on his face. "Is it because you have to help Prince Tali and Zoric?"

"Yes, that's one reason," said Kevin as he reached out and rubbed the hair on Kane's head, "and the other reason is to look for a special birthday present for a ten-year-old."

A big smile came to Kane's face. "That's not for another two months."

"I know, but I don't know when I'll be going back to town again."

"You better hide it real good so I don't find it."

Kevin laughed. "I know the perfect spot."

An hour later Kevin entered the dining room. Zoric and Prince Tali were waiting for him. "This is the first time I've seen you dressed up, McKade. What's the occasion?" Prince Tali asked.

"Just wanted to get rid of that ball and chain for a day, and I plan on going shopping for a special birthday present."

"We don't have to worry about you today, do we, McKade?" Zoric asked.

"I made a promise to my son and I'll honor that promise," Kevin said to Zoric. Then he looked at Prince Tali. "The next time there will be no promises, then you can worry. By the way, did you find what you were looking for last night?"

"I told you before, McKade, you're under surveillance twenty-four hours a day. Nothing's changed." Prince Tali stood. "Let's go."

They were silent until Zoric pulled the car to a stop about half a block from the apartment house. "What's the plan, McKade?"

"I think you both need to get out of here before someone recognizes you. I need to check another building, but I'm not sure which one, or even why, yet. I believe it's where the shooting is going to happen."

"What about the apartment?" asked Tali.

"The two men definitely have something to do with it."

Zoric counted out some money for Kevin. "There's enough for one month's rent and a four hundred dollar deposit. There's also a couple hundred extra for Kane's present."

"Thanks, Zoric. I'll spend it wisely. We'll meet at the same place around three or four." Kevin got out of the back seat of the small four-door car and headed up the street. He passed a flower shop and entered. He picked out a bouquet of flowers and waited for the clerk to wrap and put them in a box. He signed a small card—Betsy, Happy Birthday.

When he entered the lobby he looked around, amazed at how accurate Kane's drawing actually had been. No one was in sight, so he tapped the small bell sitting on the counter.

Betsy emerged from behind the drawn curtain. When she saw who it was, a big smile appeared on her face.

"Nice to see you again. I don't believe you told me your name."

"It's Kevin, Kevin McKade."

"Kevin, that's a nice name. I have bad news, Kevin. The two gentlemen returned last night and paid for two months."

"That's all right, Betsy. I decided I would take the apartment across the hall for a month, if it's still available."

"It certainly is."

"Good. This is for you." He handed her the box containing the flowers.

"Oh, they're lovely, but how did you know this was my birthday?"

Kevin shrugged his shoulders and smiled at her. "Could I see the apartment again?"

"Sure, why don't I just give you the key and you can go up and look around. Take your time and I'll start the paperwork."

Kevin rode the elevator to the top floor. The presence of the two men, not only on the elevator, but in the lobby and now in the hallway was felt strongly by him. *I'll never get used to this hollow, scared feeling that goes through my body when this happens.*

Kevin opened the door to the apartment. It wasn't very large, but it was cozy and comfortable in a homey sort of way. He left the door open as he entered the hallway. It didn't take him long before he found the door that led to the roof. A sign on it read 'Door locks automatically from outside.' Kevin pushed it open and lowered the foot knob at the bottom to prop it open. As he stepped out on the flat surface, a cool breeze greeted him.

A three-foot wall surrounded all four sides of the roof. Kevin walked to the edge that overlooked the street where the parade would take place the following day. He took a deep breath, realizing for the first time in his life that he was not fond of high places. He realized something else, too. This was not where the shooting would take place. *Okay, Kevin, get your act together. Figure out what the hell is going on here.* He walked to the side and looked down on the building next door. It was much smaller...only about four floors high. He walked to the back. *Nothing here but the alley and parking lot for the tenants.* He felt something pulling him to the other side of the roof. The building on that side was the same height, but longer and not as wide as the one he was on. The two buildings butted up against each other, making access to that roof very convenient. It was not a flat roof like the apartment dwelling, but dome-shaped. There were three large vents toward the middle. Then Kevin saw it. By the third vent, facing the main street below, was a small attic-type steeple with small windows. *That's it. Someone could probably hide inside and never*

41

*be seen. Well, I've done my part. Zoric or Tali will have to check it out now. This is where my bravery ends.*

Prince Tali and Zoric watched as Kevin walked down the street and entered the small flower shop.

"What the hell is he doing?" asked Prince Tali.

"You worry too much."

It was only a few minutes before Kevin came out carrying a small box. He entered the apartment building.

"Be right back," said Zoric.

A few minutes later he returned. "He bought a small bouquet of flowers with a card for the landlady of the apartment building." Zoric smiled. "You have to admit he's a classy guy. Have you decided on how we're going to handle these guys that are behind this mess?"

"There's only one way. I thought about letting the police in on it, but there's nothing they could do if no crime is committed. If they arrest these guys, they'd even be more determined than ever to eliminate us," Tali looked at Zoric. "I'd sure like to know who these creeps are."

Zoric could hear the concern in Prince Tali's voice. "We'll know soon enough. I'm sure McKade will find something."

"He finally made a believer out of you. Is that what you're saying, little brother?"

Zoric laughed. "It's damn spooky, the way they see things happen before they do. If I hadn't seen it with my own eyes, I wouldn't have believed it. Speaking of eyes...the way theirs change color—you have to admit when you see that happen, it scares the hell out of you."

Prince Tali laughed. "It sends chills up my spine. Mani was totally freaked out and he doesn't even know why. He just thinks McKade is weird."

The two men laughed at the memory. It was two hours later before they saw Kevin emerge from the apartment building.

Kevin left the roof and returned to the lobby. Again no one was there. *Quiet little place.* He tapped on the small bell. Betsy pulled the curtain aside. "Come in."

Kevin walked around the counter and stepped through the doorway, entering a small, but organized, office.

"Sit down, Kevin. Coffee?"

"Yes, thank you. Black is fine." He sat in the small chair across from her desk.

"This is a standard month-to-month lease," she said, as she handed him his coffee and sat down across from him. "If you decide to stay longer, it needs to be dated and re-signed."

"Sounds simple enough." Kevin picked up the piece of paper and read it. He signed it and reached into his pocket for the money. He also removed the letter to Amanda. After he had counted out four hundred for the rent and four hundred for a deposit he asked, "Would you have an envelope and a stamp I could buy? I need to mail a letter to the United States."

She opened the door on her desk and removed an envelope, handing it to him. He addressed it to A.D. Farly, in care of Lawrence Farly, P.O. Box DR321 Vermont USA. There was no return address.

He slipped the letter inside, sealed the flap, and picked up the stamp she had placed in front of him.

"Is there somewhere I could mail this?" he asked.

"There's a basket that tenants use for outgoing mail on the counter." She glanced at her watch. "They should be here to pick it up within the hour. Let me put it out there for you."

"Thank you." He handed the letter to her. "How much do I owe you?"

"Nothing." She smiled at him. "It's the least I can do to thank you for the lovely flowers." She placed the envelope in the basket and returned to her chair. "You never did tell me how you knew it was my birthday."

"A lucky guess." He smiled at her.

Three cups of coffee and an hour later, Kevin left her office just as the man picked up the mail. Kevin felt a sense of relief. It was almost like he'd done something illegal and gotten away with it. He smiled at Betsy. "Thanks for the coffee. See you later this afternoon." He reached out to shake her hand.

"Thank you, Kevin. By the way, if you decide you don't want that apartment on the top floor, I have one available on the third floor. It's a corner unit, facing the main street."

"Maybe I'll take a look at it when I return." He waved good-bye as he left the building. *Nice lady. All I have to do is figure out how to*

43

*save her life.*

He walked toward the car, opened the back door and got in. "I see you two didn't get very far."

"Did you see the gunmen?" asked Zoric.

"No. Betsy, the landlady, said they came back last night and paid two months in advance. They're brothers."

"Did you get their names?" Prince Tali asked impatiently.

"Yes, they are Basil and Cyril Dooron."

Zoric looked at Prince Tali. "Do you know them?"

"Yes. I haven't seen or heard from them since I kicked them and their family off the island a couple of years ago."

"Why?" asked Zoric.

"You name it! They were bullies, beating up on the younger kids, stealing money from them, destroying other's property. I warned their family that if it continued, they'd have to leave the island. The father pleaded with me to give them another chance. Things were quiet for about a year; then several robberies happened. I wasn't real sure who was behind them until they robbed Mr. Demetrius' liquor store and beat him up pretty badly."

"I remember who they are now," said Zoric. "We took Mani and a couple other guards, along with a moving truck. Packed up the family belongings and escorted them to the mainland."

"That's them." Prince Tali nodded his head.

"I remember something else," Zoric said. "You told them if they ever tried to come back on Tali Island, they'd never see another sunrise."

Kevin looked at Prince Tali. "Would Kane ever have had an opportunity to meet them?"

Prince Tali thought for a moment. "He could have. I'm not positive. He accompanied me and Raul several times into Tali Town. Is that important?"

"Could be. Don't know yet."

"What else did you find out?" asked Zoric.

"When I was telling you about the dream, I said no one realized that both of you had been shot for several minutes. I now know why. It seems there was an accident and it drew the attention of the people around the apartment building."

"Do you know what happened?" asked Prince Tali.

"Yes." Kevin laid his head back, resting it on the seat, and closed his eyes. "The shooting doesn't take place on the apartment building's roof, but the building on the west side." Kevin told them the layout he'd seen. "One of the men hides behind that small window. He has a gun with a scope attached to the top and a silencer on the end. The other man is on the apartment building roof, hiding behind one of the vents. He's waiting for Betsy, knowing she plans on watching the parade from there. She steps out onto the roof, carrying a folding chair. She works her way to the other side, setting her chair up in the far corner. The man closes the door to the roof and puts a heavy board under the knob. He braces it to the floor so no one else will be able to enter onto the roof. He waits until he sees the signal that your car is approaching, then he walks up behind her and speaks. Startled, she stands and he pushes her. She falls to the ground."

Kevin opens his eyes slowly. They had changed color.

Prince Tali took a deep breath. "Then what happens?"

"As the people are gathering around her, your car is about half a block away. The gunman in the window is holding the gun. It is pointed directly at you." Kevin's voice becomes shaky. "He fires once, hitting Zoric. The second shot hits you. You're both dead."

Zoric and Prince Tali looked at each other. Kevin noticed how pale they both looked.

After a few minutes, Zoric asked, "What happens to the men on the roof?"

Kevin leaned back again and closed his eyes. "The one on the apartment roof jumps to the other roof. He helps his brother crawl out the window. Then they go to the back where there's a fire escape ladder down to the ground, and they both crawl over the side and down the ladder. They get into a car, laughing and smiling as they drive away. The ambulance arrives, but it's too late. Betsy and the two of you are dead."

The three men sat there, each consumed with his own thoughts. It was Kevin who finally broke the silence.

"I have to keep Betsy from getting on that roof." He knew it was something Prince Tali didn't want to hear.

Finally Prince Tali spoke. "If we catch these two tonight, or before the parade begins, it's something you won't have to worry about."

"You're putting a lot of emphasis on 'if'," Kevin said. As he sat there in the back seat, he realized Prince Tali wasn't going out of his way to help Betsy. He would have to do it himself. "I need to check out another apartment. I haven't figured out why yet, but I'll do that this afternoon. Now I want to go shopping. Do you gentlemen want to join me?"

Prince Tali turned to look at him, a smug look on his face. "Zoric will go with you." Turning his head toward his brother, he said, "Drop me off at the office. When you finish, both of you meet me there and we'll decide what to do."

Zoric nodded his head in agreement, started the car and drove off. Fifteen minutes later he pulled up in front of a very exclusive building. Prince Tali got out as a doorman approached.

"You might as well sit in front with me, McKade," Zoric said.

Prince Tali waited until Kevin changed seats. Then he closed the car door. He watched Zoric drive off down the street before turning and entering the building.

He opened the door to his penthouse suite and walked in. This was the only place, besides his home on the island, that he felt safe. He opened the French doors that led to the balcony. The fresh air gently greeted him.

He sat down in the big overstuffed chair. His mind went over everything that happened the last two days, wondering if there was any possible way McKade could be wrong. He had a hard time accepting the fact that someone wanted him dead—that they would kill Zoric just to get to him.

He walked out on the balcony, his eyes scanning the city below. *McKade's right. There will be the death of two brothers tomorrow and it sure as hell isn't going to be Zoric and me. All I have to decide is what to do with the bodies—use the quicksand pit or the deep blue sea.* Prince Tali smiled to himself as he made his way inside and headed toward the wet bar. After fixing himself a drink, he called and ordered a late lunch for the three of them, then sat back down in his favorite chair. His mind went back in time to the first killing he'd witnessed. He was thirteen.

"You're old enough to know now," his father told him. "We protect what is ours."

Prince Tali remembered trying to be brave, but inside he was terrified. He asked if it was necessary to kill the man. His father explained, "Yes, it is. This man, Hemly, killed your big brother, Boris, by picking him up and throwing him through a plate glass window. Boris bled to death before help could reach him. Hemly will be punished by Tali law."

Prince Tali remembered the fear leaving his body, another emotion replaced it. He wanted to kill the man himself.

His father took him to the guard quarters where Hemly was strapped to a chair, his legs and arms bound securely to its frame with his palms up. His mouth was taped shut. Prince Tali heard again the words his father spoke, looking straight into Hemly's eyes.

"You think you're such a big man, picking on someone half your size. My son was only sixteen. You laughed as you watched him bleed to death, begging for help. Now, you will die the same way."

I watched as my father pulled the knife from his pocket and opened it up. Hemly squirmed in his chair, his head twisting back and forth. My father lowered the knife, making a deep slash just above the man's right wrist. Blood spurted out. I walked up to my father and held out my hand. He gently laid the knife in it. I looked into the eyes of this killer and saw fear and tears. The hatred for him swelled up inside me. I lowered the knife and slashed his left wrist. My father and I pulled up chairs and sat in front of him, watching him die.

When it was over, my father untied him, threw his body over his shoulder and carried him outside to where the horses were. He laid the body across one of them, then saddled two more horses and we headed for a place on the island that was strictly off limits to everyone, including me—The Tali Island Jungle. My father warned me again never to come there unless it was absolutely necessary.

It took almost an hour before we reached the sand pit. Getting down from our horses, we removed the body. My father took the arms and I picked up the legs, swinging the body into the pit, watching as the earth consumed it.

We were silent on the ride back to the estate. Then my father said to me again, "We take care of our own." Nothing of what happened that day was ever spoken of again.

When I was eighteen and Zoric was fourteen, we found our grandfather's body washed up on shore. We thought he had died from natural causes until my father received a card that same day. 'Maybe you're a better swimmer than your old man. Stay out of our way or the same thing will happen to you and your sons. The Island no longer belongs to you. Get off!'

The next day my father took Zoric and me to the guardhouse and there strapped in a chair was a stranger. My father told us the man admitted killing our grandfather and he must die according to Tali law. My father didn't know who this man was or his name. He didn't care.

We built a box and my father drilled about four, three inch holes in the bottom. With his arms and legs bound, the three of us put him in the box then carried it out to our truck and headed for the dock where we kept our boat. We loaded the box and sailed out to sea. The man was screaming and begging the whole time. Finally, bringing the boat to a stop, we lifted the box overboard and waited until it sank.

It was a year later when a shot was fired that killed our father. It turned out the killer was related to the man we buried at sea, his uncle.

As Prince Tali remembered the past, a strange feeling passed through him. The faces of the two men Kevin told him about took on a different meaning. *There's something about them that seems familiar.* The feeling passed as quickly as it arrived. He remembered how he and Zoric shot the man that killed their father. Prince Tali made his second trip to the pit; Zoric, his first.

He sat there in his chair thinking about McKade. His father had showed him the letter from Jeffrey McKade after the death of Tali's grandfather. He made Tali promise that no matter what happened, he was to keep looking for a male McKade related to Jeffrey. Tali promised.

"You'll know he's a true McKade by his eyes," his father told him.

Tali traced the McKade family from Ireland to Scotland, then lost track of them. It was a year later when he learned of the death of Kevin's parents, but no trace of Kevin could be found.

Then, as if a gift from above, he and Zoric were walking down the street when they noticed a small boy hopping around inside a barber shop. They were drawn to him first because he was close in age to Prince Tali's son, Raul. Then they noticed his eyes. Prince Tali couldn't keep his own eyes off the boy. It was only a few minutes before a man picked up the small boy and left the shop, his eyes the same color as the boy's.

"Let's pick him up and ask a few questions. If it's not him, we'll let him go. No harm done," Prince Tali told Zoric. "But first, go in and see what you can learn about him."

Zoric entered the barber shop, approaching a man at the counter. "Are you in charge here?" he asked.

"Yes. What can I do for you today?"

"Can you tell me who that man was who just left with the little boy?" Zoric flashed three large bills.

"Sure, he's come in here a few times. Nice man. Name's Kevin, Kevin Kincade. He mentioned having a daughter. I believe he's a gardener and his wife, a teacher. That's all I know."

"Thanks." Zoric handed him the money. "I've never been in here, no matter who asks. Understand?"

The man nodded his head. "No problem." He smiled at Zoric as he put the money in his pocket.

Zoric walked out of the barber shop and looked around. Prince Tali was nowhere in sight. Zoric got into his car and drove to the corner. He saw his brother about halfway down the next street. He pulled the car up beside him and Prince Tali got in. Zoric told him what he had found out.

Prince Tali remembered the look on McKade's face when he came up beside him as he walked down the street.

"Hello, McKade."

"Sorry, you've got the wrong man. My name's Kincade."

"Like hell it is. I'm only going to say this once. I want you and your son to get in the car. Your wife and daughter are fine. As long as you co-operate, they won't be hurt. That's a promise, but if you give me any trouble or try to escape, you'll be responsible for what happens to them." Prince Tali opened the back door of the car. McKade and his son got in.

For the next two days, Prince Tali and Zoric tried to find out information about McKade's wife and daughter, but they found nothing. Prince Tali kept searching for another year. One of his investigators suspected they were dead or had fled the country. There was absolutely no trace of them.

Now, over eight years later, as Prince Tali sat there, he tried to sort out his feelings for McKade. *I damn well respect the man. He gave up his life for that of his son and family. Could I kill him if I was faced with the choice?* Prince Tali thought for several minutes. *Yes...yes, I would do it if it meant protecting Raul and Zoric. I wouldn't like it, but I'd do it. Let's hope I'm never put in that situation. If I don't let down my guard and keep him under surveillance, I should never have to make that kind of decision.*

# Chapter 5

It was close to twelve-thirty when lunch arrived. Zoric and Kevin showed up about ten minutes later. As the three of them ate, they talked about the next day.

"When you see us being shot, McKade, can you tell me where the bullets hit?"

Kevin thought for a few minutes, then closed his eyes. That always seemed to help when he had to concentrate very deeply. "It seems you're both hit in the heart. The man's an excellent shot."

"I sure am glad to hear that." Zoric laughed. "I always demand the best, no matter what it is."

Kevin joined in his laughter. It helped relieve some of the tension. Kevin yawned.

"You going to make it?" asked Zoric.

"One more thing I have to take care of, then I'll be ready to head back to the island."

"Have you figured out what it is?" Prince Tali asked suspiciously.

"Something to do with a lock," Kevin lied. "I need to see this other apartment. I still don't know why, but I will." He reached his hand into his pocket and pulled out the key Betsy had given him. He handed it to Zoric. "I'll go in first and have Betsy take me to see this other apartment. If you want to check out the place, this would be a good time. This is a nice office you have here, Tali. You should stay here more often. Now, if you'll excuse me, I'll use your bathroom and then be ready to go."

Zoric pointed and said. "Down the hall."

He waited until Kevin couldn't hear him, then asked, "Got a plan?"

"I want everything to go along as originally planned. I'll have two guards take our place. They'll be wearing bullet-proof vests. You and Mani will wait in the back of the building. Once you have captured the men, I'll drive up in the limo. We'll put them in the back, bring them to the island for a decent burial."

"And the woman?"

"Like I said, everything is to go along as originally planned." Prince Tali leaned forward to look at Zoric. "Sometimes, little brother, sacrifices have to be made. Pick me up here when you're through."

They rode in silence until Zoric pulled the car to a stop close to the apartment house. "Is there anything you can do to help this woman, McKade?"

Kevin was touched by the concern he heard in Zoric's voice. "I'll do what I can."

Kevin entered the lobby. Again, no one was around. He touched the bell and Betsy appeared from behind the curtain.

"Kevin, I was hoping it would be you."

"I think I'll look at that other apartment. Do you have time now?"

"Sure do."

It was larger than the one on the sixth floor. Kevin liked the view of main street much better. At least his stomach wasn't turning in circles.

"Can we talk for a minute?" Kevin asked as he sat down at the small kitchen table.

"Okay." Betsy sat in the chair next to him. She looked into his eyes and a peaceful, contented feeling passed through her.

"What is it, Kevin?" she asked softly.

"I hope I can explain this in a way that won't let you think I'm totally insane. Have you ever walked down a strange street and felt you've walked down it before; or went to answer the phone and knew who was on the other end of the line; or met a stranger and knew it was their birthday?" He couldn't help but smile.

Betsy chuckled. "Well, one out of three. What are you trying to tell me?"

"Yesterday I entered this building for the first time in my life." Kevin held up his right hand. "I swear," he said, "it seemed familiar. Then, since you showed me the apartment those two men rented, I've had this strange feeling about them." Kevin leaned forward and looked directly into her eyes. "I don't trust them. I've never met them, couldn't begin to tell you what they look like, but they're bad news." Kevin picked up her hand and held it in both of his. "I want you to make me a promise."

"What kind of promise?" she asked.

"I don't want you to go up on the roof tomorrow to watch the parade."

"Don't be silly. I always watch the parade from the roof. It's a great view."

"Couldn't you watch if from this room?"

"Probably, but I'd like to know why."

"If I told you something was going to happen today and it came true, would you then promise you'll stay off the roof tomorrow?" Kevin had a big smile on his face.

"What's going to happen today?" she asked.

"It's something that will make you extremely happy...well?"

Her curiosity finally won. "Okay, I promise. What is it?"

He turned her hand over, then turned it back again. "You don't have any children of your own, but you have a stepson whom you care about as if he was your own."

Her other hand went to her heart. A shocked look appeared on her face. "How did you know?"

His eyes met hers and he shrugged his shoulders. "You haven't seen him in what, three years now?"

"That's close enough. I haven't seen him since he married a girl he met when he was in the Philippines. I didn't want him to marry her and we got in a big argument. That was the last time I talked to him."

Kevin could see the sadness in her face. "They're coming to see you today. They want their son to meet his grandmother."

Happiness spread through her. "Are you sure about this, Kevin?"

"I hope so. It feels right. You won't forget about your promise?" Kevin stood.

She sat there, looking up into his eyes. The trust she felt for Kevin could be seen on her face. She stood. "No, I won't forget my promise."

Kevin smiled at her. "Good. I have to leave now. I'm late for an important business meeting. Have a wonderful birthday." He folded his arms around her.

She hugged him back. "How can I ever thank you?"

"Save me a piece of birthday cake." He kissed her forehead. "You'd better go and get ready, they'll be here in a couple of hours. Actually, I think they might enjoy staying in this apartment for a few days."

They were standing in the hall, waiting for the elevator. When it arrived and the doors opened, there stood Zoric.

Kevin smiled. "Oh, here's my driver now, right on time."

As they walked down the street, Kevin said, "She's probably watching us." A big grin appeared on his face.

"Shit," Zoric said as he opened the back door for Kevin and waited until he got in. Then he got behind the wheel. He glanced at Kevin in the rearview mirror. "Next time I'll bring my chauffeur's hat."

"You better, or I might have to fire your ass." They both laughed.

"Everything go okay?" asked Zoric.

"I hope so. How about with you?"

"Didn't see or hear anything, great view of the alley."

"I thought so," said Kevin.

Zoric called Prince Tali on the car phone. He was waiting outside when they arrived.

"Everything okay?" he asked Zoric as he got in the front seat.

"Fine."

"And you, McKade. What was so important about this other apartment?"

"Nothing to do with you, but I had to make sure. It seems Betsy's going to have some unexpected company and the lock on the roof door was sticking, nothing a little oil won't cure. I do believe my services are no longer needed." Kevin stretched his body out on the back seat and in minutes was sound asleep, not waking until they were back on the island.

The next morning, Kevin watched from his garden as a limo with Zoric and Prince Tali drove away. Behind them was another car with Mani and two other men. Then he saw the blue convertible limo with 'Tali Island' stamped in gold lettering on both sides. J.J. was driving and accompanied by another guard. *Don't tell me I'm alone.* Kevin glanced around. *Who am I kidding! They probably left some trigger happy punk with a 'shoot first, ask questions later', attitude.*

Kevin yawned. He hadn't slept well the night before, worrying about Kane, but no dreams came to either of them. He walked back to the Estate. Kane and Raul were probably finished with breakfast by now. The boys had a full day planned. Their teacher was taking them to see the parade and later that afternoon J.J. would start their first fencing lessons.

Kevin waved good-bye to the boys and walked back to his living quarters. He slipped off his shorts and shirt and stretched out on his bed. He thought about the letter to Amanda, wondering how long it would take before she received it. He smiled to himself. *I'll know. Sometimes this gift has its advantages.*

It was close to one o'clock in the afternoon when Kevin opened his eyes. He heard again the scream from Betsy, but this time she was standing in front of a window in the apartment on the third floor. She screamed as the body fell from above, crashing to the ground below. Her family was there to comfort her as she cried uncontrollably. "That could have been me, that could have been me."

Kevin heard the gun shots—four. He realized it wasn't coming from his dream, but here on the estate. He jumped out of bed, pulled on his clothes and ran down the hall, then out the back door onto the veranda. He saw Prince Tali and Zoric load two bodies into the back of a pickup truck down by the guard house. They drove off in the direction of The Tali Island Jungle.

Kevin looked around, but no one else was in sight. He barely made it back to his bathroom before the urge to vomit overcame him. When he finished, his body felt completely drained. He lay back down on his bed, not waking again until early evening.

*I'm so thirsty. What crawled in my mouth and died?* After drinking several glasses of water and brushing his teeth, Kevin made his way to the living room.

Kane watched as he sank down in his favorite chair. "You okay, Dad?" He smiled at his father. "I tried to wake you, but you were really zonked."

"I'm fine. How did it go today?"

"It was the greatest." Kane put down his drawing tablet. He went over, sat down by Kevin and told him about the parade and his fencing lessons. There was no mention of any dreams or killings, only the events of one day in the life of a nine-year-old boy.

"Zoric brought you some dinner. He put it in the oven to keep warm."

"That was nice of him. Did you eat?"

"Yep, with Raul. Zoric said he'd come by later to see if you wanted to play a game of chess."

Kevin went into the kitchen and opened the oven door. *Yum! One of my favorites, corned beef and cabbage.*

Kane showed Kevin the moves he learned from his first fencing lesson. "Prince Tali stopped by and fenced with the teacher. I was surprised, he's pretty good."

"I think I'd like to learn, too," Kevin said. "Do you think you could teach me what you learn?"

A big smile came to Kane's face. "Sure."

It was close to ten o'clock when Zoric knocked on the door. "I come bearing gifts." He held up a bottle of very expensive brandy. "Ready for another lesson in chess?"

"Sounds good. Maybe this will be my night for winning."

"Maybe."

Both knew that when the evening was over, Zoric would walk out the door as the winner. He was the one who taught Kevin, Kane and Raul how to play. Zoric loved the game and Kevin was the only one on the island that gave him any competition.

Kevin checked on Kane. He wanted to make sure he was sleeping before he and Zoric talked.

When he returned, Zoric had poured them both a brandy. He handed one to Kevin. "My thanks go out to you again, McKade."

They sat down at the table, setting up the game of chess between them.

"Who was the man that fell from the roof?" Kevin asked.

Zoric leaned back and took a drink of brandy before answering. "It seems he was a long-time tenant, lived there about five years. The police think he had a heart attack and fell. They'll be checking it out so I'll let you know what they come up with. I do know they called Betsy's brother. He's a doctor and gave her some medicine to calm her down. Everything else happened just like you said. I've gotta tell you, McKade, it's the spookiest damn feeling to see things happen...things you know are going to happen."

"You should be on this side." Kevin couldn't help but chuckle.

Zoric shook his head, then slapped the palm of his hand against his forehead. "Right! What the hell am I doing, telling you." He was silent for a moment, then spoke. "McKade, I have to ask you a question. If it had just been Tali, would you have told us?"

Kevin looked directly into Zoric's eyes, thinking about his answer before he finally spoke. "Honestly, I don't know. I will never forgive your brother. He took away the few years I would have had with Kane's mother. She's dead now. I don't know if I would be capable of taking a father away from his child."

Zoric knew he was talking about Raul.

"I will tell you this. I will escape someday and Kane will be by my side. Now I have to ask you a favor."

"What?"

"I want you to go see Betsy for me."

"I don't think that's a good idea," said Zoric.

"It's the least you can do for my saving your life."

"You trying to lay a guilt trip on me, McKade?"

"Yes, if that's what it takes."

Zoric laughed. "All right, it worked. What do you want me to do?"

"I want you to go see Betsy, tell her I had to leave town, family emergency or whatever. Tell her to keep the money from both apartments because the tenants won't be returning. Tell her the view from the roof is beautiful this time of year. Enjoy it. Oh, one more thing, tell her to save me that piece of cake. I will be back."

"That's it?" Zoric asked.

"I think so. I'll let you know if there's anything else."

"I'll do this for you, McKade, but I'd like to wait a day or two till things cool down."

"Sounds fair." Kevin held up his glass. "To my kicking your ass and maybe I'll even win at chess."

Zoric threw back his head and laughed. "In a fair fight, McKade, you might be able to kick my ass, but you'll never beat me in chess."

It was three o'clock in the morning when Zoric said goodnight, the winner of all four games.

Kevin awoke the next morning, feeling at peace with himself. He didn't know if it was from the brandy or because no dreams invaded his sleep.

*Carole A. Sheller*

# Chapter 6
## TALI ISLAND
## THREE YEARS LATER,
## ON A SATURDAY MORNING IN JUNE

Kevin opened his eyes and closed them again. His head throbbed with pain. This was the first true vision he had ever had of his daughter, Katy. There had been one other, years ago. Small bits and pieces of a tiger and a small boy. He knew Katy saved the boy's life.

This vision was more vivid. Kevin could see a man swing a bat, hitting two small boys, probably his sons, and a woman. Blood was everywhere, especially around the woman. Then the man is hit with the bat and Kevin knows the man can no longer hurt the two boys or the woman. The vision fades.

All these years Kevin had tried to block Katy from his mind. He knew if something happened to her and he was not there to protect her, he would go crazy. A smile came to his face. He knew she could protect herself. There were people who loved her. Kevin was sure one of them was Meg's sister, Elizabeth Riley. Kevin didn't know who the man was, but he was much too young to be Katy and Kane's grandfather, Matthew Riley. Whoever he was, this man loved his Katy and would protect her.

Kevin opened his eyes, the headache slowly faded away. He tried to picture what Katy looked like, but couldn't. The image of Meg was always there.

He wondered again, as he'd done a thousand times before, if he had made the right decision. Well, right or wrong, now that he knew Katy was absolutely safe, he needed to tell Kane about her. *If something happened to me, they might never find each other. I have to find some way of telling him and soon...think McKade, think, think, think.* Kevin drifted back to sleep.

# KANE
# EARLY THAT SAME
# SATURDAY MORNING

"Are you sure you won't change your mind and ride in the race today?" Raul asked.

Kane looked at his friend and smiled. "I'm sure."

The sun was just coming up over the horizon. Kane watched the coloring of the clouds begin. This was his favorite time of day. He wished he was sitting on the hill by the lake, instead of here at the corral, helping Raul load his champion horse for the big race in Tali Town today.

"I'd be glad to meet you in the winners' circle and share half the prize money."

"You really think I'll win, Kane?"

"Of course, there's not another horse in the whole country, hell, probably in the whole world that can beat Sassy." Kane touched the horse's nose. "Ain't that right, Sassy?"

The horse shook her head as if saying yes. Both boys laughed. Kane could see the confidence building up in Raul.

"You two punks ready yet?" Mani asked as he walked up to them.

Raul smiled at him and started hopping around as if he was a boxer throwing punches in the air. "I'm a rowdy teenager now, Mani, and next month Kane's going to be one, too. We just might be able to knock you on your fanny."

Kane joined Raul, hopping and boxing around the corral.

"You two are punks, always have been, always will be, " Mani said as he turned and walked toward the guard house.

"I get the feeling Mani doesn't love us. You feel it ,too, Kane?"

The boys were still laughing and joking around when Mani returned an hour later.

"Let's go."

"I thought J.J. was taking us?" Raul said.

"Last minute changes." Mani said. "He'll ride over later with your father. I'm driving you."

The smile faded from Kane's face. "That's a downer."

Raul shook his head in agreement.

They were silent on the ride over to Tali Town.

Kane helped Raul unload Sassy. "Don't let Mani ruin everything. This is your day, Raul. Your dad's going to be so proud. One more thing..." Kane smiled.

"What's that?"

"It's the only thing you're good at."

The tension left Raul's body, replaced by laughter.

That was how J.J. found them about an hour later.

"How's my little champ?" J.J. asked as he smiled and patted Raul on the back.

"Nervous. I'm sure glad you're here. Where's Dad?"

"Over at the lodge. He wants you and Kane to meet him there and get a bite to eat. I've got a package to deliver on the mainland, then I'll pick up Kevin. We'll be back here in time to see you win that race."

The boys watched him drive away. "Have you ever wondered why your dad doesn't drive?" Raul asked Kane.

"Not really. You ever wonder why *your* dad doesn't drive?"

"He's a Prince, that's why."

"Well, maybe my dad's a King," Kane said with a smile on his face.

"King Kevin, I like it. Come on, let's go meet the Prince."

Kane picked up his drawing tablet. "No thanks, I'll catch you later. I'm working on something real important. I'm going to find a tree that's looking for someone to lean against, like that one over by the picnic table."

Raul laughed. "Okay. I'll bring you back a worm sandwich, with spoiled cole slaw on the side, and a piece of maggot cake with buffalo chips on top for dessert."

"Umm, sounds great." Kane rubbed his stomach. "I'm starving."

The boys headed in separate directions.

Kane propped himself against the tree and opened his tablet to the drawing of Raul's horse, Sassy, and started to draw the winning lei that circled Sassy's head. He looked over toward the stables where the veterinarian and his assistant were checking the horses. He knew who they were by the official bands they wore around the top part of their right arms.

Kane yawned, then looked at his watch. *Two hours yet before the race. Think I'll stretch out and take a little nap.* He yawned again, moving away from the tree. He lay on his back on the soft grass, putting his tablet behind his head. It wasn't his hill by the lake, but it would do. Within minutes his breathing became regular and a deep sleep swept him into dreamland.

Kane awoke, sitting straight up. His breath came in quick, heavy intervals. The weather was hot, making him sweat, but his hands were ice cold, his mind swirling from the vision he'd just had.

He glanced at his watch. *Forty-five minutes before the race. I've got to keep Raul off Sassy!* He knew what he had to do...find Prince Tali.

He stood, looked around the arena, and spotted Tali who was walking in the direction of the stable. Raul was nowhere in sight.

"Prince Tali!" he screamed as he ran toward his friend's father.

By the time Kane reached Prince Tali, he was shaking and could hardly catch his breath. Tears were streaming down his cheeks.

"What is it, Kane?" Prince Tali asked. Panic spread through him as he looked into the strange-colored eyes of the boy. He put his hands on Kane's shoulders, trying to comfort him. "What do you see?"

"It's Raul. You have to keep him from riding Sassy in the race."

Prince Tali heard the fear in Kane's voice. "Why?"

"After Sassy wins the race, she goes crazy, bucking off Raul and stomping him in the head with her front hoofs."

Kane sobbed uncontrollably as Prince Tali wrapped his arms around him. "It's going to be all right, Kane. I'll take care of everything."

Prince Tali waited a few minutes before he spoke again. "I want you to go and wait in the car. Put these on." He handed Kane his sunglasses.

"I need to call my father," Kane said.

"We'll call him from Zoric's car. If your father's not at the Estate, J.J. probably picked him up and they're on their way here."

Prince Tali glanced at his watch. *Thirty-five minutes before race time.* "Let's hurry, Kane."

Prince Tali picked up the car phone and called J.J. first. "Where are you?"

"Just getting ready to turn onto the Island entrance road. I should be able to pick up McKade and be there in time to see Raul win."

"Good." Prince Tali then dialed the estate. When Kevin answered, Prince Tali could hear the urgency in his voice. "Everything is fine, McKade. Kane got to me in time. Raul won't ride in the race."

"Thank God. Where's Kane?"

"Right here. I'll let you talk to him. I'm on my way to find Raul." He handed the phone to Kane.

"Dad."

"Are you okay, son?"

"I think so. It was so horrible, Dad. What would make Sassy do that?"

Kevin could tell Kane had been crying. "It's all right. Nothing's going to happen to Raul. Prince Tali will take care of everything. Where are you?"

"In Zoric's car."

"Stay there. I'm waiting for J.J. and we'll be there as soon as we can."

"I'm so scared."

"I know you are, son. Try to relax...walk around...take a few deep breaths. You saved Raul's life. Did I ever tell you? You're my hero."

Kane chuckled. "Oh Dad, you're silly. Anyway, it's not me who will save Raul, but Prince Tali."

They talked until Kevin heard the horn honk. "J.J.'s here. I'm on my way." Kevin hung up the phone, put on sunglasses and headed out the door.

Kane sat in the driver's seat, his hands on the wheel. He laid his head back, closed his eyes and thought about Raul. A smile came to his face. Prince Tali got to Raul in time. *I think he's just a tiny bit upset.* The smile faded, replaced by a frown. A feeling he'd had several times, of someone pulling at him, entered his body. *Who are you? What do you want? I know you're out there somewhere.* The feeling lasted longer this time. Kane opened the car door, he needed to find Raul.

"I'm going to ride Sassy in this race. I don't care what you say." Tears stung Raul's eyes as he hollered at his father.

"No, you're not...not in this race! Look at me." Prince Tali touched Raul's shoulder. Their eyes met. "You know I've been with you all the way on this, maybe even pushing you too hard to win. I wouldn't keep you from racing and winning if it wasn't extremely important. Trust me on this, Son."

Raul glared at his father, wanting to tell him he hated him, but he couldn't. He loved his father more than anything.

He lowered his head, breaking eye contact. "Are you sure there's nothing I can say that would change your mind?"

Prince Tali smiled, pulling his son toward him. "I'm sure. I know this is breaking your heart. Mine too. I'll make it up to you, somehow. Why don't you go find Kane. I'll take care of everything here." Prince Tali watched Raul slowly walk away, then he turned and headed for the stables.

He found Sassy, along with her new trainer, Berto. He was a six-teen-year-old, tall, skinny, quiet kid. "How's she doing today?" Prince Tali asked as he stroked the horse's neck.

"She's ready to race. Where's Raul?"

"There's been a change of plans. Raul's not feeling too good, so I'm pulling him and Sassy out of the race."

"But sir, if Sassy doesn't race today, she'll be disqualified for the rest of the year. I could ride her."

Prince Tali studied the boy for a few minutes before answering. "Are you sure you can handle her?"

Berto's face lit up. "Yes, sir."

"Okay. I'll inform the officials of the change in riders."


J.J. pulled the car up alongside Zoric's. Kevin was out of the car before he could turn off the engine.

Kane saw his father and ran toward him.

Kevin wrapped him in his arms. "Are you okay?"

"I am, but I don't know about Raul. He said he wanted to be left alone."

"Where is he?"

"Over there." Kane pointed. "Standing by the fence. The race is about to start, but he doesn't want to watch it."

"Let's go keep him company."

Kane smiled at his father. "Okay."

When they reached Raul, Kevin touched him on the shoulder. "I'm sorry this had to happen, Raul."

"I don't understand why my father is doing this to me."

"It's not you. It's the horse. There's something wrong with Sassy and your father had to keep her out of the race."

They heard the firing of the gun, which signaled the start of the race.

The three of them stood there in silence, far enough away to barely hear the announcer over the noise from the crowd, but they heard J.J. hollering at them. "Hurry! Come and watch! Sassy's winning!"

"What?" the three of them said at the same time, as they started running toward J.J. They got there just in time to see Sassy cross the finish line. Then they watched in horror as the horse went crazy, throwing the young rider off, rearing up and coming down with her front hoofs on the boy's head.

The crowd became silent. The only noise came from the snorting sound made by Sassy. A scream echoed through the crowd, bringing everyone back to reality.

Kevin was the first to react. "J.J., get Sassy! Take her back to the stable, check her out, and be careful. Kane, you and Raul go with him." Kevin ran toward the boy, Berto. He knelt down beside him, checking his pulse. "He's alive. Someone get a doctor and an ambulance. He's bleeding badly."

A crowd had gathered. A voice could be heard from the back. "Let me through. I'm a doctor, let me through."

Kevin stood and waved his arms in the air. "Over here, doctor."

People separated to let the man through. He knelt down by the boy. "Has anyone moved him?"

"No," answered Kevin, kneeling down beside him.

"Good." The doctor checked the boy over as best he could. "He has a good heartbeat. We won't know the extent of his injuries until we run tests. He needs to be taken to the hospital on the mainland. He's lost a lot of blood."

"No," came a voice from behind them. "We have a clinic here. That's where he'll be taken."

Kevin turned. Prince Tali stood there. Before anyone could stop him, Kevin rose from the ground with all the power he had. "You bastard," he said as his fist connected with Prince Tali's jaw, knocking him backward through the air. Tali landed flat on his back.

Zoric and Mani grabbed Kevin before he could do any more harm.

"Cool down, McKade," Zoric said.

Kevin was leaning over Prince Tali's body. "I'm going to be sick and unless you want me to puke all over him, you should let me go."

Zoric knew he was telling the truth. "Let him go, Mani."

Kevin looked at Zoric. "Thanks! Even my puke is too good for him." He turned and walked away, not getting very far before he became violently ill.

That was where J.J. found him. "You and Kane must have eaten the same thing. The kid is really sick. Maybe the doctor should have a look at both of you."

"We're okay, J.J. Where is Kane?"

"On the other side of the stable, lying in the grass."

When Kevin found him, Kane was sleeping soundly. Kevin laid down beside his son, touching Kane's cheek softly with his hand, then rolled over on his back. Within minutes he, too, was sleeping soundly.

"How long have they been asleep?" asked Prince Tali.

"Two, almost three hours," answered Zoric. "You want me to wake them up?"

"No, let them sleep." He touched his left jaw. "McKade packs a pretty mean right."

"Be thankful he didn't hit you with his left. It's a killer." Zoric laughed, his brother joining in.

"What's the punishment for knocking Prince Tali on his ass?" asked Zoric.

"Why, the pits, of course." The laughter began again, but after a few minutes the smile left Prince Tali's face. "I really feel bad about the boy."

"I know you do, brother. What about Sassy?"

"Whoever put those burrs under her saddle knew what they were doing. It wouldn't matter who was riding her, she would have reacted the same."

"I'll talk to McKade tomorrow when he's feeling better," Zoric said.

"Okay, little brother. I think I'll go back to the estate. Would you stop by the clinic and see how the boy is doing. Tell that doctor, or whoever is in charge, that if they think he should be sent to the hospital on the mainland, it's all right. I want what's best for him."

Zoric watched his brother walk away. He wanted to ask him why he let Sassy race. In fact, he had a lot of questions he'd like answered, but they would have to wait. *I've got more important things to take care of.* He walked over to J.J. "Keep an eye on our sleeping beauties. I'm going to the clinic to check on the boy."

Kane slowly opened his eyes. It took a moment before he realized where he was. The ground was hard under him, making his body stiff. A smile came to his face as he turned his head and saw his father lying beside him, sound asleep. He stood and stretched.

"It's about time you woke up, sleepyhead."

Kane turned toward the familiar voice. "J.J., what's going on? Where is everybody?"

"Prince Tali and Raul are back at the estate. Zoric's at the clinic, checking on the boy."

"I hope he's okay."

"Me too," said J.J.

"I guess I'll wake up Dad and see what he wants to do. Father, wake up, wake up."

A moan came from Kevin's throat as he opened his eyes.

"How long have I been sleeping?" he asked as he pushed himself up to a standing position.

J.J. looked at his watch. "About two hours."

Kevin looked around, then watched as Zoric drove up in his car, stopped and got out.

"I've been at the clinic with the boy. It doesn't look good."

"Is there anything we can do?" asked Kevin.

"They're asking for blood donors. I volunteered while I was there." He looked at Kevin. "They're expecting you and J.J. to do the same. I'll take Kane home."

"All right. Do you know where this clinic is, J.J.?" asked Kevin.

"Yes, I do."

"Ask for Doctor Stevens." Zoric told them. He looked at Kevin and smiled. "Try to behave yourself, McKade. Come on, Kane, let's go."

The clinic was located in the center of Tali Town. The main entrance was one level which attached to another two level, half-moon-shaped building.

Kevin took in all the sights. This was his first time in Tali Town.

J.J. parked the car. They walked through the entrance marked emergency.

"Can I help you?" the lady asked as they approached the information desk.

"We're looking for Doctor Stevens. Zoric Tali sent us to donate blood for the young boy, Berto," Kevin said.

"Come this way. I've been expecting you."

They followed her down the hall to a room marked for blood donors. Inside were several reclining chairs. The one at the end of the room was occupied by a man. His chair was opened almost to a flat position and the necessary equipment for drawing blood was attached to his arm.

"Do you know what your blood type is?" the lady asked them.

J.J. reached into a pocket for his wallet and took out a medical card. He handed it to her.

"Type O positive. Good, and you?" she asked Kevin.

"Sorry, I don't know."

"No problem." She smiled at him. "We'll find out, then let you know."

"Thanks."

"I do need both of you to fill out a card with just your name. I need to attached it to the blood container when we send it to the hospital on the mainland. Zoric gave me all the other information." She handed them each a small clipboard, along with the card and a pen.

They filled out the card and handed it back.

"Johnny Jacobson and Kevin McKade. Thank you, gentlemen. Why don't you find a comfortable chair and I'll be back in a few minutes. There's a restroom down the hall with soap and water. It looks like you both could use some." They watched as she walked away.

J.J looked at Kevin. "You're not going to get sick or faint when they show you that needle, are you, McKade?"

Kevin smiled. "I hope not, Mr. Johnny Jacobson. To tell the truth I can't remember ever getting a shot."

"Are you serious?" asked J.J.

"It's the truth," Kevin said as he walked around the room. "I'll take that chair by the window, but first I think I'll take her up on that soap and water."

As Kevin looked in the mirror, a strange nauseous feeling swirled around in his stomach. He splashed cold water on his face and took several deep breaths. As he looked at his reflection, his eyes lowered to his belt buckle. His fingers reached down and touched the outline of the eagle. Meg consumed his thoughts. Then, as if a shot of electricity passed through his hand, he removed his fingers. He stood there several seconds before reacting. *So that's how you've done it all these years,Tali.* Kevin didn't know whether to be angry or relieved.

He unbuckled his belt and removed it from around his waist. He inspected the buckle very closely. *Somewhere on this belt is a microphone so that Prince Tali can hear everything I, or anyone standing by me, says.* A smile came to Kevin's face. *Well won't I have fun now.*

J.J. hollered at him. "They're ready for us, McKade."

"Be right there! I want to wash the dirt off my belt buckle first." Kevin ran some water in the sink. With a big grin on his face, he dropped the buckle into the water then turned around, and closed the door behind him.

"Remind me, J.J., not to forget my buckle. I left it soaking." He walked over and sat in the chair by the window. The nurse was attending to J.J. in the chair next to him. They were flirting with each other and it brought a smile to Kevin's face.

"There, all done," she said.

"Thank you, pretty lady," J.J. said, a big grin on his face.

She walked over to Kevin. "Your turn."

He laid back in his chair and closed his eyes.

"First I'm going to take a small amount so that we can check your blood type while we draw the rest.

"Okay," Kevin said without opening his eyes.

It only took her a few minutes. "All done. Now you two handsome men relax. I'll be back to check on you shortly."

Kevin opened his eyes and turned his head toward J.J. "You just met the future mother of your children."

"In my dreams. Why would a pretty girl like her want anything to do with me?"

"Beats me. All I know is that she's going to be your wife. Whatever made you take this job, J.J.? You don't seem to fit the qualifications."

"You know I'm not supposed to talk to you about these things."

"I know, and if we were any other place, I'd never ask you and put your job in jeopardy."

J.J. looked at Kevin, knowing what he said was true. "When I was hired it was to be your and Kane's personal bodyguard. I was told you were on the island for your own protection. I know now that's not true. You seem more like prisoners. I don't want to know the reason. I like it here. I like you and Kane and Raul. You don't ever cause trouble. Well, until today, that is." A smile came to J.J.'s face. "I might have to protect you from Prince Tali. After you knocked him on his ass, he probably wants to string you up."

Kevin laughed. "He won't do anything. He was wrong and he knows it. I do want you to know one thing. The reason I'm on this island is my decision and I will stay until I know it's time to leave. The day will come when I will leave here a free man. For now just stay my friend and we will never talk again about any of this."

J.J. gave him the okay sign. They both laid back in their chairs and closed their eyes.

J.J. thought about the pretty little nurse.

Kevin thought about the belt buckle Meg had given him. *How could I've not known all these years?* Kevin thought about the time he slammed Mani into the post and threw him down the stairs, banging Mani's head on the ground. Prince Tali told Kevin he'd heard everything and repeated word for word what Kevin had told Mani. *Yes, I was wearing my buckle that day.*

He thought about other times in his life. There were the two days he went to the mainland. Prince Tali and Zoric had kept him under very close surveillance. *No, I was not wearing my buckle those two days.*

Kevin opened his eyes and looked out the window overlooking Tali Town where it backed up to a small mountain range. There was a waterfall along one side of a larger mountain. It was truly a beautiful view. As he admired the scenery, he could see a beautiful home built on the opposite mountain that faced the waterfall. *How could I see these things and yet not know about the microphone built into my buckle? Because I'm an idiot, that's why. I'm not paying enough attention to more important things. Well, that's going to change. I've always given human interest more priority when it comes to this 'gift'. That won't change. But now I'm going to try using it in other ways...if possible.*

"Beautiful view, isn't it, Mr. McKade?"

Kevin turned his head toward the male voice, and watched as a stocky-built man with a smiling, caring face approached. Kevin wondered where he had met him before. Then he remembered. He was the doctor that tended to the boy, Berto. There was something else about the man that reminded Kevin of someone.

"Yes, it's very beautiful. How's the boy, Berto, Doctor—-?"

"Stevens, Doctor Stevens." He reached out his hand and touched Kevin's wrist to take his pulse.

The minute he touched him, Kevin knew this was Betsy's brother. "How's Betsy?"

Shock appeared on the doctor's face. "Why, she's fine. How do you know my sister?"

Kevin smiled. "It's been a few years. I met her when I was looking for an apartment. But things didn't work out and I had to leave. In fact, it was her birthday and she promised to save me a piece of cake. Tell her 'hello' for me, and tell her that I will come by and see her."

The doctor looked at Kevin. Then as if two brain cells finally united, he exploded with happiness. "Of course, you're the Kevin McKade who saved her life."

Kevin glanced over at J.J., who was listening to their every word.

The doctor laid his hand on Kevin's shoulder. "I'm sorry! I should have recognized your name. She talks about you all the time. It's an honor to thank you in person for all you've done. I've never seen Betsy so happy. Her stepson and wife are living with her. They have two children, boys. In fact, the youngest was named, in a way, after you. His name is Mac."

Kevin smiled. "I really didn't do much. Actually, Betsy did it all by herself."

"We all know she would be dead now if it weren't for you. We all thank you very much."

"Well, you are all welcome, and I will try to visit her."

"Good, she'd like that. The reason I didn't recognize your name right away is because I was more interested in your blood type. From what Nurse Sally told me you didn't even know what it was. Is that

71

correct?"

"Correct," Kevin confirmed.

"Well, it's rare, very rare. OBA negative is found only in one out of every one million humans. I'm having some extensive testing done on yours. So far it shows that you're extremely healthy. We usually recommend to people with rare blood types to put a pint away every few months or once a year in a blood bank, in case they have an accident or for some other reason they might need a blood transfusion. We'd also like to put you on the blood line circuit. It's becomes available to hospitals all over the world; you would be available to donate blood if someone needed your rare type. Which was why I was so interested in yours.

"There's a young girl from Russia, fifteen years old, a dancer, ballerina, with so much talent they say she is destined to be the world's best. She needs open heart surgery to repair a hole in her heart. Even with the surgery there is no guarantee she will live, but without it she will surely die. She's becoming weaker and weaker everyday. She might live ten days at the most. Your blood is a perfect match."

"How many other people are available?" asked J.J., completely absorbed in the conversation now.

"They're still checking," the doctor said sadly. "Six people with this blood type died in the past two years. Three people are positive HIV carriers, so they've been removed from the list. Two people have sicknesses of their own. So far they have four people, but they need at least ten pints of blood going into surgery. They would prefer twelve. The four people from whom they have already received blood will be able to give another pint before surgery. That makes eight. With yours, it will be nine."

"Can you take another pint from me?" asked Kevin.

"Maybe, but it's really too soon."

"Doctor, I think my son might have the same blood type."

"Are you sure?" asked the doctor hopefully.

"No, not positive, but I think there's a chance."

"When could I test him?"

"I'll go get him now," said J.J.

"Okay," said Kevin. "Explain everything to Zoric. He'll probably want to come back with you."

The nurse, Sally, came in the room. She unhooked J.J. and gave him a large glass of orange juice. "Relax for about ten minutes." She smiled at him. "I'll be back in a few minutes to take care of Kevin," she informed the doctor and left the room.

"Doctor Stevens," Kevin said. "There is one slight problem. You won't be able to use my name in any way. The information you've learned about me today must never leave this room. All records and information that has been recorded must be destroyed."

"But why?" Doctor Stevens asked.

"My life and the lives of the people I love depend on it." Kevin reached out with his left hand and touched the hand of Doctor Stevens. "Please believe me."

A frightening feeling passed through the doctor's body as he looked at Kevin, believing everything the man had said. "I will do as you ask."

"Thank you," Kevin said. "Then my blood is at your disposal."

Feeling a sense of relief, the three men laughed.

"How old is your son?" Doctor Stevens asked.

"Almost thirteen."

"He's awfully young."

"Don't worry, Doctor. He's a strong and healthy young man. He looks a lot older than he is."

Two hours later, Kevin was sitting in the same chair, reading a magazine, when the door opened and J.J. entered with Kane at his side, followed by Zoric.

Kane smiled at his father. "You okay, Dad?"

"Fine, Son. Do you know why you are here?"

"Not really. Something about you and me having the same blood."

"That's close enough." Kevin smiled at him, and explained the best he could about blood types. "Do you understand, Son?"

Kane reached out his hand and touched his father's arm. "Did it hurt?"

"A little, but it's for a good cause. This young girl needs my blood. It's not enough though, so that's why we need you. They'll test you first to see if you have type OBA negative."

"Okay, I hope I do."

"Good. Let's get started," said Doctor Stevens. "You look like your father." He smiled at Kane. "You both have extraordinary eyes. Why

73

don't you hop up here and we'll begin. This is Sally, the nurse who will draw your blood."

"Hi, Kane, I promise not to hurt you too much. Can I get you to lie down? You'll be a lot more comfortable."

"Sure." Kane smiled at her. He stared at her face as she inserted the needle into his arm. "Are you going to marry J.J.?"

Kevin watched the blush spread across J.J.'s face and chuckled.

The question took Sally by surprise. "I don't know. He hasn't asked me yet." She chuckled.

Kane motioned for her to lean closer, then whispered so no one else heard. "He will."

"I think you are hallucinating and I haven't even drawn any blood yet."

Kane laughed.

"I'm going to take this sample and have it tested. You lay there and take it easy."

"Okay, I will," promised Kane.

She winked at J.J. as she left the room.

It was twenty minutes later when the doctor returned. "Great news. Kane's blood type is the same as yours, Kevin, healthy and strong. I think our young girl has a real good chance of making it, thanks to you two. I brought a photo to show you. Her name is Julianna." He handed it to Kane, who looked at it for a long time. Kevin finally asked him. "Is everything all right, Son?"

Kane handed the photo to his father. "She sure is pretty."

Kevin studied the photo of the young girl in her ballerina costume with large, sad, dark eyes. "Yes, she is." He handed the photo to Kane.

"Can I keep this?" Kane asked the doctor."

"Of course."

"When do you need us again?" asked Kevin.

"Can you leave a number where I can reach you?"

Zoric handed the doctor a card. "Call me and I'll make whatever arrangements that are necessary."

"Good." The doctor put the card in his breast pocket.

Zoric turned to J.J. "Why don't you take Kevin and Kane with you when they're finished here. I need to talk to the doctor in his office. If that's okay with you, Doctor Stevens."

"Certainly. It was nice to meet you, Kane and Kevin. I'll see you again soon, and thanks for everything."

Zoric followed the doctor into his office. He sat down in the chair across from him. "I need to have all records from what went on here today. There is to be no record of any kind that would connect Kevin McKade to this place."

"May I ask why?" Doctor Stevens asked.

"The laws on Tali Island are not the same as they are on the mainland. We protect all who live here with the right to privacy. When you were invited to come here, I'm sure you read the agreement before you signed it."

"Correct."

"You've enjoyed your stay here and the accommodations have met with your approval?"

"Absolutely."

"You only have two weeks left on your commitment. We would like very much to invite you back again next year for two months. Everyone here seems to like working with you and your medical qualifications are what we're looking for."

"I would be very honored to come back again. It has been more of a vacation than work." The doctor stood and picked up a large sealed envelope and handed it to Zoric. "I think you'll find everything in order. These are the transactions of what occurred here today, right down to the sticky notes."

A big smile appeared on Zoric's face as he reached for the envelope. He stood to shake the doctor's hand.

"Now that's the way I like doing business."

The doctor touched his breast pocket where he put the card Zoric had given him. "I will keep this and I promise I'll never use it unless it's a matter of life and death."

"Or if you've got a free afternoon for a round of golf, or we could meet at the lodge for a game of chess."

The doctor laughed. "Both sound great. I'll give you a call."

"Doctor Stevens, it's been a real pleasure."

"Likewise."

Zoric left the doctor's office and returned to the room where Kevin, Kane, and J.J. were about ready to leave. Zoric looked at Kevin and breathed a sigh of relief as he looked at the familiar buckle attached to the belt wrapped around Kevin's waist.

Kane sat in the back seat, his father in the front with J.J. He was holding the photo of the girl, Julianna. "Dad, when our blood is put in her body, will she be my sister?"

Kevin turned his head toward Kane. "No, Son, but you will have a special bond with her. I'm very proud of what you did today."

"Thanks, Dad, I can hardly wait to tell Raul. He's going to freak out when I show him this picture of Julianna. He'll probably fall madly in love, just like J.J. did today with Sally," Kane said teasingly.

"He'll probably have lots of babies, too," Kevin added.

"I wish you two would knock it off," grumbled J.J. "First you marry me off, now I'm a father."

Kane and Kevin were still teasing J.J. when they arrived at the estate. Zoric's car was already there.

"I'm going to find Raul," Kane said as he closed the back door of the car.

"And I'm going to the bunkhouse to clean up for my big date tonight," said J.J. with a wide grin on his face.

"Have a good time my friend," said Kevin, "see you tomorrow."

Instead of using the side entrance as he always did, Kevin walked around to the front. It was closer to Prince Tali's office. When he arrived, he opened the door without knocking.

"You wanted to see me?" he asked.

Zoric stood and left the room without saying anything.

Kevin walked over and sat in the chair Zoric had occupied. He knew it irritated Prince Tali when he entered without knocking and taking a seat without being invited. Kevin knew something else, too. It made Prince Tali very uncomfortable when he stared at him, which he was doing right now.

Prince Tali acted as if he was putting the finishing touch to a letter. Kevin knew he was stalling until he felt in control. Finally Tali put the paper down. He stood, went to the wet bar, and fixed himself a drink. He returned and sat down in his chair, then took a drink of the bourbon he'd just poured. Finally he spoke.

"I know you're not going to believe this, McKade, but I really didn't think that boy would get hurt."

Kevin stared at him without saying a word.

"I will do everything in my power to see that the boy has the best medical help available." He took another drink of his whisky. "I'm only going to tell you this once. Don't ever take another swing at me."

Kevin stood and looking down on Prince Tali, he said, "Then don't ever give me a reason." He turned to leave and, before he closed the door behind him, he heard Prince Tali say. "Damn you, McKade."

It brought a smile to Kevin's face.

*Carole A. Sheller*

# Chapter 7

Kane found Raul in the stable, brushing the neck of his horse. "How's Sassy doing?" He could tell from Raul's blood-shot eyes that he'd been crying. Sassy was stretched out on her side sleeping.

"The next twelve hours should tell. The vet wanted to put her down, but Zoric wouldn't let him. Zoric called another vet who gave her something to help her sleep. He also pumped her full of antibiotics and removed the poison burrs. I don't understand why someone would want to kill Sassy."

Kane reached out and stroked the horse's neck. "She's going to be all right, Raul. I promise you."

"How do you know?"

"I can feel it," Kane said as he looked at Raul.

"I believe you, Kane," said Raul as he looked into the caring eyes of his best friend. "Where have you been, anyway?"

Kane smiled. "You're never going to believe this."

He told Raul everything that had happened that day. Then he showed him the picture of Julianna.

"Wow, she's pretty. Do you think you'll ever meet her?"

"Maybe. Dad and I might have to give more blood when she's operated on."

"Will she be okay?"

"Yeah, she's going to be okay, just like Sassy is going to be okay."

"Good," said Raul. "Maybe I'll marry her and you can be my best man."

"Bull! I'm going to marry her and you can be my best man, or do you mean you're going to marry Sassy?"

Kevin could hear the laughter as he approached the stable. "Hi, boys."

He knelt down and rubbed his hand across the horse's nose and down her neck. "She's going to be fine, Raul."

"I know. Kane already told me."

Kevin touched Raul's shoulder. "Kane and I will find out who did this. In the meantime I think I'll set up camp in here. Keep an eye on our champ."

Fear sounded in Raul voice. "Do you think they'll try to kill her again?"

"Yes, I think there's a good possibility."

"But why?" Tears stung Raul's eyes as he blinked rapidly, trying not to cry.

"I wish I knew." He wrapped his arm around Raul, trying to comfort him.

"I want to stay in here with you, Dad."

"Me too," said Raul. "I was going to spend the night in here anyway. Now I'll have company."

Kevin nodded his head in agreement. "I'll go round up everything we'll need. I'll get Zoric to help me. You boys stay here. Don't let anyone touch Sassy—not anyone. I'll be back in about an hour."

"What the hell are you talking about, McKade," Zoric hollered. "There isn't any way someone could get on this island and hurt that horse."

"What if it's someone who's already on the island?" asked Kevin.

Zoric thought for a moment before answering. "I'll stay out there with you."

"Whatever. I'm making a list of what we'll need."

"Give it to me when you're finished. You go back and stay with the boys."

Kevin finished the list and handed it to Zoric, then turned and headed for the stables without saying another word.

It was early evening when they finally had everything organized for the night. Raul wanted his sleeping bag in the stall with Sassy. Kane put his in there, too. They ate cold sandwiches for dinner. Then the boys played checkers.

"You up for a game of chess, McKade?" Zoric asked.

"Sure, it will help pass the time."

Zoric won—again. "I'm the champ, always will be." Kevin watched a cocky smile appear on Zoric's face as they set the game up for round two.

Kevin studied the board and, for the first time in playing this game of chess, he felt himself drift into a deep state of concentration. Then it happened. He could see what move Zoric would make after he made his.

"Wake up, McKade." Zoric's voice brought him back to reality.

80

A sly grin spread across Kevin's face. "I'd like to make a wager on this game."

Zoric laughed. "You think you can beat me?"

"Yes, I do, if you play by my rules."

"There's only one rule you could make that would let you beat me and that's if I play blindfolded."

Kevin laughed and so did the boys. "I never thought of that, but if you're willing."

Zoric studied Kevin's face. "What's going on in that devious mind of yours? What rules are you talking about?"

"All right," Kevin began. "First rule is that there is no talking once the game begins nor any unnecessary movement. Moves must be made within five minutes or you forfeit. That's pretty much it. Any questions?"

"What do I win?" Zoric asked confidently.

"If you win, I will tell you something that's going to happen to you in the near future."

"Something I don't know?"

"You don't even have a clue."

"Does anyone else know about this?"

Kevin thought for a minute before answering. "I really don't know. I just know that you don't."

"Okay, I'm in. Let's play."

"Don't you want to know what I'll win if you should lose?" asked Kevin.

Zoric chuckled. "Sorry, slight oversight on my part. What is it?"

"You have to be my chauffeur for a day and take me anywhere I want to go. Maybe shopping or visiting a friend. We can work out the details later."

Zoric waited a moment before answering. "Challenge accepted."

Kevin looked at the boys. "If you stay and watch you have to be very, very quiet; or you could go outside or up to the house for ice cream."

The boy's looked at each other and like a flash they were gone.

"What the hell is this about visiting a friend?" Zoric asked.

"Do you remember Betsy?"

"Sure."

"Only her and then pick up a few things for Kane's birthday."

81

"They sure do grow up fast. Hell, McKade, I'd probably do that for you even if we didn't bet."

"You might, but you know damn good and well that Tali wouldn't let you."

"You're right. So I guess I'll just have to win. Let's begin. I'll flip a coin. Heads or tails?"

"Heads."

"Heads, it is. You start, McKade."

Kevin stared at the board as a good minute went by.

Then Zoric spoke. "Come on, McKade. Let's get this game started."

Kevin looked up at Zoric with a big smile on his face. "You lose."

"What? What the hell are you talking about?"

"You talked."

"The game hasn't even started yet."

"Yes, it did. I had five minutes to decide my move."

"You asshole, but I guess that's the only way you could win."

"Double or nothing? But I still only have one thing to tell you."

"I'll play by your silly rules." Zoric took off his watch. "I'll tell you when to start."

"Okay."

Zoric waited until the second hand was on the twelve. "Begin."

Kevin concentrated on the board. It didn't take long before he knew what plays Zoric would make, depending on where he moved. It was forty-five minutes into the game when Kevin saw the last two winning moves. He moved quickly, and when Zoric moved his queen, Kevin moved his. "Check-Mate."

"You S.O.B." A smile crossed Zoric's face. "You won! I suppose there's no way I could talk you into telling me what's going to happen. Is there?"

"No way. Another time, another game."


When the boys got back, Kevin told them the good news. "And I not only won once, but twice."

"Wow, Dad, that's great. Let me shake your hand."

"I'm proud of you, too, King Kevin." Raul bowed and also shook his hand.

"Okay, guys," Zoric said sadly. "Don't overdo it."

82

Raul walked over to him. "I still love you, Uncle, even if you are a loser."

"Thanks, pal." Zoric put his arm around Raul's shoulder. "It's starting to get dark. We should call it a night. How's Sassy?"

"Sound asleep."

The boys rolled out their sleeping bags in the stall with Sassy. Kevin put his on the other side of the stall and handed Kane a stick. "If you hear anything, poke me with this. Here's one for you, Raul."

Raul took the long, thin stick and turned it in his hand. "I don't think I could hurt anyone with this."

"That's not what it's for," Kevin told him.

"I know." Raul grinned.

They all lay in their sleeping bags in total silence. Then, about two hours later, footsteps were heard outside, walking along the side of the stable, headed toward the front entrance. Kevin felt a poke from Kane's stick. "I hear it, son. You and Raul stay put. Zoric and I will handle this."

Zoric stood, without saying anything, and waited for Kevin. They moved as quietly as they could toward the front door. One stood on each side of the entrance.

The door opened slowly. A small, thin man stepped in, closing the door behind him. The flashlight in his hand guided him to Sassy's stall.

"Looking for something?" Zoric said in a loud, husky voice.

The man screamed and jumped forward, dropping the flashlight.

Kevin snapped on the overhead light. Kane and Raul opened the stall and stared at the intruder.

Zoric was the first to speak. "You're the veterinarian that wanted to put down Sassy."

"I just stopped by to see how she was doing." The man was frightened. You could hear it in his voice.

"And what else?" Kevin asked.

"That's all, I swear."

Kane walked up to him and stared into his eyes. The man became increasingly uncomfortable. "He's the one that was with Sassy about an hour before the race."

Kevin looked at Zoric. "I think this is the man responsible for putting the poison burrs under Sassy's saddle."

"You're crazy," the man said as he turned and tried to escape.

Kevin grabbed the man's arm and twisted it behind his back. "Don't try that again or I'll break your arm. Zoric, check his pockets."

Putting his hand against the man's side and feeling a bulge there, Zoric said, "What have we here?" He reached in and removed a large syringe full of some kind of liquid. Zoric found another package, containing a large needle. "What's this for?" he questioned the man.

"It's a mild sedative. I brought it in case the horse was in pain."

"Are you sure it's not something to put her to sleep permanently?" asked Kevin.

"No, I swear."

Zoric looked into the man's eyes. "Maybe I should use some of this on you, just to make sure." Even in the dim light Zoric could see the sweat on the man's forehead. There was also something about this man that reminded Zoric of someone…But who?

"Get me a rope, Raul, and help me tie his hands behind his back."

Raul did as he was told. "What are you going to do, Uncle Zoric?"

"I don't know yet. I'm going to take him over to the other stable. Your father will decide what to do."

Kevin lay in his sleeping bag and listened to the sounds of the night turn into the sounds of morning. Birds chirping, horses snorting, the breeze, that had started with the early dawn, rustling through the leaves on the trees. He heard another sound, too—the sound of a man screaming, begging for his life.

Kevin had known the minute he touched the intruder he was responsible for what happened to Sassy. Kevin knew something else, too. This man wished for the death of Raul. The thing Kevin didn't know, and would probably never know, was why.

It was an hour later when Zoric opened the stable doors letting in the bright sunlight. "Time to get up boys. Breakfast is almost ready. Did you get any sleep at all, McKade?" he asked Kevin.

"Some." He looked at Kane. "Why don't you and Raul go and get cleaned up. Zoric and I will keep an eye on Sassy till you get back."

Fear sounded in Raul's voice. "Do you think someone is still trying to hurt her?"

"No, son." Kevin put his hand on Raul's shoulder. "No one else will ever hurt Sassy again. It's only because someone should be with her when she wakes up. She'll need help standing and she'll be thirsty and very hungry. You'll have to walk her around till her strength comes back."

Raul let out a sigh of relief. "Okay."

After the boys left, Kevin walked outside. Zoric followed. "Did you find out any information before you killed that man?"

"It's something that had to be done, McKade," Zoric said defensively. "We did find out who he was. It seems he's related to the two men we had a problem with a few years ago. The men at the parade, remember?"

"I remember."

"Well, it's over now. Prince Tali will check out the rest of that man's family. We're sure he didn't plan this by himself."

He paced back and forth. "Don't judge me, McKade. We make a good team. You do your part and we'll do ours." As Zoric turned, the sun flashed across Kevin's buckle, drawing Zoric's attention. He studied it for a moment, then asked. "Is there a scratch on that buckle?"

Kevin looked down as he rubbed his thumb across it. "I tried scrubbing it off yesterday at the hospital, but all I managed to do was put these scratches on it."

"Give it to me. I know someone who'll make it good as new."

Kevin unhooked his belt, slipping the buckle off. "Take good care of it. I promised to give it to Kane on his eighteenth birthday," he said as he handed it to Zoric. He watched as Zoric put it in his pocket and walked away.

Three days later Kevin and J.J. were standing outside the small horse arena, watching Raul ride Sassy, when Zoric drove up. He got out of his car and walked toward them, a small package in his hand.

"Here you go, McKade, just as I promised."

Kevin opened the package and removed his buckle. A smile came to his face. "Looks great, thanks." He put it on his belt, then patted it with his hand. "Good to have it back. I felt naked without it."

"How is Sassy doing?" Zoric asked.

It was J.J. who replied. "Couple more days and she'll be as good as new. Raul has his heart set on racing her in the next competition."

"When is that?" Zoric asked.

"Two weeks."

"Don't see any reason why he shouldn't," said Zoric.

J.J. smiled. "Win number one coming up." He left to tell Raul the good news.

"Feel like a game of chess tonight, McKade?"

"Sure…Come by around ten after Kane goes to bed. I hate for him to see a grown man cry."

"I understand." Zoric smiled as he headed for his car. "I saw my father cry once. It was devastating." His laughter could still be heard as he drove away.

Kevin was looking through Kane's drawing tablet when Zoric arrived around ten-fifteen.

"I think my son has the potential of being a fine artist. Don't you?" He handed the pad to Zoric.

"Yes, these are good." He laughed at some. All were in cartoon form, but it was the faces that appeared to intrigue him most. "You can recognize everyone. There's you and me." He laughed. "And there's Prince Tali, J.J. and Raul." Zoric closed the tablet. "He's very talented. You must be proud of him."

"I am. Shall we begin? Same rules?"

"Of course."

Kevin let Zoric win the first one. "You're getting good at this game, but not good enough. What do we play for this time, McKade?"

Kevin thought for a moment. "If you win, I'll cancel one of my trips to the mainland. If I win, I want an art teacher to come and work with Kane. Agree?" He held out his hand.

"Agreed." Zoric shook Kevin's hand.

It was almost two hours later when Kevin finally had Zoric pinned in.

"You win, McKade. That has to be the most exciting game I've played. I will see to it that Kane has the best teacher available."

"Thanks." Kevin stood. "I think this calls for a shot of that excellent brandy you left here." Kevin poured them each a drink and sat back down.

"Well?" Zoric asked.

Kevin laughed. "Okay, I'll tell you. When I was at the hospital I was looking out the window toward the mountains. There's a water-fall."

"It's beautiful," Zoric interrupted, "one of my favorite spots."

"I can see why. That must be why you're going to be spending a lot of time there."

"What do you mean?"

"The mountain facing the waterfall has a house on it."

"There's no house on that mountain," Zoric stated.

"Not yet, but there will be. It's built on the side of the mountain with a deck running the full length in front. On one end, facing the town, are two small bungalows. At the other end there's an electric lift. It's round and seats about eight people. It runs by cable to the top of the mountain where there's another house. This one is quite small, compared to the other one. I think you use it strictly for entertain-ment."

"It's always been my dream to have my own home. I just didn't know where. I always thought it would be one of the estates or a place on the mainland, but what you've described is perfect. It was worth losing to you, then winning to learn this. I will take you to the main-land whenever you're ready."

"Don't forget the teacher for Kane." Kevin said.

"Only the best."

Two days later, in the middle of the night, Kevin awoke. He jumped out of bed, pulled on a pair of slacks and picked up his belt and buck-le. *No, not this time.* He hung it on a hook in the back of his closet. Grabbing a shirt, sweater, socks and shoes, he headed out the door. He met Zoric coming down the hall. "Let's go. I'll finish dressing in the car."

Zoric closed the front door behind him just as J.J. pulled the car up front. "I'll drive. J.J., you stay here and take care of the boys. Prince Tali's on the mainland."

Kevin touched J.J.'s arm as he went by. "Tell Kane everything's okay. I'll call as soon as I can."

As Zoric drove, he kept glancing at Kevin. "This is damn spooky, McKade."

"What is?" asked Kevin.

"The way you see things or know things or whatever the hell it is you do. It gives me the willies."

Kevin laughed. "Me, too. What did Doctor Stevens tell you."

"You mean you don't know?"

Kevin laughed again. "No, I don't, only that it has to do with that young girl from Russia."

"That's right," said Zoric. "They had to rush her into emergency surgery. She has a fifty-fifty chance of surviving. Doctor Stevens wants another pint of your blood. He's waiting at the clinic. There's a medical helicopter standing by to fly the blood to the airport where my private jet is waiting to take it to the hospital in Sweden."

Kevin looked at Zoric. "That's very nice of you. What is it about you that makes you such a softy and the next minute a cold-blooded killer?"

"I've never killed anyone in cold blood, only those that show or do harm to my family and friends."

"And the kidnapping of a young man and his baby son?"

"Don't start with that again, McKade. You haven't had it so bad and neither has Kane."

Kevin paused for a minute. "No, you're right. It's been a good life. After my wife died, when Kane was five, there really wasn't anywhere for me to go. I had no way of taking care of a family. Kane's getting a good education and he and Raul are like brothers. It would have been nice, though, if I could have taken a lady out dining and dancing. Maybe even married again."

Zoric smiled. "It's not too late. I'd be happy to introduce you to a few ladies I know."

Kevin laughed. "I could hear it now. I'd like you to meet Kevin McKade. He's a prisoner here on Tali's island. He can't go anywhere or do anything, but you could have dinner with him in his suite where everything you say and do is recorded for Prince Tali's entertainment."

Kevin slapped Zoric on the shoulder. "I'm too young to date anyway, but I'll tell you what you can do."

"What's that?" Zoric asked.

"Let me help build your home."

Zoric smiled. "I think that could be arranged."

Doctor Stevens met them at the door as they entered the clinic.

"Kevin, nice to see you again."

"You, too, Doctor."

"Follow me." He led them into a private room where all the necessary equipment was set up.

Kevin slipped off his shirt and lay down. Within minutes Kevin's blood was entering the plastic container by his side.

"You here by yourself tonight, Doctor?"

"No. Everyone else is busy. There was a small auto accident, a few people with cuts and bruises, nothing serious. Now that I've got you started, I'll see if they need my help. Relax, enjoy your stay." He closed the door on his way out.

Zoric sat in the chair next to the bed. "The doctor seems real nice. Had a drink with him the other night at the lodge, good bedside manner."

Kevin took a deep breath and closed his eyes. "Yes, he is very professional"

Zoric sat there for a few minutes listening to the even rhythm of Kevin's breathing. He stood. "I swear to God, McKade, they could put you in a tree and you'd fall asleep. I need a cup of coffee."

Kevin opened his eyes when he heard Zoric shut the door. *Alone, at last. I think this is the second time I remember being in a room where there was no one else or any security cameras or listening devices.* He closed his eyes again, savoring the few precious minutes of freedom.

The doctor and Zoric returned, entering the room together. Kevin opened his eyes when Doctor Stevens touched his wrist to take his pulse.

"You feel okay?" the doctor asked.

"Great, a little sleepy, that's all."

"You're going to be weak when this is over. I'd like to have you stay here for a couple of hours to keep an eye on you." He turned to Zoric. "You can go back home. I will call you when he's ready to leave, or you can catch a couple hours' sleep here. There's a room across the hall that's not occupied."

"I'll stay."

"Good. We'll get this precious commodity on its way to Sweden, then I'll be off duty. Would you like to join me in my office for a drink?"

"Thanks, I could use one." Zoric looked over at Kevin. "You'll let me know when you're ready to leave."

Kevin heard the warning sign in Zoric's voice. "I'm not leaving this bed until the good doctor tells me to and that's a promise."

Doctor Stevens returned about ten minutes later, carrying a tray with a pitcher of orange juice and a dish of crackers on it. "Your reward."

"Thanks, doctor." Kevin tried to sit up. Dizziness overcame him. He lay back down.

"Take it easy, Kevin. You need rest. A nurse will be here shortly to help you get comfortable. If you need me for anything, let her know."

Zoric and Doctor Stevens watched the helicopter take off, then walked down the hall toward the Doctor's office. Zoric sat down in the same chair he used before.

Doctor Stevens walked over to the small wet bar, opened the shelf door, and took out two glasses. He noted the powdered substance in the bottom of one. He put two ice-cubes in each glass, then poured scotch in each. The powder dissolved instantly. He opened a small bottle of drinking water and filled his glass. Then he handed Zoric his drink, along with an unopened small bottle of soda water.

Zoric mixed his drink. The doctor held up his glass. "To the young, beautiful, and talented Russian dancer."

Zoric touched his glass to the doctor's. "Do you think she'll make it?"

"At least now she has a fighting chance. Without Kevin and his son's blood she would surely die. It was a miracle the day you sent Kevin here. I'm truly grateful."

"Do you know this girl personally?"

"I was fortunate to see her dance in England in the production of Camelot. I was invited backstage to meet the performers. I took an interest in Julianna when I was told of her heart problem. That was two years ago."

"Is Kevin in any danger?"

"He could be. The body only holds five to six pints of blood. We should have waited at least a month before taking more. He'll be weak, could become anemic, have an iron deficiency, shortness of breath. That's why I want to keep him here. The nurse will check his

90

vitals every half hour. He's probably on oxygen now, maybe even an I.V. If I thought he was in any real danger, I wouldn't have done it. The same for his son, Kane. If he had been of small structure, thin and underweight, we wouldn't have been able to take his blood at all, but he's very mature for his age, tall, stocky, healthy. He looks more like fifteen or sixteen."

"He's one in a million." The doctor could hear the pride in Zoric's voice. "Going to be a real heart breaker."

The doctor nodded his head in agreement. "It's the eyes that attract your attention first. They're extraordinary."

Zoric laughed. "Yes, they certainly are that."

Ten minutes later they left the doctor's office and walked down the hall to Kevin's room. The nurse had just taken his blood pressure.

"How is he doing?" Doctor Stevens asked.

"Sleeping like a baby. I put him on oxygen and started an I.V."

"Good." The doctor looked at Zoric. "You can probably take him home in two or three hours. He'll need to come back every day for a week or so for me to make sure he's doing okay."

"I'll talk to Palo," Zoric said. "He runs our clinic. I'll have him send a nurse over to the estate to take care of him."

"Excellent," Doctor Stevens said, nodding his head in agreement. "She can check Kane, too, while she's there."

Zoric yawned. "Excuse me."

"Why don't you go lie down for a while." The doctor pointed to the room across the hall. "I'll wake you if there are any changes."

"I think I'll do that." Zoric yawned again. "Please leave the door open if you would." He walked across the hall, slipped off his shoes, and laid down.

The doctor glanced at his watch. *Ten minutes and he, too, will be sleeping like a baby.* He left Kevin's room and went back to his office. He washed the glasses and made himself a cup of coffee, then sat down in his chair. *There is too much secrecy going on around here, and I'm going to find out why.* He smiled to himself. His sister, Betsy, always kidded him, saying he would make a better detective than a doctor. He considered that quite a compliment since he knew he was a damn good doctor.

He finished his coffee, walked back down the hall and checked on Zoric first. *Sound asleep, good!* He entered Kevin's room. He was surprised to see him wide awake, sitting up in bed and drinking his orange juice. He smiled. "How do you feel, young hero?"

Kevin smiled back. "Weird, light-headed, weak."

"All normal. I wanted to know if there is any reason why I can't ask you some personal questions?"

Kevin studied the doctor for a moment before asking, "Zoric?"

"He was having trouble sleeping, so I gave him a little something to help."

Kevin looked at Doctor Stevens, knowing that for the first time in a long time, this man standing before him was someone he could truly trust. *Where do I begin?* "You might as well sit down, Doc, and make yourself comfortable."

The doctor pulled a chair close to the center of Kevin's bed. He wanted to be able to see into the room across the hall. He smiled at Kevin. "I want you to know that whatever you tell me will not leave this room unless you want it to."

Kevin started out slowly, trying hard not to miss anything. He explained, as best as he could, the 'curse' that plagued the McKade men. He told the doctor about his first vision, the death of his parents, meeting Meg, the twins and of his life since the kidnapping. "Now here I am back at the clinic, giving blood for the second time." It had taken Kevin almost two hours to tell his life story. The doctor sat patiently, listening to every word.

"There has to be something I can do to help you escape...anything."

"Nothing. I can't take a chance until Kane is older. I do have a favor to ask."

"Anything," said Doctor Stevens.

"I'd like to write a letter to Amanda if you could find me some paper, pen and an envelope."

"Of course. I'll be right back."

The doctor left the room, checking on Zoric first before going to his office. His mind went over, and believed, everything Kevin had told him.

He returned to Kevin's room and handed him the items he'd requested.

"Zoric is still asleep. He shouldn't wake up for a couple of hours. I'll check back with you in a while."

"Thanks."

Kevin started his letter.

*My beautiful darling. I think of you everyday. I know you're doing well. Raul still shows me the cards you send. I have good news. I've found a special friend. His name is Doctor Roberto (Rob) Stevens. I've told him everything. He has agreed to help in any way he can. He will be our link for communicating with each other.*

Kevin told her about the boys, and J.J.'s new girlfriend. Six pages later he finished the letter.

*I know it's been seven years, but my feelings toward you haven't changed. I still dream of coming to America. I hope that when I do you'll be there waiting for me. Please write.*

Kevin folded the letter, slipping it into the addressed envelope. He waited for Doctor Stevens. When the Doctor entered his room, Kevin handed him the envelope. "I didn't seal it because I want you to put a note in with the information on where she's to send her letters."

"I'll take care of it. Why don't you try resting."

Kevin yawned. "I think I'll do that." He held out his hand. "Thanks."

The doctor shook his hand. "You're welcome."

A feeling of freedom and contentment passed through Kevin as he closed his eyes and drifted to sleep.

An hour later he awoke to see Zoric sitting in the chair by his bed. "How do you feel, McKade?"

Kevin stretched. "Hungry. Have you been sitting there all this time?"

"No, I slept for a few hours in the bed across the hall. Best night's sleep I've had in a long time." Zoric reached over and pushed the buzzer for the nurse. "Let's get out of here."

It was three weeks later when Zoric gave everyone the sad news. The boy, Berto, died in his sleep. The next day Zoric took Kevin, who was not wearing his buckle, to the mainland for his visit with Betsy. It was there Kevin read his first letter from Amanda.

She told him about her life in Vermont, how happy she was teaching school, and about her beautiful daughter, Victoria. She told him the most important thing he wanted to hear—that she still loved him.

Life took on a new meaning for Kevin. He was more confident and more determined than ever to escape from Tali Island.

A week later he was working in the garden when Kane approached him.

"Father, do you have time to talk with me?"

Kevin looked around to see if anyone was near. He was glad he'd not worn his belt buckle. "Of course, Kane. Come sit down beside me."

"I've been having strange dreams again. There is someone very close to me who I can't see or touch. What does this mean, Father?"

Kevin touched his son's shoulder. He made Kane promise that what he was going to tell him, he was not to repeat to anyone—not even Raul. Kane promised.

Kevin told him about how he met Kane's mother, their marriage and how Meg had given birth to two babies. "Yes, Kane—you and your twin sister, Katy. I've never told you this before because I knew if certain people found out, they might kill her. When you are older we will try to find her. In the meantime, think of her as much as you can and remember that when we do find her, we'll know her right away because she has the same color eyes as we do."

Kane lay in his bed that night thinking about what his father had told him. He was confused. He wanted to ask his father more questions, but for now all he wanted to do was think about his sister, Katy.

# Chapter 8
## FOUR YEARS LATER

Kane awoke feeling nauseated, his mind reliving the vision of Raul's tortured body. *It's over. Why doesn't this dream go away? Raul's going to be okay. Am I missing something that I was supposed to see, or am I losing my mind?* Kane got out of bed and walked to the bathroom. He splashed cold water on his face, then drank a glass of water. Feeling better, he returned to his bed. He lay there, thinking about Katy. *I'll find you, Katy. I promise I will, but first I have to help our father.*

Tears stung Kane's eyes as his mind relived the last four weeks.

His seventeenth birthday. His father had started at the beginning, explained how they had been kidnapped when he was a baby and how Prince Tali threatened to kill his mother and sister if his father didn't play by the Prince's rules. He told about how they were under surveillance twenty-four hours a day and how their living quarters were filled with listening devices.

Now his father was dying. He had a year, maybe two, left at the most. Kane knew he had to do something, but what? When Kane closed his eyes, the dream started again. He could see Raul. Two masked men were holding him, while another masked man pounded his fists into Raul's body. He finally became unconscious, then they dragged his body over to a large tree. They taped Raul's mouth and eyes shut, then wrapped him with a rope to a tree. The men removed their masks and took out small knives from their pockets. Slowly they started to put cuts on Raul's arms, legs and stomach. Kane remembered waking from the dream with sweat pouring from his body. He jumped out of bed and jerked the door open. A fist came flying through the air. He ducked in time and the fight was on. He finally managed to push the man off balance, making him fall backwards, hitting his head on a brass table leg. Kane hit him again with a matching lamp to make sure he was out.

Kane could still feel the pain. Blood was dripping from his broken nose and the pain from his ribs was almost unbearable. Somehow he made it to Prince Tali's quarters and they were able to rescue Raul. It was several days before they knew for sure if Raul was going to live.

Kane had told Prince Tali that it was Mani and his two brothers who had done this to Raul. Kane never saw Mani again. The guard that he fought with had also drugged his father. They never saw that guard again either.

Kane learned something else about this 'gift' his father and he possessed. The mind has the ability to heal. They could see it happening with Raul. He was almost as good as new. He had become more gentle and kinder. He had placed a value on life that had not been there four weeks ago. Kane felt even closer to Raul then he had before. *I have to quit thinking about this. I need to concentrate on my father. He gave up his life for me. Now it's my turn to help him.* A smile came to Kane's face. *At least I know now why he never drove a car. Actually he never did anything by himself...there was always someone there.* Kane felt his stomach start to turn again. *This is no time to be sick. Dad needs me now.*

Kane recalled the number of times his father had been called on to give blood. It was at least twice a year since the time the doctor found out about their rare blood type, but every time his father went to the mainland, Zoric or J.J. took him and brought him back. That's been what?...About eight times now. There had been four of those times his dad had to spend the night in the hospital because he was very weak and his blood pressure was very low. Kane wondered if that had anything to do with why his father was ill.

He wondered about Raul's mother, Amanda, too. He always felt sad when he thought of her. Why hadn't she come to be with Raul when he was so close to dying? *It's because Prince Tali hadn't told her, you stupid jerk. I'm such an immature idiot sometimes.*

It was still dark outside. Kane sat up in bed and decided to get up and take a shower. The sun would be rising in about an hour and he wanted to watch it at his favorite place, on the hill overlooking the lake.

That was where Raul found him three hours later. He sat down on the blanket. "Your father wants you to help him today in the garden."

"Okay," Kane said as he handed his sketching pad to Raul. "Do any of these men look familiar to you?"

Raul studied the drawing. It was the heads of five men placed in a circle with one other man in the center. "They all look familiar, this one at the top is definitely Mani. The one on his left, I think, is his brother and this one under him is that vet. Those two on the right, I don't think I've ever seen before. The one in the middle resembles Mani and must be his other brother."

"That's right," Kane said. "Mani and his two brothers are responsible for what happened to you."

Raul looked at Kane. "I knew Mani was there. I could hear his voice."

Kane reached over and ran his finger around the circle. "All these men are dead."

Surprise appeared on Raul's face. "Mani, dead? How?"

Kane had never lied to Raul before, and he wasn't going to start now. "Your father and Zoric killed him and his brother the same way they tried to kill you."

Raul felt a chill go through his body as he looked at Kane. "Your eyes are turning that strange color again."

Kane smiled. "It'll go away in a few minutes."

Raul pointed to the vet. "Dead?"

"Yes."

"My father and Zoric?"

"Yes."

"And these two men on this side, do you know who they are?"

"I'm not sure, but I think they tried to kill your father and Zoric. We were about nine years old. Remember that parade J.J. took us to?"

Raul nodded his head.

"Those men were going to shoot your father and Zoric as they rode in the parade. My father warned Prince Tali and the two men were caught."

"How did Kevin know?"

"It's hard to explain, but someday I'll try."

"Did my father and Zoric kill these men, too?"

"Yes, I believe they did."

"What about this man?" Raul pointed to the man in the middle. "Mani's brother?"

Kane touched Raul's arm. "If you ever see him, run. Run like hell."

"Do you think he'd kill me?"

"Yes, but I'll protect you."

Raul laughed. "How are you going to do that? Look at him with those weird eyes of yours and he'll keel over dead."

Kane laughed, too. "I never thought of that. It just might work."

"What else do you have here?" Raul asked as he turned the pages in the pad. Then he stopped. The smile left his face as he stared at the drawing in front of him. "This is my mother. Why did you do this?"

"I don't really know. I've been thinking of her a lot lately. I miss her, don't you?"

Raul couldn't take his eyes off her. "Sometimes."

"She should have been here with you these last few weeks," Kane said.

"No. She doesn't care about me or my father or she would have been here."

"No one told her."

Raul raised his eyes to look at Kane. "That's not true, Kane. My father told her."

"Is that what he said?"

"He said he tried, but couldn't locate her. He left a message with her family."

Kane was sure Prince Tali had done no such thing. "Maybe it got lost. Why don't you try calling her yourself and ask her to come and visit? Take some responsibility and start acting like a man, instead of some spoiled little rich boy whose father still wipes his nose for him."

Raul laughed. "I want you to know, I quit letting him wipe my butt for me last year."

When they were through laughing, Kane stood up. He offered his hand to help Raul. The two boys faced each other. Kane was taller than Raul now by about two inches, but Raul was not considered short at five foot eleven. He had lost some weight from his ordeal, but was gaining it back slowly.

When they got back to the Estate, Raul asked. "Can I have that drawing of my mother and the one of those men, too?"

"Sure." Kane gently ripped them out. "Promise me you'll try to contact her."

Raul smiled. "I'll talk to my father about it and let you know what he says. Okay?"

"Fair enough, snot nose." Kane headed for the garden.

Kane stopped about fifty feet from his father. He studied him for several minutes. *He looks so healthy. There has to be something or someone somewhere that can help him.* He walked toward his father. "Hi, Dad."

Kevin looked up as his son approached. "Good morning Kane, have you been to the lake?"

"Yes, what are you planting?"

"Actually, I'm replanting. The flower is called Zante. I plant it in a pot in the ground in early spring. Then when the sun gets too hot I dig it up and plant it over there in the shade. Come fall she'll bud."

Kane knelt down by his father, picked up a small hand spade, and began to help. "Do you really like working out here in your vegetable and flower garden?"

"It has given me something to do and, yes, I do like seeing things grow, especially you. You've grown into a handsome, intelligent, caring young man."

Kane smiled. "Like father, like son."

It only took a few minutes to work the pot loose from the ground. Kevin lifted it out, then looked at his son. Kane could see in his father's eyes that he was asking him to be quiet.

Kane followed his father's eyes back to the hole in the ground. He watched as his father opened a plastic bag that contained what looked like a jewelry box. He snapped it open. Inside was a large amount of money. His father closed it back up and placed it in the secure plastic bag. He scooped dirt on it until it was completely hidden. He picked up another pot containing a new flower and placed it in the hole packing the dirt around it. Kane helped.

Kevin stood, "It's too hot to work outside today. I think I'll go to the lake. Would you like to join me?"

"Sure," said Kane. "I'll go tell Raul, he can join us."

"Good idea." Kevin turned and walked toward the lake.

When Kane entered the estate, J.J. informed him that Raul was in Prince Tali's office and they were not to be disturbed.

Kane smiled at him. "How was your vacation?"

"Wonderful." J.J. and his wife, Sally, had been gone for two months. J.J. asked where Mani was, he was told only that he was no longer employed there.

"Tell Raul I'll be at the lake. Thanks, J.J."

Kane went to his room to change clothes. He slipped into his swimming trunks and T-shirt. His mind kept going over what he'd just seen. *Where did all the money come from? Someone must have given it to my father to help him escape off the Island...but who and how long has he had it?*

Kane picked up one of his drawing tablets and left his room. He passed by the closed door of Prince Tali's office. J.J. was sitting in a chair close by. Kane waved to him on his way out.

As he walked toward the lake a feeling of uneasiness swept through him. He looked around, not seeing anyone. It felt strange not to have someone following him. Since the abduction of Raul, everything had changed. Surveillance cameras were set up all over the estate and could be monitored from the guardhouse, making it unnecessary for the constant companionship of the guards who Kane had become so accustomed to all his life. He was sure the new lamp posts that surrounded the estate not only contained lighting fixtures and cameras, but also listening devices. The posts were even set up around the lake.

He had always felt honored to live on Tali Island, but not anymore. He wondered what Prince Tali had planned for him and the rest of his life. He was sure it was only a matter of time before he'd have the answer to that question.

When Kane arrived at the lake he saw his father already swimming. He took off his shirt and shoes and entered the water, the feeling of uneasiness still in the pit of his stomach.

He and his father swam together in silence until they were about two hundred feet from shore.

"Do you think it's safe out this far?" Kane asked.

Kevin shook his head. "No, I don't."

Kane looked around. It was hard for him to believe that someone could hear what they said, but like his father he wasn't ready to take that chance. "When do you see the doctor again?"

"In three days. He's waiting for some more test results to come in from the United States."

"Maybe that's where you should go," said Kane. "They probably have a cure there."

"Maybe, son. That's what Doctor Stevens is trying to find out."

They talked for a while longer, then headed back to shore.

## PRINCE TALI'S OFFICE

Raul sat there, his mind going over everything his father had told him. Raul read the letter written by Jeffery McKade and handed it back to his father. Finally he spoke. "They've been prisoners on this island from the first day you brought them here?"

"Yes, Son. I tried to find Kane's mother and sister, but they just disappeared. It was rumored they died in some tragic accident. Kevin knows this is true because of this 'gift' he has." Prince Tali stood and came around his desk. He touched Raul on his shoulder. "They've had a good life here, Son. That will not change. I do want to make something perfectly clear to you. I will never let them leave this island."

"Do you actually think they would leave Tali Island?" Raul asked, disbelief sounding in his voice.

"Absolutely," stated Prince Tali. "Now more then ever. When they were first brought here, Kane was only a baby. I explained to Kevin that if he didn't do as he was told he would be eliminated and I would raise Kane as my own."

"Would you have done that?"

Prince Tali paused for a moment, then answered, "Yes."

"What happens now?" asked Raul.

Prince Tali walked back to his chair and sat down. He picked up the drawing Kane had given Raul.

"I must find this man," he said, pointing to the one in the center of the circle. "He's Mani's brother, and until he is caught, you will have a bodyguard with you at all times." Prince Tali leaned back in his chair. "Son, I want you to start learning the Tali family business. Kane too."

Raul looked at his father and, with pride in his voice, he said, "I'd like that."

"Good." Prince Tali smiled.

"There is one more thing, Father," Raul said as he reached across the desk and lifted the sheet of Kane's drawing tablet, revealing the sketch of Amanda.

Prince Tali stared at it for a moment before saying anything. "This is amazing. I can't believe Kane could remember how she looked after all these years. Why are you showing me this?"

"I want to see her."

"Why?" asked Prince Tali.

"She's my mother. I know this must sound strange, but I miss her."

"You've never mentioned this before."

"I know," said Raul. "You never showed any interest in her, so therefore, I never did either. But now I want to."

"I don't think that's a very good idea, Son," Prince Tali said. "When Amanda asked for a divorce she wanted to take you with her, back to the States. I told her no and offered her money. She took it and left. She could have had visitation rights, but again she chose to take the money instead."

Prince Tali could see the hurt look on Raul's face. "I did what I thought was right to protect you."

"I know, Father. I still would like to see her. If you don't want to call her, I will." Raul stared directly into his father's eyes. "It's not only time I took responsibility in the family business, but in my own life as well."

Prince Tali smiled at his son. "All right. I'll get in touch with her."

"Today?" asked Raul.

"Yes."

Raul stood. "Thank you, Father." He held out his hand.

Prince Tali stood, too, and as he shook his son's hand, he said, "You're becoming your own man. May the mistakes you make in life be small and few."

Raul chuckled as he left his father's office.

As Raul opened the door to his room he heard J.J.'s voice behind him. "Kane said he'd be at the lake."

"Thanks, J.J." Raul closed his door, removed all his clothing except for his underwear. He stood in front of the long mirror that was attached to his bedroom door and looked at the scars that consumed his body. Some were fading with time, but others would be there for the rest of his life. He rubbed his hand across his chest, feeling the hatred for the men who did this to him. *I'm glad my father killed you and your brother, Mani, the same way you tried to kill me. Your other brother got away, but I'll find him. I'm not going to be a coward and hide behind some bodyguard. I'm going to become the hunter. He* doubled up his fist and pounded it against his chest, making himself cough and gasp for air. *Damn, I'm going to have to wait until I'm a lot stronger before I become so brave.* He laughed to himself as he walked over to his bed and lay down. He closed his eyes and thought about Kane and his father, Kevin. He didn't know what this power they had was called, but they had saved his life. Saved it three times his father had told him today. The school bus accident, the horse, Sassy, and the rescue from Mani and his brothers. *They saved me from going insane, too.* Raul smiled to himself. After the rescue he remembered waking to total darkness, his body reeking with pain and shaking uncontrollably, and then contentment as he slipped back into unconsciousness. Then one morning he woke to find Kane sitting on one side of his bed. Kane's father, Kevin, was on the other. They each held one of Raul's hands. Raul remembered looking from one to the other. Their eyes had taken on a strange glow and Raul felt a soothing, contented feeling pass through his body. His pain subsided and the shaking, frightened feeling was gone. He felt a wonderful sense of peacefulness spread through him.

Raul knew that Kane and Kevin had saved his father and Uncle Zoric, too. *Could I let them leave this island?* He didn't like the answer he gave himself as he closed his eyes and drifted off to sleep.

It was the next day when Kane saw Raul walking toward the stables. He hollered at him. "You riding today?"

Raul stopped, turned and smiled at Kane. "Yes, would you join me?"

Kane hesitated for a minute before answering. "Sure." That strange uneasy feeling was still in the pit of his stomach.

Raul put his hand on Kane's shoulder. "I hate to tell you this, my friend, but you look like hell."

Kane laughed. "I can always count on you to cheer me up."

"Didn't you sleep well?" asked Raul.

"No, I didn't," said Kane.

"Why?" Fear sounded in Raul voice. "Is something going to happen?"

"I'm not sure," Kane said honestly. "Something is going on, but I just don't know what it is."

"Does your father know?"

"No, but he feels the same. I guess we'll have to wait and see."

The boys were silent as they saddled their horses. They didn't speak again until, overlooking a valley about a mile from the Tali Estate, Raul pulled his horse, Sassy, to a stop. "I think this is where I'll build my home and you, Kane, can build yours over there." Raul pointed his finger toward the opposite end of the valley. "We'll be far enough away from each other for privacy, but close enough so that our children can play and grow up together."

"I suppose you already have a wife picked out for me?" asked Kane.

Raul laughed. "No, but I'm sure my father does."

Kane laughed, too. "I think you might be right." Kane hesitated for a minute before asking, "How did it go yesterday?"

Raul looked away from Kane, his eyes surveying the valley before him. He took a deep breath. "My father told me everything," he finally said. "How you and your father were brought here and why. He even let me read the letter Jeffery McKade wrote to the Tali family. He told me he tried to find your mother and sister, but they had disappeared. Then he heard they had been killed. Did you know all this, Kane?"

"Not until a couple of weeks ago. I knew about the death of my mother years ago. My father told me she died when I was five. What else did your father tell you?"

"He's worried about Mani's brother. He wants us both to be very careful. I asked him about my mother, Amanda. He's going to call her and make arrangements for her to visit."

"Good," said Kane. "Did he mention my father's illness?"

The smile left Raul's face. "No, no he didn't, but I'm sure, Kane, he will do whatever he can to help."

Kane looked at Raul. "I hope so. We better head back."

Raul reached out to touch Kane's arm. "Nothing is going to change between us, Kane. We were raised as brothers, that is the way it will always be."

Kane looked at Raul, knowing what his friend needed to hear. "Yes, that's true. I will always be there for you." Kane heard the sigh of relief as Raul removed his hand from his arm.

They turned their horses around and headed back to the stable.

Kane sat up in bed. He reached over and turned on the light. He rubbed his fingers through his hair then across the back of his neck. That erie, empty feeling he felt in the pit of his stomach for the last two days was still with him. Something was going to happen, but he didn't have a clue what it was. The darkness prevented him from seeing anything. He could hear strange sounds like something cracking, but it was a whistling sound that frightened him. Then for some reason he thought of his sister, Katy. He tried to picture what she looked like. He lay back down in his bed and turned off the light. *I wonder what you're doing right now, Katy. Thinking of me, I hope.*

# Chapter 9

## 1994
## THE RANCH
### (Katy's home on the Western Slope of Colorado.)

Katy looked at the family photo again before opening the box and removing several other photos and letters her mother, Meg, had written to her before she died. There were two large unopened envelopes that were at the bottom of the box. One was addressed to 'My loving son, Kane' and the other one 'To my loving husband, Kevin.' *This will be my gift to my father and brother if—no when we finally meet.* Katy placed the two unopened envelopes back in the box.

Once again Katy read the letters her mother had left, starting with the one marked number one. She remembered the happiness she felt when finding out she had a family.

Since the death of her mother, Katy grew up with the people around her as her family. There was Sister Elizabeth Riley, her legal guardian; Ben Bennett, her Godfather; Samantha Tylar, her best friend, whom Katy loved like a sister; Samantha's father, Senator Ward Tylar; and Sister Hanna, who Katy secretly thought of as her grandmother.

Katy had been protected from her true identity and raised as Katy Kincaid. It was a promise her mother, Meg, had Sister Elizabeth make. It was only through the letters that Katy had found out her true identity. Her name was not Katy Kincaid, but Katy McKade, and Sister Elizabeth was actually her aunt.

Most of her life Katy felt the presence of someone reaching out to her. When she was thirteen, the feeling became stronger. Now she knew why. Her mother's letters told about her twin brother, who along with her father, had been kidnapped when Katy was a baby, and all because of the special gift they had. Katy had it, too, and was determined to use it to find them.

Katy finished reading the letters and returned them to the box. She left her room, closing the door behind her, and headed to the guest house to see Sami and Sami's father. As she stepped out onto the porch, a warm, early morning, July breeze greeted her.

As she walked, she waved to Sister Hanna, who was working in the garden. Five minutes later she knocked softly on the front door of the guest house. When there was no answer she went around back where she found Sami and Ward, sitting on the patio and having breakfast.

Sami jumped up when she saw her. "Oh, Katy, I'm so glad you're here. I can hardly wait to get started."

"Oh, really," said Katy. "Well, maybe your father should start by hypnotizing you first."

"No way." Sami laughed. "I'd probably tell him some of my deepest secrets, and then he'd disown me."

"Surprise, young lady." Ward smiled at his daughter. "Your father already knows your deepest secrets...you talk in your sleep. Would you like some breakfast, Katy?"

"A glass of orange juice is all, thanks."

"Okay. You girls visit for a while. I'm going to wash up a little before we begin."

Katy watched as Ward maneuvered his wheelchair around the table, then up the small ramp that led into the house. "How is he doing?" Katy asked Sami.

"If you're wondering if he's up to helping you find Kane, the answer is yes. He can hardly wait to get started. Me, too."

Katy smiled at her friend. "Let's go."

They cleaned up the breakfast dishes, then went into the den. It was a comfortable room with a fireplace, large overstuffed couch with matching love seat, and two reclining chairs. Katy sat down in one, Sami in the other.

That was where Ward found them about ten minutes later. "Are you comfortable, Katy?" he asked.

She smiled at him. "Yes, are you?"

"I'll manage. Is it all right if we record this?" he asked.

"Yes," said Katy. "Sami already asked me and it's fine."

"Good." Ward moved his wheelchair next to Katy's chair. He picked up her right hand with his and, with his left, he softly rubbed the top of her fingers as he looked into her eyes.

"This gift that God has given you is very special, frightening, too, I'm sure. When I hypnotized you in Montana, you were able to actually see a murder being committed, and with the information you gave us, we were able to get Stacey released from jail. Without you she would have spent her life in prison."

"It wasn't just me." Katy looked over at Sami. "Ben and Aunt Liz, you and Sami helped, too."

Ward smiled. "Great team work." He paused a moment before continuing. "I believe I can help you learn how to understand and work with this gift through deep concentration. I think you can do this all by yourself, without anyone else's help, including mine. I want to start out slowly, taking you back to when you were a little girl, then slowly bringing you forward to the present. I want you to think about your father and brother, now that you know they exist and have this special gift. I'm hoping you'll be able to feel their presence—maybe it will help find them. Are you ready?"

"Yes." Katy laid back in the chair and closed her eyes.

Sami turned on the recorder and made herself comfortable in the other chair.

Ward took several deep breaths, still holding onto Katy's hand, and in a soothing, deep controlled voice he began. "Your body is starting to relax, a feeling of contentment is beginning to spread through you. You feel safe as you drift deeper and deeper into a state of relaxation, but your mind is becoming increasingly alert." Ward repeated himself several times until the hand he held became limp.

"I want you to go back in time, Katy. Let your mind take you back, back to when you are a young girl, back to your first memories. Take your father and brother with you. Where are you Katy?"

A frown crossed her face. When she spoke her voice was low and sluggish. "I'm standing by someone, holding his hand." A smile came to Katy's face. "It's Mr. Ben, he's picking me up. 'Are you ready Ms. Katy?' I'm so happy. I look down. My mother is standing there. 'Be careful, Kit-Kat, do what Ben tells you.'

"He sets me on a pony. I'm a big girl now." Katy's voice drifted into silence.

Ward waited a moment, then asked, "Where are you now, Katy?"

"I'm a princess, sitting on a tall chair. There's a cake on the table in front of me."

"Are there candles on the cake?" asked Ward.

"Yes." Katy paused, then answered, "Four. They're singing to me."

"Who is singing to you, Katy?"

Katy smiled. "Mommy, and Mr. Ben. Sister Elizabeth is there. She wears that thing on her head all the time. There's another lady, she wears the same thing on her head, too. She is nice. Her name is Sister Hanna." Katy became silent again.

Ward watched as the smile left Katy's face, replaced by sadness.

"Where are you now, Katy?"

"Standing by my mother's bed. I want her to get up, play with me. She's sleeping because she's sick. Sometimes when she wakes up, I lay with her and she tells me stories. Then she sleeps again, but this time I can't wake her. Sister Elizabeth tells me that God took my mother to heaven. He needs her, but I need her too. I don't like God anymore."

Ward looked at Sami and they smiled at each other.

Katy continued. "Sister Elizabeth said God promises to take very good care of my mommy, and that I would see her soon. I think Sister Elizabeth is telling me the truth. I tell her, 'okay,' I'll like God again, but he better keep his promise." Katy paused again.

"What's happening now, Katy?"

"Mr. Ben is taking me for a ride in his big truck. I don't want to go, but he says I have to. We're taking a present to a girl named Samantha. It's her birthday and she doesn't have anyone to play with. I like her. Sister Elizabeth lets me stay overnight with her. It's fun. Sami tells me that Mr. Ben must be someone very special because he has a title—it's foreman—and only important people have titles. I tell her that he's my Godfather. She says I'm very lucky. She says she is lucky, too. Her father has a title. It's Senator. She says everywhere they go people want to shake his hand and take his picture."

Ward glanced at his watch. It had almost been an hour. He motioned for Sami to change the tape in the recorder. When she was finished, he started again.

"You seem worried, Katy. What do you see?"

"Ben shot a cat that was going to bite Johnny. Ben said it's a mountain lion. I saw it happen in a dream."

"Are you the only one that has this dream?" Ward knew it was a long shot, but they had to start somewhere. He could tell Katy was concentrating deeply. *Good.*

Katy finally spoke. "Yes, I think I'm the only one, but I feel there's others somewhere that know I had this dream. They seem far away, but I know they're out there. I can feel their presence."

Ward pressed a little harder. He didn't want Katy to lose her train of thought. "You're getting older, Katy. Can you tell me about your next dream?"

Ward thought Katy had fallen asleep. It was almost five minutes before she answered, then her body started to tremble. "It's okay, Katy, it's only a dream."

"No, first it was a dream, but then it comes true. I'm riding in Ben's truck. He's driving very fast. Sister Elizabeth is with us and we're headed for one of the farms where 'toothless' George, his wife and two boys live. Ben pulls up in front and we all get out. Ben's running into the house and there's blood everywhere. George has beaten Jan and the two boys with a bat. He starts to swing it again.

"'No', screams Sister Elizabeth. Ben runs across the room, tackling George and knocking the bat out of his hand. They fight." Katy took a deep breath and with a trembling voice told the rest of the dream that had become a reality. Then a frown appeared on her face. "My father knows," she smiled. "He's very proud of me."

Katy relaxed, took several deep breaths, then continued. "I'm thirteen now. I'm riding my horse up the trail to my favorite place. I love sitting on the large boulder and looking out over my mountains. The sun is beginning to set and the clouds become a multitude of beautiful colors. Then it happens. I feel this tugging at my body, like someone new trying to reach out to me. Who could it be? The feeling stays with me. I'm frightened. I force myself to think of something else. I think about the Ranch and how lucky I am to be able to call it home."

"You're doing fine, Katy." Ward waited until Sami changed the tape, and he started again. "You're still thirteen, Katy. How old are you when you have your next dream?"

Katy's head moved back and forth. She lowered it to her chest. Tears were streaming down her face. It took Ward and Sami by surprise. Ward was tempted to bring Katy out of the trance, but Sami shook her head. She motioned for her father to continue. They both wanted to know what would make Katy cry like this.

"What do you see, Katy, that makes you so sad?" Ward asked.

"I'm lying in bed. I wake up and look at my clock. It's ten thirty-five. I see the car accident. Sami's mother, Jill, is dead. Ward is trying to reach out to help her, but can't. His body collapses into unconsciousness. There's nothing I can do to save them."

Tears were in Ward's and Sami's eyes as they, too, relived that horrible memory.

Katy leaned her head back. "Why? Why couldn't I have seen this sooner? I'm so sick. What can I do?

"Sister Elizabeth comes to my room early the next morning to tell me something I'd known for over seven hours."

Ward tried to comfort Katy. "It's okay, Katy. It was an accident. There was nothing you or anyone else could have done to prevent it. I want you to block everything from your mind, sleep without any dreams, completely relax."

Ward waited until Katy's breathing became regular and he knew she was sleeping before he left her side, wheeling himself into the kitchen.

Sami was right behind him. "Coffee, Dad?"

"Yes, please."

"You look tired. You want to call it quits for today?" She handed him his coffee.

"I don't think Katy would want me to. What do you think?"

"I know she wouldn't, but I don't want you overdoing anything."

"I'm fine. It was just such a shock when she said she saw the accident. I didn't know."

"She never told me, either. I guess she thought it was best."

Ward nodded his head in agreement. "Let's give it another hour and see how she holds up."

"Thanks, Dad." Sami hugged her father. "You're the best."

Ten minutes later they were back in the den, ready to begin again. Ward gently picked up Katy's hand. *You've grown into a beautiful, loving, caring young lady. I will always be grateful to you for saving Sami's life.* He looked over at his daughter and smiled, then returned his attention to Katy. "You're still very relaxed, your mind is filled with new energy, searching your past, looking for your father and brother. Do you hear my voice, Katy?"

"Yes," she said softly.

"I want you to think about your life after the car accident. Do you have any more dreams?"

Again it was almost five minutes before Katy responded. She shook her head back and forth. "No. No. No. I'm going to take her to the basement and tie her up if I have to. I'm not letting her get on that train."

Even though Ward knew the answer, he had to ask. "You're not letting who get on what train, Katy?"

"Sami. She's so stubborn. I have to keep her from getting on that train to Denver. She wants to see her father. It's been a year since the accident. The doctors didn't expect him to live, but he did. Now they say he will never walk. Wrong again. I have to find some way of keeping her off that train. I see dead bodies. All the faces are blurred except one, Sami's. I swear I will tie her up and put her in the basement."

Ward and Sami couldn't help chuckling to themselves.

"I know what I'll do." Katy burst out, "I'll ask Sister Lizzie, oops, Sister Elizabeth to drive her, but we'll have a flat tire. That's okay." Katy smiled. "A handsome cowboy comes to our rescue. His name is Kord McNamera. He has this huge dog named Wild Thing—no that's not right." Katy paused. "His name is Bear. We're in the car again. Sister Elizabeth is driving. We stop and Sister makes a phone call. There's been a train accident. My dream has come true. I'm so sick. I need to lie down." Katy's voice dropped to a whisper.

"What happens next, Katy?" Ward hoped he wasn't pushing her too fast.

"I'm so weak. I need food. Where am I? Sister Elizabeth is here. We're at a church, staying in the convent. I meet Father James. Have I met him before? Maybe. I'm in the garden, I meet Father Tim." Katy smiled. "He's the biggest man I've ever seen. His hands are huge." Katy chuckled. "His mother is there, she's so tiny. I'm tired. I need to sleep. The smile left Katy's face. "No, not another dream. I must tell Father Tim that his mother is hurt. He has to go to her right away." Katy's voice faded. "I can't believe it, I'm going to be sick again."

Sami waited for an okay sign from her father before she changed the tape in the recorder.

"Where are you now, Katy?"

"I'm at the Ranch. Sami is so happy that her father's coming home. Ben tells us about the train accident. He flew a rescue chopper. He saves a lady and her son." Katy paused again. "Ben takes her to one of the cottages for her safety. She's under the Witness Protection Program. Her name is Jennifer DeValladero and her son's name is

Luke. She's homely until she takes her disguise off. She's really pretty." Katy smiled.

"I'm reading the letters my mother left me." Katy became very excited. "Sister Elizabeth is really my aunt. I have a twin brother named Kane and my father, Kevin, might still be alive. I have to find them, but first we have to help Jenny. She slips in the mud, falling down a cliff. We have to let her parents, sister, and brother know she's okay.

"Ben and I fly to Montana. There's trouble. Jenny's husband, Victor, is there. We fly Patty and Lou Mason, Jenny's parents, and her sister, Stacey, and brother, Mike, back to be with Jenny. They're so happy to see each other.

"Stacey and Mike go back to Montana with Ben. Stacey is arrested for the murder of Jenny's husband. I fly with Ward, Sami, and Sister Elizabeth to Montana. The real murderer is caught. We're back at the Ranch. Now all I want to do is find my brother and father." Katy paused again. "I'm sleeping, dreaming again. The dream is so strange. I see someone tied to an object. They're hurting him, I feel pain in my body and face. My nose is bleeding. I think it's broken. I jump out of bed, look at myself in the mirror. I'm okay, but I still feel the pain. I don't understand. I lay back slowly and close my eyes. The person tied to the round object is cut free. I still feel the pain. I'm so sick I need to sleep. I open my eyes. The pain and nausea are gone. I tell Sami about the dream. She thinks it has something to do with my brother and father. I think she's right. I need to find them because if I don't, one of them might die. "Katy started crying uncontrollably.

"Everything's all right, Katy. We'll find them. Relax, take a deep breath. When I count to three I want you to wake up, remembering everything that's happened. You will feel calm and rested, one, two, three."

Katy slowly opened her eyes.

Sami handed her a tissue. "You did good, Kit-Kat."

Katy laughed. Her legs felt stiff from sitting. "How long have we been at this?"

"Four hours," Ward replied.

"Are you all right?" Katy asked, concerned.

"Never felt better. Are you aware of what happened here today?"

Katy thought for a moment before answering. "Yes. I think so.

What's next?"

Sami interrupted. "I have a question to ask you, Katy." She stood by her father, placing an arm around his shoulder. "Do you really see my father walking again?" She could feel her father draw a deep breath as they both waited for the answer.

Katy looked at them both. She knew the answer they were asking for would have to be a truthful one. She laid her head back against the chair and closed her eyes.

Ward took Sami's hand. When Katy opened her eyes again, they both noticed the slight change of color in them.

"Yes, Ward, you will walk again. You still have a lot of hard work ahead and one of your legs is weaker than the other, but with the proper brace and a cane for a couple of months, you will do quite well. Soon you won't even need them." Katy could see the happiness on both their faces.

Sami hugged her father. "I knew it. I just knew you would walk again."

"If you were so sure, why did you have to ask Katy?" Ward asked with a big grin on his face.

"I wanted you to have that second opinion." Sami was so happy that she danced around the room. "Will he walk me down the aisle and dance at my wedding?

"Oh, that reminds me, Dad, I asked Ben to bring Stacey back with him tonight. He's going to the cottage to take Jenny on a picnic. Just the two of them all alone."

Ward laughed. "Maybe we should be thinking about dancing at Ben's wedding."

"Wouldn't that be wonderful?" Katy replied.

Sami and Ward nodded their heads in agreement.

"Enough horsing around, girls. Right now, Katy comes first." Ward reached over and picked up her hand. "We will find your father and brother."

Katy smiled at him. "I wish I could close my eyes and see the answer. I don't understand. Why can't I see them?"

"You were very young then and you didn't even know they existed until a few weeks ago. Now you feel their presence. I thought the session went very well today. I think we should listen to the tapes. Talk about what you're thinking when you hear them. Sound like a plan?"

Ward asked.

"Yes, it even sounds like a good one," Katy said, teasingly. "I think it's enough for today, though. I'll take the tapes with me. When Ben gets back maybe he and Aunt Liz, oops, I mean Sister Elizabeth, will want to hear them."

"I'm sure they will," Ward replied.

"Okay," Sami said to her father. "Off to the therapy room you go. I'll fix you a light lunch, then more therapy. By then you'll be ready for, and need, a hot shower. I'll fix something so you and Stacey can enjoy a late supper."

Katy laughed. "That sounds like a plan."

Sami shrugged her shoulders. "I guess I do get a little carried away sometimes. I can't help it, I'm just so happy."

"I have an idea, Sami. Why don't you come up to the house tonight? I'm sure Ward and Stacey wouldn't mind being alone for a while."

The smile left Sami's face. "I don't know. What do you think, Dad?"

Ward thought for a moment. He didn't want to hurt his daughter's feelings. She had become so devoted to him.

"Well, I've learned to take care of all my personal needs. Thanks to you. I don't think I would make too big an ass of myself. It wouldn't be as if you were leaving me alone, but I'll let you decide. Whatever you feel comfortable with, sweetie."

"I'll let you know later," Sami said as she handed the tapes to Katy.

"Okay." Katy bent down and gave Ward a hug, then rubbed the top of his head. "That's for luck. Thanks for everything."

After Katy left, Ward touched the top of his head. "I think Ben shaved my head because in reality he's a very mean person."

Sami couldn't help laughing. "He does get a little overprotective at times. You're still a handsome guy. He couldn't change that." Sami snickered. "One thing for sure, without Katy and Ben, our lives would have been very boring."

"We mustn't forget Sister Elizabeth. What can you say about a woman that runs a large corporation. Flies a plane or helicopter. Farms a ranch, rides a wild horse, and a  motorcycle, and drives an eighteen-wheeler. She speaks at least four or five languages. Her karate is something to admire from afar. She's terrific at baseball or chess, a killer when it comes to pool, and the best darn poker player I ever met. She's also one of the most caring, kindly, loving women in the world, and being a nun is the most important thing in her life, besides Katy."

Sami agreed with everything her father said. "We are very lucky to have Katy, Ben, and Sister Elizabeth in our lives. Do you think the session went well today?"

"Unbelievable is more like it. Katy makes it so easy. She's a little frightened of the unknown, but once she learns she has some control through deep concentration, she'll be okay. Right now she needs me to help her, but that won't be for long."

"Don't be silly, Dad, Katy will always need you."

Ward smiled at his daughter. "Us, you mean, and we'll always need her. Shall we get started on my torture for the day?"

"Let's go."

Ward approached his therapy with a new eagerness, knowing it wasn't with a maybe, but with a definite yes. *I will walk again. Thank you, Katy.*

Katy walked slowly back to the ranch house, her mind going back over everything that had happened this morning. Her whole life seemed clearer by remembering what happened to her years ago. She thought about the first time she met Samantha. Ben had held her little hand as he introduced her. "Katy, this is Samantha Tylar. These are her parents, Jill and Senator Ward Tylar."

"So this is the little princess Ben's told us so much about. I'm very happy to meet you," Ward said as he bent down and took Katy's other hand. "What a beautiful little princess you are. Please call me Ward."

Katy remembered giggling and saying, "Okay."

She thought about Ben. He had been there her whole life to protect her. He was like a father to her and she loved him very much.

"Hi, Katy."

She turned when she heard the familiar voice. "Hi, Father Tim." She smiled and waved to him. *I'm so happy his home is The Ranch now. He's going to play an important part in everyone's lives in the years to come.*

She could see Aunt Liz walking toward her. All her life Katy had felt a certain closeness to Sister Elizabeth. The day she read the letters and found out about her brother and father, she also learned that Sister Elizabeth was her mother's sister. It was the happiest day of Katy's life.

Katy ran toward her. "Oh, Aunt Liz, I wish you could have been there. It was awesome. We taped it all so you and Ben can hear everything."

Katy's happiness was contagious. Sister Elizabeth wrapped her arms around her. "I can hardly wait. Maybe we can listen to the tapes tonight when Ben gets back."

"I was thinking the same thing," Katy replied.

# Chapter 10

Ben sat on the blanket across from Jenny. He couldn't take his eyes off her. "You're so beautiful."

She smiled at him. "You just think that because you saw me in my disguise and I was so homely."

Ben laughed. "I'll never forget the look on Katy's, Sami's, and Sister Elizabeth's faces when you removed it in front of them."

Jenny joined in his laughter. "Sometimes, Ben, I think you have an ornery streak inside you."

"Maybe." The smile left his face. "One thing for sure, you'll never have to wear it again."

She reached over and touched his face. "Thanks to you."

He took her hand and kissed it softly.

"Do you think I'll ever be able to go home to Butte, Montana, Ben?" Jenny asked. "Will my son be safe?"

"You and Luke are both safe as long as you are here."

"We can't stay in a secluded cottage forever, Ben. Luke needs other children to play with. I need to find a job, but I don't even know what name to use. With my husband and father-in-law both dead, would anyone else try to kill me if they found out I was alive?"

"What about your mother-in-law?" Ben asked.

"She married Vincent DeValladero because she loved him, not because he was a high class gangster. Victor was her only child. As far as I know she has no family except a grandson she knows nothing about."

Ben could hear the sadness in Jenny's voice. "You liked her very much, didn't you?"

"Yes, I did."

"Come here," Ben said as he gently pulled her close. She laid her head on his shoulder. His hand touched her cheek and he gently moved her hair behind her ear. "Maybe we should pay her a visit."

Jenny smiled up at him. She put her hand on the back of his head, pulling it toward her until their lips met. Their kiss became more passionate until Ben reluctantly pulled away and looked into her eyes. "I think I better make an honest woman of you."

She smiled. "An honest woman out of an ex-wife of a gangster?"

Ben smiled, too. "I'll give it my best shot." His lips lowered to hers again.

It was late afternoon when Ben dropped off Jenny and picked up her sister, Stacy. An hour later Ben pulled his truck to a stop in front of The Ranch guesthouse. "Sit tight. I'll open the door for you." He smiled as he held out his hand to help her out of the truck.

"Thank you, Ben," Stacey replied.

"My pleasure."

Sami met them at the door. "Hi, Stacey, Ben."

"Hi, Sami. Thank you for inviting me," Stacy said. "It's so beautiful up here."

"Come in and make yourself at home." Sami reached for Stacey's overnight bag. "I'll take that, Ben, and show Stacey where her room is. Dad's finishing his shower. He'll be right out."

"I'm going to leave," said Ben. "I'll be at the ranch house if you need me."

"Okay, tell Katy I'll be there in half an hour." Sami could see the surprise on Ben's face. She winked at him.

"I'll tell her. Bye, Stacey. See you tomorrow."

After Ben left, Sami showed Stacey what she had fixed for supper. "I don't think you'll have any trouble. Dad will help you. If you need me, the number for the ranchhouse is by the phone. Don't worry about the dishes, enjoy yourselves."

"You don't have to leave, Sami."

"I know, but if you don't mind, I'd like to go for a couple of hours."

"Of course, I don't mind. Have fun."

They both turned when they heard Ward's wheelchair coming into the room.

Ward looked at one, then the other. "Hello, you two beautiful women."

"Hello, Ward," Stacey said, smiling at him fondly.

Ward smiled back. When she made no effort to move in his direction, he moved toward her. "I think I like the way you said 'hello' in Montana much better."

Stacey didn't hesitate. She walked up to him, bent down and looked into his eyes. "Hello, my hero." She kissed him tenderly.

Sami smiled. "I can see you two don't need me hanging around here. I'll be at the ranchhouse."

When she arrived, Sister Elizabeth, Katy, Ben, and Father Tim were waiting for her in Sister Elizabeth's office. "Hi, everyone."

Katy handed her a notepad and pen. "In case you want to take a few notes."

"Thanks," Sami replied.

It was two o'clock in the morning when Sami returned to the guest house. She peeked into her father's bedroom, and found him sleeping soundly. She thought about checking on Stacey, too, but changed her mind.

As she got ready for bed, her mind went over the tapes again. *I know Katy's brother and father must still be alive. For how long is the question.*

For the next two weeks, every evening when Katy went to bed she was thinking the same thing.

They had listened to the tapes in sections, as Ward suggested, but it didn't seem to be helping, so he wanted to hypnotize her again. She had tried it on herself the night before, but something scared her. It was a strange noise. A very frightening, whistling sound traveled through the darkness. An erie feeling went through Katy's body. *It'll be a long time before I try that again.* She thought about her boyfriend, Kord, and hugged her pillow. It had been three weeks since she last saw him. *I miss him.* She closed her eyes and drifted off to sleep.

The morning came too soon as far as Katy was concerned. She struggled to get out of bed. *Coffee is what I need and lots of it.* After taking a shower, she slipped on shorts and a sleeveless blouse, brushed her hair back in a ponytail, and headed out the door toward the guest house.

Ben was waiting for her outside. "Hi, sweetie."

"Hi, Ben."

"Want some company today?"

Katy smiled. "Sure. How's Jenny and Luke doing?"

"Great. I'm flying her parents and sister, Stacey, home to Butte, Montana, tomorrow afternoon. I'm bringing Jenny and Luke back here to stay. I don't want to leave her alone again at the cottage."

"Don't we have someone scheduled to stay in Cottage One this month?" asked Katy.

"Yes, that's another reason I'm bringing her back here. The cottage is leased out from August tenth to September tenth. Ben paused for a moment, reached out his hand and placed it on her shoulder. He turned Katy to face him. "I want you to know, Katy, that helping to find Kane is at the top of my list. That's why I wanted to see what happens today."

Katy put her arm around him. "Thanks, Ben, you're the best."

Ward and Sami were ready for her when Katy and Ben arrived. She settled into the recliner as she had done before, but for some reason she felt more at ease. *I think it's because that handsome Godfather of mine is here with me.* She winked at Ben, laid her head back against her chair, and closed her eyes.

Ward picked up her hand. "I'm going to take you to your favorite place. You will start to feel relaxed as the tension leaves your body. Let my voice be your guide, your protector."

Ward talked to her until he felt her hand become limp in his. "You feel so much peace within yourself, yet your mind is extremely alert. I want you to feel the presence of your father, Kevin, and your brother, Kane. They are with you as you let your mind go back in time. Take them with you. They've always been at your side, keep them there. I want you to remember your dream about Johnny and the lion. Can you feel the presence of your father with you?"

A frown appeared on Katy's face, then was replaced by a smile, but no answer. Ward continued, "You're twelve years old now, Katy, and you are having another dream. Two boys and their mother are hurt." Ward could feel Katy's body stiffen. "They're okay, Katy, relax. Who is there with you?"

Katy was slow to answer. "Sister Elizabeth, Ben and my father. He's proud of me." Katy smiles.

"Is your brother, Kane, there?"

"No. He's not."

"You're older now, Katy. I want you to feel Kane's presence. Can you tell me how old you are?"

Katy turned her head from side to side. "He's calling to me from far away. I know it's him now. I'm not afraid anymore."

"How old are you, Katy?" Ward asked again.

"Thirteen." Katy snickered. "Sami says I'm a witch."

"Why does she say that?"

"She likes to tease me. She's so funny."

"Katy, I want you to remember when you turned seventeen and the dream you had of someone tied to a round object. You feel the pain in your face and ribs. I want you to tell me what happens, but you will not feel any pain. Do you understand Katy?"

"Yes."

"The person who feels the pain is your brother, Kane. Is this true, Katy?"

"Yes. He tells someone, but I don't know who it is."

"Where is your father?"

Katy was silent for a moment. "He's sleeping. He's very sick and needs me. I must find him." Katy pleaded for help. "Please help me find him."

"It's okay, Katy, relax. Everything is going to be all right, I'm going to wake you on the count of three. You will remember everything, but you'll feel in control. One, two, three."

Katy slowly opened her eyes. Her body was sweating. "My father's not well! I have to find him."

Ben walked over to her. Taking her hands, he gently pulled her up from the chair and wrapped his arms around her. "We'll find them, Katy, I promise."

"But how?"

Ben pulled her from his embrace and sat her back down in the chair. He kneeled in front of her and smiled. "I have a couple of ideas," he said.

"Like what?" Katy asked.

"I'm going to get in touch with Father James. He played a big part in your mother's and father's lives. He was there when they first met, he was the priest who married them, and he was responsible for helping your mother bring you home to The Ranch. I'll have Father James make a list of all the places your parents went and we'll go there. What do you think?"

"Sounds wonderful. We have to start somewhere."

Sami interrupted, "Who's going to be the brave one and tell Sister Elizabeth about this master plan?"

Silence fell around the room. They looked from one to another.
Ben chuckled. "I guess I'll be the one. Is there anyone here that
thinks it's a bad idea?"

Ward was the first to respond. "It seems the only logical thing to do.
I don't think Katy would be in any danger as long as we don't ask
questions that would make someone suspicious."

"How would we find them then?" asked Sami.

"We have to depend on Katy," Ward replied. "Maybe she will feel
their presence more strongly in some places."

Katy looked at him. "You'll have to go with us, in case I need to be
hypnotized. I tried it on my own last night and all I could feel was
myself in total darkness with this cracking noise and frightening,
whistling sound."

"Do you think it's a vision of something that's going to happen?"
Concern sounded in Ben's voice.

"I don't know."

"If it happens again," Ward replied, "let me know and we'll try
bringing it out in the open."

Katy smiled at him. "Okay."

For the next two hours they discussed Ben's plan. Katy decided it
was up to her to tell Sister Elizabeth. "After all, besides Kane being
my brother, he is Aunt Liz's nephew."

Later that evening Sister Elizabeth and Katy sat on the porch of the
ranchhouse, going over the plan to find Kane and Kevin.

Sister Elizabeth knew there was no way she could say no to Katy.
"I think you're on the right track, but we'll have to take every precaution to protect your identity."

Katy was so excited. "Oh, thank you, Aunt Liz. I'll do anything you
say, dress as a nun, wear brown contacts, anything."

She smiled at Katy. "Let me sleep on it tonight. We'll talk again
tomorrow." She had to admit to herself it did sound exciting. "No matter what decisions are made, we have to get our passports ready to go,
and check with Dr. Daniel to see what shots we need."

"How long will it take?" asked Katy.

"By the time we get everything ready, I'm thinking it'll be about a
week or week and a half." Sister could see the disappointment in
Katy's eyes.

"Ben needs time to go over the information Father James will give him, so that we can put together a travel plan. Tomorrow is Sunday and Ben is planning to take Jenny's parents and sister back to Montana. I think you and I should follow him to the cottage and bring Jenny and Luke back here. That way Ben could stop over in Denver when he leaves Montana and spend Monday with Father James. He can also get his passport updated while he's there.

"Since Ben won't be here, you and Sami will have to pick up the Congressman and his family at the airport in Grand Junction late Monday morning and take them to the cottage. You could go early and apply for your passport. Sami, Ward and I already have ours. We just need to get them updated and can do that when we pick up yours. I'm sure I'll have to sign something showing I'm your legal guardian."

Katy chuckled, "As fast as your mind is working, I think we'll be able to leave in about three days."

Sister Elizabeth took a deep breath. "You're right. I am getting a little ahead of myself."

Katy picked up Sister's hand. "No, you're doing great. I think everything you've suggested is perfect."

They sat there in silence for a few minutes, then Katy finally asked, "Something's going on in that mind of yours, Aunt Liz. What is it?"

"I was just thinking," Sister Elizabeth said, her voice sounding very serious, "that we need to fly our own plane."

"Fly our own plane, where?" Ben asked her as he stepped onto the porch and sat in a chair across from Sister Elizabeth, and Katy.

"I'd like to know the answer to that, too," replied Katy.

"My main concern," Sister said looking at Katy, "is you and your safety. I don't want to be in a strange country and have something happen. If we have to leave right away, I don't want to depend on commercial airlines."

"You make a good point," Ben said. "Something else we need to consider when we find them is how are we going to get them back here. I know I'm assuming they are still over there somewhere, but for all we know they could be here in the United States."

Katy looked at him. "Are you telling me that this is like looking for a needle in a haystack?"

Ben leaned forward. "If it was anyone else but you, Katy, I'd say yes. I do agree with Sister, though. We need to plan this very care-

125

fully. If the people who kidnapped your brother and father because of this special 'gift' were to find out you have it, too, you could be in danger."

"No one will find out, Ben." Katy said reassuringly. "I promised Aunt Liz that I would do whatever I'm told."

"That's my girl." Ben smiled at her.

Sister Elizabeth explained to Ben what Katy and she had been discussing.

"How many people are going to be involved in this?" asked Ben.

"For right now the three of us, along with Father Tim, Ward, Sister Hanna, Sami, and Father James." Sister looked at Katy and then Ben. "But I will keep an open mind. I do realize there might be others we will have to take into our confidence."

"Like Kord?" Katy asked with a big grin on her face.

Sister smiled back at her. "If necessary. When do you plan on seeing him again?"

"I'm not sure. He's supposed to call me around ten." Katy glanced at her watch. It was almost nine-thirty.

"Kord has a passport, doesn't he?" asked Ben.

"I'm sure he does. His mother lives in England and he flies there at least twice a year," replied Katy. "Why, what are you thinking?"

Ben smiled. "Just exploring all options."

Katy stood and walked over to him, cupping his face in her hands. She leaned down and softy kissed his forehead. "You're the greatest, Mr. Ben," she said teasingly.

Ben smiled at her. "Say hello to Kord for me."

"I will. See you tomorrow. Good night, Aunt Liz."

They sat there for a few minutes, then Ben finally broke the silence. "How do you really feel about all this, Sister?"

"Leery, but I know it's something we have to do, and the sooner the better."

Ben studied her for a moment. "You're not just doing this for Katy, are you?"

She smiled at him. "You know me pretty well. No, it's not just for Katy. I need to find out for myself if I have a nephew. I worry, though. What if we don't find them, or worse yet, if we do and he doesn't want anything to do with us."

"That will never happen. We will find them." Ben stood and reached his hand out to touch her shoulder. "Remember, he's your sister, Meg's, son, so he has to be one hell of a nice young man."

Sister Elizabeth touched his hand. "Thanks, Ben."

"See you tomorrow."

"Goodnight." ·

Katy sat on her bed, waiting for the phone to ring, her hand holding the locket that hung from her neck. Kord had given it to her on her seventeenth birthday. She opened it and looked at the photo of Kord with Bear, his dog, by his side. A warm feeling passed through her as she remembered their first kiss. The ringing of the phone brought her back to reality.

"Hello."

"Hi, how's the love of my life?"

"Missing you," replied Katy.

"I miss you, too, but I have good news. My father got back from his business meeting sooner than expected, so I'll be able to come up early tomorrow, say around nine in the morning."

"Oh, Kord, that's wonderful."

"I never want to be away from you this long again, Katy."

It was an hour later when Katy finally hung up the phone and got ready for bed. She hugged her pillow close to her. *I'm going to tell you everything, Kord. I know Aunt Liz would rather I wait, but I don't want anything to come between us. I want you to know about my father and twin brother and about this special gift we have.* She closed her eyes and drifted off to sleep only to awaken to the strangest dream—of darkness, the cracking noise, and then the frightening, whistling sound.

Katy opened her eyes. The dream was the same as it had been for the last two nights. *This has something to do with you, Kane. I know it does.* Katy closed her eyes and drifted back to sleep.

*Carole A. Sheller*

# Chapter 11
## TALI ISLAND/SUNDAY MORNING

Kane stood in the shower. He pressed the palms of his hands against the wall and leaned back, letting the water flow down his body. He had spent another restless night. The same dream invaded his sleep as it had done for the last few nights. What puzzled him was the fact it hadn't changed. *Why the darkness?* Cold chills passed through him even though the shower water was as hot as he could tolerate.

He stood there for a few more minutes before reaching up and turning the water off.

Fifteen minutes later he was dressed and headed for the kitchen where he found his father having his morning coffee.

"Morning, Dad."

Kevin smiled at his son. "You're up early this morning?"

Kane poured himself a cup and sat down at the table across from his father. Almost as if in a trance, he stared at the swirl made with his spoon as he stirred sugar into his coffee.

"Kane, are you all right?" Kevin asked, concern sounding in his voice.

Kane smiled at his father. "I'm fine, just a little tired."

"Since you're up early, how about going to mass with me this morning?"

Kane looked at his father. *Why not.*

"Sure," Kane answered. He watched as the smile spread across his father's face.

"Wonderful. J.J. should be here in about twenty minutes to drive us. How about some breakfast?"

Kane stood. "I'll just have cereal. I'm not really hungry."

As Kane was getting the milk out of the refrigerator, a knock sounded on the door.

"McKade, you up?" Zoric hollered as he opened the door.

"In the kitchen," answered Kevin.

"You're both here, good. I have some news." Zoric helped himself to coffee and sat down. "Prince Tali is planning a little party for Raul this afternoon and he wants you both there."

"Will there be any girls?" Kane asked.

Zoric chuckled. "Yes, several just for you and one of them is special."

"Why, is she the one Prince Tali has picked for my future wife?"

Zoric heard the bitterness in Kane's voice. "No son, not this time. You'll probably wish it was, though. Doctor Stevens called yesterday to inform me that Julianna, the young girl you both donated blood to, is in town. He's bringing her to the party. She'd like to meet both of you and thank you for what you did."

Kane sat there for a minute before saying anything. "Wow, that's great. I haven't thought of her for a long time. Is she still dancing?"

"Yes," answered Zoric. "In fact she's quite famous, a very talented young lady."

Another knock sounded on the door. "There's J.J." said Kevin. "Come in."

Kane stood. "Let's go, Dad, before I change my mind."

"Where are you two going?" asked Zoric.

"My son's accompanying me to church today," Kevin said with pride. He placed his arm around Kane's shoulder. "Let's go." He noticed Zoric glance at his belt buckle as they walked out the door.

Kane sat in church with his father on one side, J.J. on the other. A feeling of contentment passed through him as he looked around. He thought of his sister, Katy, and for some reason, felt closer to her than ever before. He even felt a closeness to the mother he'd never known. *It's probably because she was going to be a nun. Maybe that's what Katy's going to be. Whatever it is, she's close to people involved with the church and, for some reason, I feel the same closeness.* He reached over and touched his father's hand. When their eyes met, Kane knew his father felt the same. They smiled at each other.

Later that afternoon Prince Tali and Zoric sat on the verandah and watched the party get underway. On one side of the large yard a tent was set up to protect people from the sun. Some were swimming, some playing tennis, others were dancing to the music of a small band. Everyone seemed to be enjoying themselves.

"My son is an excellent dancer," Prince Tali stated as he watched Raul twirl a pretty young girl around.

"Yes, he is. I think Raul is healing quite well on the outside as well as inside."

"I want him to start learning the family business, Zoric. You will help, of course."

"I'll do what I can. What about Kane?"

Prince Tali looked at his brother. "Do whatever it takes to make sure he's at Raul's side. I want to find him a wife as soon as possible and hope he has several sons."

Zoric laughed. "I hope you have better luck with him than you did with me."

Prince Tali joined in the laughter. "I hope so, too." He paused for a minute before asking, "Do you think you'll ever marry?"

Zoric glanced out over the crowd. "I always wanted to and haven't given up hope, maybe someday. What are you doing about McKade?"

"There isn't much that can be done. It doesn't look good, he might have a year left."

"Damn," said Zoric. "I've always considered him a good friend. I often wonder if we did the right thing by bringing him here."

"We did. You know we'd all be dead if he hadn't been here. He's finished now, and Kane is the only one I'm concerned about."

Zoric didn't like to hear his brother talk like that. He stood up. "I think I'll go down and join the party."

As he walked down the stairs, he watched J.J. bring the limo to a stop. He went over to greet Doctor Stevens who emerged from the car.

The doctor held out his hand. "Zoric, nice to see you." He turned to help the young lady. "I'd like you to meet Julianna. This is one of our hosts, Zoric Tali."

She held out her hand. "Thank you so much for letting me come to your beautiful home."

"We're very honored to have you." Zoric smiled and gently placed a kiss on the back of her hand. He was reluctant to let it go as he stared into her eyes. "The doctor said you were very pretty. I think he meant to say beautiful."

He folded her arm around his. "Please let me be your escort and introduce you to everyone."

"Thank you."

Kane and Raul started walking toward them. "Do you think she's too old for me?" asked Raul.

"For you, yes. For me, no," answered Kane.

"Asshole," Raul said under his breath so no one could hear him other than Kane.

They stopped in front of her.

Zoric chuckled. "Let me warn you about these two, Julianna. They're two vultures that live on the island. This one is Prince Tali's son and my nephew, Raul."

Julianna smiled. "Hello, Raul."

"Julianna. Maybe I could show you around the island later."

"That would be nice. Thank you."

"And this here…" Zoric motioned toward Kane. "…is someone you personally came here to meet. This is Kane."

Julianna dropped Zoric's arm and moved closer to Kane. She was tall, about five foot nine. She reached up her hands and placed them on Kane's face. They stared at each other for several seconds before she spoke. "I wanted so much to thank you in person for saving my life." She rose up on her toes and pulled his face toward her. She gently kissed his lips, then dropped her hands. "Thank you."

A smile came to Kane's face. He raised his hands and placed them on her face as she had done to him. "I wanted so much to tell you in person that you're welcome." He lowered his head and his lips pressed against hers. "You're welcome."

"Why don't the two of you take Julianna and introduce her to your fathers," Zoric said.

"Our pleasure," said Raul as he took one of her hands and Kane took the other.

"I have to be the luckiest girl in the world to have such handsome men for my escort."

Two hours later, Julianna was standing in the shade of the tent and talking to Prince Tali, with Raul and Kane not far away, when Kevin came up behind her. "This must be the beautiful and talented Julianna."

She turned and looked into the eyes of one of the most handsome men she had ever seen. "You must be Kevin. Kane has your eyes."

Kevin took the hand she extended in both of his. He studied her for a moment, then asked, "How are you feeling?"

The concern she heard in his voice touched her. She smiled. "I'm doing very well, thanks to you. Could we go somewhere and talk?"

"Of course," Kevin said. He noticed Prince Tali glance at his belt buckle as he led her away.

They found a table under a tree where they could have privacy. That was where Kane found them an hour later. "Can anyone join this party?" he asked.

She smiled up at him. "Come, sit down beside me."

"Okay."

She slipped her arm through his. "I hope someday we will all meet again. Maybe you could see me dance."

"It's a date," Kane said.

Kevin stood. "I think I'll find Doctor Stevens, see how he's doing."

They both watched him walk away. "Your father's very nice."

"Yes, he is, but I'd rather talk about you."

She looked into his eyes. "I'd rather you kissed me again."

He wrapped his arms around her. "Me, too."

Kane had kissed other girls before, but this was different. He really liked this girl, and he could tell she felt the same.

When their kiss ended he looked into her eyes. "You know, I've had a crush on you from the first time I saw your picture." He reached into his pocket and pulled out the photo Doctor Stevens had given him.

She giggled. "Oh, no, that was taken years ago. I was so young, fourteen, fifteen maybe."

You were beautiful then and you're more beautiful now. Would you like to go for a walk. I'd like to show you my favorite place on the island."

"I'd love to."

Kevin watched them as they walked toward the lake with their arms around each other's waist. He smiled at Doctor Stevens. "I think they like each other."

"It does look that way," Doctor Stevens said as he looked around the island. "It certainly is beautiful here." *I guess if you're going to be held a prisoner somewhere, this would be my first choice.* "I'm hungry, shall we eat?"

They were having dessert when the Doctor said, "I'm glad to see you still have a good appetite, Kevin." He wanted to tell him about the news he'd received from a doctor friend of his in the states, but knew he couldn't say anything until he learned more. The operation, a bone marrow transplant, required a perfect match. He had checked Kane, and his didn't match. He also checked Julianna with no luck. He wanted more information about the procedure, then he'd talk to Kevin.

"Don't forget that you need to see me tomorrow at ten."

"I remember," Kevin replied.

Julianna rested her head on Kane's shoulder as he told her about growing up on the island. "Will you ever leave here, Kane?"

"Yes, and soon." He told her about the sickness that would soon take his father's life.

"I'm so sorry, Kane. Is there anything I can do?"

He looked at her. It was so good to talk to someone. "I don't know if we'll see each other again. Your dancing takes you all over the world, and I have to help my father."

Julianna knew what he was saying was true. "Can we write to each other?"

"I'd like that." He pulled her close and kissed her. "I better get you back before the Doctor misses you." He smiled at her and kissed her again. "I have a feeling we will meet again."

Saying good-by was difficult, but they promised to write to each other.

After Doctor Stevens and Julianna left, Kevin excused himself and retired to his room. He lay on his bed with his eyes closed, his mind going over the vision that consumed his thoughts. *Something tells me the darkness only concerns me. I feel as I'm floating in space, it's so dark and quiet.* The feeling stayed with him for a long time before he heard the sound of a female voice calling to him from far away. *Who is it? Why can't I see whoever it is?* Kevin opened his eyes. *I've never heard that voice before. Could it be...could it be Katy?* He got out of bed and decided to take a shower. Twenty minutes later he laid back down and within minutes was sound asleep.

It was three hours later when Kane checked on him, happy to see his father sleeping peacefully.

Early the next morning found them both well rested. No vision had invaded their sleep, but it was only the quiet before the storm. Later that day the vision played hell with them both, and by late Monday afternoon Kane knew exactly what was going to happen. He would have to handle it by himself. His father lay in a hospital bed after Doctor Stevens demanded that Kevin be kept overnight for observation. He knew something was definitely wrong after he had examined Kevin earlier that morning. The one thing he didn't understand was why Kevin would suddenly drift into unconsciousness.

Kane had been at his father's bedside all afternoon, drifting in and out of sleep, when the vision finally took on a total meaning. Kane didn't want to leave his father alone, but knew he had to. He had to get back to the island.

J.J. stood up when he saw Kane leave Kevin's room. He had never seen Kane's eyes like that or the frightened look on the young man's face. "Is your father okay?"

"He's stable. We have to get back to the island right away." They didn't speak again until they were in the car. "J.J., I want you to trust me and do as I ask."

"What is it, Kane?"

"After you drop me off at the estate, go and get your wife and children. Take them to the mainland where they'll be safe."

"What the hell is going on?" J.J. was frightened now.

"We don't have much time. Mt. Vicco is about to erupt. We need to get buses and trucks and evacuate the island."

"How do you know? Are you sure about this?"

"Please trust me, J.J. If my father were here, he'd be telling you the same thing."

"Don't you think Prince Tali and Zoric should make the decision on how to handle this?" The look Kane gave him sent chills up his spine. "Why the hell are your eyes like that?"

"It doesn't matter. I need to know you believe me. Many lives depend on it."

J.J. took a deep breath, "Okay, I'll do as you ask."

"Thanks, J.J."

"How much time do we have?"

Kane closed his eyes and rubbed his hand across his forehead. "I'm not sure. It's dark, so I assume we have until the sun goes down."

J.J. glanced at his watch. Ten after five. "Doesn't give us much time. There's only about four hours of daylight left."

Kane banged his head against the back of his seat. "God, J.J., what are we going to do?"

"The best we can, that's what we're going to do." J.J. reached over and touched Kane's shoulder. "We'll get the evacuation started, then get you back to the hospital. You need to be with your father."

A smile of relief showed on Kane's face. "Thanks, J.J., but I need you to make me a promise."

"If I can."

"Don't let Prince Tali keep you from getting those people off the island."

"I'm sure he won't let anything happen to innocent people, Kane."

"I'm not so sure, just promise me."

"I don't understand how you know what's going to happen. Can you give me some kind of explanation?"

Kane looked at J.J. He smiled and shook his head. "I certainly can't blame you for thinking I'm a real nut case."

"You and your father both," chuckled J.J.

He listened as Kane explained as best as he could about the 'gift' he and his father had.

"Like knowing Sally would be your wife." Kane smiled.

"You're absolutely positive about Mt. Vicco?"

"Yes, I am."

"Can you tell me what you see, Kane?"

Kane leaned his head back and closed his eyes. J.J. thought he had fallen asleep, but a few minutes later Kane spoke. "At first, there's total darkness. It's spooky. There's no noise and I can't see anything at all. Then there's this crackling sound, made by the heat at the top of the volcano, followed by a whistling noise as it spits out the hot lava which gushes down the mountainside. The rumbling from under the ground creates a chain reaction of small earthquakes all over the island. Electricity is out and gas lines break, starting fires. People are running from their homes screaming, but no one is there to help them." Kane couldn't continue. He could see dead bodies. One of them was Sally, J.J.'s wife. The tears started streaming down his cheeks and within minutes he was sobbing uncontrollably.

Tears stung J.J.'s eyes too, but he didn't know what to do or say to help comfort Kane. One thing for certain, he didn't have any doubt left in his mind that Kane was telling the truth. *The boy is actually seeing this happen before it does.* He pressed his foot down on the accelerator.

Prince Tali sat in his viewing room and listened to the conversation between Kane and J.J. He finished the whiskey he had poured earlier, then picked up the phone. He dialed the number to J.J.'s car.

J.J. clicked the speaker phone on. "Hello."

"J.J., I heard everything. This is what I want you to do. Go get your wife and children, then go to the lodge. Zoric should be there. Tell him to meet me at my apartment on the mainland. I'll have one of the other drivers take Raul and me there. Bring Kane and your family there, too. Do not take Kane to the hospital. I'll have Zoric do that."

"Is there anything I can do to help start evacuating the people?"

"No, I'll take care of it. You just do as I've told you. What's Kane doing?"

J.J. looked at Kane. "I believe he sleeping, sir."

"Good. Don't wake him."

"Yes, sir."

J.J. clicked the phone off. *Kane was right, you son of a bitch. You have no intention of helping those people, except maybe the rich ones who live in those fancy estates.* He glanced at Kane and smiled, glad to see the young man's eyes the color they were supposed to be as he woke up. He gave him the okay sign. Kane smiled back and did the same.

A few minutes later J.J. drove the car up an old abandoned road. He pulled it over to the side and stopped. Leaving the motor running, he quietly opened his car door and got out. He motioned for Kane to follow him. They walked up a small embankment that overlooked the road where the gate opened for access to the island.

"I think we can talk here," J.J. said, "without being heard, that is unless our bodies are bugged."

Kane smiled. "It wouldn't surprise me, everything else is, even my father's belt buckle."

The memory flowed back into J.J.'s mind of the first time he and Kevin had donated blood and Kevin had made the remark about washing his buckle. It was the first time Kevin talked to him openly about anything. "Do you think Zoric will help us?"

Kane looked at J.J. "Yes. What's the plan?"

"We need to get at least six buses from the mainland to start transporting the people. Women and children first, of course." J.J. smiled. "We need to find out who has knowledge of gas lines and electricity."

"What about the patients at the clinic?" asked Kane.

"Good point. Sally should be able to help there. We might need an extra ambulance or two." J.J. could see and hear the relief in Kane.

They heard the gate open, and turned to watch the limo drive through. Prince Tali and Raul could be seen in the back seat from the driver's window as he reached out and pushed the button to close the gate behind them, then drove off.

A few minutes later J.J. drove through the same gate and headed down the road toward Tali Island.

J.J. was happy to see his good friend, Ali, on guard duty at the entrance to the island. He pulled his car to a stop. He and Kane got out and approached him. "Ali, we need your help."

"Sure, J.J. What is it?"

He explained to Ali, as best he could, what was about to happen and watched the fear grow on Ali's face. "Prince Tali told me to handle everything and not to call him unless it was an emergency. Did he talk to you when he left here a few minutes ago?"

"No, he didn't. I need to let my family know."

"Of course, but we don't want to cause a panic. We have time." *I hope.*

"Call your family, tell them Prince Tali is evacuating the island. Have them go to other homes and spread the word. Do you know anyone with buses that could help."

"No, I don't. Sorry."

"That's okay. If they want to know the reason for the evacuation, tell them you don't know, only that Prince Tali wants it done. I'm on my way to find Zoric. He should be able to help find housing for everyone on the mainland. We'll all gather at the park. Everyone is to be there no later than nine. You have all the numbers to the estates?"

"Yes." answered Ali.

"Good. Start calling them. Make sure you emphasize it's Prince Tali's request. If they don't have any transportation, use whatever is available from Tali's estate. Have the guards pick up anyone that needs a ride. If there are trucks that can be used for transporting people, I'm sure we can get drivers, men or women. Any questions?"

"Are you sure Mt Vicco is going to erupt?"

J.J. looked at Kane, then back at Ali. He knew his friend would be able to handle the situation better if there were some doubt. "No. It's not a sure thing. For all we know Prince Tali could be using this as a test to see how well people obey his orders, or he might be doing it to see how long it does take to evacuate his island in case something like this would happen in the future."

Ali chuckled. "These people will move their asses a lot faster because Prince Tali said to, then to the possibility of Mt. Vicco going boom."

J.J. and Kane joined in his laughter. "I think you're right, Ali. So just tell everyone it's Prince Tali's order. It'll save us a lot of problems. I'll try to keep the car phone open in case you need me."

J.J. and Kane got back in the car and headed for Tali Town. Ali picked up his phone to make his first call.

Kane turned to J.J. "You handled that like a pro, great idea to make it Prince Tali's request." Kane slapped J.J. on the shoulder. "Way to go."

They found Zoric at the lodge where Prince Tali had told them he'd be.

Surprise showed on his face when J.J. entered with Kane. "What's going on? Is your father okay, Kane?"

"He's stable, but in a deep state of unconsciousness and Doctor Stevens doesn't know why. He's keeping him at the hospital. Is there someplace we can talk in private?"

Zoric looked closely at Kane's eyes. *Good.* "Let me see what I can do." He walked away, returning a few minutes later. "The poker room is available, follow me."

After they sat down, J.J. started telling Zoric everything that had happened that day.

"Are you absolutely sure about all this, Kane?"

Kane looked straight into Zoric's eyes. "I can only tell you what I see. You're the one who is going to have to decide whether you believe it or not. You can stay and help us save these people or leave and join your brother as he has commanded you to do. Whatever you decide, we need your answer now. We're running out of time."

Zoric smiled at Kane. "You're turning into a good, strong, young man. I'm proud of you. If I had a son I'd want him to be like you."

Kane relaxed and smiled back. "Thanks, Zoric. Now I must tell you the really sad news. I hope you enjoyed your golf game today. That golf course won't be there tomorrow." Kane started laughing. It didn't take long before Zoric and J.J. joined in.

When the laughter died down, Zoric asked Kane. "How much time do we have?"

"I'm not sure. I do know that it will happen when it's dark. We better plan on when the sun goes down."

"All right, I'll get some buses in here and make sure the main gas line is turned off. We'll keep the electricity on until the last. I'll have the girls here at the lodge start making calls, find these people a place to stay, compliments of Prince Tali. One thing we can be grateful for—we only have about four to five hundred people on this island.

"That was a good idea, J.J., you had about gathering at the park. There's plenty of outdoor toilets, games for the children and lots of green grass to sit on. Let's get started."

Within half an hour the gas line was shut off, and six buses were on the main road to Tali Island, where a small group of people already had started to gather.

Zoric called in a helicopter from the mainland. He wanted to go up and take a closer look at Mt. Vicco. "Kane, would you like to come with me?"

Kane stared at him in surprise. He felt as if someone had just offered him his first taste of candy. "Are you sure?"

"Come on," said Zoric. He put his hand on Kane's shoulder.

As the helicopter sliced through the air, Kane could not believe the sensations his body felt. It was a thrill beyond belief. Then a strange thing happened. For some reason, Katy flashed into his mind and he knew she had experienced these same feelings.

The helicopter circled around Mt. Vicco, then hovered high over the small opening on top where they could see something was definitely going on and could even feel the heat that penetrated the air.

"Let's fly around the island," Zoric said to the pilot. He wanted to take one last look. *No telling what it's going to be like tomorrow.* He glanced at his home, not knowing if he was looking at it for the last time.

When they returned, Zoric asked the pilot to get clearance to land at the hospital in about an hour. He would take Kane with him. J.J. was to take his family to Zoric's apartment on the mainland.

As the sunset and dusk fell over the island, Zoric, J.J., and Kane stood by the gate, watching the last bus drive off down the road.

Ali came up to them. "We believe everyone's accounted for, sir."

Zoric held out his hand. "Thank you, Ali. A job well done. What happens now, J.J.?"

"Ali's going to stick around for half an hour to see if any strays show up, then he'll give the signal for all the power to be shut off. He'll wait for the person doing that, then the two of them will head for the mainland. Last report from the park was there were only about sixty people, plus the ones on the bus that just left, who need rooms. My understanding is that shouldn't be a problem. There are plenty of rooms available. The people have been told to have one member of their family, or someone else to represent them and return to the park by ten tomorrow morning where Prince Tali, or yourself, would talk to them. I've also placed two men at the main entrance. They're not to let anyone back on the island unless okayed by one of us."

"Hell of a job, J.J.," Zoric remarked.

Kane slapped him on the shoulder. "That's right, J.J., hell of a job. One more thing, thanks for believing me."

J.J. smiled. "It's those weird eyes of yours that did the trick. They scared the hell out of me."

Zoric put his arm around Kane's shoulder. "I know exactly how you feel, J.J., I've been there."

"I hate to break up this little party," Ali said. "But it's time to shut her down."

Zoric and Kane walked toward the helicopter, J.J. toward the limo where his wife, Sally, and their children were waiting.

Ali waited until the chopper was in the air, then gave the signal.

Kane and Zoric watched from above as the island went dark. The only light was the soft glow that escaped from the top of Mt. Vicco. They were both thinking the same thing. *How can something that beautiful be so deadly.*

Kane sat by his father's bedside, holding his hand and talking softly. He told him about the evacuation and that everyone was safe, then he told him about his ride in the helicopter.

Zoric sat in a chair across from Doctor Stevens. "You're saying you don't have any idea why he is still unconscious?"

"Not a clue. I've never seen anything like this before. There's no logical explanation. He was fine Sunday, good appetite, seemed happy. We ran several tests today. All came back fine. There's a possibility he could wake up and have no effect from this." Doctor Stevens pounded his fist on the desk. "Damn, I just don't know what else to do."

"Could he die?"

Doctor Stevens didn't know if it was concern or guilt that he heard in Zoric's voice. "Anything is possible. We have him on medication to control high blood pressure. A special IV is used to prevent him from becoming dehydrated. We also use it for feeding. He's hooked up to a catheter and a heart monitor. If anything happens, we'll know right away."

Zoric glanced at his watch. It was after eleven. "Kane would like to stay with his father. I'll give you my private phone number. Call me immediately if there's any change. I'll leave a guard posted outside the room. You can let him know if you need anything."

Zoric opened the door of his car and slid in behind the wheel. He sat there, trying to clear his mind as he went over everything that had happened. *I wonder why my brother hasn't tried to call me. Damn you, McKade, don't you die on us. That boy needs you. Hell, who am I kidding, I need you, too. After all we've been through together we've become good friends.* Zoric started his car and headed for his brother's place.

# Chapter 12

Raul lay on the couch in the living room, looking up at the ceiling. *I wish I knew what was going on. I've never seen my father drink this much before.* He stood up, waving his arms. The smell of cigarette smoke was strong in the air. He looked at his father, who was on the other couch in the study, sleeping or passed out, Raul wasn't sure. *I should just leave him and go to the hospital to be with Kane.*

Raul heard the key turn in the lock. "Uncle Zoric. God, am I glad to see you."

"I hope that's not you smoking those cigarettes."

Raul chuckled. "I think I inhaled most of the smoke, believe me, not by choice."

"Where's your father?"

Raul pointed to the study. "In there. How's Kevin?"

"No change." Zoric walked over to look at his brother. "How long has he been like this?"

"Since early this morning."

"Let's go out on the balcony. I have to talk to you."

Raul followed him out. "I knew there was something going on. I kept asking Dad, but he said it didn't concern me."

"He's only trying to protect you, Raul."

"Protect me from what—life—or is he treating me like a prisoner, like he's done with Kane and his father all these years."

Shock appeared on Zoric's face. "You know?"

"Don't look so surprised, Uncle. Dad told me everything—how he threatened to kill Kevin if he tried to escape and raise Kane as his own, about the killings, the pit, everything. You know what really disturbs me more than anything. He justified everything he's done, and I am my father's son. I'm not so sure if I was faced with those situations I would not have handled them exactly the same."

"We protect what is ours, Raul. We have our own laws on Tali Island. People respect and obey them, or they get the hell off—one way or another." Zoric sat down and motioned for Raul to do the same. "How much do you know about this 'gift' of the McKades?"

"Everything. I don't understand how it works. I mean, how can someone see into the future, and when their eyes change color, it's so weird."

Zoric agreed. "That's what happens when they have these visions. So far every time it's come true. Like today with Kane."

"I knew it." Raul slapped his knee. "Kane's been acting strange. He told me something was going to happen, he just didn't know what. Is it about his father?"

"No. There's no explanation why Kevin is in a coma. This has to do with Tali Island and Mt. Vicco."

Zoric told Raul everything that happened that day and what was planned for morning.

"What can I do to help?" Raul asked.

"Right now we both need to get some sleep. I've got a feeling we won't be getting too much of that in the next few days."


Zoric had been asleep about three hours when Raul woke him. "Uncle Zoric, J.J.'s on the phone." Raul couldn't remember ever seeing his uncle move so quickly.

Zoric picked up the receiver. "J.J. what is happening?"

"Mt. Vicco erupted an hour ago and the media is already asking questions. Turn on your TV to the National News."

"Okay. Hold on."

Zoric heard his brother's voice from behind him."What's going on?"

"You better watch this."

One of the news helicopters was showing live footage of Mt. Vicco. The three of them listened as the reporter spoke.

'We are looking at Tali Island where a small volcano has erupted in the middle of the night. We do not know what damage there is or if any deaths have occurred. We'll keep you updated as the information becomes available. Our sources tell us several underground tremors have occurred, but again we don't know the extent of the damage. Please stay tuned for additional information.'

"J.J., call the station and set up a meeting with them in half an hour. Tell them a representative of Tali Island will brief them on what is going on. Call me back." Zoric hung up the phone. "Raul, tell your father what's happened. I'm going to take a quick shower."

Fifteen minutes later Zoric walked back into the room just as the phone rang. He picked it up. "J.J?"

"The station is expecting a representative. Do you want me to handle it?"

"No. I'll take care of it."

"I thought you would. I'm about five minutes away. Pick you up out front."

"I'll be waiting." He turned to his brother. "I can't talk to you right now. There's a meeting at the park at ten. I think you should attend. I'll be back to pick you up."

Zoric started to walk out the door when Prince Tali asked him, "Where is Kane?"

"At the hospital with his father."

"I gave J.J. orders to bring him here."

"I took Kane there myself. I posted a guard by his room. They'll call here if anything happens." Without another word Zoric left, closing the door behind him.

Zoric slid into the front seat when J.J. pulled up. "You look like hell."

J.J. chuckled. "I feel like it, too."

"Did you get any sleep at all?"

"Couple of hours."

"You can drop me off at the news station. Go get cleaned up. We'll stop and have breakfast when you pick me up. I don't think this should take more than an hour. Have you heard anything from Kane?"

"I called the hospital. No change in Kevin. They said Kane was sick in the middle of the night, but is sleeping like a baby now." J.J. pulled up in front of the station and looked at his watch, four-twenty. "See you in an hour."

Zoric watched him pull away. He took a deep breath and looked in the direction of Tali Island. The early dawn reflected off the haze over the island, causing a beautiful golden glow.

He walked up the few steps to the front entrance and pressed the button that unlocked the door and gave him access into the building. A short, heavyset man stood by the information desk. "I'm Zoric Tali."

"Come this way. We've been expecting you."

Zoric followed the man down a hall where he opened a door to a large room. "In here please, Mr. Tali. Make yourself comfortable. There's coffee made, help yourself."

Zoric waited until the man left, then poured himself a cup and sat down. He looked around the room. It was comfortable, with two cameras set up facing the lounge area.

The door opened and an attractive lady walked in, carrying a note pad. Zoric recognized her. She did the early morning news. She held out her hand. "I'm Lousetta Napollas, Mr. Tali. Please call me Lou."

Zoric took her hand. "Please call me Zoric."

"All right. Let's sit over here where we'll be more comfortable. Have you ever done a live TV interview before?"

"Better live than dead, I suppose." He smiled at her. "Little TV humor. Yes, I have."

They talked for about twenty minutes. She told him what questions she'd be asking as they waited for the crew to set up the camera. "Ready?" She smiled at him.

"Ready."

The camera focused on her. "Good morning, everyone. I'm Lousetta Napollas, your early morning newscaster. I'm here on special assignment to bring you an update on the volcano that erupted early this morning, northwest of Greece on the small-populated Tali Island. The Tali family has owned the Island for several generations. I have here with me Zoric Tali, who will give us any information he can on what's happened. Thank you for being here, Mr. Tali." The camera focused on Zoric, then back to her. "What can you tell the people? Do you know what damage there is, or if there are any injures or causalities?"

Zoric looked right into the camera. "As far as any damage, we won't know until we can safely go back on the Island. Yesterday afternoon when my brother, Prince Tali, was informed that Mt. Vicco might erupt, he evacuated the Island. It's not highly populated, so it took only a couple of hours. He put the families in hotel and motel rooms at his expense. He'll also pay for all meals. There have been owners that donated rooms and also several restaurants offered free food. I want them to know we greatly appreciate it, but it's not necessary. This is not a major disaster, only a slight inconvenience for the residents of Tali Island."

"I want to thank you so much for taking the time to talk with us. I know I am certainly relieved to hear what you had to say as I'm sure all our listeners are, too. I hope you can stop by again and give us an update on how things are going."

"Be happy to."

"Now back to our regular programming."

Zoric waited until everyone except Lou had left the room. "I'll call you if there's anything newsworthy."

"Thank you, again, for stopping by."

They shook hands and Zoric walked out without saying another word. He was glad to have a few minutes alone as he waited outside for J.J.

Later that morning J.J. dropped him back off at Tali's apartment. They agreed to meet at the park around nine-thirty. Zoric would drive Prince Tali and Raul there himself, stopping by the hospital first to see how Kevin and Kane were doing. J.J. would check the Island from the helicopter.

Zoric had expected Prince Tali to be upset, but he wasn't prepared for the show of anger he displayed in front of his son.

"I will not tolerate my orders being disobeyed, not by anyone, including you."

Zoric glared at his brother. "Then handle the situation yourself."

"I was handling it, but you screwed it up, so you can finish what you started."

"Please, Dad," Raul pleaded. "Calm down before you have a heart attack."

Prince Tali turned toward his son and the anger faded from his body. He put his hands on Raul's shoulders. "You're right, but you have to understand that, if Tali Island is going to run correctly, my orders must be obeyed."

"I understand, Dad, and I think, no I'm sure, it was handled exactly like you wanted. You just weren't in any condition to give anyone orders last night."

"You're right. Believe me, I'm paying for it this morning." He turned and held out his hand to Zoric. "Shall we start again?"

Zoric accepted his hand, knowing it was the closest thing to an apology he would get.

They arrived at the hospital shortly after eight-thirty. The guard moved aside to allow them access into Kevin's room. There was soft music coming from the radio by Kevin's bed. The drapes partially opened to let in the morning sunlight.

Prince Tali walked over to Kevin's bed first, making mental notes of all the tubes hooked to his body. The monitor registered his heartbeat and blood pressure as normal. He moved to Kane's bed. The boy was in the same deep sleep as his father.

An hour later Zoric pulled the limo into the park. A small crowd had already gathered around J.J. and Ali, helping themselves to coffee.

"Anything we should know about?" Zoric asked J.J.

"Reports of small ground tremors are still being reported. They're not as serious as they were earlier, and they're farther apart. From the air I could see damage to several buildings. The clinic was the worst. It looks like the south side has extensive damage. The haze is clearing out rapidly, so we should be able to get a better look in a couple of hours."

Zoric looked around. "It looks as if we can get started."

Prince Tali interrupted. "I'll start, say a few words, then turn it over to you."

Zoric nodded. "All right."

Prince Tali walked over to where J.J. and Ali had assembled a small platform. "Could I have everyone's attention?" The people turned toward him. A few started clapping. The rest joined in. Prince Tali held up his arms. The crowd became silent. "It should be me applauding the people of Tali's Island. You all did one hell of a job with no injuries or deaths occurring. I know you're curious about what's happening, and my brother, Zoric, is going to speak to you. Thanks, again, to you, your families, and all the residents of Tali Island."

Prince Tali stepped down and Zoric took his place. "Good morning everyone. It's been a rough night for all of us, so I'm going to get right to the point. Mt. Vicco erupted around three this morning, causing damage not only from the hot lava, but from the earth tremors as well. The last report is that the tremors are very mild and occurring farther apart. The island was inspected by air this morning and some minor damage could be seen to several buildings. The haze prevented a clear view, but it's moving out and that will help. No damage was reported to any of your homes. Prince Tali and myself are taking the helicopter up as soon as this meeting is over. We'll do another aerial flight around noon and, if possible, a ground inspection around one or two.

I'm asking that this same group"… Zoric moved his arms around the crowd…"return here at four for another update. There will be someone in this area all day to help any resident from Tali's Island.

"We are trying very hard to keep this out of the media before they turn it into a circus. The fact that the island was evacuated and no one was hurt is a plus. I did a TV interview this morning and I'll tell you exactly what I told them. 'This is not a national disaster, only a slight inconvenience for the residents of Tali Island.' I hope everyone is finding their accommodations satisfactory. Please remember to tell others to keep their island residence identification cards with them at all times. Use them for charging meals to their rooms or at restaurants that are posting signs honoring the cards."

Zoric paused before continuing. "We all need to be thankful that our families are safe. Life can't be replaced, material things can. So let's get to work. It's up to you to spread the word to the others. I would like all of you to please leave your name and card number with Ali in case we need to contact you. See you at four."

# Chapter 13
## KATY / THE RANCH
## Monday Evening

Katy sat at the table in the family room across from Ben and Sister Elizabeth. She was studying the list Ben had given her from Father James about the places her mother and father had visited while in Europe.

It seemed most of their time was spent in Greece, then Spain, then Italy, and back to Greece again. "What is our flight schedule?" Katy asked Ben.

"Our last fuel stop will be the Netherlands. Then it's a straight flight into Spain. Our passports will be ready to pick up tomorrow, one each for Sister Elizabeth Riley, Sister Kathleen Riley, and yours truly, Benjamin Bennett. Senator Ward Tylar, daughter, Samantha Tylar, and the Senator's assistant, Kord McNamera, will take a commercial flight and meet us there. I also have in my possession Father James' new passport." He handed it to Sister Elizabeth. "...and my bag of magic tricks."

Sister laughed when she looked at the photo. "Our Father James, who was once cleaned-shaven, blue-eyed, and had sandy-colored hair, now has a beard, gray hair, and brown eyes.

"It's starting to all come together, isn't it?" Katy asked as she looked first at one, then the other.

Sister Elizabeth smiled at her. "Yes. We're going to find them and our family will be together at last."

"It's such a wonderful feeling, Aunt Liz." They sat there in silence. The only noise came from the television across the room. It was on low and they could barely hear the strange sounds it made. Then something caught Katy's attention. She stood and walked toward the TV. Reaching down, she turned up the volume and stepped back. The news was on, but it was the sound in the background that held her attention. The sound ended and she listened to the newscaster. "That's all the we have on this unexpected eruption of Mt. Vicco. Please stay tuned. We will interrupt our regular broadcasting to bring you any additional information as it becomes available."

"What is it, Katy?" Sister Elizabeth asked as she came and stood by her side.

Katy's voice trembled. "I don't know."

Ben was glad to see Katy's eyes hadn't changed color, but he could see something else in them—something had frightened her.

Katy reached down and clicked the TV to another channel. Nothing. Then on the national news station she heard, "Please stay tuned for a special report."

"Maybe this is it." The three of them sat down on the floor in front of the TV and waited. After several minutes the newscaster began. "A small volcano has erupted on a little island off the northwest corner of Greece. This is what we know so far. The island is called Tali Island and has been owned for several generations by the Tali family. It is not a largely populated island. The volcano erupted around three o'clock Greece time. Several ground tremors were reported, but have since diminished to almost none. Damage to the island is not yet known. It's confirmed there are no fatalities, we repeat, no fatalities. We have an interview, which was recorded earlier, with one of the owners of Tali Island, Zoric Tali. Here is that interview now." You could hear him speak, but the report only showed a photo of Zoric's face.

The newscaster came back on. "Here is some footage from our news helicopter that flew over the island in the early dawn hours. As you can see, this is considered a very small eruption. The area just left of the volcano and down toward the right of your screen is called Tali Town where they believe there might be some structural damage. The good news is there are no fatalities."

As Katy looked at the light escaping from the top of the mountain, she didn't realize she was holding her breath. A tingling sensation passed through her as she gasped for air, scaring Sister Elizabeth and Ben half to death.

Ben grabbed and shook her. "Breath, for Christ's sake. What the hell's the matter with you?"

Sister Elizabeth shouted, "It's okay, Ben. She's breathing."

Katy took several deep breaths. "I'm okay, really. I was looking at the glow from the volcano and I had the weirdest feeling. It's Kane. He saw the same thing. I think he was in that helicopter or some other plane."

"Come over here and sit on the couch." Sister held on to her as she guided her in that direction.

Ben knelt down in front of her. "Please don't ever do that again."

Katy smiled. "I'm sorry, Ben, Aunt Liz, I didn't mean to scare you."

Sister Elizabeth touched Katy's cheek softly. "Can I get you anything, water, soda?"

"Water sounds good."

"I'll get it." Ben stood and walked toward the kitchen.

"Relax Katy, breathe deeply."

Ben came back and handed the glass to her. "Here, sweetie."

"Thanks, Ben." Katy took the glass and looked up into his eyes. She could see how worried he was. She sipped the water slowly. "I feel much better. I think I'll go to bed."

"If you need me I'll be right here."

"Thanks, Aunt Liz." She gave them a hug and went to her room. She was glad Ben was staying at the main house. He had moved his things in early that evening so that Jenny and her son, Luke, could live in his house. Katy liked having her Godfather close by.

She thought about Kord as she lay in bed, hugging her pillow. Sunday she had told him about her life and about her twin brother, Kane, and her father. When she finished he had held her tight and kissed her, not once but several times. It had made her feel all warm and loving inside. He promised to help her find them. Now she had three men in her life, whom she knew and loved, helping her find the other two men she loved. It was that she just didn't know them—yet.

There were times she felt closer to Kane than she did toward anyone. *It's as if I know about special foods he likes or certain things he does, like watching a sunrise or sunset or flying in a helicopter.* She smiled to herself. *That was pretty weird tonight on TV. Oh, who am I kidding. The only thing that's weird around here is me.*

She rolled to her other side so she could look out the window at the stars. After her mother had died and they told her she was in heaven, Katy would look up at the stars wondering which one was her mother. She always picked the brightest one. Katy felt content as she closed her eyes and drifted off to sleep.

It was early the next morning when Katy jumped out of bed, grabbed her housecoat and ran down the hall, screaming. "Aunt Liz. Aunt Liz." She swung the door open.

Sister Elizabeth sat up in bed. "Katy, what is it?" She noticed right away that Katy's eyes had not changed color. *Thank God.*

"Hurry, get dressed. I'm going to wake Ben. I know what happened last night when we were watching TV."

Katy raced out of the room and down the stairs toward the guest bedroom in the back of the house, yelling Ben's name all the way.

Ben swung the door open before she got there. "My God, Katy, what happened?"

She flew into his arms. "I have great news." She pulled away and smiled up at him. "I'm going to get dressed, you too, then I'll tell you all about it." Katy could smell the fresh brew of coffee. *Sister Hanna must be out in the garden already.*

Sister Elizabeth and Ben were waiting for her in the kitchen when she returned fifteen minutes later. Relief was felt by both when they saw the happiness on her face.

She slowly walked over to get a cup of coffee, humming to herself. She knew she was driving them crazy with curiosity. "Beautiful morning, don't you think?" She sat down at the table.

Ben watched her as she picked up the cream and sugar. *Two can play this game.* "It is a beautiful morning. If you ladies will excuse me I think I'll mosey on down to the house. I bet Jenny is making her delicious pancakes this morning."

Katy laughed. "Don't you dare move."

Sister Elizabeth touched her hand. "You better talk to us then or I think I'll go with him."

Katy looked from one to the other. "You're not going to believe this, but I know where Kane and my father are, well at least Kane, but I'm sure my father has to be close by."

"Where?" both asked at the same time.

"On that island, Tali Island, where the volcano erupted."

"How do you know?" Ben asked.

"You know those weird dreams I've been having the last few nights about the darkness and crackling, whistling sounds?" They both nodded. "That was from the volcano, except for the darkness, which doesn't feel right. There must be something else going on with that. I was holding my breath so I could hear the sounds in the background. They were so faint and far away. Then I felt Kane. I knew he had seen the same thing in a plane, looking down at not only the volcano, but the island, too. That man they showed the photo of—Kane, and I believe my father—know him."

Sister Elizabeth sat back in her chair. Her head moved from side to side. "This is unbelievable, fantastic, but unbelievable."

"It probably has a lot to do with the fact they're twins, being able to sense things about each other. It's very common." Ben looked at Sister Elizabeth. "Don't you think?" He was trying very hard to come up with something that sounded logical.

"You're right, Ben. I'm so excited. When can we leave?"

"Aunt Liz, isn't that supposed to be my question?" They all started laughing.

That was how Sister Hanna found them when she came into the kitchen. "This is a happy lot I have here this morning."

Katy jumped up and threw her arms around her. "Oh, Sister Hanna, I've got great news. I know where my brother, Kane, is."

"Oh, Katy, I'm so happy for you. It's a miracle."

"Sister Hanna, everything is a miracle to you," Ben said jokingly. "The sun comes up, the sun goes down, it's a miracle. The rain turns to snow, it's a miracle. You wake up each morning, it's a miracle."

"That one for sure is the truth." Sister Hanna laughed. "Don't you be a teasing me, Ben. I have a protector now, you know."

"Speaking of protectors," Ben asked, "Where is Bear?"

"Outside with his best girl." Ben stood and looked out the window. Bear, Kord's dog, and Ben's dog, Sara, were lying on the grass side by side.

"Father Tim took them for a run up the hill this morning." said Sister Hanna.

"Speaking of Father Tim," said Ben. "Here he comes now, all six foot seven of him."

Father Tim ducked as he came through the door. "Good morning, everyone."

"Good morning, Father Tim," they said together, sounding like a class of students in school.

Father Tim smiled. "Such a nice thing to have so early in the morning, obedience and respect."

The phone rang. Ben reached over to answer it. "Hello." A big grin appeared on his face. "Good morning, Jenny." He paused, listening to what she had to say. "Everyone's here, let me ask. Jenny wants to know if we'd all like to come to breakfast? She's whipping up a big batch of blueberry pancakes." Before Ben knew what happened, the four of them were out the door. Sister Hanna turned and shouted at him, "Last one there does the dishes."

"If you look out the window, Jenny, I think you'll have an answer."

He could hear Jenny laughing on the other end. "Luke, look who's coming for breakfast." He could hear Luke clapping and yelling in the background.

"I'm on my way, too. Save some for me." He hung up the phone, running to see if he could catch up. *Damn, I'm going to have to do the dishes.*

Father Tim thanked Jenny. "Ben was right, those are the best pancakes I've ever eaten."

Sister Elizabeth agreed. "But you really didn't have to trouble yourself."

"No trouble at all, Sister. I like cooking." Jenny looked over at Ben and winked. "Besides, someone left a hint in the refrigerator."

Ben looked at Father Tim. "Did you do that, Father?"

"Not this time, but I'm sure I'll be guilty of it in the future."

"Any plans for today, Father?" Sister Elizabeth asked him.

"Yes." He glanced at his watch. "I better get going, one of the farms needs work done on their barn door. I offered to repair it and sure could use some help." He looked over at Luke.

"I could help!" Luke said as he jumped off his chair and came around to stand by Father Tim.

"Well, I don't know. Are you pretty strong?"

"You bet." Luke showed him his muscle.

"Wow, that's strong all right. How much will I have to pay you?"

Luke thought for a moment. He put his little fist up to his chin and tapped his index finger on his bottom lip. "A dollar."

"Um, a dollar. I think that's fair. The first thing you have to do is get permission from your mother. You don't ever want to go with anyone unless she says it's okay."

Luke looked at her. "Mom, okay?"

"Okay. Wash your hands and brush your teeth first."

Luke turned back to Father Tim. "When we're finished working, can we stop and see Center Ward and Sami?"

Everyone laughed.

Jenny stood. "Come on, Luke. I'll help you."

After she left the room, Ben turned to Father Tim. "It looks like we're going to be leaving sooner than expected. It seems Katy knows where her brother is. I'll explain everything later this afternoon."

Father Tim looked over at Katy. "I'm so happy for you. Let me know if there's anything at all you want me to do."

"I will." Katy smiled at him. *I'm going to have to change that to four men I know and love.*

Luke came running into the room. "Okay, boss man, I'm ready."

Father Tim stood. "Give your mom a hug and we're out of here."

"Oh, do I have to in front of everybody?"

"No, you don't have to, but I will." Father Tim bent down and folded her in his arms. "Thanks, Jenny, I'll have Luke home early."

Luke stood there and watched as everyone else hugged her, too. Then he climbed on a chair. "Okay, I'll hug her. Come here, woman," he said with a big grin on his face.

"Luke, where did you get that from?" asked Jenny.

He shrugged his shoulders and wrapped his little arms around her neck. "Bye mommy, love ya."

"Love you, too."

Everyone left except Ben. "Remember I told you I would be out of town a few days. Well, I'll be leaving sooner than expected."

"When?"

"Tomorrow morning."

She looked into Ben's eyes, knowing not to ask any questions. He told her what he wanted her to know and that was enough for her. "I'll miss you."

He pulled her close and kissed her. "Maybe when I get back we could have that serious talk with Father Tim." He kissed her again. "I'll stop by later today. I'm heading for Center Ward's bunkhouse." They both laughed.


Jenny watched him walk up the road, turned and went back into the house. *This is going to be my home.* She twirled around the room. *How did I ever get so lucky?* She stopped and looked around, realizing this was the first time she'd been alone in quite awhile. She missed the cottage. *I wonder if Ben would put a hot tub in here.* A smile came to her face. *Like the one in the cottage.*

Ben heard the excitement coming from the guesthouse at least half a block away. He picked up his pace. After everyone had settled down it was time to get serious again. "Can you two really be ready to leave by tomorrow?"

"We think so," said Sister Elizabeth. "We'll know for sure by late this afternoon."

They heard Ward hang up the phone. "Thursday is still the earliest flight we can get. We fly out of Denver at eight-thirty, directly to Kennedy. We have a three-hour layover there, which gives us time to change planes. Then it's direct to London where we have approximately a five-hour delay. Kord will have time to visit with his mother. She's going to meet him at the airport. Then we're off again, next stop, Athens, Greece.

"Are you sure this isn't to much for you?" Katy asked.

"Are you kidding, I can hardly wait. In fact I'm ready to leave today—right now—this minute." He leaned over and held out his hand. Katy reached over and took it. "Everything is going to be fine. We're leaving Wednesday afternoon and driving into Denver. Father James is meeting us at Gaetanos Restaurant for dinner, then we'll all get a good night's sleep and be refreshed and ready to go by Thursday morning. Remember, Kord will be with us. He'll do all the driving and help Sami with me. I really don't have anything to do, but enjoy myself."

"You're right." Katy smiled at him. "I think you're a teeny, weenie bit spoiled."

"Yes, but I'm worth it."

"When will Kord be here, Katy?" Ben asked.

"No later than ten. That will give him most of the day to work with Ward, learning how to transfer him, lift him or whatever else Sami needs help with." Katy looked around the room. "Since we're all here I want to thank each of you. I'm sure if it was anybody else, you would be hauling me off to the loony farm."

"Actually," said Sami, "that was our first choice, but we did it the American way and voted. It was three to two. We decided to take advantage of this trip first. Then we'll take you to the loony farm."

The rest of the day was spent in running errands and getting things organized. By eight that evening the decision was made. Katy, Sister Elizabeth and Ben would leave at daybreak—Katy would be on her way to find her brother.

*Carole A. Sheller*

# Chapter 14
## TALI ISLAND

The helicopter lifted off the pad and headed toward Tali Island. Four people were on board, the pilot and the three remaining members of the Tali family, Prince Tali, Zoric, and Raul.

"I hope this thing stays in the air," Raul said jokingly, "or they'll have to re-name the island."

Prince Tali thought about what his son had said. "It probably isn't a wise thing, the three of us together like this."

"I was only teasing, Dad. Anyway, I'm sure Kane would let us know if there's a problem. That's what we have him around for, isn't it?"

Zoric heard the bitterness in Raul's voice, but Prince Tali heard something else, his son accepting why Kane was here on the island and telling his father he approved. *If Kevin dies, so be it, but Kane will never leave the island.*

They flew over the south side first, where Tali Estate was located. It appeared not to have sustained any damage. The same went for the other estates. Tali Town was a different story. The clinic showed the worst damage. Zoric wondered. *How many people would have died if we hadn't gotten them out in time? Even one would have been to many.*

The damage, from minor to extensive, ran in a straight line. "That must be from the worst of the underground tremors," Prince Tali stated. "We'll get a ground crew in there this afternoon. Truthfully, it doesn't look that bad to me."

They could see where the hot lava spread across a section of the golf course and settled in and around the Tali Jungle.

Zoric was relieved to see his house still standing.

They flew around one more time. "Look, Father," said Raul, "see that valley down there. That's where Kane and I decided to build our homes. I'm going be on the east end, Kane on the west. We'll put stables, a swimming pool and tennis court in the middle so we can share."

"It sounds as if this is something the two of you have given much thought to." Prince Tali smiled at his son.

"Some. When we get back, I want to go to the hospital and be with him."

"All right, but I want the two of you to come back to the apartment—together. I don't want Kane spending the night at the hospital again. He could probably use a decent meal and a good night's sleep."

Zoric wondered if his brother's concern for Kane was because he cared for the boy or because he couldn't keep him under surveillance good enough. Zoric felt pretty confident it was the latter.

## HOSPITAL

Kane slowly opened his eyes. *Where the hell am I?* He was feeling disoriented and it took several minutes before he felt he could move. The dizziness made his body feel weak when he tried to sit up. He lay back down, groaning as his head hit the pillow. He moved his head slowly and looked around the room. *Somebody must have hit me over the head with a sledgehammer. My eyeballs even hurt.* He saw the pitcher of ice water sitting by his bed. *Thank God!* A crooked little smile escaped his lips. *One day in church and I've become a believer.* He tried again to sit up. *Ah, made it.* He poured himself a glass of water. When he finished drinking, he touched the cold glass to his forehead and took several deep breaths. He looked at his father, lying in the bed next to him, and sadness ripped through his body. "Thank God, you're still alive," he whispered out loud, truly feeling thankful. *With this gift, shouldn't I know what's going to happen to you? Where Katy is? Will I ever see Julianna again? I'm beginning to learn why the McKade's call this a curse.*

He slid off the bed and walked toward the small bathroom. He returned a few minutes later, feeling much better. *I think I just broke the record for the longest pee in history.* He drank another glass of water, then walked over to his father. "Doesn't look like you moved at all, but you look good. I'm going to check with the nurse. Don't go anywhere. I'll be back in a few minutes."

He opened the door. A chair, with a very large man in it, blocked his exit. "Excuse me, sir, I need to talk to the nurse."

"I'll get her for you. Please go lie down. You don't look like you feel too good."

Kane was too weak to argue. He returned to his bed, pulling a cover

162

over himself. He watched the guard close the door. It was only a few minutes before the guard opened it again, moving the chair to allow the nurse access into the room.

"Good morning, Kane." She glanced at her watch, "or I should say good afternoon. It's almost one o'clock."

"How's my father?"

"There's been no change. Doctor Stevens will be back later today and he'll give you a complete update. In the meantime, what can I do for you? Hungry?"

Kane smiled. "Starving."

"That's a good sign. Let's start out with some soup while I have the kitchen fix you a lunch plate. Anything else?"

Kane touched his head. "I could use something for this headache."

She reached into her pocket and removed a bottle of aspirin. "Take these," she said, placing two tablets in his hand.

"Thank you. Can you get me a cold washcloth to put on my forehead?"

Within a few minutes he was starting to feel like a human being again. He didn't know what was in the soup, but it didn't taste bad. The lunch was even better, and there was Jell-O for dessert. When he finished, he closed his eyes and within minutes was sound asleep, not knowing that halfway around the world, in the dawn of the early morning hour, a small jet would take flight high in the Colorado rockies, headed in his direction.

## THE PARK

Zoric stood on the platform with Prince Tali and Raul at his side. It was shortly after four in the afternoon. He watched the driver of a car pull off to the side of the road, turn off the motor and get out. He recognized her right away from the news interview. *Damn, what the hell is she doing here?* He didn't see any camera men or recording equipment. Nevertheless, Zoric put himself on guard.

His eyes survived the crowd. "Good. It looks like most of you that were here this morning have returned. I want to tell you first that we have a crew on Tali Island now checking the damage. From what we could tell, by air, the clinic and one or two other buildings sustained some minor structural damage. No other damage could be seen.

"We would like to take one or two members of each family back onto the island to check their homes. We will do this in three groups. If there are any repairs required, your families are welcome to stay in the accommodations they now have until they are made. If everything is all right, then by all means move your families' back. We would like to start tomorrow morning at nine o'clock. This will give us another day for the haze, caused by the ash fallout from the eruption, to clear out. The first group will consist of people whose last name begins with the letters A through H. The second group will leave at noon, that will be last names starting with I through R, and the third group S through Z, will leave at three. We expect to have all power back on sometime tomorrow. My brother and I want to thank everyone for their co-operation. Someone will be here until ten tonight and then back at six in the morning, if you need anything. Thank you."

Zoric stepped down and approached his brother. "Why don't you and Raul go to the car. I have someone I need to talk to."

"Don't be too long."

Zoric could hear the disgust in Prince Tali's voice as he walked toward the woman.

"Ms. Napollas, nice to see you again. I'm curious, though, why are you here?"

"Please, Zoric, call me Lou. I wanted to see how things were going. Several of the national news stations wanted an update. It looks as if it's going very well."

"It is."

"Good. I don't suppose there is any chance of you permitting me on the island?"

Zoric chuckled. "I'm sure you're very aware that any type of news reporter or camera is not allowed on Tali Island."

"Yes, I know, but you can't blame a girl for asking."

"Now, if you weren't a reporter, but were just a woman, whom I find very attractive, and would consider having dinner with me, I think an invitation to the island could definitely be in the near future."

"I'll be looking forward to it. Maybe you could stop by the station to do another interview and put this story to bed."

"What time tomorrow should I be there?" Zoric touched her elbow and led her to her car.

"Early as you can."

Zoric opened her car door and waited until she was seated behind the wheel. "Can I take you for breakfast tomorrow? We could get to know each other a little better."

"I'd love to. See you then."

He watched her drive away. *I wonder what the lady's up to. I'll know before I ever let her on our island.*

"What was that all about?" Prince Tali asked him when Zoric got in the limo.

Zoric told him.

"You always were a sucker for a pretty face."

"One of my weaknesses. Shall we go to the hospital?"

"Drop me off at the apartment first," said Prince Tali.

"All right." Zoric looked at his brother. "I need to talk to you about something that's not going to please you. I think we should let Kane stay at the hospital with his father. We need to let him know we care what happens to both of them. If we don't, there's going to be a lot of resentment on Kane's part, especially if his father dies."

Prince Tali thought for a moment before answering. "I see where you're coming from. Okay, tell Kane we're with him whatever he needs, but keep a tight rope on him without his knowing it."

Raul sat in the back, listening. They didn't include him in their conversation, so he offered no opinion.

When they arrived at the hospital, Zoric went looking for Doctor Stevens. Raul went to see Kane and his father. The guard didn't move when Raul approached him. After standing there a few moments and staring at each other, Raul asked. "May I go in?"

"Sorry. No one's allowed in there."

"Do you know who I am?"

The guard looked at him. "No, and I don't care."

Raul couldn't help, but smile. "Were you hired by J.J., my Uncle Zoric, or perhaps by my father, Prince Tali?"

The guard continued to stare at him, then finally asked, "Do you have some identification?"

Raul took out his wallet and opened it to his ID card. He handed it to the guard and watched him as he studied it very closely. The guard took a piece of paper out of his pocket. "You are on my list," he turned, opened the door and stepped aside. Raul entered. He was not surprised to find them both sleeping. He touched Kane's shoulder.

"Wake up. Kane, can you hear me? Wake up."

A smile came to Kane's face when he saw Raul standing there. He sat up. "That guard doesn't care who he lets in."

"Hell, I thought I was going to have to go through a strip search before he would let me in."

"Why is he out there, anyway?" asked Kane.

"Why do you think? My father's afraid you'll run away." Raul laughed. "No, really, it's because my father and Zoric are afraid that Mani's brother might try to hurt you and your father. My father will do whatever he has to, whether you approve or not. So you might as well get used to it. By the way, did you hear Mt. Vicco burped? Makes you wonder what the hell he's been eating all these years."

When they were through laughing, Raul told Kane about his ride in the helicopter, the damage to the island, and what his father and Zoric were doing.

"Has anyone heard anything about my father?"

"Zoric is trying to find out. He's looking for Doctor Stevens. How do you think he's doing?" Raul asked, as he walked over to Kevin's bed.

Kane got up and stood beside him. He touched his father's hand. "I keep hoping that whatever makes me see things before they happen would give me the answer to that question, but so far nothing. I'll have to wait and see what the Doc has to say."

Raul studied Kane for a few minutes before asking. "Can you tell me what you saw happening on the island?"

Kane sat back down on his bed. "Are you sure you want to know?"

Raul smiled. "Are your eyes going to get all weird again?"

"Probably."

Raul looked at Kane, feeling compassion for this friend. "If you don't want to tell me, it's okay."

"I think you're old enough." Kane lay back down on the bed. Raul sat in a chair next to him. Kane closed his eyes. It was several minutes before he spoke. "I'm sure the darkness I see is what my father is going through now. The cracking, whistling noise comes from Mt. Vicco. I see people running, screaming for help. Buildings are crumbling, burying people underneath. The clinic is the worst. One of the dead bodies is J.J.'s wife."

Raul saw a tear run down Kane's cheek. He touched his arm.

"Kane, stop. It's okay. Sally's fine."

Kane lay there for several minutes, taking very deep breaths. Then he opened his eyes.

Raul had seen Kane's eyes change color but never to this extreme. They actually frightened him. "I'm sorry I asked you to do that. You should look at yourself in the mirror. I don't think you've ever seen your eyes like this."

Kane got out of bed and walked into the bathroom. He stared at his reflection. *Raul is right. I've never seen my eyes change like this. My father's yes, but never mine.* He glanced at Raul. "Thanks, pal. I've just scared the hell out of myself. What's next?"

They both turned when the door opened and Zoric and Doctor Stevens entered the room. Zoric noticed Kane's eyes right away and asked. "Is something wrong?"

"No. Not unless you have bad news about my father."

Zoric stood between Kane and Dr. Stevens, hoping the doctor couldn't see the strange color of Kane's eyes and start asking questions for which Zoric didn't have answers. "Sorry, Kane, no change in your father's condition. Why don't you splash some water on your face. You look a little pale."

Kane did as he was told and entered the bathroom, closing the door behind him. He glanced at himself in the mirror, then turned on the water. He watched his eyes turn slowly back to their original color. The warmth of the water felt good against his face. He looked toward the shower and, within minutes, stripped off the hospital pajamas the nurse had given him and stood under the hot water.

It was only a few minutes before he redressed and opened the door, anxious to hear what Doctor Stevens had to say about his father.

With his eyes back to their original color, and feeling human again, he sat down in a chair next to his father's bed. Looking at Doctor Stevens he asked, "What did the tests show?"

"Not much. I'm still waiting for the results I sent to the United States. As far as your father being unconscious, it's a complete mystery. I've put him on blood thinner medications in case of a blood clot. There isn't any indication of one, so it's just a precaution. Actually he could open his eyes anytime or stay like this for days. I'll have the nurse come in and turn him every four hours, then exercise his arms and legs. They'll teach you how to do it if you'd like to help."

"Of course. Is there anything else I can do?"

"Talk to him. Let him know you're here." The doctor smiled and touched his hand. "A prayer or two wouldn't hurt."

A soothing feeling passed through Kane's body when the doctor touched his skin. *He knows.* Kane knew something else, too. This man was his father's friend and his, too. *Why didn't I realize this before. The man's drawn blood from my body, for Christ's sake.* He looked into the doctor's eyes and smiled. "A prayer or two you say...I can handle that."

The doctor said his good-byes, promising to check on them later that evening.

Zoric waited for the door to close before he spoke. "Is there anything you need, Kane?"

"I could use some clean clothes. The only thing I've got to wear are these pj's the nurse gave me."

"Where's the clothes you were wearing?" asked Raul.

"The nurse took them, said she'd have them cleaned. She took dad's, too."

"I'll check with her before I leave," Zoric replied, with a smile on his face. *Why do I think my brother had something to do with this. Probably because it would make it very difficult to escape with no clothing.* Zoric did notice, however, that Kevin's belt was conveniently rolled up on the small dresser by Kevin's bed.

"Tell me what happened today," Kane asked, as he propped himself against the pillows on his bed.

Zoric brought him up to date. "We're going to take it day by day. I don't want anyone back on Tali Island until I know it's safe."

"What about godzilla?" Kane asked, referring to the guard at the door.

Zoric chuckled. "Prince Tali's orders. He'll be your shadow while you're here. I wanted to send J.J. but I need him to help me."

"I understand," Kane replied. "I'd like to be able to walk around, though, maybe go to the exercise room."

"I'll let godzilla know. Promise me one thing, Kane, that you'll stay on this floor. It'll make things easier on everyone, especially me, if you do. By the way, godzilla's name is Yorky."

"Yorky, the large dorky." Raul said jokingly.

"I'll introduce you," Zoric said. "He's a decent chess player, in case you get bored." He walked toward the door and opened it. "Yorky, come in here."

Kane stood, watching the large man enter the room.

"You've met my nephew, Raul. This is his friend, Kane. That's his father, Kevin." Zoric pointed to the bed. "He's very ill."

Kane reached out to shake the man's hand. The moment of contact sent a hot, burning sensation through Kane's arm. Kane knew, without a doubt, he was shaking hands with a cold-blooded murderer. "Quite a grip you've got there, sir." A crooked little smile flashed on Kane's face.

The man nodded his head, turned and walked out of the room without saying a word.

Raul looked at Kane and rolled his eyes. "Little on the voodoo side, I'd say. Gee, Kane, you and him should get along great."

Kane agreed.

"I'll talk to him," said Zoric. "There will be another guard here soon to take his place. Yorky's wife is bringing their six-month-old son into the hospital. He hasn't been feeling well."

"You mean someone actually married that dork!" exclaimed Raul.

"He's a good man, dependable, keeps to himself," stated Zoric. "I don't want you two giving him any trouble. You hear?"

"Not I," said Kane. "I'll even shine his shoes if he asks me."

Zoric laughed. "He does have that effect on people." He turned toward Raul. "It's time to leave."

"Okay. I'll see you sometime tomorrow, Kane. Call me if you need anything." Raul smiled at his friend and followed his uncle out the door.

Kane shouted after them, "Don't forget to have someone bring me that chess game. When my father wakes up it will give us something to do until he's better. Bring my drawing tablet, too, okay?"

"I'll have it sent to you right away," Zoric said, understandingly.


They had only been gone about ten minutes when Yorky opened the door, a dinner tray in his hand. He set it down and turned to leave the room without saying a word when Kane asked him, "Did you sample everything first to make sure it wasn't poisoned?"

Yorky turned, a smug look on his face. "Of course."

Kane couldn't help, but laugh. "Thank you, I appreciate it. Would you leave the door open, please." He watched Yorky leave the room and return to his chair.

Kane had just finished his dinner when a nurse came into his room, carrying the chess game, tablet, and a box of drawing pencils.

"Zoric sent these for you." She handed them to him.

"Thank you."

He set the board on the end of the bed, opened the box containing the chess figures, and placed them in their correct spot. He moved a chair to the other side of the bed across from him.

"Sir," he opened the door and said to Yorky, "would you like to play a game of chess?" Yorky nodded and entered the room, sitting in the chair Kane had placed there for him.

"Since you're my guest," Kane said with a smile, "please go first."

It was a close game. Kane found Yorky a worthy opponent, but finally lost to him.

"Best two out of three?" Kane asked.

Yorky, without saying a word, set up his figures. He made the first move and waited for Kane.

Kane looked into the cold, dark, uncaring eyes of the man across from him. With a new sense of determination he had never felt before, Kane made his first move. An hour later he made his last as he placed his queen in place. "Check mate."

A noise in the hall made them both turn. A lady with a baby in her arms appeared at the door. Kane could see the strain and worry on her face. He watched Yorky move toward them, taking the baby, then wrapping his arms around her.

"How's my boy?"

Kane couldn't believe the change that came over this cold-blooded murderer. He was kind, gentle, and loving toward his family.

Yorky touched his wife's cheek. "We can leave when my replacement gets here." He glanced at his watch. "He should be here any time now."

Kane stood, moving his chair around to the other side. "Please come in and sit down."

The lady didn't hesitate. "Thank you."

Kane could tell Yorky didn't approve, but he said nothing. Yorky walked over and sat in the chair he had just occupied.

Kane went over and stood beside him. Smiling at the baby, he said, "Hi there, little one. I'm sorry to hear you're not feeling well." Kane reached out and touched the top of the little boy's hand with his finger. The baby instantly grabbed it. "Wow, that's quite a grip you have there. You got that from your father, I bet."

"Sorry I'm late, Yorky," J.J. said, entering the room.

"J.J., I didn't know you were going to be here," said Kane.

"Only until the other guard arrives. Yorky and his wife have an appointment with Doctor Stevens. I hope he finds out what's wrong." He looked at Yorky then his wife. "He's a good doctor."

Kane waited until they left before he asked, "He doesn't talk much, does he?"

J.J. laughed. "No, he doesn't. How is your father?"

"The same."

They talked until the other guard arrived. J.J. said good-bye, promising to stop by the next day. He closed the door behind him when he left.

Kane sat on the edge of his father's bed. "I see we didn't keep you awake today. It would have been nice if you had joined the conversation though. Well, maybe tomorrow. Night, Dad. Wake me if you need me."

Kane lay down on his bed. He closed his eyes and thought about Yorky's son. *What is making you sick, little one? Are you in pain?* Kane rubbed the finger the baby had grabbed hold of. *Tell me, little one, what's wrong. Maybe I can help.* Kane drifted off to sleep, thinking about the little baby that touched not only his hand, but his heart as well.

He awoke when he heard the nurse enter the room to check on his father. It was only a few minutes later when Doctor Stevens came in.

"How's our patient?" he asked her.

"Same. I'll check on him again in a couple of hours. Anything I can get for you, Kane?"

"No, thanks." He stretched when he got out of bed. "I need to give my legs a little exercise." He looked at Doctor Stevens. "Maybe you could show me the exercise room."

"Right this way." The doctor smiled at him. On the way out the doctor told the guard where they were going. The guard stood and followed them down the hall.

"How is Yorky's baby?" Kane asked.

"This hasn't been my week. I can't find anything wrong with him. I've checked everything. I know the little guy is hurting, but I honestly don't know why."

"He has a headache." Kane stated.

"What?" The doctor stopped and looked at Kane. "What did you say?"

"I said, he has a headache."

"How do you know that?"

"He told me." Kane smiled.

The doctor stared into Kane's eyes. It was several moments before he spoke. "What else did this six-month-old baby tell you?"

Kane chuckled. "It does sound pretty strange, doesn't it?"

"I don't know if that's the word I would use, but it'll do for now."

They entered the exercise room. Kane looked around, then walked over to the middle of the room and stepped onto the treadmill. He noticed the guard had stayed by the entrance. Kane was pretty sure he couldn't hear them. "It has something to do with the boy's ear."

"I checked him for a ear infection. Everything was fine."

"It doesn't, I don't think, have anything to do with the inner ear. There is something like a lump, cyst, or pimple that's behind his right eardrum. When he lays on his back or right side, it presses on a nerve or maybe even the eardrum, causing the little guy to have a headache. If he lays or sleeps on his left side, there is no pressure, therefore, no headache. Oh, and one more thing, doc. If it isn't removed, the boy will be deaf in his right ear in a few months."

The doctor walked around the room, thinking about what Kane told him. *How in the hell could he know something like this? Why am I even questioning this? Undoubtedly Kane has this special gift, too, like his father.*

Kane laughed as he watched the doctor throwing his arms in the air and mumbling to himself. Finally the doctor came up to him. "We better get back."

They were silent until they arrived back in Kevin's room. Doctor Stevens pointed to Kevin's belt buckle and looked at Kane.

"Do you think he can hear what we say?" Kane asked the doctor.

"Yes, I definitely do." He looked at Kane, both knew—that the other knew—they were talking about Prince Tali.

"I wish I had some idea of what is happening to your father, Kane. Maybe we'll know tomorrow. Keep talking to him though, and let him know you're here. I have to leave. I forgot to tell one of my patients a very important thing—to sleep on his left side. See you tomorrow. Try to get a good night's rest. Have someone page me if there's any change at all." He touched Kane on the shoulder and left the room, closing the door behind him.

Kane went over to his father. "If you need me tonight, Dad, call my name. I'll be right here next to you."

After spending a restless night, Kane woke early the next morning. *What day is this, anyway? Oh, right. It's the first day of the rest of my life.* He didn't remember where he read that saying, but he liked it. For some reason it meant more to him today. He closed his eyes, then quickly opened them again, turning to look at his father. He breathed a sigh of relief when he saw his father still in bed. The nurse had turned him on his side during the night, but Kane had not heard a thing. *Why would I imagine seeing an empty bed? What's even weirder, my bed is empty, too. Does this mean my father is well? Are we back on the island?* Kane didn't want to think about any other possibilities.

There was something else strange going on inside his head. For some reason Katy seemed closer than usual. *Where are you, Katy?* He closed his eyes and thought about his twin sister. *She is getting closer, I can feel it, but why?* Kane always wondered if he would know her if he passed her on the street. He wondered, too, what she was doing at this exact moment. Sleep overtook him, but not for long. His eyes popped open and a huge grin appeared on his face. *She's coming here. I know it. I can feel it. She's coming here to help us. How does she know where we are? She doesn't, I'll have to help her, but how?* Hundreds of questions were floating around in Kane's mind. One thing he knew for sure—he had to be extremely careful. *If Prince Tali found out about Katy—no I won't let that happen.*

Kane got out of bed and walked over to the window. He opened the drapes and was greeted by a beautiful sunrise. He glanced at his father. The sun cast a golden glow across his face. *You almost look like an angel.* Kane smiled to himself. *The only thing missing is a halo and wings.*

Kane walked over and sat in the chair by his father. He picked up his hand and held it tightly. Then Kane closed his eyes. *Please, Father, try to wake up. I need you.* He wanted to tell him Katy needed him, too, but they were words he couldn't say out loud—only think them.

After a few minutes Kane stood. "I'm going to take a shower. Don't go anywhere." He picked up the clean pajamas the nurse left for him. I wonder if I'm ever going to get my clothes back?

Kane finished his shower and dressed. When he opened the door he noticed his father lying on his back. "I see they've been in to turn you." He looked around. *No, wait, I don't think anyone's been in here. My God, he moved by himself.* Happiness spread through Kane as he realized what had happened. *He's coming out of it, I know he is. I must find some way of letting Doctor Stevens know without anyone else finding out. I'm so tired. Why did I see an empty bed?* Kane laid back down. *I need to think, come up with a plan. Katy's the only one that can really help us. How do I let her know where we are?* Kane's mind kept jumping from one thing to another... Katy... His father... Should he trust Doctor Stevens? Then he was back to Katy again. It didn't take long before exhaustion took over and he was sleeping soundly.

It was late morning when Doctor Stevens stood outside the hospital room, talking to Yorky. "How long has Kane been sleeping?"

"All morning as far as I know. I've been here about three hours. I need to ask you something about that boy, Doc."

"All right."

"The other guard told me he heard young Kane tell you my son was having headaches. Then you called me, and my wife, telling us that's what was causing his pain and to have him sleep on his left side. It's the best night's sleep my son has had in over a month, my wife, too. I'd like to know how that boy knew."

The doctor didn't know what to say.

"I need to know, Doc. It won't go any further than me and my wife. I promise."

Doctor Stevens looked up into the eyes of the man standing before him, and seeing the determination there, he finally spoke. "I could tell you it was a lucky guess, but the honest truth is... I don't know how

Kane knew."

"But you are taking it serious, aren't you?"

"Yes, I am."

"What have you found?" asked Yorky.

"We took two more x-rays this morning of the right side behind the ear. There's a very small growth there, not much bigger than a small poppy seed. It's almost undetectable and very rare. If diagnosed early it's easily removed, with only a one- percent chance of recurring."

"And if not diagnosed early?" Yorky asked.

Doctor Stevens took a deep breath before answering. "It's a rapidly growing tumor, usually causing deafness within a year. By then, it's inoperable. Radiation has been known to help, but in most case's death will occur in three to five years."

Yorky sat down in his chair. "Sweet Jesus." He covered his face with his hands. After a moment he looked up at the doctor. "You did catch it in time?"

Doctor Stevens placed his hand on Yorky's shoulder, trying to offer some comfort. "Yes, your son is going to be fine, thanks to Kane. We'll schedule the surgery for day after tomorrow. You'll be able to take your son home the same day."

Yorky watched the doctor until he disappeared down the hall. He opened the door to check on Kane and found him still sleeping. He closed the door and sat down in his chair. He kept telling himself not to get involved. He was doing his job and getting paid extremely well, but he couldn't help wonder about the father that may or may not be dying and the devoted son who stayed by his side. Yorky had been told that their lives might be in danger and given strict orders not to let anyone in unless authorized. He also was told they weren't allowed to leave the hospital. He liked this young man, Kane, but wondered... Was it Kane, or his father, that Prince Tali was so concerned about? *Right now all I want to think about is my own son and pray he'll be all right.*

*Carole A. Sheller*

# Chapter 15
## THE PARK
## THURSDAY AFTERNOON

Zoric stood by the platform with J.J. "Everything seems to be going smoothly. We'll start moving the people back on Tali Island tomorrow afternoon. What is the status on the clinic?"

"There is more damage than we thought to the one side," said J.J. "It's going to take probably two to three weeks for repairs. The rest of the building is in good shape. Anything new on Kevin?"

Zoric shook his head. "Nothing. Prince Tali wants him moved from the hospital back to the estate. He's bringing in a private nurse, and he'll have Doctor Stevens check on him daily."

"When is that going to happen?" J.J. asked.

"Tomorrow or Saturday. Doctor Stevens wants to keep him another twenty-four hours while he checks all the test results."

"And Kane?"

Zoric smiled. "Raul is with him now. I stopped by the hospital earlier and he was sleeping. He's been to the exercise room, but didn't stay long. He doesn't like to be away from his father. I heard he played a couple games of chess with Yorky, or godzilla as the boys call him."

J.J. laughed. "Yorky doesn't say much, but he's a good man. I'm going to stop by the hospital around nine this evening to see how they're doing."

"Good. I'll see you in the morning. I've got an early dinner date." Zoric turned and walked toward his car.

Neither Zoric or J.J. paid any attention to the man that stood behind the tree and listened to their conversation, then watched as they walked toward their cars. A smile came to the man's face. *Might as well make the hospital my next stop.*

## HOSPITAL

Kane didn't want to open his eyes. Another vision was trying to form in his mind, but someone kept calling his name. He opened his eyes slowly to see the guard, Yorky, standing by his bed. A doctor that Kane had never seen before stood at Yorky's side. Raul was there, too. "What's going on?" Kane asked as he got out of bed.

"Doctor Stevens called the nurse's station and left word he was sending up a doctor to take a sample of blood from you and your father. He needs it for another test of some kind. Doctor Stevens also wants him to give you both an anti-bacterial shot."

Kane knew right away something was wrong. "Did you talk to Doctor Stevens personally, Yorky?" Kane asked.

"No, I didn't, just the nurse."

Kane looked at the doctor. Something about the man, wearing dark-rimmed glasses and a thin mustache, seemed familiar. "I'm sorry I didn't catch your name." Kane held out his hand.

"Doctor Cougar."

The minute Kane shook the doctor's hand he knew who he was—Mani's brother.

Yorky grabbed Kane's arm. "Are you all right?"

"A little dizzy, that's all. I think I stood up too fast." Kane glared at the man that called himself a doctor. "Doesn't this man look familiar to you, Raul?"

"As a matter of fact he does." Raul said, as he stepped forward. "Have I met him somewhere before?"

A smug smile came to Kane's face. He looked at Raul. "You never pay any attention to me when I tell you something important. I told you, if you ever saw this man, run, run like hell, and here you stand." Kane threw his arms in the air. He lunged toward Mani's brother, but Yorky was quicker. Within seconds the man was flat on his stomach, on the floor, with his arms behind his back.

Kane and Raul stood listening to the vulgar language coming from Yorky. Finally Kane spoke. "Yorky, I didn't realize your knowledge of such a large vocabulary of words."

Yorky looked up at both boys. A big grin appeared on his face and he started to chuckle. "This man doesn't realize how lucky he is. If he had hurt either one of you, I'd have killed him with my bare hands."

"Maybe you should do just that." Raul said, slipping his shirt off and revealing his chest. "He did this to me. By the time my father and I get through with him, he is going to wish you had killed him."

Hate reappeared on Yorky's face. He grabbed the man, jerking him to his feet. "You bastard," Yorky said, swinging his powerful fist into the man's jaw, knocking him back to the floor unconscious. "I'll go call your father."

After he left, Kane went over to Raul. "Are you okay?" he asked, putting his hand on Raul's shoulder.

"No. I'm not," Raul said, looking up at Kane. "It's taking everything I've got not to kill this man for what he did to me, and was about to do to you and your father."

Kane glanced at his father. "I'm afraid you'd have to stand in line." He looked back at Raul. "I think, if Yorky has his way, there won't be anything left to pass around."

Raul started to grin. "Can you believe that punch. Hell, if he hit me that hard, you'd be looking for me back on the island, probably already in my own grave."

Clowning around helped relieve some of the tension both boys felt.

Yorky stood outside the door. He had to pause for a minute, take several deep breaths, and wait for the nausea he felt in the pit of his stomach to pass. The picture of Raul's scarred body flashed in his mind. *What kind of monster would do such a thing to a nice kid like that, and why? Well, he'll never be able to hurt anyone again when I'm through with him."* Yorky walked over to the nurse's station and picked up the phone to call Prince Tali.

His phone rang only once before Prince Tali picked up the receiver. "Yorky, is my son all right?"

Yorky paused for a moment before answering. "Yes sir, he's fine. So is Kane and his father. We had an intruder."

"I know. Where is he?"

"Taking a little nap on the floor, sir."

Prince Tali chuckled. "Good. Keep him like that. I'm on my way."

Yorky heard the click from the other end of the line. *Now I know the reason for tight security. The room is even monitored.* Still Yorky was puzzled. *Had this man planned to kill or torture young Kane like he had Raul?* Yorky felt his jaw hurt as his teeth ground together from the anger that was building up inside him. *I hope Prince Tali lets me finish this creep. Hell, I'll even do it free of charge.*

Yorky walked back into the room. He found Kane standing by his father's bed. Raul was standing over the man that young Kane called Mani's brother. "Did he give you any trouble?" asked Yorky.

Raul shook his head. "No, but if he had I would have done this." Raul swung his leg back, then forward, kicking the man in his ribs. "Ouch," screamed Raul as he jumped around on his other foot. "Son of a bitch, I think I broke my toe." He fell across Kane's bed. "Why do you let me do crazy things like that?" He looked over at Kane and found his friend laughing uncontrollably, and even worse he heard the laughter behind him. Raul didn't know whether to laugh or cry. "Hey, I could use some sympathy here." That just made them laugh even harder. Raul couldn't hold it back any longer. His laughter joined with theirs.

By the time Prince Tali arrived, they had calmed down. "Did he give you any more trouble, Yorky?"

"No, sir. I would like to put an end to this situation though—permanently."

Prince Tali knew exactly what Yorky meant. "I appreciate that, but this is something my son, Raul, and I have to take care of—personally."

Yorky nodded his head. "I'll go get a wheelchair."

When he returned, Kane helped with Mani's brother. When they turned him over, his jacket fell open, revealing the gun the man had concealed there in a shoulder holster.

Kane looked at Yorky and smiled. "Look at this, Raul. I think there's a dent in the barrel of his gun."

Raul hobbled over to take a look. "Funny, Kane, but if you look real close you'll notice which way the gun is pointing. If my aim had been more accurate, and the gun had fired, you would not be helping to move Mr. Macho, but Ms. Mademoiselle."

Prince Tali couldn't help but smile when he heard the laughter coming from the three of them. Especially Raul. He liked to see his son happy. He would ask him about his limp later. What surprised Prince Tali was Yorky. He couldn't remember ever seeing the man smile. *Maybe this is who I need to replace J.J. I'll talk to Zoric and see if he wants J.J. to work for him.*

Prince Tali planned on firing J.J. when everything got back to normal on the island. J.J. had not followed his orders and that was something Prince Tali didn't tolerate. *Yorky has proved his loyalty to me by offering to kill someone. That not only takes guts, but honor as well.*

The only thing Prince Tali didn't know is that Yorky's loyalty was not to him, but to Kane. Yorky knew Kane was responsible for saving his son, maybe even his life as well, along with Raul and Kane's father. If Yorky had to protect young Kane, he didn't care who he had to destroy—even the Prince himself.

"Does anyone even know this man's name?" Raul asked.

"No," said Prince Tali, "and no one needs to know. Kane, I put another guard on duty. I don't think there will be any more trouble. I'm taking Yorky. He will accompany me and Raul back to the island. Call Zoric if you need anything. Oh, I almost forgot to tell you, I'm moving you and your father back onto the island tomorrow. I'll have Doctor Stevens hire a private nurse." Prince Tali saw the concern on Kane's face. "You'll both be safer there."

Kane waited a few minutes after everyone left, then opened the door. He informed the guard he was taking a nap and didn't want to be disturbed.

Kane walked over to his father's bedside and picked up his hand. "You missed out on all the excitement again. I know you'll be coming back to me soon. Maybe going back to the island is a good idea. J.J. and I can wheel your bed out on the patio. The fresh air and sunshine will do you good. I'll even pick some of your favorite flowers for you." *But what will we do about Katy? How is she going to find us there? What am I thinking? How is she going to find us here?*

A warm sensation ran through Kane's body as he felt a soft squeeze from his father's hand. Tears stung his eyes. "Everything's going to be all right. I know your mind is out there in space somewhere, but it's here with me, too. We'll get through this together." *You, Katy, and me.*

Kane talked to his father a while longer. "I think I will take that nap before they bring dinner." Kane walked over to his own bed and laid down. His mind went over what happened earlier. He knew Prince Tali would take the life of Mani's brother before the day was over. *The man has some valuable information. I'm sure Prince Tali will find out what it is, one way or another.*

Kane's thoughts turned to Katy. *She's getting so close. Instead of using this gift to help others, we must use it to help ourselves to find each other.* Kane closed his eyes and drifted off to sleep not knowing that, high in the air above the city, a jet circled, waiting for clearance to land.

# Chapter 16
## KATY
## THE PLANE TRIP

Ben sat in the pilot's seat with Sister Elizabeth as co-pilot at his side. Katy sat behind her, her face pressed against the window.

"I think that's Tali Island just ahead and to the right," said Ben. "You can still see some haze from the volcano."

Katy was so excited and nervous. "I know they're down there somewhere. I wish I could point to the exact spot and say there they are." Katy sighed. She looked down at Tali Island. "It looks beautiful."

Sister Elizabeth smiled. "Yes, it does." She covered her mouth with her hand, trying to control the yawn that escaped from her tired body.

They had all taken turns flying, trying to give each other time to get some sleep. The flight was long, over fifteen hours, plus they lost nine hours due to the time changes. Several hours were spent at the different airports for fuel fill-up and maintenance. Having to wait for clearance to land wasn't helping either. They were six hours off their schedule, but they were finally at their destination. It was Thursday afternoon.

Katy reached down and turned off the tape machine, ejecting the cassette it held. "I guess we won't need these anymore." They had been listening to 'Learn How to Speak Greek' in four easy lessons. It was a refresher course for Sister Elizabeth, but Katy seemed to pick it up easily, too, probably because she spoke Italian so well and the languages were similar. Ben was another story, a few common words were about his limit. He didn't seem worried about it, though. Father James promised him a translator if he needed one.

Katy took the compact out of her night bag that contained her brown contact lenses, and carefully placed them on her eyes. She combed her hair back into a braid, then placed the white nun's head covering on her head. She had changed from her jeans into the nun's habit at their last stop. She picked up the last article of her disguise, a pair of plain eyeglasses and slipped them on.

"All set."

Sister Elizabeth and Ben turned to look at her.

"I can't believe you're our Katy," Ben replied. "You look like you're about fourteen."

Finally the airport controller came on and gave them permission to land, then guided Ben into a private hanger about four blocks from the main terminal.

Ben brought the plane to a stop and breathed a sigh of relief as he shut off the engine. He turned and looked at Katy. "Are you ready to go find that family of yours?"

A big grin appeared on Katy's face. "You bet, let's go!"

They departed the plane and were getting their luggage out of the storage area when a man and woman, occupying a baggage cart and beaming with happiness, drove into the hanger and pulled to a stop next to them. The man hopped out and extended his hand toward Ben. "Welcome, my friends, to Greece. I am Damon. My brother, Father Anthony, asked me to meet you. I work here at the airport and I'm at your disposal. This is my wife, Lorena." He turned and pointed toward the smiling woman who was getting out of the cart.

They exchanged casual greetings. You could see the respect for Sister Elizabeth on Damon's face as she conversed with him in Greek. "Have you been to our beautiful country before?" he asked her.

"No," Sister answered. "I've been wanting to come here for years, though."

The smile left the man's face. "I'm sorry the reason for your visit is not a pleasant one. My brother told me you're here to transport a very sick person back to the United States."

"Yes. That's true," Sister Elizabeth confirmed.

"I'm here to help in any way I can," Damon said.

As they were talking his wife, Lorena, walked over to Katy and touched her shoulder. Katy turned to look into Lorena's smiling face and couldn't help but smile back.

"Do you speak Greek?" Lorena asked in Greek.

"A little," Katy replied.

"I don't mean to be rude, but you look too young to be a nun."

Katy touched Lorena's hand. "Thank you. I'm not nearly as young as I look. I'll be eighteen, and I'm not a nun yet. I'm a novice, study-ing to be one."

Sister Elizabeth came up to them. "I'm going to check inside the plane and make sure we got everything."

"I'll go with you," said Katy.

When they were inside, Katy could hardly wait to tell Sister the news. "I know why Lorena and Damon are so happy, Aunt Liz."

"Really, why is that?" Sister asked as she turned toward Katy.

"Lorena is going to have a baby."

"She told you that?" Sister Elizabeth asked.

Katy laughed. "No. It's one of those things I just know." She paused before continuing. "She does need to be careful and get a lot of rest."

"Will Lorena and the baby be all right?" Sister asked, but had to wait a moment before Katy answered.

"They're going to be fine."

They finished checking the plane and returned to the others.

Sister Elizabeth looked over at Lorena just as the woman was bending over to pick up one of their suitcases. "No. No, Lorena. I will get that." Sister hurried toward her. "Didn't the doctor tell you not to pick up anything heavy?"

Damon walked over to his wife and put his arm around her shoulder. "Why would the doctor tell her that?"

Without thinking, Sister Elizabeth blurted out, "Because she has to be careful now that she is pregnant."

Sister watched the happiness disappear from the couple's faces. The sadness she saw there startled her. "What's the matter? I don't understand."

Damon lowered his head. "I'm sure you don't. We've been married for eight years. More than anything in this world, we wanted children. We've been tested and re-tested. The doctors told us that it was never going to happen. We finally accepted that was the way it was."

"I'm so sorry," Sister said understandingly. She looked at Katy and saw the smile on Katy's face. Sister turned back, took one hand of Damon's and one hand of Lorena's. Would you do me a favor?" she asked.

They both looked at her and smiled. "Of course," said Lorena.

"Go see your doctor again. Please promise me you will. That beautiful glow on your face usually only appears on a woman with child. If I'm wrong, then I'm truly sorry. But in the meantime, rest and please don't pick up anything heavy."

Lorena smiled at her. "Okay."

"Do you know when they're scheduled to come by to fuel the plane?" Ben asked.

"Between four and ten in the morning." Damon replied. "Unless you need it done sooner."

"That will work fine." Ben paused before continuing. "I hear there has been some excitement around here with the eruption of Mt. Vicco."

Damon nodded his head. "Yes there was, but it's pretty much over now. Tali Island, where Mt. Vicco is located, is not largely populated. The people of the island were evacuated the night before."

"We heard about it on the news," Ben said, "before we left the States. They showed pictures of the volcano, then some man came on to say everything was fine. His name was Tali. I guess the island is named after his family."

Damon laughed. "It's not only named after the Tali family. It's owned by the Tali family."

"The whole island?" Ben acted surprised.

"Yes indeed. No one is even allowed on the island unless they have special authorization. The people who live and work there have ID cards to get back and forth. They have to obey and respect the laws of the island or they're no longer allowed there."

"Who makes up these laws?" Ben asked.

Damon laughed again. "Why, the Tali family, of course, and the laws are passed down from one generation to the other. Prince Tali is in charge now and there's his brother, Zoric. He's the one you probably saw on television. Prince Tali has a son, Raul. That's it. There's just the three of them."

Damon was telling more of what he knew about Tali Island when Ben interrupted. "Where did the people go when they were evacuated?"

Damon thought the question odd, but answered anyway. "The Tali family found places for them to stay in hotels, motels, whatever was available. They even paid all expenses."

"They seem like nice people," Ben stated. "Have the people been able to move back to their homes?"

Damon hesitated. "I'm not sure. They might have started today."

"How do they know it's okay?"

*Americans sure ask strange questions,* Damon thought to himself, then answered. "One of the local TV stations gives updates every couple of hours. I also heard that the Tali family has something set up at the local park. They meet three times a day and someone from the island informs the people on what is happening. Do you know when you'll be leaving?" Damon decided it was his turn to ask questions.

"Two or three days probably. Sister Elizabeth wanted to volunteer if the people of the island needed any help while we were here."

*That's why all the questions and interest in Tali Island.* Damon felt a little foolish. "That's very nice. I'll do some checking and find out for you."

"Thank you. Well, I think we're ready to go."

It was only a few minutes when Damon pulled the cart to a stop next to a small station wagon. "This belongs to my brother, Father Anthony. He wants you to use it while you're here."

"That's so nice of him," replied Sister Elizabeth.

"I have a map for you, too." Damon reached into his pocket and spread the piece of paper across the hood of the car. "This is the hotel where I understand you'll be staying. This is where we are." Damon showed Ben the best way to get to their destination. He pointed out some other points of interest he had circled.

"This is the park I was telling you about." Damon circled it, too.

Ben noticed the park wasn't that far from where they were staying. *Maybe, if my girls aren't too tired, we'll go by there and see what's going on.*

Damon put his phone number, and his brother's, on the front of the map. "I know you're all tired from your trip so I won't bother you this evening. Please call me, though, if you need anything."

"We will," said Sister Elizabeth. She turned toward Lorena. "Please let me know what the doctor says."

"I will." Lorena smiled at her. "I hope it's good news, but I'm not going to get my hopes up too much."

Sister wrapped her arms around the young lady. "I know."

Then Lorena walked over to Katy and hugged her, too. "See you tomorrow, Sister Katy."

"Get some rest," Katy told her as she walked away. *She is definitely pregnant.*

It took about twenty minutes for Ben to drive to their hotel, and within another twenty, they were in their rooms.

Sister Elizabeth and Katy were busy unpacking, laughing and talking about Lorena and Damon. "I don't think in my whole life I've ever met any couple that was so perfectly matched or that smiled so much, except when I told Lorena she was pregnant. I sure hope you're right about that, Katy."

"I am." Katy sat down in the chair by the window that overlooked the view of the city. "I wish I could be that sure about my father and brother. I mean I'm sure, or pretty sure, they're out there somewhere. I want to be able to walk right up to them and say, "Hi, I'm Katy, your sister and daughter. I'm here to take you home."

Sister Elizabeth came over and stood by her. "We'll find them. I think going to the park is a good start."

"Me, too." Katy looked up at her. "I have a really good feeling about it, Aunt Liz. I wish Ben would hurry up and get here."

"It won't be long. He probably took a shower. He wanted to call Father Anthony to let him know we arrived and to thank him for the use of the car."

Ben stood in front of the mirror, towel drying his hair, another towel wrapped around his waist. He was putting, or trying to put, all the information he'd received in the last week about Katy's father and brother into some kind of perspective. He laid the towel down and ran a comb through his hair, then walked over and sat in a large, comfortable, overstuffed chair. His mind went over, again, the information he had. *Katy's pretty sure her father and brother are in Greece. She knows her father is, or will be, very sick and she knows her brother, Kane, was looking down on Mt. Vicco from a helicopter or plane. She wasn't sure which.*

*So what does all this mean? Hopefully, Katy will be able to add a few more pieces to the puzzle before the night's over. All I can do is be here to help and, God forbid, protect her if needed.* Ben took his job of Katy's Godfather, very serious.

Ben closed his eyes, his mind drifting back in time. The only home he'd known until he came to the Ranch was a place called The South Valley Orphanage. It was a decent place to grow up, everyone was kind and understanding. When he was fourteen, his counselor told him why he had been brought there at the age of four. Ben's father had shot and killed Ben's mother, sister and grandparents. Ben was staying with one of his friends on a sleepover when it happened. He ended up staying at his friend's for over a month before the authorities took him away. In time Ben's memory of his family faded.

At the age of fifteen, Ben decided that when he was old enough he'd leave and find a job on a farm or ranch. He had told his friends at the orphanage he was going to ride tame horses, wear a cowboy hat, and chase wild women. Well, two out of three wasn't bad. He remembered the day he walked onto the Ranch and met Sister Elizabeth's grandfather, Matthew Riley. Ben knew this was where he wanted to spend the rest of his life. Over the next couple of years, Mr. Riley became the father Ben had never known, and Elizabeth Riley, his sister. Then Mr. Riley's other granddaughter, Meg, returned home with her daughter, Katy. Katy's true identity had been kept from her. It was a promise they all made to Meg, but Katy would find out through the letters her mother left her to read, when she turned seventeen, about who she was and about the father and brother who she had never known.

Ben stood. *Enough remembering.* He got dressed and walked out of his hotel room and down the hall.

When Sister heard the knock on the door, she walked over and opened it.

"Hi, Ben. How's your room?"

"It's fine. It's down the hall, two doors to the right. When they arrive, Sami will have the room adjoining yours, and Ward's is next to mine. You girls ready to check out the city?"

They walked along, not saying too much of anything. They did comment on how friendly the people seemed to be, smiling and saying hello.

They walked about two blocks, when Katy came to a stop and looked at the buildings that surrounded her.

Ben touched her shoulder. "You've got that look again. You are breathing, aren't you?"

Katy looked up at him, and for reasons she couldn't understand, she started to giggle uncontrollably. Ben stepped back as Sister Elizabeth came up and put her arm around Katy.

A few minutes later Ben looked up at the sky. *Here I stand in the middle of a strange city, hell, a strange country, with two nuns in front of me who have both completely, totally, lost it.* He knew he had to ignore them and walk away before he, too, would be right there, joining them. He noticed an outdoor café about a block away and walked toward it, taking a seat at a table where he could keep an eye on them. He ordered three coffees and waited.

When they finally joined him he looked from one to the other. "Can someone tell me what just happened with you two?"

Katy took a sip of her coffee. "It was the strangest thing. When I looked up at those buildings, this eerie feeling came over me. It was like de ja vu. I knew I'd been there before." She smiled at Ben. "Then you touched my shoulder, bringing me back to reality, and the look on your face, I couldn't help it." Katy took another drink of coffee. "Lack of sleep probably had something to do with it, too." She reached over and touched Ben's arm. "We embarrassed you, didn't we?"

Ben patted her hand. "A little. You okay now?"

"I think so. I've never had a feeling quite like that before. It was as if I stood in that same place and looked at those same buildings. I know it's not me, though." Katy looked at Ben, then Sister Elizabeth. "I think it was my father."

She waited to see if there was any reaction from either one of them, and when there wasn't, she continued. "I think he stood in that spot long before I was even born. It's like this special gift God has given to me. My father has it, too. I think about the other genes my father passed on to me, his eyes for example. I definitely have his eyes. Couldn't it be possible he passed his memory genes down to me, also."

Sister Elizabeth looked at Ben, then back at Katy. "To be honest with you, Katy, I never thought about it. It certainly would explain a lot of things, like when people know how to do something they've never done, or they stand in a room, talking to people, and get the feeling they've done that before."

Ben scratched his head. "Memory genes, I guess that's a possibility."

"Good, I'm glad you both think so, because I would like to go to the church where my mother and father first met. Do you know where that is, Ben?"

He smiled at her. "I'm sure it's on that list I have back at the hotel that Father James gave us. First things first, let's go to the park. See what kind of trouble you can get us into there."

Katy stood. "Actually, I do feel a little mischievous. Let's go."

## HOSPITAL

"Kane, wake up. Can you hear me? Wake up, you're having a bad dream."

Yorky pulled his hand back when Kane opened his eyes and saw the strange color they had become. Kane knew immediately what was happening. He faked a smile. "It's okay, Yorky. My eyes change color when I've had a bad dream. It's pretty weird isn't it?"

Yorky stared at him, then finally answered. "I do believe it's the weirdest thing I've ever seen."

Kane looked at his father. No change. Then he looked out the window and realized it was early evening. "Why are you here? I thought you were going to the island with Prince Tali and Raul."

"I did. I drove them there. Prince Tali decided he and Raul would probably stay there tonight. Then he'll drive them back tomorrow afternoon. I wanted to be here when they operate on my son in the morning."

"Have you seen, or know, where Zoric or J.J. might be?" Kane asked.

Yorky glanced at his watch. "They're both probably at the park."

"I need to talk to one of them, Prince Tali, too." Kane stood. "I'll use the phone at the nurse's station and call Prince Tali. You get a hold of Zoric."

Kane listened to the ringing at the other end of the line. *Damn, where is everybody?* Finally a click and the answering machine came on. 'Leave a message.'

"This is Kane. We have a big problem. Don't drive any of the cars. Get everybody away from the estate. Go down to the stable. We're trying to find Zoric. Someone will be there to pick you up." Kane hung up the phone and looked around for Yorky, but he was nowhere in sight. Kane started to walk back to his room when the phone rang. He hurried back to answer it.

"Hello."

"Kane?"

"Zoric, where are you?"

"At the park. My beeper went off, urgent from Yorky. What's going on?"

"Have you heard about Mani's brother?"

"Yes, I believe that problem is being taken care of as we speak."

"Not entirely. It seems he's leaving some presents behind, the kind that go boom."

"Bombs? Are you sure Kane?"

"I wish I could say I'm not. But I can't. It looks like there's three. Somehow Mani's brother got on the island. One of them is in a car, one is in the estate. I haven't figured out where the third one is, yet." Kane told Zoric about the message he left. "Check yours and J.J.'s cars, too."

"Okay, you and Yorky stay close to the phone. I'll call back in about ten minutes."

Kane hung up the phone, folded his arms on top of the counter, and laid his head down. The feeling he had about Katy kept getting stronger and stronger. *I know she's close by. I can feel it, and there's not a damn thing I can do about it right now. I can't leave my father and I have to figure out where the third bomb is.*

Yorky touched his shoulder. "I'm back. You okay, Kane?"

"Not really. I think it's going to be a long night. Why don't you sit down?" Kane pointed to the chair behind the counter. "Zoric will be calling back. He told us to stay close."

"What's going on?" Yorky asked as he walked around and sat down in the chair.

Kane told him what was happening. "Zoric should be calling any minute to let us know what plans he's made."

"No one knows where the third bomb is?" asked Yorky.

"Not yet."

"Do you think that scum could have left it here in the hospital somewhere?"

Kane paced back and forth. "No. I don't think he would intentionally hurt innocent people."

Yorky studied Kane closely, then asked, "Why are you so involved in this?"

"It's pretty complicated. I'm sure Zoric, or Prince Tali, will tell you what you need to know."

"I doubt that. I have a feeling you know more about this than they do. Like the way you were with my son."

Kane smiled. "I do my share. I'm going back to my father's room. Can you stay here and wait for Zoric's call?"

Yorky watched him walk away, *I keep telling myself not to get involved, but I can't help it. There's something strange going on around here, and I'm going to make sure no harm comes to young Kane.*

Kane turned back. "Yorky, if you see the nurse, tell her to bring my clothes, clean or dirty. I want them right away."

# Chapter 17
## KENNEDY INTERNATIONAL AIRPORT
## NEW YORK

Ward noticed people staring at him. He didn't know if it was because they thought he looked familiar, and recognized him as Senator Ward Tylar, or because he was in a wheelchair. He looked over at his daughter, Samantha, who sat across from him, her hair tucked under a baseball cap and dark glasses on. Ward couldn't help but smile. He knew she didn't want to be recognized especially by the media. So far, so good.

Ward had relinquished his seat in the United States Senate because of the car accident. He had made up his mind to put his political career on hold until he knew what was going to happen in his life. For now all he wanted to do was to help Katy find her father and brother.

"Is there anything you need, Ward?" asked Kord.

"I'm fine. Why don't you take Samantha and get something to eat. I'm going to sit here and catch up on some reading."

Kord smiled. "I know they're serving dinner on the flight, but I could use a snack. How about you, Sam?" he said as he stood and walked over to Sami, taking her hand and pulling her up from her seat.

"Do you really think I look like a boy?" she whispered.

Kord took a step back. His eyes moved from her face down to her feet and back up again. He whispered back. "There's no way in hell anyone would mistake you for a boy."

Sami chuckled. "Why, thank you. Can we bring you back something, Dad?"

Ward glanced at his watch. They would start boarding in a little over an hour. "No, thanks. You two go ahead." He watched them walk away. Ward liked this young man of Katy's, everyone did, even Sister Elizabeth.

Ward rolled his wheelchair over to the window. He could see his reflection in the tinted glass, and smiled. *Hell, nobody is going to recognize me. I don't even recognize myself, thanks to Ben.* Ward rubbed his hand across his chin where his beard was starting to grow back, so was the hair on his head. He lifted his hat and scratched the top of his head, then replaced the hat. He could see people moving around behind him. He opened the folder that was sitting on his lap, the one that Father James had given him. It contained information on Katy's parents when they lived in Greece. There were even copies of Katy's and Kane's birth certificates, along with American citizenship papers showing both children born to an American mother while traveling in Greece.

Ward had been reading for about fifteen minutes when he started yawning. He missed the afternoon nap he'd become so accustomed to. He looked up, his eyes surveying the reflection of the people behind him. There were only about a half dozen or so new faces. As he looked around the room his eyes flashed back to the attractive short, blonde standing at the check-in counter. Something about her seemed familiar. He turned his chair to get a better look at her. He finally realized who she was, but for the life of him couldn't remember her name. Ward knew her brother quite well. She had accompanied him to several charity dinners. *She even had lunch with my wife, Jill, a few times. Why can't I remember her name.*

Ward watched her as she walked away from the counter and sat down in a chair on the other side of the room, away from the other people. It was going to drive him crazy until he could remember. *Well, there's one way to find out.* He turned his wheelchair around and headed in her direction. He watched her look up as he approached, then look back down at the book, lying open in her lap.

He pulled his wheelchair up close to her. "How's your brother, Larry?"

She looked up, startled. "Excuse me," she said.

Ward smiled. "I asked how your brother, Larry, was?"

She smiled back. "You must know him quite well. No one calls him Larry, not even our parents."

"I do know him quite well. In fact, my wife and I joined you and your brother at several charity events. I know this is going to sound weird, and I feel like an idiot, but I can't remember your name."

A big smile appeared on her face. "It's Amanda."

Ward's hand came up and slapped his forehead, almost knocking his hat off. "Of course, Amanda Farly, sister of Lawrence Farly,

United States Congressman from Vermont."

Amanda chuckled. "Now, I feel like an idiot. I have no idea who you are."

"I want you to know I'm very disappointed you don't recognize me. I'm Ward Tylar." Ward watched as the smile disappeared and the look of shock replaced it. Both of her hands came up to her face. She stared at him for several moments.

Ward became concerned. "It's all right, Amanda." He reached up and took one of her hands, holding it tight in his.

She finally spoke. "I can't believe it's really you. I tried to find you after the accident. Oh Ward, I'm so sorry about Jill. Larry told me you weren't expected to live. We heard you were paralyzed and in some rehabilitation hospital, then it was as if you disappeared off the face of the earth. You've changed so much. Are you okay?"

Ward patted her hand. "Yes, I'm okay. The reason you didn't know me is because I'm traveling in disguise. No beard, glasses, head shaved. The only thing that's real is this wheelchair. I hope by the time my hair grows back, I won't need this anymore." He patted the arm of his chair."

"What do the doctors say?" asked Amanda.

Ward smiled. "I have it from a very reliable source… I will walk again, probably with the aid of a cane or leg brace."

"That's wonderful news, Ward. I'm so happy for you. Are you on this flight to London?"

"Yes, I am. My daughter, Samantha, and my assistant are traveling with me. You remember my daughter?"

Amanda was surprised. "Why yes, I do. I haven't seen her for, let's see, three, four years."

"You won't recognize her, either." Ward chuckled. "Are you traveling to London on business or pleasure? If you don't mind me asking?"

"Actually…" Amanda glanced around the room, hesitating a moment before she answered, "London is only a stopover, I'll catch another flight to Greece."

"Really." Surprise sounded in Ward's voice. "Me, too. I wonder if we're on the same flight." His hand reached into his breast pocket. "I have my schedule here somewhere." As he moved around, the folder on his lap slid to the floor, spilling the contents within.

"I'll get those," Amanda said, bending over. Her hand froze as she touched the top paper. The words Tali Island glared back at her. The touch of Ward's hand on her shoulder and the sound of his voice brought her back to reality.

"Amanda, are you all right? You're white as a sheet." Ward could see her hands tremble as she tried to pick up the pages and return them to the folder.

She sat up and placed the folder on his lap, a weak smile appeared on her face. "I'll be fine. It's just that I don't care for flying. I think I need a stiff drink."

"I understand completely. My daughter's the same way." Ward glanced at his watch. "There's a lounge close by, I think I could use one, too."

Sami watched her father as he entered the lounge, the blonde lady at his side. *Please don't let her be some nosey reporter.* She glanced up at Kord. "It looks like we got back just in time."

"Really," said Kord. "In time for what? You're too young to drink."

Sami stopped and Kord did, too. "Someday I'll tell you horror stories of what my father, mother, and I went through almost every time we went somewhere. Never any privacy. Someone always taking your picture. Microphones shoved in your face. The only normal life we had is when we were on the Ranch."

Kord smiled at her, trying to understand what she was saying.

"Let's go check her out." He touched Sami's arm, leading her toward the lounge.

They arrived just as the waitress set the drinks down for her father and the lady.

Sami walked up and stood beside her father, placing her arms protectively around his shoulders.

"Samantha." Ward smiled as he looked up at his daughter. "Do you remember Amanda?"

Sami looked at Amanda for a moment, then answered, "Of course, you were a friend of my mother's."

"It's nice to see you again, Samantha. Your father told me I probably wouldn't recognize you. I didn't recognize him either. Your disguise is great."

Sami smiled at her. "Thanks. This is my father's assistant, Kord

McNamera. Kord, Amanda Farly."

They were exchanging small talk when an airline assistant approached their table. "Excuse me, Mr. Tylar, Ms. Farly, we'd like to get you both aboard before we make our first boarding announcement."

Within fifteen minutes they were all settled in their seats in the first class section. Ward and Sami in the front row, Kord behind them. Amanda was four rows back on the opposite side.

The stewardess served champagne to all of them. Two glasses later the plane was ready for takeoff.

The seat next to Amanda was vacant, and for that Amanda was grateful. She didn't feel like talking to anyone. She was still trying to sort out her plans for when she arrived in Greece. No one knew she was coming and she wanted to keep it that way. She was sure if Prince Tali found out he would keep her from seeing her son, Raul, but Raul wasn't the main reason she was going to Greece. She needed to see Kevin. Doctor Stevens had reached her, telling her about Kevin's illness. Tears stung Amanda's eyes as she remembered what Doctor Stevens had told her—he didn't know if Kevin would live or die. The words kept repeating over and over in her mind. She went back in time to the first letter she received from Doctor Stevens. Inside the envelope was another sealed envelope, containing the letter from Kevin. It had been one of the happiest days of her life. She realized that it didn't make any difference how many miles or years that separated you from someone you loved, if that love was honest and true, it remained with you. She didn't know how she was going to do it, but she wanted to be at Kevin's side for whatever time he had left.

Amanda looked out the window. The plane had taxied onto the runway and quickly gained speed. Within moments it lifted smoothly off the ground. She thought again about the papers that had fallen off Senator Tylar's lap. *Why would Ward have information on Tali Island? What was he looking for? Is that why he's going to Greece? I guess the only way I'll know the answer is to come right out and ask him, and that's exactly what I'm going to do.*

Ward held his daughter's hand as the plane took flight. "You okay?"

"I feel great. A couple glasses of champagne, it's the only way to fly. I think Katy has something to do with it, too. I mean, if we were going to crash into the ocean or on the other side of the world, she would have told us. I've decided I'm not going to be afraid to fly anymore. From now on I'll get flight information ahead of time from our very own, see into the future, little witch." Sami paused, then asked, "It was nice to see Amanda again. Were Mom and her good friends?"

Ward thought for a moment before answering. "I think, for the short time they knew each other, they were. I know your mother liked her very much."

"I wonder why she never married?"

"Actually," Ward said, "I think she was married when she was very young. It lasted several years, then she divorced him and took back her maiden name."

"Any children?" asked Sami.

Ward's other hand came up and he rubbed his fingers across his chin. "I'm not sure."

"Is she traveling to London on business or pleasure?"

"It's only a stopover. She's catching another flight."

"To where?"

"To Greece."

"Why?" Sami asked, sitting up a little straighter in her seat.

Ward started to laugh. "I don't know. Are you wearing that disguise and asking all these questions because, in reality, you're a reporter working for one of those snoop magazines?"

Sami joined in his laughter. "God, that's exactly what I sound like, but all kidding aside. Why is she going to Greece?"

Ward looked at his daughter. "I don't know. I do know something is troubling her. When I found out where she was going, I checked to see if we were on the same flight. The folder Father James gave me slid off my lap. She picked up the papers and put them back into the folder, but her hands were trembling and she turned very pale. I thought she might faint. When I asked if she was okay, she told me flying made her nervous."

"I can relate to that," Sami acknowledged.

"I think it's a little more than that," replied Ward.

"Hm-m, I think I have the solution to this problem," Sami stated. "If Amanda is on our flight, or even if she's not, we'll make arrangements for her to meet our favorite little witch, and when Katy shakes her hand, presto. She'll tell us everything we want to know." Sami looked up at her father and saw the troubled look on his face. She patted his arm. "I'm just kidding, Dad, really."

"Good, you had me worried there for a moment."

Sami turned serious. "It's just that all we've been talking or thinking about for days has been Katy and how to find her father and brother. It was nice to think about something else for a change."

"You're absolutely right, Samantha. If Amanda needs someone to talk to, why not me? It's a long flight. I've asked her to join me when they serve dinner. You don't mind sitting with Kord, do you?"

"Of course not, Dad."

When the plane finally reached its flying altitude, the captain's voice came over the speaker, welcoming everyone and informing the passengers they were free to move around the cabin, but to please keep their seatbelts on when seated.

Sami moved to the seat next to Kord, where she found him sleeping. She couldn't help but smile when she saw the cute little grin on his face. *Must be thinking about Katy.* Sami made herself comfortable, then picked up the headset and placed it on her head. She turned the knob until she found something she liked. *Ha, country music, nothing like the voice of Willie Nelson to sooth the soul.* Within minutes she, too, was sound asleep.

Amanda had just finished the letter to her daughter, Victoria, when the stewardess approached her. "Ms. Farly, Mr. Tylar would like you to join him at your convenience."

"Thank you." Amanda slipped the letter into the already addressed envelope and sealed it. She would mail it from London as promised. A smile came to her face as she thought about her daughter, the joy of her life. She opened her wallet and removed the photo of Victoria, taken only a month ago. Everyone said she looked exactly like Amanda, and even Amanda could see the resemblance. There was something, though, that Amanda saw in her daughter that reminded her of her son, Raul. *I think it's that mischievous little grin that appears every now and then. It's hard for me to believe that Raul is seventeen now. So is Kane.* She tried to picture what they looked like, but the memory of two five-year-old boys was all she saw.

Amanda slipped the photo of Victoria back into its holder and returned it to her purse, along with the envelope. She was feeling more relaxed now that she had time to think about everything. Even the papers Ward had, on information about Tali Island, didn't bother her as much. *After all he could have a dozen reasons for wanting to know about the island. Maybe he knows someone there. Or, God forbid, he actually knows my ex.* Amanda smiled. *Wouldn't that be a shock?*

She stood and made her way up the aisle. "May I join you?"

Ward smiled up at her. "By all means. Are you okay?"

Amanda sat down in the seat beside him and buckled her seatbelt. "Much better."

The stewardess offered them more champagne. "I believe a toast is in order," Ward said as he raised his glass to hers. "I checked, and we are on the same flight to Greece."

"That's wonderful." Amanda touched her glass to his. "How long will you be there?" she asked.

"My return flight is open," Ward replied. "I'm not sure, and you?"

Amanda took a sip of her champagne. "Same."

For the next half hour their conversations was casual, relaxed, and sometimes humorous.

"I don't think I've ever known anyone that was able to turn your heart inside out like Larry."

Amanda chuckled. "That's my brother, one in a million. When was the last time you saw him?" she asked.

"Let's see." Ward leaned his head back. "It's been about three years. He was master of ceremony for the Children's Hospital fundraiser. They expected to raise about one hundred thousand and, if I remember correctly, they doubled that, thanks to Larry. You were there with some gentleman. Are you still seeing him?"

"We go to dinner once in awhile, nothing serious."

"Is there anyone special in your life," Ward asked. He could tell by the way she acted it was not a subject she wanted to talk about. "I'm sorry, Amanda, I didn't mean to pry. If you'd like to talk, it won't go any further then here."

Amanda looked at him, then smiled. "I'll tell you what, Ward. I'll tell you my deep, dark secrets if you tell me yours."

Ward smiled back. "I don't know, I have so many. I don't think we have nearly enough time."

The stewardess stopped to talk to them. "I'll be serving dinner in about half an hour. Can I get you both another glass of champagne?"

"I'd like another one. How about you, Amanda?"

"Yes, I'd like another one, too."

They were silent until the new glasses of champagne were placed in the holders by their seats.

"Well, is there someone special in your life?" Ward asked.

Amanda really did want to talk to someone. *Why not Ward? We'll probably never see each other again once we land in Greece.* "As a matter of fact, there is. That's why I'm on this flight. I'm on my way to see him. His health has taken a turn for the worst. The doctor's not sure what's going to happen."

Ward could hear the sadness in her voice. "I'm sorry, Amanda. Does he live in Greece?"

"He's in the hospital in Athens. I haven't seen him for a long time. Years, actually. We've been writing to each other." Amanda paused and took a deep breath, then continued. "We love each other very much. I wanted him to come to the States, but he has a son he's raising. His wife died and, because of uncontrollable circumstances, it was impossible for them to leave Greece. Now, what about you? Is there someone special in your life?"

Ward rubbed his hand across the stubbles of hair growth on his head.

"I was feeling guilty about my feelings toward this woman. It had only been about eighteen months since my wife, Jill, died and the attraction happened so unexpectedly." Ward looked at Amanda. "Do you know anything about the DeValladero family?"

Amanda sat up straight. The look of sadness disappeared from her face. "You're talking about *THE* DeValladero's, the crime family?"

Ward chuckled. "That's the one. How much do you know?"

Amanda settled back down. "Well, let's see, I know the father, Vincent, died in prison, and the son, Victor's, wife died a few years ago in a boating accident. Then Victor was killed just recently. His dead wife's sister was arrested for his murder, but was released when Victor's new wife and bodyguard were arrested. What do they have to do with this new attraction in your life?"

"Oh, where do I begin?" Ward reached over and touched her hand. "You will keep what I tell you in strict confidence?"

"I promise. I can't wait to hear this."

"Okay." Ward smiled at her. "I promise to keep your secrets confidential, too. When Victor's sister in-law, Stacy, was arrested I went to Wyoming with, I'll just call them my team, to see if we could be of any help to the police department."

"You were quite involved over the years, trying to put the DeValladero family in prison. Weren't you?" asked Amanda.

"Yes, but we never had any luck until we got our big break from Victor's first wife, Jennifer."

"The one killed in the boating accident?"

"Yes, well, kind of killed."

The stewardess approached. "Dinner is served."

"I guess, I'll have to keep you in suspense for a while," Ward replied.

"Oh, I don't know if I can stand it."

"Stand what?" Sami asked as she poked her head between Ward's and Amanda's seat, with a big grin on her face.

Amanda laughed. "Stand to eat all this food when I've had all this champagne to drink."

An hour later, Sami reached over and touched her father's shoulder. "I'm going to read for a while, Dad. Try to get some rest."

Ward patted the top of her hand. "I will, sweetie."

Sami opened her carry-on bag, lifting out the novel she had purchased at the gift store. She glanced at Kord just as he was yawning. He smiled at her. "Wake me if your father needs me."

"I will." Sami replied.

"You and your daughter seem very close."

"We are," Ward answered. "We were always close. It was hard for both of us after Jill died. Then a couple months ago, I almost lost Samantha."

"My God. What happened?" asked Amanda.

"We were supposed to meet in Denver. Did you read about the train accident they had in Colorado?" Ward asked.

"Yes, I did read about that."

"Well, Samantha was supposed to be on that train, but her best friend, Katy, and Katy's aunt were driving into Denver and Katy talked Samantha into riding with them. It's always hard to lose some-one you love, but to lose a child. I don't think I could handle that. Do you have any children, Amanda?" Ward could swear he saw a flash of sadness in her eyes, but it was replaced quickly by a warm smile.

"Yes, I do. We'll talk about that later. I want to hear more about the DeValladero family."

Ward chuckled, then continued his story. "Well, like I was telling you, we knew the DeValladeros were responsible for several murders. We just couldn't find enough evidence to convict them until Jennifer overhead her husband, Victor, and her father in-law, Vincent, planning the murder of this woman. The FBI, with the help of Jennifer and the woman, set up video and recording equipment in Victor's hotel suite and were able to get enough evidence to arrest them. In the meantime, the FBI staged Jennifer's boating accident. They put her in the Witness Protection Program, changed her name, and shipped her off, pregnant, to God only knows where."

"She was pregnant?" Amanda asked, sounding surprised.

"Yes. Of course, she didn't realize it at the time, but about eight months later she had a son."

"Then what happened?" asked Amanda.

"Her husband, Victor, was released from jail because his father con-fessed and told the judge his son didn't have anything to do with any of the murders. Victor found out there was a possibility his wife was still alive, so he had some of his friends bug Jennifer's family's homes and work places. It didn't do any good because her family believed she was dead."

"Did Victor know about his son?"

"No." Ward shook his head. "And thank God he didn't. He was a cold-blooded killer. He wouldn't have hesitated one minute to kill Jennifer and raise his son as a DeValladero."

Amanda spoke almost in a whisper. "It's amazing how much Jennifer's and my life resemble each other."

Now it was Ward's turn to sound surprised. "Why is that?"

"Sorry, I was thinking out loud."

Ward studied her for a minute, then asked, "Why would you think Jennifer's and your life have similarities?"

Amanda looked at him. "I'll tell you, but first I need to ask you something."

"Anything," Ward replied.

"Why are you going to Greece and why the interest in Tali Island?"

Now Ward was surprised. "How did you know about Tali Island? Oh, right, the papers from my folder."

"I didn't mean to pry," Amanda said, apologizing. "The only thing I did see was Tali Island, and it caught my attention. Not too many people even know the island exists."

"That's true," Ward acknowledged. "I certainty didn't until this past week when Mt. Vicco erupted."

*Of course, I feel like such a fool. I'm so paranoid, what was I thinking.* Amanda confessed, "I just wondered why someone like you had taken an interest in the island. Maybe you could answer the first question. Why are you going to Greece?"

"Would you believe me if I told you a vacation?"

"Is that why?" she asked.

Ward looked at her. "No, that's not the reason."

*Maybe I'm not a fool.* "Is that one of your dark secrets you're not going to share with me?"

Ward shook his head. "No, I'll tell you. After all, you did tell me why you were going to Greece." Ward paused. He was getting tired. It had been a long day. No nap or exercise, plus the loss of hours, was starting to give him jet lag. "Remember Samantha's best friend, Katy, I was telling you about?"

Amanda nodded her head.

Ward continued. "Well, Katy's mother died when she was very young. Katy grew up thinking she had no family. On her last birthday she was given a box that her mother left for her, containing letters she had written to Katy. The information in those letters revealed that she had a twin brother and that her father and brother might still be alive. Katy believes her father is ill, like your friend. So we're going to see if we can find them. Katy's parents traveled around from Greece to Spain to Italy and back to Greece. Without a trace, Katy's father and brother disappeared. So that's why we're going to Greece."

"I wish you all the luck in the world," Amanda said.

"Thanks. We have a few good leads."

"I'm going to return to my own seat and get some rest. You look tired, too, Ward. Is there anything I can get you before I leave?" Amanda asked.

"No thanks," he answered. "I think some sleep is what I need, too. Thanks for the company. If you don't have any plans for the layover in London, we'd like you to join us."

"Thanks. Goodnight, Ward."

"Goodnight, Amanda."

She started to leave, then turned back toward him. "Ward, it's all right to tell Samantha, if she asks, why I'm going to Greece."

Ward smiled up at her. "Thanks."

After Amanda left, Ward turned to check on Samantha. She was sound asleep, her headset still on her head. The book she'd been reading lay open in her lap. *My sweet little angel. Guess I'll try to get some sleep, too.* Ward made himself as comfortable as he could, then closed his eyes. His mind kept going over the conversation he'd just had with Amanda. *I wonder what it was about Jennifer's life that reminded Amanda of her own. It definitely must have something to do with her ex-husband, and the similarity of why we're both going to Greece. She's going to visit a sick man—I'm going to look for a sick man. Her sick man has a son—my sick man has a son. Wouldn't that be a kick in the ass, if all along, we're talking about the same sick man and his son.* Ward smiled to himself. *No way. It's impossible.* Ward tried to remember if she had mentioned a name. *No, I'm sure she didn't. I know I didn't. Maybe I should just casually drop the name Kevin and see what reaction I get from her. Now I'm really being ridiculous. I'd better get some sleep before I go completely crazy.*

Amanda sat down. She let her mind drift back over the conversation she had with Ward. She thought about Jennifer and the similarities in their lives. *Her husband was a murderer; my ex-husband could be one. He had threatened to kill Kevin if he tried to escape the island. Jennifer has a son her husband didn't know exists—I have a daughter—who—my ex-husband knows nothing about. Would he kill me and take our daughter to live with him on Tali Island? I don't think he would kill me, but I'm positive he would try to take our daughter.* Fear passed through Amanda's body, followed by a rush of cold chills. *No, I will never let that happen.*

Amanda thought about the reason Ward was traveling to Greece. *Wouldn't it be something if all along we were talking about the same man and his son?* Amanda chuckled to herself. *There's no possible way on earth that could be true. First of all Kevin never mentioned having a daughter.* She chuckled again. *Kane has a twin sister? I am being ridiculous and, if this Katy is Samantha's best friend, I'm sure they must be about the same age, and Samantha's at least twenty. Oh, why am I even thinking about such nonsense. I have other things on my mind a lot more important.* Amanda opened her wallet and took out a photo, but this time it wasn't of her daughter, Victoria. It was the photo of Kevin with her son, Raul, on one side and his son, Kane, on the other, taken over twelve years ago. *This is what's important, finding some way to help Kevin.* Amanda put the photo back into her wallet. She closed her eyes. She could see Kevin's face so clearly and his eyes, his beautiful eyes. Amanda fell asleep, remembering again that special night that she and Kevin had spent together so many years ago.

# Chapter 18
## KANE
## THE HOSPITAL

Yorky had been sitting at the nurse's station about ten minutes when the nurse finally showed up. "I hope you don't mind me sitting in your chair, I'm waiting for a phone call."

She smiled at him. "No problem. I'm only here to check on my patient, then I'll be gone again. I'm helping out in another station."

"Before you go, young Kane needs his clothes. Could you get them for him?"

"I'm sorry, I can't. I was given strict orders not to."

Yorky glared at her. "That's changed, I'll take the responsibility. Please get them before you leave."

She walked over to one of the empty rooms and opened the closet door, removing both Kevin's and Kane's clothes. She returned, handing them to him.

He smiled sweetly at her. "Thank you. No one needs to know you did this."

"I would appreciate that." She turned to leave when the phone rang.

Yorky reached for it. "I'm sure it's for me," he said, picking up the receiver. "Yorky speaking."

"Anything new?" Zoric asked.

"No, sir. Kane's in with his father. No change there, either. His father's still unconscious."

"Tell Kane I'm flying to the island to pick up Prince Tali and Raul, then we'll come by the hospital."

"I'll tell him, sir." Yorky heard the click as Zoric hung up the phone. He looked at his watch. *Three hours before my replacement gets here.*

Kane was sitting by his father's bed when Yorky entered the room. "Here's the clothes you requested. I'll hang them in the closet."

"Thank you, Yorky."

"If you need anything else, I'll be right outside your door."

Kane picked up his father's hand. "It's time to come back to me, Dad. I need you. There's something going on with Mani's brother.

He set three bombs. I know where two of them are, but the third one... I haven't a clue. I really could use your help on this one. *And more important, Katy's here somewhere.*

## KATY
## THE PARK

They were about a block from the park when Sister Elizabeth spoke. "Ben, Katy, let's stop here for a minute. Remember, Katy, I want you to let Ben and me check things out. If we have to tell anyone who we are, you're my niece, Ben is your uncle and my brother."

Katy smiled at her. "Aunt Liz, I think you're worrying too much. We have to take a few risks, or this whole trip is wasted. I know Kane is in this city somewhere. This is just a place to start. One place I really want to see is the church where my parents met. Tomorrow Ward and Sami will be here with more information from Father James. Then we need to check out this man, Zoric Tali, that we saw on the television. We have to find out if, in fact, he knows my father and brother or if it's just a feeling I had. Hopefully, he'll be here tonight. If not, we'll come back in the morning. Remember. I'm not going to do anything if you don't approve."

"You're right, Katy. Let's go."

Zoric was standing by the platform talking to J.J. "Where the hell is that pilot?"

"We'll find him. I would never have sent him home, Zoric, if I knew we needed him tonight."

"It's not your fault, J.J. We've got several people trying to locate him. I'm sure he'll show up any minute. I have to be truthful with you, this whole thing frightens the hell out of me. Kane still doesn't know where that third bomb is and, if I know my brother, he's already taken care of Mani's brother."

Sister Elizabeth spotted the man she saw on television when they first entered the park. "I'm sure that's him. What do you two think?"

Katy agreed with her. Ben wasn't so sure. "Maybe it's the other brother."

"No, I'm pretty sure it's him. Katy, you wait here with Ben."

Sister walked toward the platform, saying hello to several people as she worked her way through the small crowd that started to form. The man had his back toward her. She reached out and touched his shoulder. "Excuse me, Mr. Tali?"

Zoric turned. When he saw the nun standing there, the frown left his face and was replaced by a soft smile. "Yes, can I help you?" Zoric always appreciated looking at a beautiful woman, even if she was a nun.

Sister smiled fondly at him. "I was wondering if there was anything I could do to help?"

"That's very nice of you, but unless you can fly a helicopter, I don't think there is."

The remark startled her, and she couldn't help but laugh. "You probably won't believe this, but you're looking at one of the best chopper pilots around, registered, certified, and licensed, plus I have a terrific co-pilot." She pointed her thumb upward, letting her eyes roll toward the sky.

Zoric stood there and stared at her. For the first time in his life he was speechless.

"You don't have a problem flying with a woman pilot, do you?"

"I've never had the privilege. I think I could handle it, though."

He studied her for a moment. "You are serious, aren't you?"

"Absolutely."

A big grin appeared on his face. "Look at me. Here I stand, asking a nun if she's telling the truth. You'll have to forgive me, Sister. It's been a long day."

For reasons she couldn't understand, Elizabeth felt compassion for this man. The smile left her face. "I'm sure this past week has been hell for you. If you feel uncomfortable with me being a woman, my brother is here with me. He too, is a licensed pilot."

Zoric looked at her. "I think you'll do fine."

"How long will we be gone?"

"Probably an hour."

"I'll let my brother know. Be right back."

Zoric watched her walk away. He turned toward J.J. "Now, that is one beautiful woman."

J.J. nodded his head in agreement.

Sister explained to Katy and Ben what was happening. "I should be back in an hour. Do you want to wait here?"

"I think we'll go back to the hotel," Ben said, "and get the information on where this church Katy wants to visit is located. Are you sure you don't want me to fly the chopper?"

Sister could hear the concern in Ben's voice. "I'm sure. Don't worry, he seems like a nice man. Shall we meet back here?"

"I guess these are the risks Katy was talking about. Be careful."

"I will." She turned and walked back toward Zoric. "Are you ready, Mr. Tali?"

"Would it be all right for you to call me by my first name, Zoric?"

"Zoric, I'm Sister Elizabeth." She held out her hand.

"And this," said Zoric, "is J.J. He'll drive us to the helicopter."

"Is it far away?" she asked.

"No, it isn't."

They had only driven about two blocks when J.J. pulled the limo onto a large field. He stopped about ten feet from the chopper and waited for them to board. "I'll see you at the hospital," he said, then drove away.

Sister settled herself into the pilot's seat and put on her headgear. Zoric sat next to her. She spent the first few minutes checking everything, then started to switch on buttons. Within seconds the chopper was ready for take-off.

"I'll handle the radio," Zoric informed her, then notified the local airport about their destination—Tali Island. He gave her directions as she lifted the chopper off the ground. Twenty minutes later he told her where to land. She set the helicopter down with total ease, then turned everything off.

She looked over at Zoric, who sat there with a big grin on his face. "You are an excellent pilot," he complimented her.

"Thank you."

"Please, wait here. We'll be leaving right away with two more passengers, my brother, Prince Tali, and his son, Raul."

Zoric started walking toward the estate stables when he heard a car coming from the direction of the Tali Jungle. He waited until it pulled up beside him and stopped. His brother and nephew got out.

"Why are you here?" Prince Tali asked.

"You haven't heard the message from Kane, I take it."

"No. What's happened?"

"It's what's about to happen." Zoric explained, telling them everything.

"Kane is still trying to figure out where the third bomb is. Did Mani's brother say anything?"

"No, but I didn't ask him either. Who's flying the chopper?"

Zoric smiled. "An excellent female pilot. I'll explain later. Right now, we need to get the hell out of here."

They boarded the chopper. Zoric introduced them to Sister Elizabeth. Within minutes she had the chopper in the air and headed back toward the mainland, when they heard the explosion. Zoric asked her to circle back. They all looked down, in shock, at the car on fire that Prince Tali and Raul had just occupied.

"Let's get out of here," said Zoric. "Sister, do you think you could land this on the rooftop of the hospital. They have a landing pad available?"

"Yes. I can do that." *I wonder why Katy didn't know about that car exploding. Maybe I'm expecting too much from her, or maybe it's time for her to meet a member of the Tali family. No, not unless absolutely necessary.*

She set the chopper down smoothly and shut off everything. She looked at her passengers. "Is everyone all right?"

"We'll be fine," Prince Tali replied as he opened his door. He waited until everyone was off, then walked over and placed his hand on Sister Elizabeth's shoulder. "Zoric said you were an excellent pilot. Thank you for getting us here safely. There is one more thing. For the safety of my family, I ask that you keep what you saw this evening to yourself. I know who was responsible and it has been taken care of."

"You have my word. My family and I will only be staying in your city for a day or two, then we'll go back home. If there's anything I can do, please let me know. If I don't see you again, I wish your family well."

Prince Tali smiled at her and, without saying another word, turned to enter the hospital.

Sister looked over at Raul, who was standing and staring into space. She walked over to him. "Are you okay, Raul?"

He forced a smile and looked at her. "Besides being a failure to my father, I'm terrific."

Sister glanced over at Zoric, who looked puzzled by Raul's remark. She took Raul's hand. "You seem like a very nice young man. We can't always do things just to please someone else. You're at a time in life where the decisions you make will turn you into the man you'll soon become."

"You sound like my best friend. He's here in the hospital with his father, who's not doing well."

"I'm sorry to hear that. I'll pray for him."

Zoric walked up to them. "Sister, come with me. We'll get J.J. to drive you back to the park or anyplace else you'd like to go."

"Thank you."

The three of them entered the hospital and took the elevator down to the third floor, where the door opened into to a small lounge area.

"Raul, why don't you go ahead. Tell J.J. to meet me here."

"Okay, Uncle Zoric. It was nice meeting you, Sister Elizabeth. I hope we see each other again before you leave."

"I hope so, too." She watched him walk away down the hall to where a man was sitting in a chair. The man stood when Raul approached and opened the door, giving Raul access into the room. Sister turned back toward Zoric. "He's a nice, good-looking, young man. Do you have any children?"

"No, but I haven't given up hope. You said you were here with your family. Anyone else beside your brother?"

Sister knew he was just making small talk until J.J. arrived. "Yes, my niece is with us."

"Vacationing?"

"Business. I wish we could spend more time. Maybe sometime in the future."

"If you do return, please call." Zoric reached for his wallet and removed a card.

Raul told Kane and J.J. what happened and about the nun who flew the chopper. "She's good and real pretty, much better than that man pilot we have."

"Is she still here?" asked Kane.

"She's waiting for J.J. Zoric wants him to drive her wherever she

214

needs to go."

"I guess I better get down there before Zoric wonders where I am."

Kane followed him to the door and peeked out. The nun was standing with her back toward him. He got the strangest feeling that he knew her. *It probably has something to do with the fact my mother wanted to be a nun.* He watched as J.J. led her to the elevator. Within seconds, she was gone.

Zoric walked toward him. "How's your father doing?" he asked.

"Same."

Zoric looked around the room. "Where's my brother?"

"Haven't seen him," replied Kane.

Yorky spoke up. "He was here about ten or fifteen minutes ago, said he was going to see Doctor Stevens." *And no, he didn't ask about young Kane or his father.* Yorky was beginning to dislike Prince Tali more and more.

"I saw the nun you were talking to," said Kane. "I wish you would have let her come down here and say a prayer for my father. He would have liked that."

"Sorry, Kane," Zoric said, an expression of regret on his face. "If she comes back, I'll definitely see that she stops by."

Yorky interrupted. "Zoric, since you're here, I'd like to go get a cup of coffee. Can I bring anyone anything?"

"When is your replacement expected?" asked Zoric.

Yorky looked at his watch. "Should be here in about an hour."

"Why don't you go ahead and leave. I'm sure you'd like to be with your family tonight."

"Yes, I would. See you tomorrow." Yorky closed the door behind him when he left.

Zoric looked at Raul. He could tell there was something deeply troubling his nephew. "Want to talk about what happened today? I heard your conversation with Sister Elizabeth. Maybe we can help."

Raul looked at Zoric, then at Kane. "You'll both think I'm a real sissy chicken if I tell you. Anyway, Kane probably already knows. That's his job. Isn't it, Uncle Zoric?"

"You'll have to ask him."

Raul looked at Kane. "Well?"

Kane came over and stood by his friend. "I'm afraid I've let you down. I don't know what happened. I've been so worried about where that third bomb is, I haven't thought much about anything else. So why don't you tell me what happened." Kane sat down on his bed and motioned for Raul to sit by him. Zoric took a chair close by.

Raul started, slowly telling about leaving the hospital with Mani's brother tied up in the back seat. "He seemed real nervous until we got to the island and headed for Tali Jungle. We pulled him out of the car. The guy didn't even resist, he just stared at my father." Raul continued, telling them what happened next. "Then my father took a gun from the glove compartment of the car and put it in my hand. He went over and ripped the tape off the guy's mouth and told him, "You're going to die for what you did to my son, but not like your brothers did... I tortured them... It was a slow death. I don't have time to give you the same luxury.'

"All the man said was, 'Take your time, he wasn't in any hurry. My father was going to die before the week was over, no matter what happened to him.' My father looked at me. I stood there, pointing the gun at the man's heart." Raul's voice trembled. "I couldn't do it. No matter how much I wanted to, I couldn't take his life. I handed the gun to my father and saw the disappointment in his eyes. I fell to my knees and cried. It was only a few minutes before I heard the gunshot My father told me that the least I could do was to help him get rid of the body. We dragged it over to a place that looked like a big hole filled with sand. We picked up the body and threw it in. It was quicksand. Within minutes, the body disappeared. We got into the car and drove back to the Estate. That's when we saw you..." He looked toward Zoric. "...there with the chopper." Raul took a deep breath. "You know the rest."

Kane waited for Zoric to say something but nothing happened. Was he disappointed in Raul, too. Kane couldn't tell. He said, "I'm proud of you, my friend. I couldn't have done it either. I'm not saying the man shouldn't have been punished in some way, but not with his life."

"What if they had succeeded and Raul was dead?" Zoric asked, disgust sounding in his voice.

"I probably would have killed him myself, but that didn't happen." Kane stood. "No man should put a gun in his son's hand and expect him to kill someone in cold blood."

Zoric stood there, glaring at Kane. He wanted to defend his brother, but deep down inside he knew Kane was right. If Raul's father, or

216

even he himself, wanted this man dead, so be it, but it never should have been the responsibility of a seventeen-year-old innocent boy like Raul.

Zoric's voice softened. "Kane's right, Raul. I'm glad you didn't do it, too. Your father will come around in a few days."

Raul breathed a sigh of relief. "Thanks. What happens now?"

"I need to go for a walk in the fresh air," Kane said, moving toward the closet. "Let me put my clothes on."

"When did you get your clothes back?" asked Raul.

"They've been hanging in a closet all along. Give me five minutes." Kane went into the bathroom and closed the door.

Zoric touched Raul's shoulder, "I'll let the nurse know we'll be leaving for a while. I want her to check on Kevin while we're gone."

Prince Tali walked into Doctor Stevens' office without knocking. "I hope you have something strong to drink, besides coffee."

Doctor Stevens looked up from the book he was reading. "As a matter of fact, I do." He opened the bottom desk drawer and took out a bottle of Scotch he kept there, along with two glasses. "I'm glad you stopped by. I finally heard back on Kevin's tests I sent to the States. It's good news." Doctor Stevens waited for Prince Tali to finish his drink, then poured him another one. "There's an eighty-percent chance of complete recovery on Kevin's part, if we can find a compatible donor and do a bone marrow transplant, which is a relatively new operation for this procedure. The doctor explained, as best he could, how it worked. "I tested Kane. He doesn't match. I'd like to see if there's anyone out there that does. I'll start testing people right away."

Prince Tali finished his drink and set the glass on the desk. They heard a soft knock on the door.

"Come in."

Yorky opened the door. "Sorry to bother you, Doctor Stevens. I wanted to let you know I'm leaving. I'll see you early in the morning."

Prince Tali stood. "Who's with Kevin?"

"Zoric."

"I'll need you to drop me off at my apartment," Prince Tali said as he walked toward him. He turned when he got to the door. "I'll think

217

about what you told me and let you know my decision sometime tomorrow afternoon." He walked out of the room. "Let's go," he said in a voice of authority.

Yorky noticed the puzzled look on the doctor's face when he glanced his way before closing the door.

The doctor sat there, thinking about Prince Tali's remark. *Unbelievable, that man actually thinks he owns Kevin and his son. They truly are prisoners.*

# Chapter 19
## THE PARK

Katy stood next to Ben. They watched as Sister Elizabeth was driven away in the limo.

"You're sure she's going to be all right?"

Katy chuckled, trying to relieve some of the tension. "I think you mean to say, 'are they going to be all right'. Remember, we are talking about Sister Elizabeth."

"Of course. What was I thinking." Ben felt better. He smiled at Katy. "What do you say we go back to the hotel. See if we can find out how to get to that church where your parents met."

"Okay, but let's sit here for a few minutes." Katy pointed to an empty bench. She sat down, Ben beside her. "What time do we pick up Sami and Ward tomorrow?"

"One fifteen."

"Will you do me a favor, Ben?"

*Oh, oh, what now?* "If I can."

"Cut me a little slack. Talk to Aunt Liz. I know I had a feeling when I saw that man, Zoric Tali, on television. I felt he knew my father and brother, but if I don't meet him—you know touch him—we might not find out anything. However if my feeling isn't right we could be wasting valuable time. Am I making sense?"

*Damn, she's right.* "I'll talk to her."

"Thanks. I knew I could count on you."

They both watched in silence as the helicopter, in the distance, sliced through the air, headed in the direction of Tali Island. When it was out of sight, Katy turned toward Ben. "It looks like Aunt Liz sees something on fire. From a distance," she added right away. "It's okay, Ben. Let's go get that address and the car, then we'll come back here and wait for her, so she can go with us."

An hour later they returned. They didn't have to wait long before the limo drove up and Sister Elizabeth got out, waving to the driver as he drove away.

"I guess I won't be meeting the famous Zoric Tali tonight."

Ben heard disappointment in Katy's voice. "The night's not over yet. Is it?

Katy smiled. "You're right. It's only just begun."

As they drove to the church, Sister told them everything that happened. "They seem like a nice family. I hope no harm comes to them."

"Maybe." Katy glanced at Ben, then back at Sister. "If I met them, I'd be able to help."

"Don't even think it," Sister blurted out.

Ben pulled the car to a stop in front of the church. "Here we are. What now, Katy?"

"I want to walk around the grounds first, then go inside."

"Okay. Sister and I won't be far behind, in case you need us."

Katy got out of the car and closed the door. She walked around the front of the church and knew she had been there before. With her mind completely focused on her father, she started up the stairs. Her hand moved along the banister. About a third of the way up, she stopped and her body, as if frozen in time, knew her father had stood in this same place. *Father, I know you're here somewhere. Please try to help me find you. Father, can you hear me. It's Katy. Please answer me, Father, please."*

## HOSPITAL

Kevin's eyes popped opened. He lay there, his body not able to move. The dim light in the far corner cast shadows around the room. *Where am I? Katy, are you here?* He raised his head up from the pillow and noticed the tubes attached to his arms. *I'm in the hospital, but why? What happened?* He lay his head back down. *Was Katy here in this room or was it my imagination? No. She's here somewhere.*

Kevin turned his head from side to side, his eyes surveying the room. He noticed the pajamas, laying at the end of the unmade bed next to his. *My son has been here with me. He spent the night—or was it two nights? How long have I been here?* He turned his head to the other side. He felt contentment as he looked at his belt buckle. *I see you've been here with me too, Meg.* He turned his head back when the sound of voices came from outside his room. He closed his eyes and listened. A man and woman entered. He recognized the male voice as Doctor Stevens', who was talking to a nurse. Kevin heard more voices coming down the hall, his son, Kane, Raul's, and

Zoric's.

"Hi, Dad. I'm home."

It took everything Kevin had to control the laughter that wanted to escape from inside him.

"Have you received the results back from the tests yet?" asked Kane.

The doctor smiled. "Yes, as a matter of fact I have, and it's good news."

Doctor Stevens explained to them about the bone marrow transplant.

Kane sat down on his bed. "Are you sure I'm not a match. Maybe you should test me again."

"I did check it, three times. We'll find a match. Now that we know what we're looking for, it's much easier."

"I think this is great news," Zoric butted in. "Hell, if we have to, we'll test everyone before we let them back on the island. Raul and I will be at the front of the line, I promise you."

"I'll save everyone the trouble. I'll be the perfect match." Raul put his hands on his hips and swelled up his chest. "You can call me Macho Match."

After the laughter died down, Kane stood up. "Now that that is settled, I need something to eat. Who wants to go with me to the cafeteria?"

"Why don't you and Raul go? I'll join you as soon as the other guard gets here." Zoric glanced at his watch. "Should be anytime now."

After the boys left, Doctor Stevens told Zoric about his visit with Prince Tali. "Your brother wasn't as enthusiastic as you. He told me he'd let me know his decision sometime tomorrow afternoon." The Doctor walked over to Kevin's bed. "Might as well check to see how he's doing while I'm here. I hear you're moving some of the residents back on the island tomorrow."

"Maybe, or we might have to wait till Saturday."

They heard the knock on the door. "Mr. Tali... "

Zoric turned. "Ali, what are you doing here?"

"I need to talk to you. I'm taking Yorky's place until one of the other guards can get here."

"I was just leaving," said Doctor Stevens. "I'll go down, see how the boys are doing."

Kevin had laid very still while the doctor checked him. He didn't want anyone except Kane to know he had gained consciousness. *My God, I've been like this for over three days. That was the darkness I couldn't explain. And what about Katy? She called out to me. I know she did, that's what woke me. She's here in the city somewhere. I must find her—or help her to find me.*

"What did you need to talk to me about?" Zoric asked Ali, after Doctor Stevens had left.

"We found another bomb."

"Where?"

"Under Prince Tali's bed. It was set to go off at three in the morning. It's been dismantled and destroyed. We've gone over every inch of the estate, that was the only one we found."

"Damn. There's still one out there somewhere." Zoric paced the room. "All of the vehicles have been checked?"

"Yes, sir. Two or three times." They both walked toward the door. "I'll stay until one of the other guards get here. If you want I'll check the cars again."

"I don't think that's necessary. It looks like this guy spread them around. Prince Tali is who he's after. He figured if he didn't get him in his car he would in his bed. There's no way the guy could have broken into my brother's apartment or office. That pretty much leaves the island, and we don't know when the bomb's set to go off. It could be tonight, tomorrow, or next week."

Kevin heard the door close when the two men left the room. He slowly opened his eyes. *Ah, alone at last. It sounds like there's a lot going on, but all I'm going to think about is Katy.* He sat up very slowly and waited for the dizziness to pass, then swung his legs over the side of the bed. He could feel a tingling sensation in his toes as the blood flowed through them. He wanted to stand, but couldn't because of all the tubes attached to his body. The catheter was the one that worried him most. *Will I be able to disconnect it without causing problems—like infection.* He lay back down. *I better wait for Kane.* He closed his eyes and thought of Katy. *I'm here, Katy. The closer you get, the more you'll feel my presence. Concentrate Katy, follow your instinct.*

Zoric sat with Raul and Kane while they finished their dinner. "Did you get enough to eat?"

"I'm still hungry," said Kane. "I think I'll take a couple of sandwiches back to my room for later. Do you know who's on guard duty tonight? I hope it's not the one that snores all night. Between him and the nurse coming in every couple of hours, it's a wonder I get any sleep at all. That's probably why I don't know where that third little present's at."

Zoric could tell by Kane's voice that the boy was exhausted. *No wonder, not knowing if his father is going to be okay, all this stuff with Mani's brother, constant guards watching his every move.* "It's the same guard that usually replaces Yorky. I'll have him move across the hall and I'll tell the nurse to check on Kevin at ten tonight, then at three, and seven in the morning."

"Thanks, Zoric." Kane stood. "See you tomorrow, Macho Match."


Kane walked down the hall toward the guard stationed at his father's room. He offered him one of his sandwiches, but the guard declined. "Zoric is going to let you move your chair across the hall. You could probably open the door to that room and watch television, if you want. But check with Zoric first." Kane entered his room, closing the door behind him.

He set his food on the dresser by his bed. "Hi, Dad. Well, you slept through another exciting day." He kept talking as he walked around the room. He glanced at his father. When he saw him laying there with his eyes open and a big grin on his face, Kane jumped back. His hand went to his heart.

Kevin raised his arm, bringing his finger to his mouth, then pointing toward the buckle to remind Kane of the listening device.

Kane walked over, leaned down and hugged his father. Then he took the belt buckle into the bathroom and placed it in the tub, covering it with towels. He pulled the shower door shut and walked out, closing the door and returning to his father's side.

Kane whispered. "Thank God, when?"

"About two hours ago. Katy's here."

"I know, but how do we find her?"

"We'll find a way, but first we have to find some way of getting out of here."

"There's a guard outside the door, and the nurse will be in to check on you at ten, then three and seven. It's eight-thirty now. Can you wait till ten?"

"Yes. You better put the belt back."

Kane did as he was told. "I don't know why I keep talking to you, Dad, but the doctor tells me there's a good chance you can hear me. So I'm going to tell you again everything that's happened since we got here. We might as well exercise your legs, too."

He started about when they first arrived at the hospital on Monday, when Kevin had an appointment with Doctor Stevens, and ended with dinner that evening with Raul in the cafeteria.

Kevin listened to every word, finding it hard to believe all that had happened without his knowing any of it. The pride and love Kevin felt for his son was overwhelming. He knew something else, too. They couldn't be prisoners any longer. No matter what happened, even if it cost him his life, it was time to rescue his son from the clutches of Prince Tali.

Kane stood and walked around the room. "I don't know why I'm so wound up tonight. I think I'll call Doctor Stevens and see if he can give me something to help me get a good night's sleep. I could sure use one." Kane picked up his tablet and wrote; *Maybe I can find a way to give the medication to the guard, so he can have a good nights sleep, too.*

Kevin nodded his head.


The guard turned when he heard the door open. He had put his chair inside the room and was watching television. "You need something?"

Kane walked over to him. "Could you find Doctor Stevens? Tell him I need to see him." Kane turned, went back into his room and closed the door before the guard could ask any questions. He walked over to the dresser where the radio was. "Maybe I should turn on some soft music for you. I know how much you like it."

It only seemed like minutes before they heard a knock on the door and Doctor Stevens entered. "Is everything all right, Kane?"

"I don't know if it's all right, but everything is the same. I was wondering if you might have something to help me sleep." Kane picked up the tablet and wrote; *Please don't say anything, we need your help.'*

A smile came to the doctor's face. "I think I could handle that." He walked over to the hand Kevin extended to him and took it firmly in his. "I might as well check your father while I'm here."

"I exercised his legs already, so the nurse won't have to do it," Kane said.

"Good. I'll let her know."

"Zoric was going to tell her to check on my father at ten, three, and seven."

The doctor looked at his watch, nine-forty-five. Kane handed him the tablet again. It read; *The guard could use some sleep, too. We need help with the tubes.*

"Your father's the same, no change. I'll be back in a few minutes."

He closed the door and walked across the hall. He recognized the guard from before. "I'm going to get some coffee. Can I bring you some, or a soda, scotch?"

The guard smiled. "Tempting as the scotch sounds, I better not. Coffee is okay, sugar, no cream."

"I'll be back in about twenty minutes."

The doctor entered his office. He put what supplies he needed into his medical bag and waited. He didn't want to put the sleeping pills in the guard's coffee until the last minute. *I wonder what they've got planned? How are they going to escape without anyone seeing them? Where will they go?* He opened his desk drawer, took out the extra key to his apartment and wrote his address down on a piece of paper. He took some money out of his wallet and rolled it up with the key in the piece of paper. He placed it in his medical bag and glanced at his watch, ten fifteen. *The nurse should be finished by now.* He poured two cups of coffee, dropping two tablets into the one with sugar. He put cream in his, so he'd be able to tell them apart. He handed the guard his coffee.

"Thanks, Doctor Stevens. I hear you're operating on Yorky's boy tomorrow. I hope everything goes okay."

"It will. The surgery is at six in the morning, so I'll be staying here at the hospital tonight. If you need me for anything, call my office."

"I'll do that. Thanks again for the coffee."

Doctor Stevens knocked on Kevin's door before entering. "Has the nurse been here?"

225

"You just missed her," Kane informed him. "I told her she didn't need to come back till morning, but if she had to, it was okay."

"Here, this should help you sleep." The doctor opened his bag and handed Kane the rolled up piece of paper. "This is for later in case you need it."

Kane smiled and put it in his pocket. "Maybe you could help me turn Dad before you leave."

"Sure." The doctor removed all the tubes attached to Kevin, then cleaned and placed bandages over the places from where he'd taken the needles out. "That should do it. I think he looks comfortable. Don't you?"

"Thanks, Doctor Stevens," said Kane.

The doctor looked at Kevin and shook his hand again." I'll be here at the hospital all night, Kane, in case you need me for anything. Goodnight."

"Goodnight, doctor."

# Chapter 20
## THE CHURCH

Ben glanced at his watch, eight-thirty. Katy had wanted to go into the church by herself. That had been half an hour ago. "Well, what do you think? Are you going to introduce her to one of the Talis?"

"Let's wait and see what she says," replied Sister Elizabeth.

Neither one of them noticed a car slowly driving by, then turning around and parking behind the station wagon; nor did they see the two occupants who got out and walked toward them.

"Sister, Sister Elizabeth."

She turned. "Zoric, Raul, what a nice surprise."

"We were on our way home and saw you standing here," Zoric explained. "Is everything all right?"

"Of course. We like to visit churches when we go to a new city. The architecture of this one is beautiful. It must be very old."

Katy walked out of the church and sat on the step. She recognized the man talking to Aunt Liz and Ben, but she didn't know who the young man was. She needed to gain control of her emotions before she went any farther. She knew where her father was—in a hospital somewhere—but which one? *Where else could he be? The answer is so obvious. Where do sick people go, dummy.*

Sister introduced Ben to Zoric and Raul. "My niece is inside. We were just getting ready to join her."

"We won't detain you then," said Zoric. "It was such a surprise, seeing you standing here. We wanted to make sure you were all right. If you get a chance to come by, we'll be in the park at nine, then at noon tomorrow. We always have plenty to eat, and you never know, I might need a good pilot."

"You could have your pick. There's three licensed pilots here, Ben, myself, and my niece."

"Your niece can fly a chopper?" Raul sounded stunned.

"Yes." Sister chuckled. "I think she's even better than Ben or me."

"You're talking about the young girl sitting on the steps up there?" It was Zoric's turn to sound surprised.

Sister turned to look. "Yes, that's her."

"I need to talk to her." Raul walked away before Sister could stop him. He approached the bottom stair, looking up at her. "There's no way you're old enough to fly a chopper."

Katy smiled. "Not only a chopper, but small planes, including up to ten-passenger jets."

"Unbelievable, but you look so young."

"I'm probably older than you."

"I don't think so." Raul laughed. "I'm almost eighteen."

"Me, too," Katy said. "In about ten months."

Raul sat down on the step and turned to face her. "When did you start flying?"

"When I was thirteen, but I couldn't get a license until I was sixteen. I'm supposed to have a licensed pilot with me until I'm eighteen. It's a wonderful feeling up there, looking down."

"I think I would like to learn to fly. Then my father and Uncle wouldn't have to depend on others to fly them everywhere."

Katy was sure this must be the nephew of Zoric Tali. "Is that one of them down there?"

"My Uncle Zoric. I had the privilege of flying with your Aunt today. She's very good, pretty too, and real nice."

Katy smiled at him. "I think so, too." *Well, here it goes.* She held out her hand. "I'm Sister Katy."

He reached up. "I'm Raul Tali."

Katy felt the warmth of his hand, against her cold one, as his life flowed into her body. This was her brother's best friend, the one that had been tied to a tree and tortured. Katy felt the pain. Tears stung her eyes and she pulled her hand away from his.

Raul stood. "Are you not feeling well?" Concern sounded in his voice.

Katy forced a smile and even a little chuckle. "I've never met the son of a prince before, and your hand was so warm." She took a deep breath. "I don't think I've ever felt better in my life."

Her happiness was contagious and Raul smiled. "My uncle invited all of you to come to the park tomorrow. I hope to see you there. Maybe I could talk him into letting you fly me around in the chopper, with your aunt as co-pilot, of course."

"Of course."

"Good-night."

"Bye." Katy waved and watched him walk away. *Everything is happening so fast, but at least we know.* Katy felt the presence of her father again and smiled. *I'm on my way. At least I have some idea of where you are.* She watched the car drive away with Zoric and Raul. She stood up and walked down the steps. Aunt Liz and Ben were waiting for her. She started dancing around in circles.

Ben looked at Sister Elizabeth. "I think we have a happy girl on our hands."

"Me, too." Sister Elizabeth let out a sigh of relief. "I was so scared." She held out her arms to Katy.

The three of them stood there with their arms wrapped around each other.

"Okay, okay," said Ben. "Tell us what happened. I can't wait any longer."

Katy pulled them both toward the car. "I'll tell you on our way back to the hotel. Then we'll decide what to do next."

"I can't begin to describe the feeling I had, standing there and knowing my father and mother had been here before. I could feel their presence, especially my father's. It was almost like I could reach out and touch him. Then it was like a spark going off in my brain. Father is sick and where do sick people go, to the hospital."

"Of course," said Ben. "It was right there in front of us."

"I know. I feel like such a idiot." Katy revealed. "And Raul—do you know who he is?"

"Who?" They both said at the same time.

Katy laughed. "I'm glad you're sitting down. He's Kane's best friend. He was the one tied to the round object. It was a tree." Katy's voice went sad. "He was tortured, but Kane saved him."

Ben drove into the parking lot of the hotel. "What now?"

Sister spoke first. "It makes so much sense now."

"What's that?" asked Katy.

"What Raul told me earlier at the hospital. He was there to be with his friend because his friend's father wasn't doing well. If he was talking about Kane and your father, that means they're at that hospital on the third floor in the room where the guard was stationed."

"I think you're right," said Ben.

229

"I know you're right, Aunt Liz," Katy confirmed.

The three of them sat around a small table in Ben's hotel room. "Okay, let's try to put this in some kind of perspective. We're going to assume that Kevin is in the hospital sick, on the third floor, in the room with the guard. Why the guard? For his protection or is he under guard because he's a prisoner. Is it possible Kane is still there with him?"

"The guard could be there for protection, if it's connected in any way with the explosion of Prince Tali's car on the island." Sister Elizabeth hesitated for a minute, then continued, "I just realized something. There weren't any other people on the third floor of that hospital like nurses, patients, or doctors."

"That is strange," said Ben, "and will make it more difficult to get access into his room. What do you think, Katy?"

"Everything's happening so fast. I've got so much spinning around in my head. I wish Ward was here." She smiled. "He could hypnotize me. I'd be relaxed and then everything could be put in perspective and make some kind of sense."

Sister Elizabeth touched her hand. "We could wait till tomorrow, when he's here, and try to get a good night's sleep. Maybe everything will look better by then."

"I wouldn't be able to sleep. The one thing I know for sure is I have to find some way of getting into that hospital room tonight."

"Then that's what we'll do."

Ben was surprised to hear Sister Elizabeth agree. "Okay, let's get started." A big grin appeared on his face.

An hour later found them pulling up in front of the hospital. Sister Elizabeth would remain in the car. Ben was dressed as a heavy-set older man with a beard and cane. A hat covered his dark hair. Katy remained dressed as a nun. They were to walk into the hospital as if they had been there a hundred times before and take the elevator up to the third floor. Sister Elizabeth's exact words were, "Let's just go for it." If anyone asked questions, Katy had a speech all prepared. If this didn't work, plan two was to find a way to the roof and take the elevator down to the third floor.

"Come on, Grandpa," Katy said, teasingly.

With one of Ben's hands on the cane and the other wrapped around

Katy's arm, off they went.

Sister Elizabeth watched them until they disappeared through the main door. She made the sign of the cross and said a prayer. A smile spread across her face as she looked up toward heaven.

Her eyes glanced around the hospital grounds. *What's the worst that could happen? They might get asked to leave, maybe even arrested and thrown out of the country.* She chuckled to herself. The walkie talkie Ben gave her laid next to her. If she saw anyone that looked like trouble she was to use it, and Ben and Katy would leave the hospital immediately. Ben promised he would keep it on, in case there was anything she should hear.

## KANE

Kevin walked slowly around the room, gaining strength with every step. Kane walked behind his father ready to grab him if he started to fall. Kevin sat down on the chair to rest. Kane handed him half of a sandwich, then walked over to the door to check on the guard, who was now laying on the bed, sound asleep. *That guy can snore louder than any human or animal I know.* Kane looked across to the nurse's station in the mirror that hung in the corner. It was round and made things appear distorted, but he could see down the hall toward the elevator without leaving the room.

Katy and Ben walked across the main lobby and turned down the hall where the elevators were located. It was more crowded than they thought it would be, but Sister Elizabeth was right, no one paid any attention to them. They stepped into the empty elevator and Katy pressed the button marked 3. "This is going to be easy, Ben."

"Or… we're just too good." He patted her hand.

Kane was startled when he heard the bell sound that indicated the elevator was stopping on their floor. He closed the door just enough to see into the mirror and turned, motioning to his father to get back in bed. He peeked out the door again, into the mirror. He watched two people get off. *Someone is on the wrong floor.* He couldn't quite make out who they were. *It looks like a nurse—I think, helping some old man.* Kane closed the door softly and crawled into his bed. *I'll give them about five minutes before they realize they're in the wrong place.*

Ben and Katy walked down the hall, stopping when they heard snoring coming from the room where the television was turned on low.

"Do you think that could be a guard?" Katy asked.

"He's completely dressed. I guess it could be him."

Katy smiled. "He takes his job real serious. According to Aunt Liz that should be my father's room." She pointed to the door Kane had just closed. She took a deep breath and place her hand over her heart. *My father might or might not be in that room. If he is in there, he might be dying. Be prepared for anything, Katy, stay focused, confident, and whatever you do—don't cry.*

Ben gave her a hug. "I'll be right here, keeping an eye on sleeping beauty." He pointed at the guard.

She let go of his arm and walked slowly to the door, turning and giving Ben a smile. She reached down and opened the door as quietly as she could and stepped into the room, then closed the door behind her. Through the dim night light she could see two beds. They both looked occupied. She stood there frozen, not able to move. The person in the bed closest to her pulled off the covers, swung his legs over the side and stood. Katy knew right away it was her brother, Kane. The tears flowed down her cheeks. She placed her hands over her eyes, not able to control the sobbing that rocked her body.

Kane stood there dumfounded, then stepped forward to offer comfort to the young girl.

Katy took her hands away from her face. Kane was standing in front of her. She reached up and threw her arms around his neck.

The second she touched him, Kane knew it was Katy. His arms went around her waist, lifting her off the ground, hugging her tight. The tears flowed freely from his eyes, too. After a few minutes he pulled away and set her back on the floor. Then he drew her close again, whispering in her ear. "Don't say anything, the room is bugged." He reached over and turned on the main light. His hand came up and touched her eyes.

Katy reached in her pocket and took out the holder she had for the brown contacts she was wearing. She looked up at him and smiled. *He's so handsome.*

Kane looked down at eyes the same color as his and smiled. *She's beautiful.* He turned, taking her by the hand, leading her to their father. Kevin was sitting on the side of his bed. She stepped forward, letting him hold her in his arms. Kane went over, unplugged the radio, and picked up the belt buckle. He took them into the bathroom, plugged the radio back in and turned it on. He then set the belt buckle in the shower stall, like he'd done before, placing a towel over it. He walked out and closed the door. He put his arms around Katy and his father and whispered, "together at last." He waited a minute before continuing. "Who's with you?"

She touched Kane's face softy with her hand. "Someone you and Dad can trust." Goosebumps spread across her skin. *Dad, what a beautiful word.* She reached over and touched her father's face, too. "Let's go someplace where we can talk."

Ben watched Katy enter the room. After a few minutes, when she didn't return, he walked over and sat in the chair in the room where the guard was asleep on the bed. He sat there for a few minutes before he got up and rolled the man on his side. *Enough of that noise, it could drive a person insane.* He sat back down, wondering what was happening behind the closed door. He was sure Katy's father was in there. All the facts pointed in that direction. *I wonder if I'll like him.*

Ben was experiencing emotions he never felt before. Katy was like his daughter. Now he'd have to share her with her real father. *Is this jealousy I'm feeling? No, that's not it. Katy's happiness is more important than anything.* Ben knew what really bothered him. *Why hasn't Katy's father tried to contact her in all these years? For the longest time I truly thought he and Kane were dead. He could have let her know, somehow, they were both alive, but I'll give him a chance to explain. I'm a fair man. Kevin does have one important thing in his favor—Meg. Katy's mom had loved him deeply.*

Ben stood when he heard the door open and saw three people step into the hall, closing the door behind them. He turned the walkie talkie on. "She found them. I'll leave this on so you can hear."

Ben couldn't help but smile when he saw the happiness on Katy's face. There was no doubt this was her father and brother. They all had the same color eyes, and as Ben looked at Kane, a shiver passed through him. Something about the boy reminded him of Meg. Kevin was in the middle with his arms on Katy's and Kane's shoulders. Ben could see the weakness in Kevin's face. He stepped forward. "Can I help?"

Kane was the first to speak. "There's no one in the room next to us. If you could open the door, we'll go in there and talk."

It only took a few minutes before they had Kevin sitting on the bed, Katy and Kane at his side. Ben pulled up a chair in front of them and sat down.

"Ben, I want you to meet my brother, Kane." Katy said. Kane shook Ben's hand, a big smile on his face.

Ben couldn't help but smile back. He noticed the young lad was reluctant to let go of his hand. "Was there a reason we couldn't talk in your room?" Ben asked.

"It's not safe," Katy stated. "Someone might be listening. We can check it out later. I want you to meet my father, Kevin."

Ben noticed Kevin, too, was reluctant to let go of his hand. He noticed something else, too, relief on the man's face."

Kevin finally spoke. "Now I can put a name and face to the person who has loved and protected my Katy. You're the lion killer." A big smile came to his face.

The remark took Ben by surprise as he recalled the memory from so many years ago.

Kevin continued. "It was one of the first visions I had of Katy and knew she was safe with her Aunt Liz, but I didn't know who the man was until now."

Kevin studied Ben's face for some kind of reaction. When it didn't happen Kevin smiled understandingly. "I know you have a lot of questions. Someday I hope I can answer them, but for now I want you to know what you're up against. Kane and I were kidnapped, when Kane was just over a year old, by the Tali family. We were taken to Tali Island. It's very secluded. There's only one entrance, by land, onto the Island and it's heavily guarded. The one in charge goes by the name of Prince Tali. From the very first day we arrived on the island he made it very clear that if we tried to escape he would kill me and raise Kane as his own. He told me if I cooperated he would do no harm to my wife and daughter, and I would live to see my son grow into a man. We had no money and were under surveillance twenty-four hours a day. Guards following us became a way of life."

Katy and Ben sat there and listened to Kevin as he told them about Prince Tali.

"He'd kill you if he knew you were here. I'd like to tell you more, but we're running out of time. The nurse is scheduled to check on us at three, then again at seven."

Ben looked at his watch, one forty-five. Kevin had been talking for over two hours. Ben understood now why Kevin hadn't contacted Katy. The respect he felt for this man was overwhelming.

"That doesn't give us much time." Ben stood and started to take off his disguise. Kevin and Kane sat there in a state of astonishment. "Do you think you can make it outside with Katy's help and this cane?" Ben asked Kevin.

"I know I can. What about Kane?"

"He'll leave with me." He looked at Kane. "Your Aunt Elizabeth is outside, waiting in a car. You said there might be a listening device in your room?"

Kevin was the one to answer. "I know for a fact there is. Kane will show you."

"Okay, but I'll check everything, anyway." Ben reached into the pocket of the coat he'd taken off and took out the small detector. He clicked it on and it started to buzz. It took all of them by surprise. He turned it off, and looked at Kevin, then Kane. "Would you mind standing on the other side of the room, Kane?"

Ben turned on the detector again and moved it around Kevin's body...nothing. He walked toward Kane. The buzz started softly, then got louder as Ben approached. The buzz was the loudest around Kane's head. Ben turned it off. "Do you wear a hearing aid?"

"No. Nothing."

Ben turned it back on, moving it around Kane's head. It made the strongest sound on his right cheek. "Open your mouth, please."

Kane did as he was told and the buzzer went crazy. Ben turned it off. "Have you had any dental work done lately?" he smiled, hoping to ease some of the frightened look he saw on the boy's face.

Kane thought for a moment. "Yes, about a year ago. I went with Raul. We both had a check-up. The dentist found a small cavity in my back tooth and filled it."

"Katy, would you hand me the small flashlight? Come over here and sit down, Kane. You don't mind if I have a look, do you?"

"Do you have a license for dentistry?" Kane asked jokingly.

Ben smiled. "Of course. I have a license for just about everything. Open wide. There's only one tooth clear in the back that's filled. I'd say that's the culprit we're looking for."

"What is it?" asked Kane.

"I'm sure it's some kind of tracking device. In other words, someone has a machine they can turn on at anytime and know where you are. It can reach one block, one mile, or a hundred miles. We're all positive this has Tali's trademark on it, so we have to assume it's for at least a hundred miles or more."

Kane took a deep breath and looked into Ben's eyes. "How do we get rid of it?"

"Let me think about that for a while."

He placed his hand on Kane's shoulder. "We'll figure out something. In the meantime, let's go check the other room. Make sure there's no more surprises. Katy, why don't you stay here and help your father put his new clothes on."

Kane opened the door quietly and looked around. "All clear."

Ben followed him into the other room, checking everything along the way. When he opened the bathroom door the buzzer on the detector went crazy. Ben turned if off right away. Kane lifted the towel and picked up the belt buckle, showing Ben where the listening device was, then put it back and covered it again with the towel.

They returned to the other room to find Kevin ready to go.

Ben smiled. "Good girl. He looks great. I want you two to leave. I'll stay here and take Kevin's place."

"What about the nurse?" Kane asked.

"It'll be your job to try and keep her away from me. If that doesn't work, we'll think of something else." Ben smiled.

Kane looked at his father. "Are you sure you can make it?"

"I'm walking toward freedom. I'll make it. I'll worry about you, and Ben, until you're by my side again." Kevin put his arms around his son. "Be careful."

"You, too, Dad."

Ben removed a small pair of pliers and two different screwdrivers from his coat, then helped Kevin put it on. "See you on the outside."

Ben and Kane watched them until they got on the elevator. Katy waved, then closed the door. Ben took the walkie talkie out of his breast pocket. "Katy and her father are on their way, Sister. Let me know when you see them."

It was almost ten minutes before he heard her voice. "Here they come now, walking very slowly. I'm going to drive up in front and pick them up."

"Be careful, Sister."

"Always."

"Why do you call her sister?" asked Kane. "Is she a nun?"

"Yes. She is."

"I knew it. She's the one that flew the chopper. Isn't she?"

"One and only." Ben chuckled. "That's our Sister Elizabeth or Aunt Liz to you and Katy."

"Raul said she's a terrific pilot and real pretty."

"Actually," Ben said, "she's beautiful, and she's not the only one that can fly a chopper. Katy can, too."

Kane was so surprised, he didn't know what to say.

Sister's voice came back on the walkie talkie. "Ben?"

"I'm here."

"Kevin's a little tired, but doing fine. What happens now?"

"I'll have to turn off our communication for a while. I'll contact you again when it's all clear."

"Be careful, Ben. Remember I'm right here if you need me."


Ben made himself comfortable in Kevin's bed. *When was the last time I slept?* He couldn't remember.

It was half an hour later when Kane heard the door open and the nurse came in. He got out of bed and motioned for her to leave the room. He followed her out into the hall. "We're okay, but I wanted you to know I told the guard to lay down. He wasn't feeling well. Are you the one that comes back at seven?"

"Yes" she answered.

"If he's still sleeping, you need to wake him before the other guard gets here." Kane yawned. "Excuse me. Doctor Stevens gave me something to help me sleep. I'll see you in the morning." Kane went back into his room, closing the door behind him. He crawled into bed and waited. After a few minutes, he breathed a sign of relief.

He lay there thinking about everything that happened earlier. His hand went up and touched his right cheek. He felt such contempt for Prince Tali. *Ben kept the pliers, so I guess it won't be in there very long. If I didn't think Prince Tali would send Yorky, or J.J. after it, I'd take my tooth to the zoo and put it in the animal waste dump.* Kane chuckled to himself as he pictured Prince Tali sorting through manure.

Getting back out of bed he walked over and touched Ben's shoulder. When Ben jumped, Kane realized he'd been asleep.

Kane was careful and checked the hall before they went into the room next door. He walked over and sat in the chair, holding onto the arms very tightly. "Okay, I'm ready."

Ben looked at him with a puzzled look on his face. "Ready for what, Kane?"

"For you to pull my tooth."

Ben laughed. "That's not why I kept the pliers. I would only do that as a last resort. Your father said Doctor Stevens is here tonight in the hospital and we can trust him. I was hoping he could give you something to numb the area before he pulled it. You might need something for pain if he has to take a stitch or two. Can you call him?"

Kane let out another sigh of relief. "I sure can." He walked over to the nurse's station, picked up the phone, and called Doctor Stevens' direct line. He heard the doctor's groggy voice on the other end. "It's me—Kane. I've got a real bad headache. Can I come to your office and get something for the pain?"

"Of course. Take the stairs to the second floor. I'm in the first room to the right. I'll be looking for you."

Kane found Ben in the bathroom. He was taking the belt buckle apart. When he finished, he placed the listening device on the tub. Kane reached for the belt and put it around his waist. He picked up his drawing tablet and walked out of the room. Ben followed.

Doctor Stevens' office door was open. He was surprised to see the stranger with Kane and even more surprised to see the belt buckle around Kane's waist.

"It's okay."

Ben took out his detector again and checked the doctor's office. "All clear, except for this." Ben held it up to Kane's cheek and it started buzzing.

Kane explained to Doctor Stevens what he needed done and why.

Ben was impressed as he watched the doctor take control, moving around and gathering what he needed. Within minutes Kane's mouth was numb, the tooth removed, stitches taken, and medication given for pain. Ben picked up the bloody tooth. "Is there a restroom close by?"

"In there." Doctor pointed to the closed door.

"Would you like the honor?" Ben handed the tooth to Kane. The next noise they heard was the flushing of the toilet.

"Thank you." Ben shook the doctor's hand. So did Kane. "We'll be in touch." They walked out without saying another word.

"Did you get everything you need?" asked Ben.

"Yes."

Ben reached into his pocket and took out a baseball cap. "Put this on, keep your head down like you're in mourning."

"What do you mean?" Kane put his hand on his cheek. "I am in mourning."

They took the stairs to the main floor. Ben put his arm around Kane's shoulder and guided him across the main lobby, talking to him. He showed comfort to the young man at his side until they walked out the front door.

Ben took the walkie talkie out of his pocket. "We're here at the front door. Flash your lights." He looked around. "Okay we see you."

The car was about half a block away. Sister Elizabeth was standing outside by the front fender, watching them walk toward her.

Kane stopped in front of her. "Aunt Liz?"

Her breath caught in her throat as she noticed the same thing Ben had, the resemblance to her sister, Meg. She hugged him tightly. "You look a lot like your mother."

"My father thinks I looked like her, too."

Katy got out of the car and stood beside Kane. "Are you okay?"

He tried to smile. "I will be, I had to get a tooth pulled."

Sister and Katy said at the same time, "Ben, you didn't?"

Kane laughed. "I'm sure glad I'm not the only one who thought he'd do it. But, no, it wasn't him. Doctor Stevens was kind enough to take care of it."

He looked down at Katy and smiled. "How's our father?"

She smiled back. "Resting. We made him as comfortable as possible. We should get him to the hotel. What do you say we get out of here?"

Ben got behind the wheel. He didn't have to worry about keeping awake with all the talking and laughing. He was surprised Kevin slept through it, and felt bad when he had to wake him to help him to their room.

They put Kevin and Kane in the adjoining room next to Ben's.

It was five in the morning when Ben excused himself and went to bed. He awoke at eleven and decided not to disturb anyone. He could go to the airport alone to pick up Ward and Sami.

# Chapter 21
## LONDON AIRPORT

Ward woke up when he heard the captain, telling of their arrival in London. He couldn't believe he'd been able to sleep.

Sami moved to the seat next to him. "Will you be all right until we land?" She noticed he used the urinal bag supplied to him by the airline.

"I'd like to stand and stretch my legs," he said, jokingly.

Sami reached into her jean pocket and took out an envelope. "Amanda asked me to give you this."

"Thanks." Ward opened it and read the note.

*Ward,*

*Thank you for the terrific company. You made the flight very interesting. I'm going to decline your offer of spending the layover with you and Samantha. I have some personal business to take care of. Please join me for pre-flight drinks.*

*Warmest Regards,*

*Amanda.*

"Bad news?" asked Sami.

"Amanda won't be joining us until flight time. She'll meet us for drinks."

Kord's mother was there to welcome them at the terminal gate. She rented a hotel room close by so they could shower and clean up.

The time went by quickly and, before they knew it, they were back at the airport. Kord would be staying in London with his mother. He would join them again on the flight home, but he was there to help put Ward on the plane. They didn't see Amanda until ten minutes before takeoff. When she boarded the plane, she stopped and made her apologies. "Ward, I'm so sorry. I lost track of time."

"That's okay, Amanda. We were late, too."

"I'll see you later." She handed him another note and walked toward her seat.

*Ward,*

*I'm going to try and get some sleep. If I don't talk to you again before we land I'll be staying at the Greek Manor House Hotel. Please call and we'll make arrangements for dinner. If things work out the way I'm hoping they will, I'll be able to introduce you to my son.*
*As Always, Amanda.*

Ward reread the note again to make sure he had read it correctly. He showed it to Sami to see her reaction. It was the same as his. "A son in Greece?"

Sami knew why Amanda was on her way to Greece. Her father had told her everything. "Oh, the plot thickens."

Ward took the note back. "You've been around too many reporters," he teased.

"You said she married young. Her ex-husband must live in Greece. Maybe they share custody, you know, six months with her, six with him, and she's here to pick her son up."

"I don't think so," Ward replied. "She made it pretty clear her main reason is to see this man she cares very deeply for. I noticed she's staying at the same hotel we are." Ward grinned. "I think we must have the same travel agent. Would you tell her we're staying there, too, and we have someone picking us up. We'd be happy to give her a lift."

Sami was only gone for a few minutes. "She said she would really appreciate the ride."

The time went by quickly, and before they knew it, the pilot's voice came over the intercom to announce their arrival in Athens. They would land in half an hour.

## ATHENS AIRPORT

Ben stood by the door waiting for it to open. Once all the passengers unloaded, they would let him go aboard to help with Ward. He couldn't decide whether to tell them about Kevin and Kane or surprise them when they got to the hotel. Ben couldn't believe how fast everything was happening. He did know it wasn't over yet. They wouldn't be safe until they were all home at the Ranch. Even then he wouldn't

242

let his guard down. *Tali must be one pissed off guy by now. I wonder what he did when he found out the good news.*

## HOSPITAL – 8 A.M.

Prince Tali stomped up and down the hall. "What the hell do you mean they just disappeared? Kevin was unconscious, for Christ sake. They had to have help. I want this town turned upside down until we find them. I want every access checked and re-checked."

Zoric had never seen his brother so mad. He had arrived at the hospital at six-thirty to check on Yorky and to see how Yorky's son was doing after the operation. Doctor Stevens said it had taken only twenty minutes to half an hour and the prognosis was excellent. Zoric was proud of Kane—again. And it showed.

"Zoric, are you listening to me?" Prince Tali shouted at him. "I want a list of everyone on duty last night. I already fired the guard that fell asleep on the job. According to the nurse on duty, she checked on Kevin and Kane at three o'clock and they were both sleeping. The guard said they were sleeping at five, then he fell asleep and when he woke at six, they were gone. I don't believe either of them. I'm going to the island to check on a couple of things. I'll be back no later than ten and I want some answers." Prince Tali stormed out of the hospital, taking Raul with him.

"Aren't you worried about that third bomb that's out there somewhere?" asked Raul. "You better slow down. You're driving the car like a crazy person. I would like to see my eighteenth birthday."

Prince Tali pulled off to the side of the road and stopped the car. "You're right, son. I need to think this through calmly, but damn... " His voice got louder. He slammed the palm of his hand against the steering wheel. "Did you know anything about this?" He saw the hurt look on Raul's face as he turned to look at him.

Raul lowered his head. "No. I can't believe Kane would just leave without telling me. Something must have happened and he's protecting us. I'm sure he'll call. Maybe he went back to the island."

"How would he get there? No money, no clothes or transportation, his father unconscious—or maybe not. They could have been planning this for a long time. I know one thing, someone's helping them."

243

"Maybe they were kidnapped," Raul said smugly, "and their lives are in danger."

"I'll find them." Prince Tali didn't tell Raul about the listening device he found on the tub. *I wonder how long McKade has known about that. It doesn't make any difference, he's a dead man. There's no way I'll support any kind of bone marrow transplant now.*

Neither one spoke again until they arrived on the island. "I'm going to check on Sassy," Raul said, walking away before his father could stop him.

Prince Tali went into the viewing room. An hour later he walked out after listening to the tapes from the hospital. He was fairly sure Kane and Kevin were in the room at three in the morning. There was no indication the guard ever was. He held what looked like a small lap top computer under his arm. He opened the door to his office and his eyes scanned the room. A feeling of uneasiness surrounded him. Without the protection of McKade and Kane, what would happen to them, especially Raul?

He walked over to the wet bar and made himself a large, stiff drink and sat down at his desk, placing what he called his locator in front of him. He opened the lid and turned it on. The screen on the top showed the city of Athens and surrounding areas. He switched on the button marked tracker—nothing. It was programmed and guaranteed to pick up a signal within three hundred miles. *Where in the hell are you, Kane.*

He'd been sitting there, staring at the screen for at least ten minutes, when he noticed a dim flicker of light flashing, then fading. He waited. It happened again. A grin came to his face. *So you're still in the city somewhere. Well, guess what? I'll have you both back on this island within twenty-four hours. Neither you, McKade, or you Kane, will ever be allowed to leave again—for any reason..* Prince Tali had never told Zoric, or anyone else, about the tracking device he had the dentist put in Kane's mouth, disguised as a tooth filling. It was his secret and he planned on keeping it that way, at least for a while. He finished his drink. *Time to get back to the city and find our little escapees. I'll drop Raul off at the park first.*

# HOTEL
# KANE

Kane opened his eyes. It took him a minute to realize where he was. He looked over at his father and found him sitting in the chair by his bed. "What are you doing up so early? Are you all right?"

Kevin smiled. "I've never felt better. Do you realize this is the first time in sixteen years we're free?" Kevin threw his arms in the air.

Kane started laughing. He had never, in his whole life, seen his father so happy. They talked for a while. Kane told his father how Katy, Aunt Liz, and he had stayed up until seven in the morning, talking.

"What time is it?"

Kane looked around for the clock and found it across the room on a small shelf. Eleven-fifteen. "Four hours sleep and I feel great. Zoric invited Aunt Liz, Katy, and Ben to join him in the park for lunch. Katy and Aunt Liz are going, but Ben has to go to the airport and pick up Katy's friend, Samantha, and her father, Ward. He's in a wheelchair." Kane was telling his father all about them when they heard the knock on the door.

"It's Katy. Can I come in?"

"Of course."

"Good morning, you two sleepyheads." She was dressed in nun's clothing, her brown contacts in her eyes, and glasses on. She was carrying a large tray of food.

"Are you sure you're our sweet Katy?" asked her father, watching her set the tray down.

"Only on the inside." She walked over and gave him a hug. "You look like you're feeling stronger today."

"I feel wonderful."

Kane picked up his tablet and gently tore the top sheet off. He folded it down and wrote on the front 'To Zoric Tali.' He handed it to Katy. "Do you think Aunt Liz could find some way of getting this to him?"

Katy smiled. "One thing you'll learn about our Aunt Liz is she can do most anything and she's not afraid of anyone. She actually has a very devious mind. She'll think of something."

"I'm sure glad she's on our side." Kane smiled. "She can read it

245

first. You, too."

"Okay." Katy took the piece of paper and put it in her pocket. "We should be back soon. We're not planning on staying. I want to be back when Sami gets here."

Sister read the note out loud to Katy.

*Zoric,*

*I apologize to you and Raul for any trouble I might have caused, but my father comes first. I'm not going to tell you where we're going. I will tell you this, I'll be back. Tell Raul I'm sorry for leaving the way we did, but we had no choice. I know I'm taking a big chance writing this letter, but I needed to let you know where to find the third present. It's in the park, taped to the underside of the platform, and it's operated by a detonator. I have no idea where the detonator is. It could be where the man lived or he could have had it with him. I do not see it causing any potential danger, but you should dismantle it.*

*Kane*

*P.S. Tell your brother I found a new dentist.*

Katy and Sister Elizabeth walked toward the park. Katy hummed a song as they strolled along.

They were surprised to see the park so crowded. "It looks like they're going to take people back to the island." Sister pointed to the buses parked along the side. "There's Zoric and Raul over by the first one."

It was about ten minutes before Zoric saw them and walked in their direction. They both noticed the strained expression on his face. "It looks like you have your hands full this morning. Is there anything we can do to help?" Sister asked.

"That's very kind, but I think we have it under control."

"We won't stay then."

"You don't have to leave. Have lunch with us." Zoric paused and looked around. "I don't see your brother."

"He's at the airport, picking up some friends of ours. We wanted to come by and let you know we're here if you need us. Maybe we could stop by later today."

Zoric smiled at her. "That would be nice, thank you."

They turned to leave. "See you then." Sister walked about five feet when she turned back. "Oh Zoric," she called to him. "I almost forgot." She reached into her pocket. "A young man asked me to give this to you."

Zoric recognized the paper right away. It was from Kane's tablet. He reached for it. Sister placed it in his hand, turned and walked away.

Zoric read the note, then hurried after her. "Sister Elizabeth, please wait. Who did you say gave this to you?"

"He didn't tell me his name. He asked if I was the one that flew the Tali helicopter yesterday. I said, 'yes', then he asked if I would give you that letter. I hope it's not bad news."

"No. No, it isn't. Can you tell me what he looked like? The color of his hair, his eyes?"

"He was tall and from what I could see, I would say, he's a very handsome young man. He had a cap on and sunglasses. His hair was light-colored, kind of like, well kind of like Sister Katy's. I couldn't see his eyes. He said he was late for an important meeting, thanked me and left."

"Did you happen to notice which way he went? Did he get into a car?"

"I'm sorry I didn't pay more attention, Zoric." Sister said, apologetically. "Did you notice which way he went, Sister Katy?"

"He walked across the park in that direction." Katy pointed in the opposite direction of their hotel. "I don't know if he was driving a car."

Zoric smiled, thanking them both. "See you later."

He walked up to Raul and showed him the note. Zoric noticed the look of relief on his nephew's face when Raul handed it back to him.

"I knew Kane wouldn't leave without letting me know. I want to tell you something, Uncle Zoric. I would have helped him if he'd asked me."

Zoric touched Raul's shoulder. "I know." He knew something else, too. He had to call his brother and tell him about the note, but first he needed to take care of the problem underneath the platform.

Prince Tali sat in his office. He had a meeting scheduled in five minutes with Gus, the man he purchased the tracking device from. He sat there, staring at the screen. The dim light still flashed every few minutes.

Within ten minutes, Gus had pinpointed the area where the light was coming from. They were walking out the door when Prince Tali's private phone rang. He was sure it was Zoric. "That's just my brother. I'll call him when we get back."

It was two hours later when Prince Tali returned to his office—alone. That guy's an idiot. How could that tracking device end up in the sewage plant. It must be picking up a signal that belongs to someone else. He noticed the flashing red light on the phone. When he checked, there were three calls from Zoric. He was getting ready to pick up the phone when it rang. "Zoric?"

"Yes. I've been trying to locate you."

"I had some personal things to take care of. What's going on?"

"I have a note here I need to read to you from Kane." When he finished he asked his brother, "What did he mean, he found a new dentist?"

"I'll explain later. How did you get that note?"

Zoric told him. "I've taken care of everything. We're on our second run to the island. Everyone should be back in their homes by late evening."

"Everyone except McKade and Kane. They're in this town somewhere. Did you have Doctor Stevens' apartment checked?"

"Yes, nothing. I've got someone posted outside. When he returns to the hospital, we'll go in and have another look."

"I want the surveillance equipment turned back on and operating on the estate as soon as possible," Prince Tale informed Zoric, then hung up the phone.

# Chapter 22
## AIRPORT

The airline attendant escorted Ben onto the airplane. Sami greeted him with a hug. Ben noticed the attractive blonde standing behind her.

Ward was the one that introduced them. "Ben, I'd like you to meet Amanda Farly."

"Any relation to Lawrence Farly?" Ben asked as he shook her hand.

"My brother." She smiled at him. "I hope you have room for another passenger. I'm staying at the same hotel and Ward has offered me a ride."

"My pleasure."

"You seem awfully happy, Ben. What's going on?" asked Sami.

He put his arm around her. "I missed you."

"You're up to something, I can tell."

Ben looked at Amanda. "Sometimes I get the feeling they don't trust me. I can't understand it."

"Watch him close, Amanda," Ward said. "He's the one that gave me this haircut and shave."

Amanda laughed. "I think you did an excellent job, Ben."

"Thank you."

An hour later Ben pulled up in front of the hotel and went to find someone to help Amanda take her luggage to her room. She was on the opposite side from them and promised Ward she would call and try to get together for lunch or dinner the following day.

Ben knocked on Katy and Sister Elizabeth's door. "We're here."

Katy swung the door open. The two girls acted like they hadn't seen each other for months. "Did Ben tell you the great news?"

"What news?" asked Sami.

Katy looked over at Ben. He was shaking his head, no. "I'll have to show you." She grabbed Sami by the hand and led her across the hall. "It's me," Katy said and opened the door, pulling Sami into the room.

Kane stood and looked at the person with the cap on her head and dark glasses on, standing next to his sister. He smiled.

Sami let go of Katy's hand, reached up and took off her glasses.

She looked at Kane, then Kevin, who was sitting up in bed. *My God, their eyes are exactly like Katy's.* Sami didn't hesitate. She ran across the room, stood on her tiptoes and wrapped her arms around Kane's neck. "You're alive. Thank God." Her hands cupped his face as she kissed his cheeks, his lips, then his cheek again. She stepped back. "God, you're handsome." She started to snicker when she saw the blush spread across his face. Her hand touched his cheek. "I'm Sami. Katy's like a sister to me and I feel like you're my long lost brother, too. You'll get used to me, and I think we'll like each other a lot."

Kane touched her hand. "I know we will. I've heard a lot about you already and I liked you, anyway."

Sami laughed. "We're going to get along great." She turned and walked toward Kevin. She sat down, gently, on the bed by his side. "How are you doing?" She touched his hand.

"I've never been better, Sami. That must be your father, Ward."

Sami moved so that Ward could maneuver his wheelchair close enough to shake Kevin's hand. "This is quite a surprise. I can hardly wait to hear how you all found each other."

That was how they spent the rest of the afternoon, telling Sami and Ward everything that happened from the time they arrived in Greece.

"Maybe," said Sami, "the reason you slipped into unconsciousness is because, subconsciously, you knew Katy would be able to help you escape more easily off the island."

Kevin smiled. "You could be right, Sami. I'm getting my strength back and I want to thank all of you. This feeling of freedom is something I can't even explain, it's so wonderful. I must tell you, though, Tali must be furious. He won't take this lying down. He's going to turn this town upside down, trying to find us."

Ben was the first to speak. "When we all agreed to come here and help Katy find you and Kane, we weren't really sure what we would be facing. We didn't have any idea what your situation was. I think we took everything into consideration, especially Katy's welfare and safety, which was top priority. We got this far. I think if we're all careful, and work together, we'll make it."

Everyone agreed. "What happens now?" asked Kane.

Ben smiled. "As you all know, I'm a master of disguises."

"Oh no," said Ward, "here it comes."

"I can't really take credit for this one, Ward. It was your idea."

250

"It has to be good then," Ward replied.

"I've made a few little changes." Ben heard the moans. "Wait, wait till you hear me out, then we'll vote. First, Kevin and Kane will not be able to leave this room until we're ready to fly out of here. I've got Father James' passport, so for the next couple of days Kevin will become Father James."

"I knew a Father James a long time ago," said Kevin.

"One and the same," Ben confirmed. He handed the passport over to Kevin. "He looks a little different than you probably remember, but I'll have an easy time making you look like that. Kane's going to be a little tougher. We've got Kord McNamara's passport. We'll all have to think about that one." Ben yawned. "I know one thing. I'm starving and I need some sleep."

"I'll order up some room service," said Sister Elizabeth, "then Katy and I are going back to the park to see how things are going. Would you like to go with us, Sami?"

She looked at her father. "No, I better not. Dad needs some exercise and..."

"No more ands," said Ben, "I'm sure Kane and I can torture him and take care of anything else he needs."

"He's right, sweetie." Ward smiled at her. "You go ahead, please. It will give us guys some time to talk."

"Are you sure?" asked Sami.

"Positive."

"I'll go and get cleaned up."

Half an hour later Katy, Sister Elizabeth, and Sami walked toward the park. Sami couldn't believe how great it felt to be herself and not worry about being recognized.

When they arrived, only a few people remained. Zoric was there with another man. Sister Elizabeth recognized him as the guard she'd seen at the hospital. She mentioned it to Katy and Sami. "Why don't you two sit over there on the picnic bench. I'll be back in a few minutes."

Zoric smiled when he saw her walking toward them. "I thought you might not make it."

Sister looked at Zoric. "We won't be staying long. I'm starting to feel jet lag, but I wanted to see how you were doing."

"Everything went smoothly. Do you know how long you're staying?"

"We haven't made any definite plans. Samantha, that's her sitting with Sister Katy, and her father want to spend some time sightseeing. Samantha's parents were in a tragic auto accident. She lost her mother and her father, Ward, is in a wheelchair. We plan on staying until his assistant arrives."

"I'm sorry to hear that. Maybe we could make arrangements to take them up in the chopper. Show them the islands."

"How nice of you. I have your card. Is that the number where I can reach you?"

Zoric heard someone call his name. He turned.

"Telephone call, said it's important."

"I'd better answer that. Please call."

"I will." Sister Elizabeth walked away toward Katy and Sami.

Kane and Kevin sat in their hotel room, waiting, while Ben helped Ward change his clothes. "Did you get unexpected vibes when you met Sami and Ward?" Kane asked his father.

Kevin lowered his head. "Yes, I did. It seems so strange, being able to talk freely. There's something I've been wanting to tell you. I've been writing to Amanda for the last couple of years. Doctor Stevens was helping us. We've fallen in love."

"Now I know why I've been thinking about her. I asked Raul to contact her. I drew a picture of her for him."

"I've been wanting to tell you."

"You don't have to explain, Dad. I understand."

"I needed to tell you. I get the feeling that Ward and Sami know her."

Kane stood and walked around the room. "I think you're right. We should ask Ward."

"Ask me what?" Ward maneuvered his wheelchair over to where Kane was standing. Just then the door opened and Sister Elizabeth, Katy and Sami entered.

"You girls are here just in time to hear Kane ask me something." Ward looked up at Kane and smiled. "What can I help you with?"

Kane sat down and studied Ward's face. "You have to realize it's hard for us to get used to speaking without someone listening."

Tears stung Katy's eyes. "You can say anything you want. You're free now."

Kane smiled at her, then looked back at Ward. "All right, my father

252

and I were wondering… "He paused for a moment, looking first at Ward then at Sami, "…if you know Raul's mother, Prince Tali's ex-wife, Amanda?"

Sami walked over to her father. They looked at each other. A shocked expression appeared on both their faces. It took a minute for everything to fall into place. Sami started laughing. "It's true. Can you believe it, Dad?"

"Unbelievable is more like it." Ward looked at Kevin. "You're the mysterious man in her life." Ward explained to everybody how he knew Amanda, about their meeting in New York, and their flight together to Greece. "You're not going to believe this, but she's staying here at this hotel."

Excitement was felt by everyone in the room. Sister Elizabeth finally spoke. "I think we need to find some way of getting her here to see Kevin, the sooner, the better." Everyone agreed.

## AMANDA

The phone rang, waking Amanda up. She reached over to answer it.

"This is your wake-up call, Ms. Farly."

"Thank you."

She had tried to reach Doctor Stevens when she first arrived, but was told he wouldn't be back on duty until six that evening. She wanted to talk to him first to find out how Kevin was, then she'd call Raul.

She called room service, ordering coffee and a salad. She showered earlier, so all she needed to do was dress then brush her hair back in a bun, apply a little lip gloss, blush and mascara.

Room service knocked on her door. She was glad they brought a large pot of coffee. Twenty minutes later she picked up the phone and called Doctor Stevens' private number. She was so relieved when she heard his voice on the other end.

"Hello. This is Doctor Stevens."

"Hello, Rob. Its Dawn." She used a short version of her middle name whenever she contacted him.

"Hello, sweetheart. What a nice surprise."

She knew right away someone was in his office and he couldn't talk. "If you're busy I can call you later."

"Things are kind of hectic around here. Can we get together later? Why don't you call me around eight. We can have a late supper together."

"Okay, I'll call you then." Amanda hung up the phone.

"Okay, honey, I miss you, too."

Doctor Stevens sat back in his chair, making himself comfortable. "I'm as puzzled as you are. Kevin was unconscious when I checked on him shortly after ten."

Prince Tali stood. "I'm sure they're here in this town somewhere. If they contact you, please let me know. They'll need all the help they can get."

Amanda picked up the phone again, this time calling Prince Tali's private number at his apartment. Her heart pounded in her chest when she realized the young man's voice on the other end of the line was Raul.

"Hello." He said it again. "Is anyone there? Hello."

"Raul?" Her voice was shaking.

"Yes, who is this? Kane, is that you?"

"This is your mother."

There was a pause before she heard his voice again. "Mom, is it really you?"

"Yes, it's me. You sound so grown up."

He laughed. "I am grown up. I'll be eighteen my next birthday. Where are you?"

"I'm here in Athens. I arrived today. I'd like to see you."

"I want to see you, too. My father didn't tell me he finally found you."

"Your father doesn't know I'm here—yet."

"You haven't talked to him?"

"Not since I left when you were five. I'm here now. When can I see you?"

"We could spend tomorrow together."

"That would be perfect, Raul."

They talked for over an hour.

"My father just came in, so we'll meet tomorrow morning at the park."

"I'll be there."

"Me, too."

Prince Tali stood there, waiting for Raul to hang up the phone. "Was that Zoric?"

"No." Raul glared at him. "It was my mother. I want to thank you for nothing. You promised. How could you lie to me like that?'

"Where is she?"

"Why? Are you finally going to talk to her after what, twelve years? How kind of you."

"You don't understand, Son. I was only trying to protect you. She could have stayed. We might even have had more children, but she chose the money instead. The checks I've sent her, every year, get cashed."

"I don't care about any of that. I want to see her."

"I won't stop you." Prince Tali walked away. *You'll see her tomorrow and that's it—one day—no more.*

Amanda felt wonderful. Her son wanted to see her. She heard no resentment in his voice, or blame, only a polite caring young man.

She was surprised when she heard the knock on her door. "Who is it?"

"It's Ward. Could I talk to you for a minute?"

She opened the door. "Of course, come in." She was surprised to see him by himself. "Is everything all right?"

"Actually, no, it isn't. I was wondering if you could talk to Samantha. It will only take a few minutes of your time."

"What's wrong?"

Ward smiled. "I would rather she told you. If you don't mind."

Amanda smiled back. "Girl stuff?"

"She has a surprise she wants to show you."

"I love surprises. Let me grab my key."


It took about ten minutes to get back to Ward's room. Sami and Katy were standing outside in the hall waiting for them. Both of them were grinning from ear to ear.

"Is this the same Samantha I met on the plane?'

"This is the real me." Sami took her hand. "I want you to meet my best friend, Katy. Oh, excuse me, Sister Katy."

Amanda held out her other hand. "It's very nice to meet you."

Katy shook her hand, then looked at Sami. "You're right, Sami.

She's everything you and Ward said she was."

Amanda looked puzzled. "I don't understand."

Sami was so happy she could hardly control herself. "You will. We just needed Katy's approval before we went any further. Come on, we'll show you." They each kept hold of her hands as they approached Kevin's room.

Katy opened the door just enough to peek her head in. Kevin was sitting in the chair across the room, "You were right, Dad." She opened the door all the way and guided Amanda in, then turned to leave, closing the door behind her.

Amanda stood there, staring. She couldn't believe what she saw.

Kevin stood. A big smile appeared on his face. He opened his arms. "Hello, my darling Amanda."

Within seconds he folded his arms around her and kissed her tenderly. "I hope those are tears of joy." He kissed her again.

"I didn't know if I would ever see you again. I had to come and be with you. I love you so much."

"I love you, too." He sat back down in the chair and pulled her onto his lap. "I've so much to tell you, but for now I just want to hold you, kiss you, and never let you go."

That was how Kane found them an hour later, Amanda sitting on his father's lap, their arms around each other. "You haven't changed a bit, Amanda. You're as beautiful as I remember."

"My God, Kane. Is that really you?" She stood. "Come over here and let me look at you." She was reluctant to leave Kevin's side.

Kane walked over to her. "I'm glad you're here."

"I always knew you would grow up to be handsome like your father."

Kane put his arms around her and gave her a hug. "I'm sure you two want to spend some time alone, but I want you to meet someone first." He walked over and opened the door. "Come in." Katy stepped into the room, now dressed in jeans, her long beautiful hair pulled back in a ponytail. Kane took her hand. "I know you met her as Sister Katy, and she really is a sister. She's my twin sister, Katy."

"She has your eyes, Kevin. She's beautiful."

Kevin smiled at Katy. "I think so, too."

"Does everybody wear disguises around here?" Amanda asked.

"Only when we have to," answered Katy. "Come on, handsome brother of mine. I think Dad and Amanda need to be alone. We'll be across the hall if you need us."

Sister Elizabeth noticed something wrong with Katy when she watched her and Kane enter the room. Kane felt it, also. "Okay, Katy, why don't you tell us what's bothering you."

Katy sighed. "Oh, I don't know. I guess I'm feeling a little betrayed." She looked at Kane. "You've had our father around all your life. I've only had him in mine twenty-four hours and now I have to share him with a total stranger."

Sister Elizabeth sat down by Katy and picked up her hand. "Sometimes I wish I had great words of wisdom to give you to take away your hurt. I can tell you this. What you're feeling is totally normal. What you have to remember is the love you're feeling toward your father needs time to grow, and it's a different kind of love Amanda has for him. I have to be truthful with you. I was feeling a little resentment toward Amanda, too."

A look of shock appeared on Katy's face. "Why?"

"Loyalty toward your mother, my sister, but she's dead, and your father deserves whatever happiness he can find."

"Do you want to meet her?" Katy asked.

"Maybe later. I'd rather spend time with you and Kane and hear more about his life on the island."

Kane smiled. "Okay, then I want to hear more about Katy's life on this place called 'The Ranch'."

Sister Elizabeth was surprised when the phone rang. It was Lorena. "I wanted you to know I'm pregnant. It took the Doctor longer because I'm not very far along. He confined me to bedrest for four weeks. I have to be very careful. He doesn't want me to lose this one. I can't thank you enough. My husband says if you need anything, anything at all, to let him know." They talked for a while longer before Sister hung up the phone.

It was close to midnight when Kane knocked on his father's door and entered. He found his father asleep. Amanda sat in the chair beside him, holding his hand. He could tell she felt reluctant to let him go. "Sister Elizabeth offered to walk with you back to your room."

257

Amanda stood, bent down and kissed Kevin on the forehead. "Goodnight, my love, see you tomorrow night."

"You could come back tomorrow morning," Kane stated.

"I'm spending the day with Raul—I hope." She watched the smile disappear from Kane's face and walked toward him. "Please don't worry. He will never know I've seen you or your father. I would never betray either of you. If it hadn't been for your father..." she paused. "Well, I'll let him tell you."

Sister Elizabeth was waiting in the hall. She introduced herself. "I understand you met my son, Raul? I'll see him for the first time in twelve years tomorrow."

"He's a nice young man. I think you'll be very proud." Sister glanced her way. "He looks a lot like you. He's polite and has a good sense of humor."

"That's nice to hear. Kevin and Kane have been a good influence on him. I don't know if you need to hear this, but Kevin loved your sister, Meg, very much. He still does. What do you think Kevin's chances are of finding a donor?"

Sister heard the fear in her voice. "Katy will be tested when we get back home. If she doesn't match... well, we'll cross that bridge when we come to it."

Amanda arrived at the park half an hour early. She came to a stop when she saw her ex-husband emerge from a limo about half a block away. A taller, thin young man followed him. Her heart beat faster. *That's my son.* She watched as he approached her, a big grin on his face.

"Mom! I can't believe you're here." He wrapped his arms around her.

His sudden show of affection surprised, but thrilled her, too. "Oh, Raul, I've missed you so much."

Prince Tali stood silently behind them. It was several minutes before Amanda acknowledged his presence. He smiled. "You're even more beautiful than I remember. I'm leaving the car and driver for you, Raul. If you don't have plans for dinner, Amanda, we would like you to join us." He turned and walked away.

"Let's sit over here... " She took Raul by the hand. "...and talk."

The park looked deserted to Raul, with only about a half dozen people walking around. "When did you say your flight was leaving?"

"It's open. I wasn't sure if you'd even want to see me."

"I've been wanting to see you for a long time. Father said the money was more important to you than I was."

They talked for a long time. Raul told her things that happened to him while growing up, Kane always at his side.

"How is Kane and his father?"

"I wish I knew." He told her about Kevin's sickness and how they both just disappeared. "Kane wants to be with his father and help him. He promised me he'd be back and I believe him. I want to show you something." He reached in his pocket and took out a folded piece of paper. He opened it and showed it to her.

"This is me."

"Where did you get this?"

"Kane drew it for me. It's very good, don't you think?"

"It's amazing." She reached up to undo her hair, letting it fall around her shoulders. She ran her fingers through it, then held the drawing up beside her. "I wear my hair like this when I'm home."

Raul looked at her, then the drawing. It was almost like she was sitting right there when Kane drew it. "You're right. It is amazing. Why don't you leave your hair down? I like it that way. How about some lunch?"

They walked to a café about two blocks from the park. Amanda was very aware of a man following them. "I see you have a new shadow. How are Mani and J.J.?"

"J.J. is doing great. He's married now, couple of kids. The new guy's name is Yorky. Kane saved his son's life." Raul told her all about it over lunch.

When they got back to the park, Raul introduced her to Yorky and asked him to look in the trunk for a blanket. Raul spread it out on the grass underneath a big shady tree. That was where they spent the rest of the day. Raul told her about Mani and his brothers. She cried when he opened his shirt and showed her the scars. "Father said he called you, left several messages, but you never called back."

"I never received them or I would have been here."

"And you haven't talked to him since you left?"

"No, I haven't. I hope this doesn't disappoint you, but I never tried to call him. He sent a check once a year with a typed note, saying everyone was fine. I want you to know, Raul, I've never spent any of that money. If you ever need it, it's there for you." She wanted so much to tell him about his sister, but knew she couldn't take the risk. *Maybe if I can get him to visit me in Vermont.* "Do you think, now that you're older, you could come to the States and spend some time with your Uncle Larry and your grandparents? They send their love and would like very much to see you."

"I'd like that." Raul smiled. "It snows a lot there, doesn't it?"

"Yes, it does."

"Maybe Uncle Larry could teach me to ski. If Kane's back by then, I'll bring him, too."

The day went by too quickly for Amanda. "Can we see each other again before I leave?"

"How about tomorrow? Would you like to go to the island?"

Amanda laughed. "I don't think your father would like that. Why don't we meet here again in the morning? Same time?"

"I'll be here." He hugged her and watched her walk away.

Amanda couldn't believe how happy she was. She would spend the evening with Kevin and tomorrow with Raul.

It was seven o'clock when she knocked on Kevin's door. She was surprised to see everyone there, waiting for her. They wanted to hear how her day went with Raul. She told them everything.

"It must have been very difficult not to tell Raul about his sister," Kane said.

"It was, but I couldn't take the chance. If he told anyone, and it got back to Tali, I'm afraid I might never see her again. Raul will find out soon enough. He wants to come and visit. Well, that's enough about me. The main reason we're all here is to help Kevin. What can I do?"

Kevin softly squeezed her hand. "Have dinner with us, relax. I think you need a good night's sleep. We'll talk more tomorrow."

Amanda left and for the next two hours different plans were talked about, torn apart and talked about again. The one thing they all agreed on, Kevin needed medical attention and they needed to get him and Kane out of Greece—the sooner—the better. The longer they remained. the more likely was the chance of Tali finding them. So they all agreed, tentatively, tomorrow Ben, along with Father James (Kevin), Kord McNamera (Kane), Katy, and Sister Elizabeth would fly in the company jet to London. There a ticket would be purchased for Father James to fly to New York, along with Ward, Samantha, Kord and Amanda.

Ben, Katy, Kane, and Sister Elizabeth would follow them there in the company jet.

Ben excused himself. He was going to call Doctor Daniel at The Ranch, explain everything and hope by the time they arrived in New York, he would have a hospital and a specialist lined up so that they could take Kevin directly there.

Ward went across the hall to use the phone. He would call the airlines, make reservations for the day after tomorrow. That would give Amanda another day to spend with her son, and Ward and Samantha could notify Ben in case of trouble.

"Aunt Liz, I have something I want to do."

"What is it, Katy?"

"If Doctor Stevens is on duty tonight, I'd like to go by the hospital and see if he can test me to find out if I'm a good donor. I need to know."

Sister nodded her head. "He might as well test me, too, while we're there."

"I'm going, too," said Sami.

Sister Elizabeth smiled. "That's my girls. Let's wait for Ben. He can drive us."

Ben picked up his detector and slipped it into his pocket. "Let's go girls."

Sister knocked on the door, opening it when she heard the doctor's voice.

"Come in."

Doctor Stevens stood when he saw the two nuns enter. Then he saw Ben and a smile crossed his face.

Ben took out the detector and checked the room. "All clear."

"I certainly didn't expect to ever see you again." The doctor held out his hand.

"My name's Ben. This is Sister Elizabeth, Katy, Kane's sister, and Samantha." Katy reached up and took out one of her brown contacts, then replaced it. "The reason we're here," continued Ben, "is Katy wants you to test her as a donor for her father. Actually you could test us all."

"Why don't I do Katy first?"

"How long will it take?" asked Katy.

"I've got everything all set up. Let me draw some blood. I'll have a pretty good idea in minutes. To be completely positive takes twelve hours."

While they waited, Ben told the doctor about Amanda, and that Kevin and Kane were fine. "Do you have an extra doctor's coat I could have as a souvenir?"

"Sure do," said Doctor Stevens. "And when you get to the States, look up this doctor." He wrote the name down on a piece of paper, handed it to Ben, along with the coat. "Tell Kevin I wish him all the best. He's a good friend."

It was only a few minutes before he turned to Katy. "Well, young lady, I would say it's ninety percent sure you are a perfect match."

Katy breathed a sigh of relief. "I had a pretty good idea I was. I just needed to hear it."

Katy knocked on her father's door before entering. Kane and Amanda were still there with Ward. "Doctor Stevens sends his best. He says there's a ninety-percent chance I'm a perfect match." Katy, Kevin and Kane looked at each other and smiled. All three knew from the very beginning she would be.

Ben shook his head. "Why do I get the feeling we just went through all this for nothing?"

Katy walked over and put her hand on his shoulder. "It wasn't for nothing. We did it for you." She started to laugh and the rest joined in.

Ben looked at Sami. "Do you get the feeling we've been taken for a ride?"

She walked over to him. "I believe you're right, but may I remind everyone the famous line from Father Tim." She and Ben said it together. "Paybacks are hell."

# Chapter 23

Raul stood there, looking at his father. "What do you mean that we have to drive to the island tonight?"

"I need your help with something. We'll drive back early in the morning. If it's not too late, we may even drive back tonight. Let's have some dinner first. I wish Amanda would have joined us."

"We could take her to the island tomorrow."

Prince Tali smiled. "If that's what you want and she would like to go. I think that would be nice."

"Thanks, Dad. Let's eat."

An hour later they were on their way to Tali Island.

"It's good to see the lights on the island again. Don't you think so, Raul?"

He had to admit it was. "Yes, it is. What is it you have to get that's so important?"

"Papers for the company lawyer. Strictly confidential. It could cost a lot of money if these papers get in the wrong hands. I have them stored in the shelter room in the basement."

Raul laughed. "You mean the playroom where Kane and I spent many happy hours?"

"That's the one." *And it's where you'll spend the next couple of days until your dear mother leaves town. She's going to find out her little trip cost her a lot more than expected. She won't get another penny from me.*

Amanda awoke the next morning with a whole new outlook on life. Everything was going along so well. Nothing could diminish the happiness she felt. She dressed with extra care, letting her hair hang loose the way Raul liked it.

She arrived at the park early, hoping Raul would, too. Soon it was nine, then nine-thirty. She was starting to get worried. *What if something happened to him?* Another half-hour passed, then she saw the limo drive up. *Thank God.* But it wasn't Raul or even his father, that stepped out of the car. It was Zoric. He walked up to her. "Sorry to keep you waiting, Amanda. You are looking beautiful, more beautiful than I remember."

"Cut the crap, Zoric. Where's Raul?"

"I see your English has improved. Please let's sit and talk. I have news from Raul."

She hesitated a minute, then walked over and sat on the bench. Zoric followed her.

"Okay, Zoric, where's Raul?"

"He's on the island. Tali called me this morning, told me you were in town and said he let Raul spend the day with you yesterday, and one day was all there would be."

"Doesn't Raul have anything to say about this?"

"No, he doesn't. Tali has his own rules. You should know that better than anyone."

"I see he still has that string tied around you. It must be tied somewhere that when he pulls on it, it hurts like hell. I bet you're still not married."

"Time has turned you into a cruel woman, Amanda. I'm here to give you a message. I thought you'd rather hear it from me than some stranger. Before I tell you, I want you to know I don't approve of you just showing up. That wasn't in the agreement. So you have no one to blame but yourself."

"Really. Why didn't Tali call me when Raul almost died?"

"He did try. You never returned his calls."

"You believe whatever he says, don't you?"

"This is the message; Prince Tali has Raul on the island. He put him in the shelter room in the basement. When you leave Greece, he'll let him out."

"You mean he's locked his own son away like some criminal. My God, and you're letting him do that! You're scum, Zoric, worse than your brother."

"I really don't care what you think of me or my brother." Zoric stood. "Do everyone a favor and get out of town."

Amanda watched him until the limo drove away. Tears stung her eyes. *What have I done?*

Zoric walked toward the limo. *I can't believe she would believe something like that.* He chuckled to himself. *I guess some women are easier to manipulate than others.*

Raul sat on the bed in the room where he and Kane had spent so many hours playing. Even though the room was cold, Raul's body was sweating. He got up and paced back and forth. He couldn't believe his father actually locked him in this hellhole. He went over and pounded on the door.

"Father, open this damn door. I'll do whatever you say." He kept pounding and screaming. He didn't know he was alone. His father was on his way to the mainland. He hated the feeling of confinement. It reminded him too much of being tied to that tree—with no way to escape. *Kane, where are you? I need you.*
His thoughts turned to his mother. *I'm so sorry.*

Kane and his father were alone in their room. Everyone else was busy, getting things organized. The only ones not leaving today on the company jet were Sami, her father, Ward, and Amanda. Kane was drawing in his tablet, while Kevin read the paper.

Kane, feeling a sense of uneasiness, glanced over at his father. "I keep thinking about Raul." He stood and showed his father what he'd been drawing. "Do you know what this is?" Kane asked.

Kevin studied the drawing closely. "It's been a few years, but it looks like the shelter room in the basement of the Estate where you and Raul used to play." Kevin knew right away something was wrong as he watched his son walk around the room with one hand on his hip and the other rubbing back and forth through the hair on his head.

"Why do I see Raul in that room?" Kane mumbled to himself.

Kevin flipped the tablet back to the beginning, thumbing through the other drawings. He stopped and looked closely at the one of a man holding a small baby. A woman sat in a chair at his side. "This must be Yorky, his wife and their baby son." Kevin smiled proudly at his son. He turned the pages back to the one of the shelter room. "Do you see Raul hiding from someone? No that's not it." Kevin looked up at Kane.

"He's in that room against his will," Kane stated. "But why?"

"It's Tali." Kevin took a deep breath. "I feel it now, too. It has something to do with Amanda."

They turned when Ben walked in from the adjoining room.

Ben stopped in his tracks and looked from one to the other. His hand rubbed his forehead. "Damn, now I have three of you. I've seen that look before. What's going on?"

Kane and Kevin couldn't help, but chuckle. "Katy's trained you well, I see." Kane walked over to him and fondly patted his shoulder. "Since Katy and Sami call you Uncle Ben, would it be all right if I do, too?"

They were close to the same height. Ben looked into his eyes. "Oh boy, this must be a real doozy."

"Let me show you." Kane walked over and took the tablet from his father, showing it to Ben. "The Tali Estate, where we lived on the island, has a shelter room in the basement. Raul and I played in there when we were children. I believe Raul is locked in that room."

"Why?" asked Ben. "Who would do that?"

"His father, to keep Raul from his mother. He thinks he's protecting him. Raul will go into shock if we don't get him out of there."

"How long do we have?" asked Ben.

"Couple of hours. Amanda's at the park now, waiting for Raul. I know Tali will have someone following her, watching her every move. That someone will be this man." Kane showed Ben the drawing of Yorky and his family.

"Is this the baby whose life you saved?" Ben looked at Kane.

"It was Doctor Stevens who saved the boy's life." Kane smiled. "I just did a little pre-diagnosis."

"How do you think we should handle this?" Ben asked him.

Kane walked over and sat by his father. "If I write a note to Yorky, could you have one of the girls give it to him?"

"Give what to whom?" asked Sister Elizabeth as she walked into the room through the same door Ben had used.

Ben shook his head. "She does this all the time. You'll get used to it."

"What do I do?"

Ben smiled at her. "Showing up exactly when I need you."

"Need me for what?"

Ben explained to her what was going on and what the plan was. He showed her the drawing.

"You're very good, Kane. This looks exactly like him. Get everything ready. I'll make sure he gets it." She handed the tablet back to him. He opened it to a blank page and began to write.

*Yorky,*

*I'm glad to hear everything went well with your son. I need you to help Raul. The woman you're following, I'm sure you know, is his mother, Amanda. Tali has forbidden Raul to see her again and has locked Raul in a basement shelter at the Estate on Tali Island. If he's not let out in a couple of hours, he'll go into shock. He can't handle being confined. You saw the reason why. When you get to the Estate, go to the kitchen. There's a door that leads to a pantry full of stored can goods. The back shelf, exactly in the middle, opens up leading down a flight of stairs. When you get to the bottom, go to your left and you will come to a room with a lock on it. A key is always left in the lock. Tell Raul I will always be there for him, and I will be back as promised. Take care of him for me until then. I know what you're feeling and what you'd like to do to Tali, but please don't. We still have that third game of chess to finish.*

*Your friend,*

*Kane.*

Kane clipped the note to the drawing and rolled it up.

"I'll get a rubberband for you," Sister Elizabeth said. "Is there anything else I need to know?"

"I think that's about it," Kane said. "Thanks, Aunt Liz."

She reached up and softly touched his cheek. "You're welcome." She turned and walked out the door, stopping at the front desk and asking for a rubberband. Then she slipped the rolled-up paper into her shirt pocket and headed for the park.

She spotted Amanda about a block away, sitting on a bench in front of a picnic table, her head lying on her folded arms.

She slowed down and came to a stop. Her eyes surveyed the area. There were only a few people there and they were on the other side of the park. She saw a couple of cars, one was a limo. She recognized the man who was sitting on the grass by a tree smoking a cigarette as Yorky.

She waited a few minutes to make sure he was alone before she continued walking. She passed close by the bench where Amanda was sitting. "Don't say anything, Amanda." She kept walking until she came to a stop in front of Yorky.

"Good morning, has anyone ever told you those cigarettes will stunt your growth?"

Yorky chuckled and stood up. "Good morning, Sister. Aren't you the one that flew the chopper?"

"Yes. I recognized you, too." She glanced around the park again.

"If you're looking for Zoric, he left about ten minutes ago."

"And left you all alone?" She smiled.

"Yes, but I think I'm finally big enough to take care of myself." He tossed his cigarette to the ground and stepped on it, then bent down, picked it up, and walked over to put it in the trash barrel. "I really have been trying to quit."

"For your son's sake, I hope you will. Maybe this can help." She reached into her pocket and pulled out the rolled-up paper and handed it to him. "Open it. See what you think."

Yorky studied it for a minute before slipping off the rubberband.

Sister watched the surprised look on his face as he looked at the drawing and began to read the note. Then she saw another look that sent chills up her spine.

"That son of a bitch," he mumbled under his breath. He looked up at her and saw the smile appear on her face. "I'm sorry, Sister. I didn't mean for you to hear that."

She reached out and touched his arm. "Believe me, I feel the same. I'm sure you can handle it. Someone has a lot of faith in you."

"I'll do my best." He rolled the drawing back up and put it in his back pocket, took out his lighter and set fire to the note Kane had written. He laid it on the ground. Both watched until the flame burned out. He took the paper from his back pocket. "Sister, nice seeing you again." He turned and walked toward the limo.

Sister watched him drive away. *I hope for Tali's sake that he's not home or we'll be attending a funeral before we leave.*

Amanda stood as Sister walked toward her. "What's going on?"

"He's going to Tali Island to let Raul out of the locked room."

Amanda sat back down on the bench. "Thank you, God."

Sister started to laugh. "I'm not quite that high on the ladder yet, but I'll pass it on."

She sat down across from Amanda, who, after realizing what she had said, was laughing, too.

Yorky pulled the limo to a stop in front of the Tali Estate. He was surprised there were no cars around. He got out and walked up to the front door. *Unlocked. Good I won't have to break a window.* He followed the instructions Kane had given him and, within minutes, he stood at the door in the basement. He reached up and turned the key, unlocking the door.

"Father?"

Yorky opened the door wide. "It's me, Raul." He saw the fear on the boy's face.

"My father sent you?"

"No. Kane did."

Raul fell to his knees and sobbed. "Kane. He came back."

Yorky pulled him to his feet. "No, he's not back. He will be— someday. He'll always be here to take care of you. How? I don't know, but he seems to be doing a pretty good job." Yorky was glad to see the smile appear on Raul's face.

"No one knows you're here?" asked Raul.

"No one, but Kane. He sent me a note."

"He's a real classy guy. Don't you think, Yorky?"

"He's got potential." Yorky handed him the key.

"We'll keep this between the two of us. I mean the three of us. I'll tell my father I had a spare key hidden in the room. I don't want you to get in trouble."

'I've never been here." Yorky waved his hand as he walked away, then pointed his finger at Raul. "Call me if you need me."

"I will. Thanks, Yorky."

Raul stood at the front door and watched until Yorky was out of sight. He reached in his pocket, taking out the piece of paper with the phone number to the hotel where his mother was staying. He walked into his father's office and sat down in his father's chair. *There comes a time in a young boy's life when he has to make a decision that will make him a man. Like Kane. He stood up and took control of his life. I'm going to do the same.* He picked up the phone and dialed the number.

"Amanda Farly, please."

It rang three times, then he heard her voice. "This is Amanda."

"Hi, Mom."

"Raul!"

"Please, don't cry. I'm okay."

"I was so worried."

"I know. Did father talk to you?"

"No. Zoric did."

Raul was surprised. "Zoric. What did he tell you?"

Amanda told him the conversation that took place.

"You don't have to leave."

"I've made a reservation on tomorrow's flight. I think it would be best for you if I go."

Raul knew she was right. "Can I come to the airport and see you before you leave?"

"I'd like that. We can talk about you coming to visit." She gave him her flight schedule. "See you tomorrow."

Raul leaned back in the chair. The words from his father kept repeating in his mind. *'It's for your protection. Someday you'll understand when you have your own children.' I wish I had eleven brothers and sisters and I was the one in the middle, and our mother was pregnant with triplets. God, what am I saying? I must be getting desperate.* He closed his eyes letting his mind go over what he would say to his father.

He heard the front door open.

"Raul, are you here?"

*Good old Uncle Zoric.* "In the office." He looked at his watch. *I've been asleep four hours.*

Zoric walked in. "I must say, you look all grown up sitting there."

"So that's why I feel older than you. It must be this chair. It certainly couldn't be because of my father, and perhaps you, now could it?"

"Is someone having a little temper tantrum?"

"No. I had that earlier when I was locked in the shelter room. In fact I think I had four or five of them."

"What? Are you trying to tell me that your father actually did lock you in that room?"

Raul studied Zoric for several minutes before he spoke. "You didn't know? Well, that's just great. It's kind of hard to be mad at someone when they didn't do anything. No, wait a minute. I am mad. You had no right to talk to my mother. She knew my father was capable of putting me in that room. Do you have any idea what I went through from last night till today? No, you wouldn't know. You're like my father. He didn't know, either. I'll explain it to you when you're old enough to understand. If you don't mind, I'd like to wait for my father alone."

Zoric stood. "I'm truly sorry, Raul. I really didn't know. I thought he wanted to scare Amanda."

"It worked. She's leaving tomorrow."

"You want me to talk to her?"

Raul shook his head. "God, no. You've been enough help, but you could tell me where my car is."

"You haven't driven your car since that night."

"Well, it's time to start. Where is it?"

"Why don't I drive you. Make sure it starts."


An hour later Raul drove his car up in front of the Estate. His father was there.

"Where the hell have you been?"

"I haven't been with Mother if that's what you're worried about."

"How did you get out of that room?"

"I had a key. Sit down, I have something to tell you. If you ever do anything like that to me again, I'll pack my bags and leave. My mother is flying back to the States tomorrow. I'm going to the airport, by myself, to tell her good-bye. If you try to stop me in any way, I'll be buying a ticket on the same flight—one way."

Raul turned and left his father sitting there. He didn't notice the smile on his father's face.

*Carole A. Sheller*

# Chapter 24
## HOTEL

Katy's eyes opened wide. *Something's happened to Raul.* She got out of bed, slipped on her bathrobe and headed for her father's room.

"Come in, Katy," her father said before she even knocked on the door. Ben looked up when she entered, noting the change of color in her eyes. "What took you so long? Kane's already taken care of everything."

She walked over by him. "Why would Tali do something like that to his own son?" She saw the concerned look on Kane's face.

"He's okay now." Kane smiled. He put his arm around her. "Yorky got there in plenty of time. I don't know about you, but I'm ready to see this paradise called The Ranch."

"We just have to make one stop first." Katy smiled at her father, then looked at Ben. "Did you call the doctor?"

"I still don't know why you ask me things when you already know the answer." He saw the sadness appear in her eyes. In a flash he was by her side. "Honey, what is it?"

She looked up into his eyes. "I don't know if I can explain, but I don't ever want not to be able to share things with you."

"That's never going to happen. You're stuck with me." He wrapped his arms around her, holding her tight. After a few minutes he let her go. He touched the tip of her nose with his finger. "Now that's the sparkle I like seeing in my girl's eyes. You ready to go home?"

They spent the next hour getting Kevin ready to go with beard, brown contacts, gray coloring in his hair, the clothes of a priest, and a walking cane.

Then it was Kane's turn, with a dark coloring in his hair, brown contacts, glasses, a distinguished-looking mustache, and the doctor's coat.

Everyone was in Kevin's room when Amanda came to tell them the good news. Ben introduced her to Father James.

"It's nice to meet you, Father." She smiled fondly and reached out to shake his hand. He pulled her forward and kissed her. "Father!" A shocked expression appeared on her face.

273

Everyone started laughing, Kevin, too. "Amanda, it's me."

"Kevin?" Her laughter joined the others. She looked over at Kane. "I would never recognize either one of you. Ben, Ward was right, you are good."

"Thank you. Why don't the rest of us go over to Sister's room? Give Amanda and Kevin a few minutes alone."

"Are you sure you'll be able to take care of everything, Sami?" Sister Elizabeth asked.

"I talked to the lady at the front desk. She'll have a special car sent to pick us up, and the people at the airport are always helpful. I'll check everyone out of their rooms tomorrow. If anything happens that you need to know about, I'll call Kord at his mother's house in London."

Ben called Damon, asking him to pick them up in two hours, at the same place where he had dropped them off to pick up the station wagon.

In an hour, they were packed and ready to go. Sami helped Ben take their luggage to the station wagon. "I'm glad you're spending the night in London. You look like you could use a good night's sleep before the long flight home." She paused for a minute. "Are they what you expected?"

"It's been—how shall I put it—rewarding, entertaining, educational, and not anything like I expected. Kane is so much like Katy. This gift they both have, I think his is a lot stronger, and Kevin, the guy's been through hell. I like them both. How about you?"

"Kane is absolutely divine. He's so good-looking and so is Kevin. I wish Dad and I could have done more to help."

"You've done a lot. If Ward hadn't met Amanda, she wouldn't be with Kevin right now." Ben closed the back end of the station wagon. His eyes surveyed the area. "See anything out of the ordinary, Sami?"

She looked around. "Only the limo."

"I think that's the guy named Yorky, leaning against the back passenger's door." remarked Ben.

"Is he going to be a problem?" asked Sami.

"I hope not. You see the size of that guy."

Sami started snickering. "You could outrun him, I bet."

Ben laughed, too. "If he came after me I could even outrun that limo." He put his arm around her and they headed back into the hotel.

"Let's just go for it. We can't sit here all day." Sister Elizabeth stood. Kane looked at Katy. "Gutsy little thing, isn't she?"

"Always has been," Katy replied. "Ready to go?"

"Amanda has been gone for what, twenty minutes?" he asked.

"Yes." Katy smiled. "I hope Yorky likes shopping."

Sister put her arm on Kevin's. "Lean on me for support. Remember your in a lot of pain."

With walking cane in one hand and Sister Elizabeth on the other side, he walked out the door. Ben, Katy, and Kane would follow in five minutes.

Ben had parked the car as close as he could to the front door. She opened the passenger door for Kevin, then heard someone call her name.

"Oh Lord, it's Zoric, and Prince Tali is sitting in their car. Don't panic," she whispered to Kevin as she helped him into the front seat.

He smiled up at her. "I won't."

She turned. "Zoric, I wasn't expecting to see you here."

"We were close by and thought maybe you and your family would like to go for that helicopter ride. We're on our way to Tali Island and would like very much for you to join us."

She closed the door and walked away from the car, hoping he would follow and he did. "I'm afraid it will have to wait until I return. Father James," she pointed to the car, "is why we came to Greece. He needs an operation on his spinal cord to remove a cyst. Were thankful its not malignant, but he is in a great deal of pain. There are only a few surgeons that are qualified to perform this type of new surgery so we're taking him back to the States. We should return in about a month."

"Well, you have my number. Please call. Have a good flight." He reached his hand out to her. "I'll be forever in your debt for being in the right place at the right time."

She smiled and shook his hand. "It almost makes you think someone planned it that way. I'll call you."

She waved to Prince Tali as she watched Zoric walk away, then glanced at Kevin, sitting in the car with a big grin on his face. She turned toward the entrance of the hotel and saw Katy, and Ben standing there, waiting. She was sure Kane was close by, too. She took a deep breath and realized her heart was beating rapidly. She walked to the car, opened the back door and got in and silently, to herself, said a prayer asking God to forgive her—-again—-for the lies she must tell to protect her family.

It was only a few minutes before Katy was sitting next to her with

Kane on the other side. Ben sat behind the wheel. Silence filled the air, then Kevin started to laugh, breaking the tension that was felt by all. It only took a moment before the sound of five people laughing echoed inside the car.

Ben finally spoke. "You know what really puzzles me. The three of you have this special gift. Why is it that not one of you knew Zoric and Prince Tali would be here?"

Kevin looked at him. "If I knew the answer to that, Kane and I would never have spent sixteen years being held prisoners on Tali Island. I didn't know I'd be dressed like this either, but, thanks to you, I am." Kevin smiled. "I'd like to see their faces if they ever find out Father James was actually me."

Damon, smiling as always, was there to meet them when Ben pulled the car to a stop. He kept thanking Sister Elizabeth over and over again for telling him about the baby his wife, Lorena, was going to have and promised he would take very good care of her. "I've already cleared your plane through the main terminal," Damon informed them. "If you give me your passports, I'll go have them checked in, too."

"The doctor won't be traveling with us," Sister Elizabeth told Damon as she handed him four passports. "Would it be all right if he rode back with you?"

"Certainly. I should be back in about twenty minutes," Damon said as he looked at his watch.

Ben waited until Damon was gone. He looked at Kane. "I hope you're not claustrophobic?"

Kane thought for a moment before answering. "I really don't know. Why? What have you got planned for me?"

"There's no way the passport we have for you will work. We're going to hide you in the compartment on the floor of the plane. It's small and the ride will be rough until we're in the air and raise the landing gear, then you can get out."

"I'll manage," Kane, said, confidently. "Please don't forget about me."

They were ready to go when Damon returned. Sister told him the doctor was called away on an emergency.

Damon thanked her again. He waited until the plane taxied out of the hanger before he got in his cart and drove away.

It took almost half an hour before they were cleared for take-off. An airline inspector stopped them before entering the road that led to the runway. He was looking around the inside of the plane when Sister Elizabeth spoke. "Look, everyone, isn't that Zoric and Prince Tali?" Shock sounded in her voice. "This must be where they keep their helicopter."

The inspector looked in the direction she was pointing. "Yes, madam, that's the Tali family." He glanced at her. "Are you the nun pilot everyone's talking about?"

She smiled at him. "Guilty as charged."

"It's a pleasure meeting you. Could I get you to sign this release slip for me?"

"Of course."

He left the plane without finishing his inspection.

Ben watched as Zoric and Prince Tali walked toward them. He glanced at Sister Elizabeth and smiled as he saw her make the sign of the cross.

Prince Tali was the first to enter the plane. "I wanted to thank you personally, Sister Elizabeth, for everything." His eyes moved around the inside of the compartment, stopping when he looked into the brown eyes of the priest setting in the back.

Ben could have sworn he saw Prince Tali's jaws grinding together as the man's eyes surveyed the plane.

Tali stepped further into the plane, stopping when he approached Katy. A smile came to his face. "You must be the one my son, Raul, told me about. He was right, you look too young to fly a plane or a helicopter. Raul was most impressed. He'll be looking forward to your return.

Katy smiled sweetly. "Me, too."

Tali turned toward the priest. He studied closely, the man sitting there looking up at him. "Father James..." Tali reached out his hand. "I'm Prince Tali." He paused for a moment before asking, "Have we meant somewhere before?"

Kevin raised his hand. "I, we have," said Kevin, the Irish brogue from his voice deep and husky, "but I was not wearing the priest clothing at the time."

For reasons Tali couldn't explain, a feeling of uneasiness passed through him. Something didn't seem right, but he didn't have any idea what it could be. He nodded his head. "I wish you well, Father." He turned and walked back toward Ben and Sister Elizabeth.

They all spoke casually for a few minutes, then Tali looked back at Kevin, turned and took Sister Elizabeth's hand. "I hope the operation is a successful one."

"Thank you." Her voice sounded a little shaky. "We look forward to our return."

"Have a good flight," Zoric replied.

No one said anything as they watched the two brothers walk toward their helicopter then stop about a half block away. Prince Tali was throwing his arms in the air, definitely upset about something. He motioned to someone to join them.

"Isn't that the inspector who just checked our plane?" Ben asked.

Everyone agreed. That's exactly who it was. They sat in silence and watched as Prince Tali pointed toward their plane and the inspector shrugged his shoulders.

Ben jumped when the intercom from the main terminal came on and gave them clearance for take-off. "Let's get the hell out of here. I wonder if Prince Tali suspects anything?"

Katy smiled. "He doesn't."

Kevin felt a strange sensation pass through him as he watched Tali and Zoric. *Something's not right with Tali, but I can't think about that now. I have my family and friends that need me.* A smile came to his face. *This flying is even better than walking off the island.* He couldn't help himself as a hardy laugh escaped from his body. It didn't take long before the others joined in.

Kane was relieved when Katy opened the hatch and helped him out. "To my rescue again, thanks."

They spent the rest of the flight talking with Kevin and getting to know each other a little better.

Their arrival in London was smooth. Kord was there to pick them up. At first he didn't recognize Katy and, because she was dressed like a nun, he was reluctant to show her any affection. He made up for it later that evening. She told him everything that happened while in Greece as they sat cuddled up next to each other.

278

# Chapter 25
## HOTEL IN GREECE

The hotel restaurant was large and cozy. Doctor Stevens sat at the bar in the far corner so he could watch the people enter. The room was dimly lit, giving it a comfortable, relaxed atmosphere. He watched the three people, an attractive blonde woman, a man in a wheelchair, and the young lady he recognized as Samantha. The hostess led them to a secluded table, not too far from him. It was only a few minutes when he saw Yorky sit down at the other end of the bar close to the entrance. The doctor picked up his drink and went to join him.

Yorky was surprised to see the doctor. "What brings you to a place like this, Doc?"

"I should be asking you that question. Why aren't you home with your family?"

"Tali business. See that lady with the man in the wheelchair."

"Yes, I noticed her when she came in, very attractive."

"That's Raul's mother, Tali's ex."

"Really?" The doctor tried to sound surprised. "She lives here in Greece?"

"No. In the States. She's just here visiting."

"I'd like to meet her. Why don't you introduce us?"

"I don't think that's a good idea. I'm supposed to be keeping an eye on her."

"She doesn't know who you are?"

Yorky smiled. "She knows exactly who I am."

"No problem then." The doctor stood. "Come on."

The doctor's forwardness took Yorky by surprise, but after he thought about it he decided—what the heck.

As they approached the table where the three were sitting, Yorky noticed the sly grin on Amanda's face. "The name's Yorky, isn't it?" she asked.

"Yes, Ms." Yorky smiled at her. "I have someone here who'd like to meet you. This is Doctor Stevens. He knows your son, Raul."

"I've heard all about you, Doctor. Raul told me you operated on Yorky's son. Probably saved the boy's life. Please, won't the two of you join us for drinks?"

"We'd be delighted." The doctor sat in the chair next to her, Yorky on the other side. Amanda made the introduction.

"How is your son?" Sami asked.

"He's doing great." Yorky smiled. "Thanks for asking."

They had only been there a few minutes when Yorky's beeper went off. "Please excuse me."

Amanda watched him walk away. "It seems like yesterday when this was a way of life, never any privacy, a guard following you everywhere you go. And Tali knowing your every move."

"Yeah, the good old days," Sami said, teasingly.

"Something like that." Amanda turned toward the doctor. "I didn't know if I was going to meet you or not." She noticed the doctor glance at Ward.

"Ward knows everything."

Fifteen minutes later she had the doctor up to date on what was happening. "I'll be leaving tomorrow with Ward and Sami. We'll meet the others in London. I'll try to write to you, I promise."

"If you can't, I'll understand."

"You've been a caring, compassionate friend to Kevin. I'm sure we'll all see each other again."

They talked a while longer, then the doctor said goodbye, walking away and feeling at peace with himself, knowing his good friends, Kevin and Kane, were in good hands.

## LONDON

A lonely, empty feeling passed through Kane as he lay in the large, comfortable, hotel bed. It was a feeling he hadn't experienced before. *Homesickness.* He had to admit it could be true. He missed Raul, J.J., and even Zoric. He certainly didn't miss Prince Tali. He missed the island and the beautiful sunrises, Sassy the horse, and his new friend, Yorky.

He glanced at his father, sleeping soundly in the bed across the room. There was a happiness on his face Kane never had really seen before. Was it Katy, Amanda, or being free? Kane knew it was all three—and more.

It seemed everything was happening so fast, and yet so slow. They had been in London two days. Amanda, Ward, and Sami arrived around noon and everyone was scheduled to fly out the following day.

Kane's thoughts turned to his sister, Katy. They had spent hours together, telling each other about their lives growing up. Katy told him about the letters, waiting for him from their mother. There was one for Kevin, too. Katy told him about her letters and how she felt when she found out about having a twin brother that may or may not be alive.

"It's like finding a part of yourself that's been missing all your life," she told him.

She shared the visions she experienced throughout her life, and expressed her gratefulness for having people around that understood and loved her. Kane felt like he already knew them all, Sister Hanna, Father Tim, Jenny and Luke. He laughed when Katy told him how she had met Kord and his dog, Bear. He told her about Julianna.

Kane and his father had talked to Doctor Daniel earlier that day. Arrangements had been made for Kevin's operation which would be done at a hospital that performed one of the first successful bone marrow transplant. The University of Colorado Medical Center was located in their home state. Doctor Daniel had assured them there was nothing to worry about. The doctor who would perform the transplant was highly qualified and he would assist, that way he would be more knowledgeable of what was required in taking care of Kevin while he was recuperating at The Ranch. Kane smiled to himself. He already knew everything would be okay, so did his father and Katy.

Kane closed his eyes. His thoughts turned to Raul. He wished he could have brought him along. *He'll be fine until I return. He's in good hands. Yorky's taking care of him.*

_Carole A. Sheller_

# Chapter 26
## THE RANCH
## ONE MONTH LATER

The helicopter sliced through the chilly mountain air. Kane looked down on the flattop mountains. It still surprised him when he saw the homes and the livestock that roamed on top. The beauty of the place he now felt comfortable calling home was breathtaking and it showed in the painting he was doing. He still did the pencil sketching of people and hoped, by Christmas he would have one of everybody on The Ranch to give them as a present.

He didn't know what he would rather do, draw or fly. Uncle Ben, as he now called him, was giving him flying lessons on days when the weather permitted, so were Aunt Liz and Katy.

"We better head back," Katy said, interrupting his thoughts. "Sister Hanna has a big Sunday dinner planned. I promised her we'd help."

Kane smiled. Sundays were becoming a favorite day for him. He didn't even mind attending mass with his family. Father Tim made it interesting and enjoyable.

During the week everyone pitched in and helped wherever they were needed, but on Sundays they all spent time together.

Kane walked into the kitchen and put his arm around Sister Hanna. "Whatever you're cooking, it smells wonderful. I hope it's apple pie."

She reached up and gently pinched his cheek. "Of course, apple and peach, cherry and rhubarb."

"Rhubarb?"

"It was one of your mother's favorites."

He smiled at her. "What can I do to help?"

"You and Katy can set up the table, buffet style. We'll have a lot of hungry people here today." She was right. Before the day was over, at least fifty people stopped by The Ranch.

It was early evening when Kane saddled one of the horses and headed up the path toward Katy's favorite place, and he had to admit his, too.

283

He sat down on the ledge overlooking the mountains to watch the sunset. He turned when he heard a horse approaching.

Katy came over and sat beside him. "When are you leaving?" she asked him.

He started laughing and lay back on the grass, looking up at the sky. "It's nice to know we can't keep secrets from each other."

"Do you want me to go with you?"

"This is something I have to do by myself. Take good care of Dad while I'm gone."

"I don't think you'll have to worry about him. I have a lot of help. There's Amanda, her daughter Victoria, Aunt Liz, and, of course, Sister Hanna and Sami."

"With all that attention, he won't even know I'm gone. Besides Amanda and her daughter are going back to Vermont. Her brother, Larry, has been taking care of everything for her, but she needs to take care of Victoria's schooling and she's applying for a leave of absence from teaching for a year. So you'll have Dad all to yourself for a while."

"Are you going to tell Raul about dad and Amanda?"

"When the time is right."

They talked for a while longer. Katy knew she couldn't talk him out of going. He had his reasons and she respected them—and wanted to help. "I'll drive you to the city tomorrow and we'll get your passport. I'm sure Ben will fly you to Denver to catch your flight."

Three days later Kevin stood by the plane, Kane at his side. He turned toward him. "You're old enough to make this decision on your own. I'll be here if you need me."

"I know, Dad. I'll call you from Doctor Stevens' apartment when I arrive." Kane hugged his father and boarded the plane.

Kevin watched until the plane was out of sight. A slight feeling of guilt passed through him, but faded fast. *There's nothing I, or Kane, can do for Tali now. The only thing that's important is Raul. Kane, and even Zoric, will be there to help him get through this tragedy—the death of his father.*

# Chapter 27
## GREECE
## FOUR DAYS LATER

Kane looked around when he got off the plane. It was almost as if he expected Prince Tali to be there with handcuffs and chains. He got in a taxi and headed for Doctor Stevens' apartment. He knocked several times. When there was no answer, he used the key the doctor had given him and went inside, making himself at home. He took out the detector to check the room, like he promised Ben he would do—nothing.

He lay down on the couch and closed his eyes. He saw again the vision of Prince Tali having a heart attack, but this time there was nothing he could do to prevent it. What was important was that he would be there for Raul.

Kane had been asleep about six hours when he heard the door open. The doctor was very happy to see him. "How's your father?"

"He's doing fine. So well, in fact, that he and Amanda are planning to be married. I'm sure they're both hoping you and your family will attend."

"We wouldn't miss it. Now I want you to tell me everything that happened, from the beginning, when you were at the hospital and who the people were that helped you. Please don't leave out anything."

When Kane finished, he asked, "Have you seen Raul?"

"No, but I know he's doing fine. Yorky told me when he brought his son in for a check-up. He always asks if I've heard from you."

"I plan on calling him to see if he'll drive me to the island."

"Are you sure that's what you want to do?"

"Raul needs me."

"Are you going to tell him about his father?"

"No. There's nothing anyone can do."

"I could run some tests, do a heart bypass. There's several things available."

"I know, and it could prolong his life for a day or two, but he still wouldn't survive. You can do whatever you think you have to." Kane smiled at him. "You're the doctor. When it's over, I plan on taking

Raul home with me. He needs to spend time with his mother and sister, Victoria, whom he doesn't even know exists."

"When will you tell him about her?"

Kane laughed. "When we're high in the air, flying over the ocean."

They talked for a while longer, then Doctor Stevens called Yorky at his home. His wife answered the phone. "Is your husband there?" He glanced at his watch, four in the afternoon.

"Yes. Is everything all right?" she asked.

"It's fine. I have a favor I need to ask him."

She handed the phone to her husband. "Hello."

"Yorky, this is Doctor Stevens. I was wondering when you were going to Tali Island again?"

"In about an hour. I'm bringing Tali back here to his apartment. He has dinner plans with someone."

"Could you stop by my place and pick up a package that needs to be delivered to the island?"

"Of course."

Twenty minutes later Yorky knocked on Doctor Stevens door. "Come in."

He stepped inside and closed the door behind him. A big smile came to his face when Kane entered the room.

"I was hoping it would be you." He held out his hand.

Kane reached for it. "Nice to see you, Yorky. I hear your son is doing well."

"Yes, he is, and your father?"

"He's going to be fine. How's Raul?"

"Growing up fast. He'll be happy to see you. We all are."

Kane laughed. "There might be one person that's not too happy."

"He'll get over it. You know he still has people looking for you. He thinks you're still in the area somewhere. I think the person he's having dinner with is some private detective he hired."

"We better get going. I wouldn't want you to be late." They talked for a few minutes longer, then Kane turned toward the doctor. "I'd like to leave this with you." He handed him a large bulky envelope. "It contains my passport, some money and Ben's detector." He handed him a smaller envelope. "It's the key to your apartment and the money you gave me."

"I'll be available if you need me for anything."

Kane shook Doctor Stevens' hand. "Thanks for everything."

Kane and Yorky were silent on the ride to the island. Yorky pulled the limo to a stop in front of the estate. "If I don't see you in a couple of days, I'll know where you are." A grin appeared on his face, "Good to have you back."

He watched Kane walk up the path to the front door. Yorky saw Prince Tali standing there, watching. *You hurt that boy and I'll kill you with my bare hands.*

Prince Tali felt relief when he saw Kane getting out of the car, but he would never let him know it. The one thing he was positive about, the boy would never be allowed out of their sight again. He waited until Kane was in front of him. "We'll talk tomorrow, Raul's in his room."

Kane watched him until he got in the limo and drove away, then he entered the estate and walked toward Raul's room. He stood in the doorway. "Hey, didn't anybody ever teach you to clean up your room?" Kane walked in, picking up dirty clothes on his way.

Raul looked up from the magazine he was reading. "I used to have this really good friend that always helped me. I knew if I cleaned it up, it would hurt his feelings, and I didn't have the heart to do that." Raul stood, and with a big grin on his face, walked toward Kane. "Hello, brother." They had their own special greeting which they shared. Instead of the traditional handshake, their hands clasped each other's forearm with their other hand placed on the shoulder.

"I'm glad you're back, Kane. How's your father?"

"He's doing okay."

Raul saw the happiness on Kane's face. "You found another donor?"

"A perfect match, but you would have been next in line."

"It was probably some beautiful female that I couldn't compete with."

Kane threw back his head and laughed. "As a matter of fact, it was."

"Do I know her?"

"You met her once, but I don't think you'd recognize her if you saw her again."

"Was it Julianna?"

"Good guess, but no, it wasn't. For reasons I think you understand I can't tell you who it was. I promise I'll confess before the month is over."

"Will I meet her again?"

"Yes. I predict you'll become best of friends."

They sat and talked for about an hour. Raul told Kane about his mother visiting and how happy he had been to see her. He thanked him for sending Yorky to his rescue and how he had stood up to his father."

Kane heard the resentment in his friend's voice. "I'm proud of you, Raul. I think your father is, also."

"He sure doesn't act like he is."

"He's just overprotective because of what happened to you. He thinks he needs to protect you from your mother, too. Locking you in that room was wrong. I think he knows that, but he'll never admit it. What you need to do is put it behind you and get on with your life."

They both became silent when they heard footsteps in the hall. Zoric walked into the room. "Welcome home, Kane. How's your father?"

"Doing well." It made Kane feel good to hear the true concern when they asked about his father.

"What are your plans? Will your father come back here to live?"

"I think you know the answer to that. No. He won't. My father's dream was to walk off this island. It didn't happen that way, but he's a free man now. Prince Tali will never see him again. As for me, I plan on staying around for a while, then I hope Raul and I can do some traveling. Take it day by day and see what happens."

Later that evening as Kane lay in his bed, his thoughts turned to the Ranch and it brought a smile to his face. He missed everyone; he now knew what the real meaning of homesick meant. To think he could have grown up there with Katy and been able to have real memories of his mother, besides the ones she left him in the letters he had read from her. He missed out on all of that because of Tali.

Kane tried to sort out the emotions he felt toward Tali. His conclusion—he just didn't like the man. He liked Zoric. To Kane, Zoric was Tali's puppet—but not for long.

It was ten o'clock the next morning when Kane knocked on Tali's office door. He was not surprised to find Zoric there, too. "Good, I'm glad you're here." He sat down in the empty chair next to Tali's desk. "I want you both to know the only reason I came back is because of Raul."

"Do you plan on staying?" asked Zoric.

"For right now, yes. I think we all need time to sort things out." Kane could smell the alcohol coming from Tali's coffee cup. He hoped his eyes weren't changing color as he looked at the man, sitting across from him, and saw death—Prince Tali would have his heart attack by tomorrow afternoon.

Tali took a long drink from his cup and set it down. "Zoric and I have been discussing putting you and Raul to work Monday morning. It's time you both take on some responsibility." He picked up a piece of paper and handed it to Kane. "I want you to pay this. I've already taken care of it, so you can make arrangements to make small monthly payments to me. I think that's fair."

Kane looked at the hospital invoice, nine thousand, three hundred and seventy-five dollars. Kane looked up and saw the smug look on Tali's face and knew exactly what the man was doing. "Once I pay this, will I be free to leave this island?"

Prince Tali hesitated a minute before answering. "Yes."

Kane stood. "I'm responsible for this and I will pay it. I won't leave until I do." He turned and walked out of the room.

Prince Tali chuckled. "That was easier than I thought it would be." He handed the paper to Zoric. "Hell, by the time he pays this off, he'll be married with a couple of kids, and a permanent fixture here on the island just like I planned."

Kane walked out of the back door and headed for the cottage he and his dad used to live in. He found a shovel and, within minutes, he held the box wrapped in plastic in his hands. He opened it up and counted the money—exactly ten thousand dollars. He counted out what he needed, putting the remainder in his pocket.

He opened the door and walked back into Tali's office without knocking. The surprised looks on both their faces made Kane smile. "Zoric, I want you to witness this." He picked up the invoice from the desk, along with a pen. He wrote, *paid in full, cash.* He wrote the amount down plus the date. "Even though this is paid, I'm still not leaving the island. Raul needs me." He was almost to the door when he turned and looked at Zoric. "One more thing. Don't ever come in my room again and go through my personal belongings." He left the door open as he walked away, a big smile on his face. *That should give them something to ponder for a while.* He headed for the stables to meet Raul.

It was two hours later when he and Raul arrived at the lake to take a swim. When Kane was finished, he lay on the blanket he'd spread on the ground, looking up at the sky. *It's such a hazy blue color, not like the beautiful clear, deep blue color over The Ranch.* Kane closed his eyes, his mind going over again what would happen to Tali. As he lay there he realized he had to tell Raul about his father. *What right do I have to keep this from him? He needs to spend whatever time they have left together, and the doctors need to do whatever they can.* Kane sat up. *Who do I think I am, God? That I can walk on that water? Hell, I'd sink just like everyone else.*

"Raul, come here. I need to talk to you." He watched as his friend reluctantly got out of the water and walked toward him. "Sit down."

Raul sat across from him. "Your eyes are spooky again. What's going on?"

"It's your father." Kane told him as gently and compassionately as he could what was going to happen. He watched as the tears flowed down his friend's cheeks.

"Is he going to die?" Raul asked.

"Let's see what the doctors say. I can't answer that now. Maybe tomorrow I can." They both stood. Kane touched his friend's shoulder. "Do you want me to tell your father?"

"No. I will, but I'd like you to come with me."

"Okay, but why don't you take a shower and spend a little time alone. I'll meet you on the veranda in about an hour."

Raul agreed as they got on their horses and headed for the stables.

Kane finished his shower and was almost dressed when he heard a knock on the door. "Come in."

Zoric entered. "Can we talk for a minute?"

Kane smiled. "Sure, friends can talk anytime."

"I'm glad to hear you say that. I want you to know I'll never go through your things again."

"Thanks, Zoric. I know it wasn't your idea. Are you going to be around a while?"

"If you want me to be."

"Raul has something he needs to tell his father. I think he would like it if we both were there."

"Okay." Zoric waited until Kane finished dressing. "You're not going to tell me where you got that money, are you?"

Kane laughed. "And take the thrill out of the suspense—never."

When the three of them entered Tali's office, he was just finishing his lunch. "If I'd known you were all here, we could have had lunch together."

"I need to talk to you, Dad," Raul said. "I have something very important to tell you."

Tali heard the concern in his son's voice. He glanced at Zoric and watched as he shrugged his shoulders, telling him he didn't know what was going on. "Please sit down, Son."

Raul sat in the chair closest to his father. He took a deep breath and, looking into his father's eyes, he began. "And you could die," he ended.

Prince Tali leaned forward, reaching out to touch Raul's arm. "I feel fine, Son. I really don't think I'm going to die. I'm not ready yet." He chuckled, trying to relieve some of the tension.

"It's not funny, Dad. I want you to go to the doctors, have them run some tests. Kane's never been wrong yet. If you get the necessary help now, maybe it will save your life. Please, I don't want you to die."

Prince Tali knew his son was on the verge of tears. He stood. "Okay, let's go."

It was several hours later while they were in the hospital that Prince Tali experienced a slight numbness in his left arm and irregular heart rhythm. They checked him into the hospital.

That evening Kane sat in the waiting room with Zoric. They both looked up when Raul entered the room. "Dad wants to talk to you, Kane."

"Okay." He stood, touching Raul's shoulder as he passed. He found Tali sitting up in bed. There were wires running from a machine taped to his chest. Tali's heartbeat flashed on the monitor.

"Looks like you were right—again. Is it serious? Am I going to die?"

Kane walked closer to him. "I think the doctors need to make that call. It looks like you're in good hands. Have they told you anything?"

"Not really. I'll know more tomorrow, I suppose." He studied Kane a moment before asking. "What about Raul?"

Kane knew what Tali needed to hear. "I will always take care of him." Kane turned to leave. "I'll send Raul back in. See you tomorrow."

The next day, all hell broke loose. Prince Tali was rushed in for emergency heart bypass surgery. The doctors did everything they could, but it wasn't enough. Prince Tali died Friday afternoon at one-twenty-four. His funeral, held on Monday, was attended by everyone on Tali Island, plus several hundred other people.

Kane was at Raul's side every day for the next week. Zoric, in the meantime, took care of everything.

On Saturday, eight days after Tali's death, Kane and Raul were sitting on their horses, overlooking the valley where once Raul wanted to build a home. "I guess I don't need to think about that anymore."

"You need to give yourself some time." Kane looked at Raul. "I want you to come with me. I'm leaving next week. We'll see your mom and my dad. There are some other people I want you to meet. Besides, I think my house should be built first."

Wednesday morning Kane and Raul stood talking to Zoric outside the front of the estate. "It's going to be boring around here with the two of you gone."

"We'll be back before you know it, Uncle."

"If you need anything at all…"

"I know—call, but we won't."

They watched as Yorky pulled the limo to a stop and got out. He had a big grin on his face. "You young men ready to run away from home?" he asked jokingly. "I sure wish I was going with you two." Raul smiled at him. "I promise you can go with us next time."

It only took a few minutes to load their luggage and say good-bye to Zoric. They joked and laughed all the way to the airport. Yorky joined in, which surprised the boys. He even hugged each of them when they said good-bye. "Take lots of pictures and keep a diary. I want to know everything that happened when you get back."

*Carole A. Sheller*

# *Chapter 28*

Kane waited until they were only a couple of hours from landing in New York. *I guess it's time to give him the good news.* "Raul, would you like to know who saved my father?"

"Are you kidding? It's been driving me crazy. Who was it?"

A big smile came to Kane's face. "My sister."

"Your what? You don't have a sister."

Kane was laughing. The look on Raul's face was priceless. "It was not only my sister, but my twin sister. You better shut your mouth before you catch something."

"My God... you're serious."

"It's true."

"My father said he tried to find your mother and sister. He was told they died. Some accident or something."

"They escaped and went back to the States. That's where my mother was born. She did die, though, when I was five, but my sister is still alive." Kane told Raul everything.

"I can't believe the young nun sitting on the steps of the church that night was your sister. That was why she acted so strange when she shook my hand."

"She knew exactly who you were and that's what helped her find me."

Raul smiled. "I guess that makes me a hero—a donor, no—a hero—yes."

"Our lives are more alike than you realize."

"What do you mean by that?" Raul asked.

"I got to meet my sister. Now we're on our way to meet yours."

"What? Get out of here."

Kane smiled and looked out the window. "I'll wait until we land if you don't mind."

Raul smiled back. "It is a big step, even for you. My mother never mentioned she'd remarried and had more children."

"She didn't remarry. Victoria your sister, is Tali's daughter. Your mother was pregnant when she left him." Kane explained as best he could what happened and why Amanda made the decision she had.

When he was finished, he opened an envelope that contained several pictures. "This is my sister, Katy. This is your sister, Victoria. This is my new mother and this is your new father."

"No, no, no. I think this altitude is getting to you. This is your new father, because he's alive and free. This is my new mother because we're finally getting to know each other. Now dumb, dumb, have you got it straight?"

Kane looked at him. "No. I'm right as usual. They're getting married."

Raul stared at him.

"Your mouth is open again." Before Raul could say anything, Kane asked. "Do you know who this is?" He handed him the photo.

"Yes, that's Sister Elizabeth."

"Well, yes and no. It's my mother's sister, my Aunt Liz."

Raul shook his head. "You're full of all kinds of surprises. Next you'll be showing me a photo of my wife and kid."

"Make that five kids."

Raul started laughing. Kane did, too, till the tears ran down their cheeks.

After a few minutes Raul finally took a deep breath. "Thanks, I think I needed that." He picked up the photo of his sister. "Do you think I'll make a good big brother?"

"The best."

"Does she know about me?"

"She didn't. When she found out, she was a little upset with her mother. I had a good talk with her, and then she told me she wanted to marry me and asked if I'd wait until she grew up. Scared the hell out of me. She looks like your mother."

Raul smiled. "I can see the resemblance. When will I meet her?"

"She'll be at the airport to pick us up, along with your mother, your Uncle Larry, and grandparents. We'll stay in Vermont a few days, then you, your mother and sister will come to Colorado with us."

"Sounds like we're in for a great time. What's that?" Raul picked up a piece of folded paper that was in with the photos. It was a drawing of a very large home with lots of bedrooms and bathrooms.

"That's the house I want to build in the valley," said Kane.

Raul smiled. "Do you really think we can afford to build this large of a house. I'm going to have five kids remember. I'll be broke."

"Well, I'm going to have seven and I need a house that large."

"Seven! You know, Kane my friend, we better enjoy all this freedom. I've got a feeling it's not going to be around very long."

Kane smiled. "Amen. Those are the truest words you've ever spoken."

# EPILOGUE

Kane's fingers touched the box that contained the letters from his mother. He wanted to read one of them another time before the wedding. He unlocked the latch and opened the lid, removing one of the most valuable possessions he owned.

He held the envelope to his nose, breathing in deeply the slight smell of jasmine.

He sat down on the edge of his bed. His eyes flashed from the top to the bottom of the page as he admired his mother's beautiful handwriting.

*My Darling Kane,*

*Words cannot express how much I miss you. It's been almost four years since I held you in my arms. I think about you all the time and hope and pray life has been, and will be, good to you.*

*Today is March twenty-first, nineteen eighty-two. It's been snowing for the last two days, but today the sun is shining and the sky is crystal blue. Your sister, Katy, is outside with your Aunt Liz, making a snowman. I picture you there at her side, and I know, deep in my heart, someday you will be.*

Kane read the rest of the letters through teary eyes. She told him about her life, growing up on The Ranch, and her much-too-short, treasured time with him, Katy, and their father, Kevin.

*This special gift you have, use it wisely and it will bring you happiness.*

*Till we meet again—and we will.*

*All my love always,*
*Your Mother*

Kane folded the last letter and returned it to the safety of its box. He walked over to the window, and as he looked out over the land, he knew his mother was right. This gift had saved Raul's life several times. Kane couldn't imagine what his life would be like without the friend he loved like a brother.

He looked up the road toward the guesthouse and saw Raul, helping Sami with her father. Ward was walking now with the help of a walker, but Raul followed him closely with a wheelchair, in case he got tired.

It had been four months since the death of Prince Tali. Raul was taking on more responsibility, learning about the Tali Corporation, and Kane was learning about The Ranch Corporation. They kept their promise to each other and were spending time traveling. Kane finally saw Julianna perform. Right now she was here at The Ranch for the wedding, and then he and Raul would accompany her back to New York on their way to Tali Island. Katy and Sister Elizabeth would join them for a two-week vacation and be there for Zoric's wedding to Lousetta.

Kane smiled to himself. It seemed like everyone was getting married. Ben and Jenny, Ward and Stacy were planning a double wedding next summer, in July, around the same time as his and Katy's eighteenth birthday.

Everyone would be there, including Zoric and his new wife, J.J., Yorky, and their families, even Dr. Stevens with his sister, Betsy.

Kane turned. He knew Katy was on her way. He walked over and opened the door. They stood there, looking at each other. Katy reached up and straightened his tie. "I do believe I have the most handsome brother in the whole world."

"And I have the most beautiful sister."

"Thank you." Katy smiled at him. "This is a big day for you. Raul will truly be your brother."

"And yours." Kane took her hand. "And we can't forget about our new baby sister, Victoria."

Katy laughed. "Talk about an instant family."

"How about meeting me in the morning and we'll enjoy the sunrise together?" Kane asked. "Our lives are going to be very different from now on. We have a lot of people who'll need us."

"I know," said Katy, "but as long as we're together we can handle anything."

Kane put his arm around her waist. "I'm so glad you're in my life. Let's go see that father of ours get married."


The next morning found them standing, again, side by side and looking out over the snowcapped mountains. Kane could feel the presence of his mother. Knowing she had stood in this same place many times sent a warm feeling through his body.

He hugged Katy a little tighter and together they watched the waking of another day as the sun spread its early morning light of beautiful color across the sky.